MANY ARE THE TRAVELERS

By William Brown Meloney

THE BOOK OF MONELLE

RUSH TO THE SUN

IN HIGH PLACES

MOONEY

MANY ARE THE TRAVELERS

Many Are The Travelers

by

WILLIAM BROWN MELONEY

APPLETON-CENTURY-CROFTS, INC.

New York

PRINTED IN THE UNITED STATES OF AMERICA

TO R.F.M. ALL HAPPINESSE
AND THAT ETERNITIE
PROMISED

MANY ARE THE TRAVELERS

One

Whenever I was introduced to anyone, it was always as Matt Tracy's cousin, John Milnor. The Tracys were such an involved family that no one, not even Matt's old Aunt Eleanor, who died several years ago, could ever be sure that they had the stories straight. My mother came nearer to understanding the ramifications of the Tracys, but Aunt Eleanor always said that was because she wasn't a Tracy—not even by marriage.

Of course, in Haviland there were very few who didn't know the truth; who didn't know that I wasn't Matt Tracy's cousin. But like any lie, if it's big enough and repeated often enough, people come to accept it, and to forget the real facts. The newcomers who drifted into the world of Haviland during the generation I grew up in were the only ones who never did know the story. In the early years they weren't accepted by the Haviland people enough to be gossiped with, and later everyone had got so used to the idea that I was Matt's cousin that they never gave any thought to it. Anyway, for many of those years I wasn't in Haviland very much—those were the years in which I was trying to escape. Matt used to laugh. He said I'd never make it; the threads that held me might not be strong, but there were so many of them that I'd never break through. There were worse things though, he'd add, that could happen to a man than to be a Tracy, and be caught up in Haviland. And I would have a drink with him and say nothing because I knew that I could get away—that someday I would get away. Matt would stare at me quietly, and as if he were reading my thoughts he would smile and we would talk of other things; sometimes, but seldom, of the war; mostly of fishing and hunting and the farm and sometimes of the books I had written and often of the book I hadn't written, the book I had begun and torn up a dozen times, the story of the family and the farm and the village of Haviland. Matt always said that someday I would write it and then he'd sing a phrase from Don Marquis' old jingle that had the line in it "skeleton rattle your mouldy leg."

"You won't open all the closets, I'll wager," he once said. "A lot of mouldy legs would come tumbling out on you, not that quite a few of them weren't damned attractive. You won't come on too much smallness or meanness, either; not because we were better than others, but because it wasn't in the blood. There'll be a lot of living in the story, good living and bad living, but most of it big living; they were a prepotent, vigorous tribe, even the women."

"Maybe somebody who's out of the tribe should tell the story," I'd said.

"No"—he shook his head—"that's where you're wrong. They'd write it to demonstrate a point, or prove a purpose. But if you write it, John, you'll write it because you want to understand a number of things, including yourself."

He was right. And yet I've never been satisfied with a way to begin to tell the story. You could start it in the year 1692 with the first Matthew Tracy who came up out of the New Haven settlement and built the first Tracy house, the little gambrel-roofed cottage that stands at the foot of the Hill Road that Will Talcott the herdsman used to live in, and other Talcotts lived in for a hundred and fifty years before him. The place has been added to since then, but you can still see the original roof line on the kitchen wing, and the floors are the wide oak boards of those days, and in the back, where they never changed the face of the house, there are the small old-time window openings that used to have side-swinging sash. The Indians liked Quakers, or thought they did; they could trust them, or thought they could. So the original Matt Tracy couldn't think of any very good reason for not being a Quaker. The Indians by that time had been sold the idea that the white man was pretty much there to stay, and like a lot of other dark-skinned people down through history, they thought that if they gave him a little land he'd be satisfied and stay on it, and stop pushing in on them. They were rather generous, but on the whole misguided about their lighter-skinned brothers.

2

Exploiting their good nature, the original Matt Tracy, in addition to his wife and two sons, voted in the graveyard. He told the Indians that he represented twenty-one others who desired to come and settle and they would need enough land for twenty-five people to live on. This was more than the Indians had bargained for; but once you've started to compromise, it's difficult to stop, as many people smarter than the Indians have later come to realize. So the chief and his sons, and Matt Tracy and his sons, paced off what came to be known as the Hill. But the Hill was more than a hill. It was two hills with a saddle of broad, fertile, watered land lying between them, and gently sloping flanks that cattle could fatten on, and in the adjoining valleys some more land just to sweeten the bargain. The Tracys were always strong on sweetening the bargain with the other fellow's sugar. And that is the Tracy farm today, a little more perhaps, but certainly not less; the Tracys are dedicated to the concept that land is something not to be sold by a Tracy.

A year or two later, when the Indains discovered that Matt Tracy's "settlement" was to be no more than just Matt Tracy and family, they resented the white man's ways; but by that time they were deeply involved with no less devious or chicane, though considerably more legitimate Quakers, on the other side of the valley. The first Matt Tracy, having no qualms or compunctions about fire arms and violence, had a little of the advantage over his gentle neighbors. The Indians let him pretty much alone while they tried to whittle down the "simple people." A lot of the names you read on the records of the First Meeting you'll still see on the mailboxes on their side of the valley. And of course on this side of the valley it's still Tracy's Corners, and Tracy's Upper Place, and Tracy's Lower Place, and the Old Tracy Place, and the New Tracy Place —new, that is, in 1790. And you'll find a few, but not many, of the Tracys themselves. As a family, they had that in them that kept most of them from living out their lives. The story might begin that way.

Or, again, it could just as well begin at almost any focal point of American history. Pick a war, or a gold strike, or the opening up of the West, or the heyday of American shipping, or even the building of the railroad empires, and you could pick up the threads of the story with a Tracy, more likely than not named Matthew.

3

The only variance with many other families of their ilk would be that the Tracys usually either died, or they came back to Haviland. They didn't breed well in other places, and even Matt's Aunt Eleanor was never able to follow out many lines of the family beyond Haviland and New York. The Tracys left their mark in far places, but they didn't leave their name to carry on.

Yes, the story could be begun in many places, or many times. It could even be begun day before yesterday, when Will Talcott came running up to our house on the Lower Place to tell me what had happened, or rather what he thought had happened. Then he and the farm help went out and brought in the bodies of my brother Matt and his wife Alyse. She looked very beautiful, too young and too beautiful to die, for mercifully the shot that had killed her had been quick, and had merely torn her heart to shreds. Only Tim Mooney and I looked at Matt—when the police were finished. But even the police weren't too difficult, and the coroner wasn't difficult at all. The Tracys were always a favored breed, a little beyond and remote from the harassments that most people know with the law at such times.

Maybe it would be a little less grim to skip that scene entirely, and start with Pop Sanford—Henry Sanford, that is—driving up the hill from Haviland to go over the matter of Matt's will with me. "It'll raise hell," Pop said. "But it'll stick. It'll stick to Dooms-day. Matt wasn't one for avoiding hell-raising, and I'm one for wills that stick. This one's tight as a well-drove bung."

As I read it, he leaned across the table. "I'll explain any part of it that doesn't make sense," he said. "Well, maybe not exactly sense—let's say that isn't clear. As far as sense goes, it doesn't make too much. But it's what Matt wanted, and no jury of his peers would ever say that he didn't know what he wanted, even if he didn't always get it."

I didn't bother to do more than waive his offer aside. Pop was long on Blackstone and clear English, and the combination leaves little room for conjecture or misunderstanding. Twice I glanced back at the date. The instrument had been written two years before, which meant that all this was something that had been a long time in Matt's mind. When I had returned to Haviland after the war, it must have been evident to him, even before I'd realized it myself,

4

that I had returned to stay; that Haviland was to be the scene of my life.

There was quite an extended paragraph. I read it twice, and then I looked up at Pop Sanford. "Was this necessary? I don't pretend to be a lawyer, but it would seem to me . . ."

"Maybe not necessary," he interrupted, "and certainly unusual. But it makes the cheese more binding. There won't be any litigation over this will. There's a lot of equity and justice in the way he wanted the cards to fall, and this way there'll be no slip-up. Come right down to it, it's no more than what everybody in Haviland has known for forty years. You were Matt's half brother. And Old Matthew was your father. And there isn't anybody, who is anybody, who doesn't have a great respect and affection for your mother. So anybody that wants to call you a bastard could have done it long since, without this will."

"I guess that's true," I said.

"And let me tell you another thing—" He looked at me for a long moment. "I'd rather be the natural son of Old Matthew Tracy than the legitimate whelp of a lot of men I can think of in this town."

I didn't argue the point. I read on through the end of the will, and finally tossed it on the table. "I've got enough without inheriting all this," I told him.

"And so have the rest of them who'll be at the funeral tomorrow, which won't stop them from wanting the Tracy land too. But Matt wanted you to have it for reasons of his own, and for reasons I suspect you know. He also wanted you to have these." Pop took two envelopes out of his pocket and handed them to me, and then he crossed to the window and looked out at the sweep down the valley. "Matt stopped by my office day before yesterday and left them with me to give you," he said.

I stared down at the letters. It can hit you where you live to hold in your hand the well-known writing of someone you've grown up with and loved like a brother, even before you knew he was your brother, and whose body is lying waiting to be buried.

"Oh, in case the thought has occurred to you"—Pop Sanford was still looking out the window—"Matt cashed all his life insurance at surrender value the afternoon he brought in those letters. He thought it was more decent and tidy that way. Matt was a tidy man about his affairs."

5

"Then you knew what he was going to do?"

"Not exactly. It was only when it happened that I realized I had known what was in his mind. Matt talked to me about a lot of things. I was his friend as well as his lawyer."

"Then why didn't you try to stop him?" I demanded with a flood of anger.

The old man drew his breath in, and held it for an extended moment before he let it gush out of him with a long whistling sigh. "It wasn't my place," he finally said. "He was of sound mind and I always respected his judgment. I didn't feel privileged to try to interfere. Not that interfering with a Tracy ever got a man very far." He made a fine business of taking a great oversized handkerchief from the side pocket of his black suit and blowing his nose and clearing his throat. I slit open one of the letters and read it.

DEAR JOHN:

I have a nasty task to ask you to do for me. When I go, I shall be leaving Joy behind me. Very often dogs with her nature and devotion can never become happy again when they have lost those they love. The grief and puzzlement of a dog is sometimes beyond the mind of man to understand. Give her a month and if she is too unhappy, take her out onto the far meadow at the upper farm, the one we've allowed to grow up to thicket and cover. If this is the course you must follow, it won't be in her heart to hunt that day, so that needless farce will not be imposed upon either of you. On the top of the knoll from which you can see out over the whole valley, you will find the mounds. That is where her people have been buried. If the spirit of a dog survives she could wish for no lovelier place to rest.

MATT

I passed the letter over to Pop; he took his gold spectacles out to read it. "Yes, Matt was very tidy," I summed up. "One of the first things I can remember about him was the top of his dresser. Everything had to be geometrically perfect and in its place. A strange quirk for a man who was so loose and large and easy in his living."

6

Pop handed the letter back to me and wiped his glasses.

"Joy wasn't with him that afternoon," I went on. "He'd put her in the kennel himself, and fed her, before he left her. She didn't eat though, and she hasn't eaten since. But I've left her in the kennel, thinking it was better that way until everything was over."

In the way he so often gave legal consideration to a problem, Pop delivered a long and inconclusive "Ummmm." A sort of a Blackstonian throat-clearing.

I dialed the barn extension and got Will Talcott on the phone. "Will, bring Matt's bitch Joy up to my house."

Pop gave forth with another considered "Ummm." This time it conveyed approbation. "That, I think, is what I would have done." A man of deep and profound respect for his own probity and judgment, that phrase was the highest praise I have ever known him to give. I have heard him give it on a trout stream, when you're puzzled between a brown hackle and a quill Gordon and finally choose the hackle. Pop likes flies with shoulders on them.

But all this was just stalling for time before I read the other letter. Pop helped me out. "How long had Alyse been sick?" he asked.

I shrugged. "Too long before they discovered it. No one held out any hope."

"It's the damnedest things that money won't buy." Pop cleared his throat again. "I was at the station the day they came back from Minnesota, from the clinic out there."

The door opened and Will Talcott stuck his head in. If he was going to say anything he didn't, because of Pop standing by the window. He just nodded and let Joy in and closed the door. The dog came across the room and put her head on my knee, and looked up at me as if I might know what she wanted to ask, might somehow be able to tell her the answer. All I could do was stroke her head, and in a moment, sensing that I was to be no help to her, she crossed over to the fireplace and sat staring into the flames, looking at whatever a dog looks at when it stares into a fire.

"When Alyse first came we used to call her the Frenchwoman," Pop said. "Nobody liked her, or, to put it more exactly, nobody liked the idea of her. She didn't seem to fit into the picture. That was when you were out West, about nineteen thirty-seven or eight, wasn't it?"

7

"Thirty-eight."

"I knew it was sometime about then," Pop said. "It was something like a couple of years after the break with Susan."

"Susan and Matt broke up in thirty-three."

"Five years between them? As long as that?" Pop scratched his chin. "Most people on the Hill and in the village thought of it as an off-again-on-again business and didn't approve. They sort of choked on the divorce. Small-town people are like that, despite the fact that Susan was a bitch."

"There weren't many people who thought so then," I reminded him.

"There are some that still don't think so," Pop said. "But for the most part, the town came to like Alyse. Of course she could have lived fifty years in Haviland and she'd still have been 'that Frenchwoman.'"

"I've been here forty years and I'm still 'that Milnor fellow,' and Elizabeth is still a 'summer resident' who rents the old house on the Lower Place."

Pop laughed. "What do you expect, to be treated like regular folks? You and Elizabeth have been here less than half a century —isn't as if you were natives, you know."

"Forgetting that I was Matt's *cousin?*"

"Only honorary." Pop chuckled. "They could hide their heads in a bushel basket and not see what they didn't want to see. When this will's probated they're going to get their ears scratched some."

"How do you think Elizabeth's going to feel about it?"

Pop sat down in the chair by the fire and let his hand slip along Joy's head. "I gave a lot of thought to that when I drew up the will," he said. "I was tempted to ask Matt to let Elizabeth and you see it, and talk it over. Matt must have read the question in my mind, for he said no, this was the better way. Matt was the head of the family, he had no living children; there was no one in his line to inherit; and there was no one closer or more rightfully the inheritor than you. Even so, he might have done something different if you hadn't come back and settled down like you were going to stay."

"You haven't said what you feel Elizabeth's going to think about the will."

"What you really mean, John, is what's she going to think about

8

what other people are going to think? Well, when a person comes of age and gets mature—that can be quite an elderly age, sometimes they can live to be a hundred and never grow up—well, when they come to such an age they just plain don't give a damn what other people think, the only important thing is what they think themselves."

"And you think that Elizabeth has reached that serene and lofty plane?"

"Yes, I think so. I've reached it. And you almost have, John. You're almost grown up, too. But look at it this way. Elizabeth was twenty-five or thereabouts when she met Old Matthew. The old business with Constance had already happened, and was finished with."

"Except that it was never finished with."

"Except that it was never finished with," Pop agreed. "Do you suppose she'll be at the funeral tomorrow?"

"Do you suppose anything but the Avenging Angel or a stroke would keep her away?"

"Knowing Constance, I don't think so. Constance is hell for occasions, and making scenes at them.—Did she understand when you told her?"

I shook my head. "I had no sense that she did. Her time machine stopped a long while back, and Matt is still a baby to her. For years now, she hasn't been able to keep Matt and his father straight in her mind. Susan and later Alyse were just more of Old Matthew's women. I tried to make it clear to her, but she kept coming back in her mind to the idea that it was Old Matthew that had died."

"Better if she hadn't been told," Pop said.

"Maybe. But you can't keep things from her. She sort of feels everything that goes on and fits it into her own strange world."

"You know what I think?" Pop asked.

"Go ahead."

"I think the Tracys overlive themselves—they don't die natural deaths like ordinary people. They either die violently, or they live forever. And what tends to complicate things, is that they have enough of this world's goods and so damned many houses that they all live together."

"It isn't the Tracys that live; it's their women," I reminded him.

"Too many damn women if you ask me," Pop further delivered

9

himself. "I think that a first-rate epidemic once a generation up on this hill would clear the air somewhat."

"It's an idea," I acknowledged. "But it's a healthy life up here, and the Tracys concerned themselves with vibrant and long-living females. However, the point is, I've got to discuss this will with Elizabeth, and she's pretty well knocked out already with what's happened."

"I was getting around to that," Pop said.

"You were taking an unconscionable time about it."

"Time is something I have plenty of." He finished polishing his glasses and put his handkerchief back in his pocket. "While we were talking, I was letting my mind go back through the years. Don't forget, John, I knew you before you were born. As a matter of plain unadulterated fact, I'm probably responsible for more of all this than I care to accept the burden for."

He paused, and I waited for him to go on. "You know the Jennings Place," he finally said. "Old Matt bought it after the fire. But you wouldn't remember the fire. That was before you were born—just before you were born."

"I know the Jennings Place," I told him. "And I know the story."

"You do, eh? Well, I suppose you do. In this sprawling patchwork of human relations up here on the Hill, I don't suppose there are very many secrets you don't all of you know about. But I suppose the one thing you don't know is that the first person Elizabeth knew in Haviland, and the oldest friend she has, is me."

"I knew you were one of her oldest friends, but I didn't know you claimed priority in meeting her."

"Well, I was the first person she met. I was at the railroad station the day she came into this town with her maid and a pile of trunks. She tripped, got her heel caught in a knothole in the station platform, and I caught her before she fell. She ripped her heel off, and caught her other one in the hem of her petticoat. She said 'damn.' Said it out loud. She was wearing one of those princess traveling suits that women used to fancy. If a woman had the figure for it, the rig sort of made her look like a princess—only there never seemed to be many women who had the figure for it. She said 'damn' again when she saw a foot or more of lace straggling from under her dress, and then she said 'thank you' and without batting an eye she lifted up her dress showing a bit more of ankle

10

than we were used to seeing in those days, and hobbled off to the Haviland House hack. Lou Henderson—he was telegrapher then, before he got to be stationmaster—let out a long, low whistle."

I smiled. "What a long memory you have. . . ."

"Too long a memory," he agreed. "My wife used to say that, if she didn't know better, she would think I was in love with Elizabeth. The first time she said it there was no little rancor in her heart, but after she came to know Elizabeth the rancor went out of her.

"A few days after Elizabeth came to Haviland she stopped by my office to inquire for a house to rent. The Jennings Place had just come on the market, and she liked it from the moment she saw it."

"This is all a long way behind us—" I called him back. "The question still is, how will Elizabeth feel about Matt's will?"

"I'm getting to that. Elizabeth had been living in the Jennings Place almost two years when she asked me to come over to see her one evening. She had some personal business to discuss, she explained; legal business, it had to do with her family in New York. I remember the way she was sitting, with the tea table in front of her, dressed in one of those loose folderol gowns. A woman might have noticed straight off how things were, but I didn't. Of course I'd heard a lot of stories. Haviland isn't the sort of place where anything can happen, or even almost happen, without there being stories."

I nodded. "What did Elizabeth want to see you about?"

"Well, you mostly. When she got up and went over to the desk to get some papers, it was pretty evident that you were an imminent addition to the vital statistics of Haviland. She talked about a lot of things that night. You see, except for Old Matthew, I was the only other friend she had in Haviland. The rest of the story you pretty much know, the broad outlines of it anyway, commencing with the burning of the Jennings Place a little while after. That was arson. It was very close to murder. Matthew moved her to this house, and you were born, and years later when he died, she stayed on living here. The truth was never denied, and a restatement of it I don't think would bother her now."

I was silent for a long moment. "The way you tell about it," I brought out with difficulty, "makes it sound so simple; and yet in

11

between there must have gone so much living, so much painful living."

"Not forgetting ecstasy," the old man said quietly.

It was a strange thought, and even a stranger word for a man of his mind and character to have used. "Why didn't Old Matt ever divorce Constance?" I went back.

"You might ask, 'Why didn't he murder her?' That would have been simpler; there was a moment when he came uncomfortably close to it. But times were different, then. Matthew's code was different. The law wasn't so tolerant; for that matter, it isn't so tolerant now, without you dodge around corners. Maybe a divorce didn't make any real difference to Elizabeth. Another man and another time, and Matthew would have picked her up and taken her away and built a new life somewhere else. But I guess he was born to this life; the place is big, bigger than any individual who ever lived on it, and it needed him, and then there was always the family. It was a big family and it needed seeing to. Constance needed seeing to, even though she was put away after the fire. She stayed in the sanitorium, you remember, until Old Matt's death. Then it was Elizabeth who saw to it that she was taken out."

That was something I hadn't known. A log crumbled into embers, and the old man got to his feet and rubbed his hands before the hearth. "Elizabeth's taking it pretty hard, I suppose?"

"Yes. She raised Matt; he seemed as much her son as I did. Go on in to see her, anyway. She'd like it, and it would do her good. I'll let you know about all this tomorrow." I gestured to the will on the desk before me. "Or do you want to take it along with you?"

"No, you keep it. It's a copy. The original is in my safe at the office."

The old man let himself out and closed the door behind him. Joy didn't stir. I sat looking into the shadows of the room, holding the unopened letter by its corners and blowing on it slightly so that it turned. I wished that Matt had never written it or that Pop had lost it. Unopened, I could more easily follow my impulse to renounce the inheritance. Opened, I was afraid Matt would be deciding for me. It was dated across the envelope on the day before yesterday, and in it he must have written things that a man would want to say when he knew that he was going to die. They would be entangling things, things that would bind me with obligations

12

to a family that was not really mine, despite the Tracy blood that flowed in my veins; they would bind me to Haviland, and to acres of land that I had not been raised to look upon as my own. What right did a man have to walk out and leave tangled skeins for others to unravel behind him? What the hell right did he have to walk out leaving a note asking me to shoot his dog if she grieved for him? I took the letter opener from the desk before me, the letter opener made from a ground-down belt knife that had been one of Matt's army souvenirs, and slit the envelope.

DEAR JOHN:

Henry Sanford will have brought you this letter, and you will have read my will before he gives it to you. Long ago our father made provision that you and Elizabeth would have all that you might ever want. Half of everything he possessed was made over to both of you, the land only being held separate and being reserved to me, in his thought that there might be of my issue a Tracy to have and to hold it. The death of Martha and my son at his birth, and my divorce from Susan, and the fact that Alyse and I could never have children have written the end of that story. And yet, in having the land devised to you, it will still remain in Tracy hands, if not in the Tracy name. There will be those, with far less right than you, who may attempt to contest this decision, so it seemed necessary to spell out in my will your relationship to the family. It's an old story which has never been really concealed, only ignored through the years. Its statement at this late date cannot, I believe, cause any deep or lasting hurt or embarrassment to either you or Elizabeth, and it will be well for the place and for Haviland and for the world to be told that you are a Tracy, and that all this is rightfully yours.

As for what I am about to do— There is no hope for Alyse. The future would be insupportable pain, or drugged months waiting for the inevitable. She has asked me to have one last go with her across the fields and up over the hill to see the sunset. It is a spot she has always loved. It will happen there.

13

Forgive me any unpleasantness that may involve you and Elizabeth in all this. So that you may know the whole story—A little while ago Alyse tried to take her own life. Afterwards she asked me to help her and I promised her that I would. She will not know when it happens—and she does not know that I shall be going with her.

The land is to be yours without any strings. If you so desire, you could turn yourself a very good thing and break it up, selling it off in small pieces. What I would wish, however, is that you would see it through, and run the place for a year or two before you decide. It is a man's work, and a good work and a useful one. Many men and many families take their living off the farm, and its produce is necessary to many more. We breed fine cattle and they are useful, and we experiment with crops and new uses of the land with the state college, and that is useful, too. As a way of life, there are those who would attack it; but I feel that we've done more good than harm. We've lived with a pretty fine democracy, and if there is a better way I have not found it. I know that you love this land, but I have loved it in a different way, for the things we possess demand their tributes of service. These things I hope you can feel, but if you do not, then all that I have said is without meaning and what will happen must happen without regret.

And now, last, there is Françoise. You have seen very little of her in the past year or two. You will probably be surprised at the way she will take this. Although she is only eighteen, she is French and the French have a supreme faculty for maturity. I must warn you of one thing: Before she left for school, she announced to her mother that she had been in love with you since she was twelve—the time you met when you came back to the place after the war. Naturally you will not take this seriously, and equally naturally it is something to be taken seriously. It is in Françoise's nature to have a very clear and inward sense of her emotions.

14

*And so good-by, my friend and my brother. We have
had much that was good between us.*

MATT

The letter was as like Matt as it was unlike any letter that had
ever been written before. I had the sense that he was sitting across
the darkened room, and that all he said was reasonable, and
charged with the quiet surge of personality that always made what
he said so hard to answer while you were with him.

I glanced at my watch. It was quarter past six. I was to drive to
Poughkeepsie to meet Françoise on the nine o'clock train from
Albany. There was time. I began to read the letter over again.

Mrs. Haines knocked at the door, and then came in. "Mr.
Mooney's waiting to see you," she announced, "and your supper
is almost ready, you should be eating something hot before you
take that drive to Poughkeepsie—and your mother would like to
see you before you leave."

"Nothing else, Mrs. Haines?"

"No, that's all." She was remarkably short of a sense of humor.
"Mr. Mooney's been drinking," she stated primly.

"Has he ever not? Or do you mean more than usual?"

"No more than usual, I daresay. But it does seem indecent that
Haviland can't have a sober undertaker."

"It's lucky enough to have one, and very lucky not to have
enough business for two," I reminded her.

"And it would be more Christian of you if you had more reverence for death. You and Mr. Matt, neither of you have a decent
respect for things, and neither of you'll end up good, you mark my
word." Her nerves were scratchy, too.

The strange thing about death is that right in the midst of it,
you can forget it. You've had the impact of its happening, and
yet the habits of living go right on, and time has to pass before you
really accept the fact that someone is gone, completely gone. It
was a full instant before Mrs. Haines heard herself. "It's so hard
to realize that Mr. Matt isn't here any more."

I knew what she meant. A half a dozen times that day I'd put
something in the back of my mind to talk to him about when I
got around to it. There were even one or two things about the

15

funeral I'd wanted to discuss with him. He'd have known how to handle details like that better than I.

Mrs. Haines emptied the ash tray and straightened up the fire. "I'll send in Mr. Mooney. —And don't you be late starting out for Poughkeepsie," she cautioned me sharply. "It's a long trip and a treacherous road."

"I won't," I promised her.

You can tell the age and generation of Haviland people by what they think about going to Poughkeepsie. For twenty years there'd been a broad cement highway over West Mountain. But to Mrs. Haines, it was still a long and adventurous journey. I could remember as a youngster when it had been an all-day trip, and the mountain road something that horses did better than the automobiles we had then. Twenty years ago the "Mountain people" lived up over the shoulder of West Mountain, the scrapings from the bottom of God's barrel. A fine mare's nest of illiteracy, inbreeding, incest and first-rate degeneracy. There were legends of highway robbery and barratry, of ingenious bear pits in the road, and pedlars and teamsters hauling freight who disappeared and were never heard of again. But there was more legend than truth in the bear pit stories. In the first place, the West Mountain people were too lazy to dig a bear pit in the road, and in the second the road was so bad that it would have been an extravagant waste of energy. What really happened was that a teamster all alone or a pedlar could, with his own mischance, break an axle or unspoke a wheel, and off he'd go for help. When he returned, about all that would be left would be his empty wagon and his naked team; they'd even steal the harness off the horses. So Mrs. Haines and her kind still worried when anybody drove over to the river from Haviland.

"Hello, John!" Tim Mooney closed the door behind him. He looked less like an undertaker than it was right for an undertaker to look. But I suppose that in a small town where you see him every day, it's better not to look like one.

"I was thinking of West Mountain in the old days," I said. "Whatever happened to the people that lived there?"

Mooney grinned. "When they opened the highway it let the sunlight in, and like lice crawling out of the seams of long woolen underwear in the spring, they all trooped down into the village."

16

"You mean that wonderful crop of good-for-nothing sons of bitches we've got in the village aren't of our own growing, they were imported?"

"Oh, we got some of our own making, too. The Mountain people were just shiftless. Ours are meaner."

"Will you have a drink?" I asked him.

"Don't mind if I do. As a matter of fact I'd mind very considerably if I didn't." He picked up the decanter from the table and was very generous to a glass. He offered it in my direction.

"I'll pour my own. I've got to drive over to Poughkeepsie."

"Picking up Francy? Must be tough her coming home to a thing like this." He held a gulp of the whisky in his mouth and let it slowly trickle down his throat. "Good liquor," he acknowledged, and glancing down at Joy he made one of those clucking sounds that men who know dogs make when they talk to them. Joy whimpered, and then put her head down between her paws. They had exchanged greetings and, like the good dog she was, she didn't have to be sentimental about it. "It's hard on dogs, too," Mooney said. "I've seen it happen a lot of times, it's hard on them. Humans can think their way through things, and most times they've got something to go on living for, but a dog hasn't. Likewise, humans forget easy, but a dog doesn't. I came up to talk over the plans for tomorrow."

"Not so many to talk over," I told him. "You've had a couple of funerals up here on the Hill, and you know how the family does things."

He took a tattered envelope out of his pocket and began to check off some of the notes written on it.

"Church is aired and cleaned. You don't ever use that church up here except for funerals and weddings, and not too many of the latter; you Tracys do your marrying in far places, or you up and do it and announce it to people about the time you're ready to have a christening. Not that I'm criticizing. I like people who herd by themselves, and don't give a damn what the rest of the world thinks."

"Then you should have a great admiration for the Tracys," I remarked.

"I do—for some of them. But you've had your sons of bitches, too. Penny was grousing. Said you people thought you were too

17

good to be buried from the church in the village. He wasn't sure that this church was consecrated any longer, or whatever it is you do in your faith to keep the franchise. More than likely he was begrudging the paint you spend up here and wishing the Tracys would foot more of his bills than they do."

"Did he make any other objections?" I asked.

"Some."

"What were they?"

"Didn't know whether he should. Anyway you look at it, you know, it wasn't just 'death by natural cause.' "

"I get what you mean. I suppose through the memory of living man this will be described as 'the year that Matt Tracy shot his wife and killed himself.' "

"Without we have another war or a real murder—but the likelihood of the one and the chances of the other aren't too great. Penny said as how his bishop wouldn't approve. I told him to keep his trap shut and not tell his bishop. The less a bishop knows about anything other than balance sheets the better. Now to get down to something important, who's coming and where do you want them sat?"

"Oh, they'll all come, I imagine. And let them sit anywhere."

"This is the first Tracy funeral you've ever run, John."

"The first, thank God, and I hope my last."

"From where you're sitting it won't be your last," Mooney said. "But I've run a heap of them, and I want to tell you if this one isn't run right you'll have the devil to pay for years. You can start more ructions at a funeral than hell is paved with. —The old lady coming?"

"Do you think you could keep her away?"

"No, but I'd sure like to. Eighty some odd is too old to be going to any funerals but your own. And beyond that, she's gotten worse. Her mind isn't what it used to be—if it ever was. She'll be burying the wrong people all the way through. She hasn't got around yet to admitting that young Matt ever grew up. God knows who she'll think Alyse was."

"Well, put her off to one corner with Mrs. Talcott," I advised him.

"More easy said than done. There's only four corners to the

18

church and you've got more than four problems. Susan'll be coming, no doubt."

"I told her not to."

"You didn't tell her strong enough. She was down at the shop this afternoon, trying to find out which graves I was opening. Sanford gave me Matt's letter of instructions. I'm doing it the way *he* wanted."

"What did Susan want?"

"She wanted a space left open for her beside Matt. Only there just isn't room. Matt's to be buried beside Martha, his first wife, and on the other side of him will be Alyse. It's like the church with only four corners. Matt hasn't got enough sides for all his women."

"Tell Susan to go to hell!"

"I did in a roundabout sort of way. I told her to take it up with you. You're going to have a time with Susan. And what about Matt's sister Adelaide?"

"What about her?"

"Look, John, this is a small church up here on the Hill. Anywhere you sit in it, you're within spitting and clawing distance of anywhere else. Adelaide can't stand Susan's guts. And the old lady can't stand Adelaide's guts, and she hates Adelaide's husband worse. You know how she can split your side imitating his 'you all' Texas accent. Well, the middle of the Twenty-third Psalm is no place to have your side split. We'll have to keep those two apart. And then there's Emmeline, in from Ohio this afternoon. She can't stand her mother or Adelaide, and that's mutual all the way around."

"No one told me Emmeline had come."

"She got off the train while I was having lunch at the station. I guess they don't recognize you as head of the family yet."

"Why should they?" I asked him.

Mooney ignored the question. "When are they going to read the will?" He glanced over on the desk. The long legal sheets were lying out before me. "It'll probably be a surprise to a lot of them."

"Aren't you taking a lot for granted?"

"Taking nothing for granted, just common sense. Sanford told me to clear things through you, which he wouldn't have told me unless the land—*and* the family—went to you. You'll be sitting in the front on the left. That's where Matt would be sitting if it wasn't

19

his funeral. After they see you there, they won't have to read the will." Mooney picked up the decanter and raised it with his glass, almost as if he were offering me a drink.

"Of course, go ahead." I nodded. "I'd appreciate it as a favor, though, if you'd stay sober tomorrow."

"I only screwed up one funeral in this town."

"Higher than a kite, from the story I heard."

"And then some," he admitted. "But my department will be all right tomorrow. Any screwing up will be done by you Tracys. Naturally I'm putting your ma and Francy beside you; that'll burn the tail feathers off some of the old biddies. Anybody else you want to sit there with you?"

"I don't give a damn where I sit."

"Maybe not. But if you don't know how to run things the Tracy way, I do—at their funerals at least. I'll get three chairs down from the big house."

I'd forgotten—there always had been an empty space where there should have been a pew in the front to the left of the aisle. Armchairs were always brought down from the house. When I was a child Old Matthew had sat there alone, and after he died young Matt and Susan, and then later it was young Matt and Alyse and Françoise.

I could remember as a child wondering why my father always sat there alone and remote, like an inaccessible god. For quite a few years of my growing up, Sundays were wonderful but confusing. Constance was "away" in those years, and Old Matt used to stay at our house. He didn't exactly live there, but he ate and slept there, and most of his clothes were there, the clothes he wore about the farm, and his hunting and fishing things; but when he met strangers he met them at the Big House, and dinner parties and the functions of the family were held there, too. But other times, all other times except when he was away from Haviland, he stayed at our house.

During those years, no matter how hard I tried on the six days of the week, I could never seem to wake up in time to go into my mother's room and have breakfast with them; except the times we went fishing, and then my father and I would eat alone in the kitchen, a breakfast of his own preparing. On all the other days, he would have been up by six thirty and out on the place before I

20

could struggle awake. Sunday mornings, though, were different. I would waken a few minutes after seven to the smell of bacon and coffee coming up through the registers—somehow the old hot-air heating system in the house took a draft from the kitchen and those wonderful food smells would come up into my bedroom. Then I'd jump out of bed and slosh cold water at my face and give a lick and a promise to my hair and go into my mother's bedroom where Old Matt slept. And if young Matt was home from school, he would come in, too. But young Matt was always late; those Sunday mornings didn't mean so much to him. Or perhaps, as I look back on it now, they meant something different to him.

Mrs. Haines was with us even then, only her name wasn't Mrs. Haines—Perry Haines hadn't come to work on the place by then— and she would bring up the breakfast trays. Mine would be served in front of the fire, and my mother and Old Matt would eat theirs across their knees in bed. Sometimes, if it was winter and the room was very cold, they would move close together—it was a huge bed-stead—and I would come in under the covers and eat my breakfast with them. I would try very hard not to spill, because Old Matt would raise hell if I got crumbs in the sheets. And I always tried to dawdle and string out that wonderful half hour, but eventually my father would gruffly tell me to eat and stop talking and get a move on, and then I would scramble out and get ready for church at nine o'clock.

I can remember, one winter Sunday morning—young Matt was there, so it must have been in the Christmas holidays—I was tucked up in the bed when he came in. He scowled at me, and threw out something about my being a sissy, afraid of the cold, and Old Matt told him to crawl in, too, and the whole damned family would eat in bed. He said, "No thank you," and finished his breakfast as fast as he could, and went back to the room we shared when he was home. Presently Old Matt told me to hurry and finish mine too, and if I got any toast crumbs in the bed he'd whale the daylights out of me. I said there was plenty of time before church, it was only quarter to eight, and Old Matt said it was "later than I thought." But I wouldn't give up my breakfast, so I took what was left of my glass of milk and my roll, and with all the dignity I could muster, I walked out of the room. Having my hands full, I didn't quite close the door properly, so I put the food down on the table in the hall and went back to close it. There was one thing Old Matt couldn't stand. If Mrs. Haines ever didn't quite close a door, you could hear him roaring from one end of the house to the other. So I went back to close the door, which had swung open a little now, and I could see that Old Matt had pushed his breakfast tray down to the foot of the bed, and my mother's too; and he was holding her in his arms, and his face was buried against the top of her night-dress, and I closed the door quietly and was glad that he hadn't heard it close. Then before I could move, there was a crash and clatter from inside, and my mother gave a little cry, with Old Matt's booming voice drowning it out: "To hell with the damned dishes, and to hell with the Derby china!" —I remember he said *"Darby,"* and years later, I found that it had stayed in my mind along with the whole memory of that morning. . . .

I couldn't hear what my mother said in answer about the tipped-over tray, but I heard Old Matt's bellowing retort: "A beautiful woman's a damn fool to use fine china when she has breakfast in bed with a man!" Then my mother laughed, and it was a very happy laugh, and it died in a smother and a little murmur of words which again I couldn't hear. But the whole house could have heard my father: "Then the Lord God Almighty'll have to wait on Matthew Tracy, and I don't think He'll mind this Sunday morning!" They both laughed, and suddenly their laughter subsided, and the room was quiet, and the house was quiet, so quiet that I tip-toed down the hall.

Young Matt was dressed by then. He was still in a bad temper and barked at me to hurry, so I hurried, but it was five minutes to nine before I was out in the hall, and young Matt was waiting on the landing outside Mother's door, looking importantly at the new watch Old Matt had given him. "We're going to be late. This family is always late," he said.

"It doesn't matter, the service won't begin until Father gets there," I reminded him. "The minister will wait, he always does."

"One of the troubles with this place is that nothing can happen until Father lets it happen—not even time."

"Well, anyway, he'll be late today," I insisted, and began to tell him what had happened, and what I'd heard while I was in the hall. I had wanted to tell him when I went back to the room, only he'd been too surly to talk to. But now I had to speak, I had to tell someone, it seemed important for me to tell it. But I didn't tell much of it. His fist doubled up, and he hit me square in the face. "Shut up, you little bastard!" He was in such a rage that his words came like a croak.

His blow had caught me off balance, but I guess he could have knocked me down even if I'd been on balance, and expecting it. The surprise hurt me more than the punch, but it was a bigger hurt because it had been Matt who hit me, and his anger seemed to have come out of nowhere. Before I could say or do anything, he started off downstairs, but he only got halfway down, and then he came back again.

"Get up," he said in a low voice. "Get up on your feet."

I didn't know whether he wanted to strike me again, but if he did, that was all right.

"Now hit me!" he said, and his hands went down along his sides, waiting. "Hit me hard!" he commanded again.

I mumbled something about maybe I didn't want to.

"Hit me, damn you! I told you to hit me, and you're going to!"

Part of me really didn't want to, but part of me boiled to get back at him for the sting and the puffiness that was building up in my lips. I closed my eyes and I let him have one. I think I must have hurt my hand more than I hurt him, but there was a scarlet red spot on his cheek.

"Do you want to hit me again?" he asked.

"No," I told him.

We both started as my father cleared his throat. The door to my mother's bedroom was open, and he was standing there. He couldn't have been standing there long, but he'd seen enough, and he was a very perceptive man. Then my mother joined him, and we all went downstairs and out into the cold snowy morning and walked up the road to the church, Matthew holding my mother's arm and Matt and I trailing along behind. Matt scrunched a handful of snow, offering half of it to me. "Put it on your lip," he said, and he rubbed some on his own cheek.

When we got to the church my father helped my mother into our pew, which was behind where his sisters sat, and then he and Matt walked up to the two chairs that waited for them before the altar. As soon as my father was settled the young minister looked up

23

from his meditation and, as if he had just decided it was time to begin, he commenced the service.

During the dull portion of the service when you didn't have to do anything but listen—and the young minister never said anything worth listening to anyway—I tried to catch my mother's attention. There were a lot of things that I wanted to talk to her about. There was something in the way Old Matt had held her that had frightened me, and I wondered if it had frightened her, too. But she didn't seem to hear me. She just sat staring straight ahead, and her color was high, maybe from the cold of the walk, and there was that strange look in her eyes that wasn't quite laughter, that came there when she was thinking of something, or remembering something special, and then the real business of church came along, like the responses, and I forgot to talk to her.

After dinner that day, I remember that my father asked Henry Talcott—that was Will Talcott's father—to bring around his favorite blacks hitched to a cutter. I thought that I'd be going with him; but he said no, some other time we would go out together alone, this time he was taking Matt. I watched them go off to the Upper Farm, taking the road that made a circuit of the whole Hill, and came back up the south valley by the Adams place. I don't remember what I did all afternoon, but I remember their return toward evening. I was reading in my room when Matt came in.

"I feel like a dog," he said, straight off, as if he'd rehearsed it to himself.

"Sometimes you don't act as good as one," I told him.

For a moment it seemed that what had happened between us before church was going to start all over again, but he held himself in and straightened up, and he looked all of a sudden like some of the pictures of Father that were about the house. "There were a lot of things I didn't understand about this morning, that I understand now," he said.

"What kind of things?"

"About men and women and what can go on between them and that sort of thing."

"What sort of thing?"

"I guess it's love," he said, "but you're too young to discuss it with. —Elizabeth asked me to tell you that supper is ready." He turned on his heel and walked out of the room. Matt had grown

24

up that afternoon. It was a full year or two before I caught up with him again, and by then, of course, all this was something that we didn't have to talk about between us.

I remember, though, that after supper that night, when it was time for us to leave the big room downstairs and go to bed, I watched Father saying good night to my mother. He would always stay down and smoke a last pipe before he turned out the lights and came upstairs. Matt kissed him first, and then I did; but I didn't go, I waited in the doorway for Mother, and I watched her go to him and I watched to see if there was anything to what Matt had been talking about that went on between men and women. All that happened, though, was that Father took her in his arms and put his lips on hers for a long time, like he always did, and his right hand came up along her side and cupped her breast, like it always did. I decided Matt had been talking through his hat. . . .

"Thinking of something?" Mooney asked.

"Just things that happened a long time back."

"Death has a way of doing that," Mooney said. "I sure hope everything goes off well tomorrow, especially for Matt's sake." He finished his glass and went to the door. "When all this is over, you and I ought to go out and get some bird shooting some morning. Matt and I used to go out together a couple of times each fall."

When he'd left I sat for a few moments staring at the fire. It was nice of Mooney to suggest a morning's shooting, a man's way to say what was on his mind. First Sanford, and then Mooney, and presently it would be the people on the place; they were still unnerved by Matt's death, but tomorrow or the next day Will Talcott and the others would be wanting decisions made, and they'd be looking for a Tracy to make them. I'd grown up in this world, and yet I'd always been apart from it. It had been Matt's kingdom, and now he was leaving it to me; leaving human relationships and obligations and duties as if they were property that could be devised as part of his estate. In England it would be different. The relationship of the Tracys to a village such as Haviland would be out in the open, and clear, where everyone could look at it. But this was a nebulous sort of thing. The Tracys never held public office, but Matt and our father before him, and his father before him, had always had no small hand in determining who would run for office, and their determination usually amounted to election. If

25

a worth-while thing for the village didn't originate with the Tracys, then it soon came to them for the aid and assistance that would make it possible. The village would raise half the money, and the Tracys would put up the other half. That was the way the library had been built, and the fire department and Grange Hall, and the Community Hall, and the water works. Old Matthew had given over Bull Pond for the water works, along with a good part of the money, and the land for the new road up the Hill—Tracy land that cost the town a dollar; and the Tracy holdings of Sheffield stock had had no little to do with the milk plant being located in Haviland. Of course, in a lot of this, self-interest might be said to be involved. The Tracys made more milk than any other one farmer in the town, and the new road certainly didn't hurt their land. But on the other hand, they had their own library, and they never went near the Community Center, and they had their own water system and didn't use the town's; so for most of it, self-interest lay in having a better town to live in. Yes, Matt had willed me more than just a farm and twenty-two hundred acres and all the Tracy clan.

I straightened the fender in front of the fire and started down the hall. I had almost reached Elizabeth's door when I remembered Joy. I whistled to her and she bounded to my side, and then I wished I'd left her where she was. Her eagerness was not for me; she thought that I was taking her to Matt.

Two

Elizabeth was in her favorite chair before the fire, a tray on a small table in front of her.

"I felt a little done in," she explained. "I thought I'd have my supper here. Would you like to have yours with me, or would you prefer to eat downstairs?"

"Here," I said. "I'll ring for Mrs. Haines."

"No need, I told her when she brought mine up to bring yours, unless you went down for it."

"That's good." I picked up the empty coffee cup off her tray.

"Mrs. Haines was going to pour it later." Elizabeth gestured to the silver pot on the hearth near the fire. "But you can have some now, if you like."

"No thanks, later will be all right. I was just looking at the china."

"It's lovely, isn't it? Derby. Matthew bought me two full sets. I'd broken two cups and a plate once, and he said the extra set was to take care of breakage. In all the years since, there's never been so much as a plate nicked. Mrs. Haines always gets it out when she thinks I need cheering up."

She was looking into the fire, and I wondered where her thoughts were. With young Matt? With my father? With the day he'd given her the china, or the morning I'd heard a breakfast tray crash on the floor?

Gently, I put the cup back. "You must remind me to begin to collect associations that will have such magic," I told her.

She shook her head. "You never know you're collecting them, or which ones have the magic," she said. "You just wake up one

27

day to discover that the things about you and the place you live in are filled with overtones. You can't do much living without that happening to you."

"I've been discovering a few overtones of my own, today."

"I don't doubt it." A faint smile touched her lips. "Henry Sanford came in to see me."

"He told you about Matt's will?"

"Yes."

"Were you surprised?"

"No. Although perhaps I was a little surprised that Matt had never talked it over with you."

"You say that as if you and he had discussed it?"

"Not concretely. When you came back to the Hill a couple of years ago, he spent a long afternoon talking to me. He knew that he would never have any children with Alyse and he felt that you would be the Tracy line, that you had returned to stay, and would live your life here. He seemed sure of that, even before I was."

"I don't know how either you or he could have been so sure of it. I'm not sure of it yet, myself."

"Maybe because there's a contentment that a man knows when he's in the right place. And once he knows it, his wanderings are over."

"You don't think I shall ever want to wander again?"

"I don't think so."

"What about yourself? Has this been your place of contentment?"

She considered it. "Perhaps 'contentment' is the wrong word," she brought out at last. "I've known love and pain, and great possession and great loss—and I've known them all with a deeper intensity and vividness than I could ever have experienced them with other people in any other place."

"It's strange that you stayed after my father died. I often wonder why you did."

"You needed roots."

"I didn't realize it at the time."

"No, and there was Matt, too," she said, "all alone here on the place, with no one really to look after him. And then there was Constance."

"That must have been difficult—Constance."

"A little. But Matthew wouldn't have wanted her to live her life

28

out in an institution. We'd talked of bringing her back here just before he died. There was no danger of violence any longer, and even her memory of what she'd done had been wiped clean."

"What it boils down to," I said, "was that you were tied here. You'd given hostages to fortune and you were held by them."

"Only in a sense. You pay for the things you have in this world, and I had had so much—the little I've done is hardly payment at all."

Mrs. Haines brought in my supper, but I wasn't hungry. I cut up a chop and fed it to Joy. She accepted a piece or two with quiet dignity, as if she were doing me a favor.

"Put some on a plate, and let her have it," Elizabeth said.

Her dog's sense of obligation vanished. She turned away, as if refusing what was on the plate could not hurt my feelings.

"Perhaps you'll both eat later," Elizabeth suggested. "I told Mrs. Haines to have something for Frankie when she comes in. You might be hungry by then and join her."

"Good." I was glad to dismiss the business of food, for there was still one question in my mind. "After my father died," I asked her bluntly, "didn't you ever think of marrying? I mean, was it because of me or Matt that you didn't?"

"No, it wasn't because of either of you. And it wasn't the false sentimentalism of being faithful to a memory. Oh, I know that women need love, but they need it most when they've never known it. Matthew and I had something from the very beginning that was marriage in its fullest sense." She smiled. "And now you had better start out for Poughkeepsie, or an old lady may shock you with her views about life and love, and men and women."

I stooped and kissed her hair, aware that it still had the same indefinable fragrance that I could remember from my childhood. She stopped me at the door. "Don't you think it would be best for Frankie to stay here at the house instead of over at the big place?"

"I hadn't thought about it," I admitted. "Yes, I suppose it would. I'll ask Mrs. Haines to attend to it."

"It's all attended to," Elizabeth said. "Mrs. Haines and I didn't want to bother you, so we just moved Frankie's things down, knowing it would save time when you did get around to thinking of it."

I laughed. "Look. Let's face it. I'm not cut out to be the head-of-the-family type. I haven't enough God-almighty complex in me.

You and Mrs. Haines had better go ahead and be the power behind the throne."

"Matt didn't want it that way."

"There are no strings on the will," I reminded her. "The whole place can be broken up into smaller acreages and sold off, and the whole damned family wrapped up in moth balls and filed away in the historical society."

"He went over those very points with me," Elizabeth conceded. "He didn't like things with strings on them. If that is ever your decision, it will be your decision and it will probably be for the best."

"By the way, Jim Fletcher called me this afternoon." I glanced at my watch and, not having eaten supper, found that I still had time to get to the station. "Like you, he didn't want to bother me now, but said he'd like to talk to me Monday about Walter Semple."

"Oh?"

I came back into the room, and leaned against the back of a chair. "Jim says the County Committee wants to bounce him out of the Assembly, and give the nomination to some younger man."

"What's your opinion of Walter, John?"

"The same as everybody else's, I guess. He's a blatherskite and a petty crook."

"I've always liked the sound of 'blatherskite.'" Elizabeth tasted the word. "It has such a nice quality of contempt."

"But damn it, I'm not ordained to decide the fate of Walter Semple. The complacent old windbag is sitting at home this minute quite satisfied that his next two years are secure. And never dreaming that if I say yea or nay, speaking for the Tracy clan, Jim Fletcher will cut his throat."

"I imagine that whether you like it or not you've been 'ordained,' as you put it; and I'll wager you'll hear from Walter Semple within twenty-four hours. He may be a crook, but he's not stupid."

"And I suppose you know what I'm going to say to him?"

"I have a pretty good idea. He'll probably make you a proposition, and it'll be sufficient excuse for you to tell him to go to hell."

"In politics you don't tell a man to 'go to hell.'"

"In small-town politics, you do. It's done every day." Elizabeth laughed. "If the admonition were effective, a considerable number of people in Haviland that Matthew told it to would be there now.

30

But even if they didn't go to hell, they didn't go to Albany, either, and at least one of them didn't go to Washington."

"Listen, I'm serious," I said. "Why don't you be the head of the family? You are anyway, and you'd do a much better job of it."

"I know you're serious. But it's a man's job, John. And it can be a worth-while one."

"Depending on the human factor, and that's pretty dangerous. Hardly what you'd call democracy—the family of power and wealth running the show from behind the curtain."

She shook her head. "You're wrong. It is democracy and it works pretty well. Never mind the power and wealth; that's secondary to respect and integrity, and a lack of self-interest. When the Tracys lose that, they won't have any contribution to make in Haviland. And it isn't just the Tracys, John. There are a lot of big and little people in the picture. Jim Fletcher and Henry Sanford and Doctor Farnley and Alf Adams down the road—they're not bootlickers and they don't need our wealth, but they have looked up to the Tracys for always standing for what seemed to be the town's best interest. And now having fully delivered myself on the subjects of love and politics, I am very certain if you don't start this instant you'll be late getting to Poughkeepsie."

"You're right. And to borrow a phrase I once heard in a play—'You're a wonderful old duck,' Mrs. Milnor."

Will Talcott was standing by the car when I got to it. "Evening, John. Just wanted to tell you that the Radiant cow dropped her calf about an hour ago. A bull calf. I suppose we'll be keeping it?"

I was about to tell him he would have to carry on with things the way he saw fit, but I realized that that wasn't the answer; he'd given me the clue. "That's one we'll certainly keep," I told him. Then something clicked in my memory. "When did she achieve her world's record?"

"Four years ago, and four lactations ago. The greatest lifetime producer in the breed."

"I remember her great—or would it have been her great-great-grandmother, when I was a boy. Old Matthew had tremendous faith in her line."

"Your father had considerable flair for cows," Will said. "That was before my time, but that original gamble of his did more for

31

the breed and for farmers' pocketbooks all over the country than any other cow in history, I guess."

I glanced at my watch again. I would just about have time to make it, but Will had more on his mind; either that or he seemed to be waiting for something. Then all at once, I knew what it was. "I'm late now," I explained. "I'll stop in at the barn and see her when I get back from Poughkeepsie."

That satisfied him. He closed the car door and leaned in the window. "You'll be mighty proud of her. She's in the end stall. I'll probably see you. I'm looking in on her every hour or so."

He waved and called as the car got under way: "Take it easy and watch out, if it's misty. The road'll be slick up West Mountain way!"

There was a cut of frost in the air and the smells of the land were sharp and pungent. From the house to the Corners at the crest of the hill was a mile and a quarter, and on both sides of the road was Tracy land. At the Corners, it was Tracy land in all directions, and the signpost reading Tracy's Corners let you know it. On the road to the South Hill, the land ran right up to Alf Adams' two hundred acres. The road to the North Hill went to the Upper Farm, and then petered out as it branched one way toward the Ten Mile and the other way over to the Connecticut line, with poor land and tumble-down houses marking where men had tried to farm and failed.

From the curve, if you slow down—and that evening I pulled to a stop to light a cigarette—you can see way out over the lower valley, and to the right the houses and buildings of Haviland itself, and near at hand the broad level fields of the Lower Farm. For as long as I could remember, it had been part of my consciousness, and it had been Tracy land. It was still Tracy land, but the man who owned it and would have to do with it would call himself John Milnor. I wondered if I would ever think of myself as a Tracy? I never had, and, except for a few years in my adolescence, I had never had any resentment about the way things were.

Only now and again in a man's life is the problem of bastardy likely to rear its head. When I was entered for school, the question either never came up or Matthew handled it in his own way. When I was nineteen, though, I tried to get a passport, and made a mess of it; such a mess that I was sent back to Haviland with a list of

32

questions that would have to be properly answered, and affidavits that would have to be executed. I was too troubled and heartsick to discuss the matter with Elizabeth; but when I went to Pop Sanford for help, he treated it as a matter of course and knew just what to do, and the passport came through in short order.

I did have some conflict within myself along in those years, though, on the matter of girls, and I had one very difficult time with a young lady in New York. I was deeply in love, or anyway thought I was; and on the night that we became engaged, or rather were about to become engaged, I told her the story of Elizabeth and Matthew. Her reaction was probably quite normal—in many ways she was an excessively normal girl. She told me that marriage was out of the question, her family and her social position would never survive the shock of the inevitable disclosure. However, her scruples did not go so far as to prevent her wanting to go to bed with me, which she did, and with such intense eagerness that for her carelessness she had some several weeks of considerable worry that bastards might be contagious, and she might be starting a long line of them. A year later she married a fine upstanding young fellow without a bar sinister to his name, and a year after that, he was sued by a show girl for beating her up and for certain other little habits, to which even the tabloid papers could only very obliquely allude. The day I read the story I happened to be in Poughkeepsie, and I got royally drunk in a bootleg joint across the street from the courthouse. I remembered later the refrain of what must have been my very dull litany to the bartender; it was that a man might be a bastard but he wasn't necessarily a son of a bitch. The bartender agreed that it was a fine point of distinction, but a valid one.

The problem naturally came up again when I voted for the first time. I didn't vote in my twenty-first year, and that in itself raised no small amount of hell in Haviland. Like many small towns, they take their voting pretty seriously. They know who does and who doesn't. It's the high sacrament of democracy, and they're all for it. So in the fall of my twenty-second year I marched into the Town Hall with no little trepidation, and feeling as if I were running the gauntlet of my fellow townsmen.

I hadn't told anybody up at the Hill what I was about, and I had picked a time when I thought the village fathers in charge of

33

such matters would have few if any applications for the franchise of citizenship. I couldn't have picked a worse hour. It was just before dinner, and it seemed that everybody in Haviland, who was anybody in Haviland, had dropped in at the Town Hall to inspect personally the health of the nation and see if the proper ratio of about eight Republicans to one Democrat had achieved their majority in the preceding year. When I saw what was stacked up against me I couldn't back out, but I made up my mind that I was going to take the first man who snickered out in the alley and beat his block off.

Jim Fletcher was sitting behind the desk, and he was flanked by old Judge Miller and Pop Sanford and both of the Allen boys from the garage and Phil Smith from the *Chronicle,* and hanging about the room was about every man I knew in Haviland. Jim Fletcher asked the questions, and before I could frame the answers he got them in ahead of me. When he came to *father,* he intoned in a loud voice *Matthew Tracy.* I must have been pretty tense at that moment, and I remember having watched the men in front of me for a flicker of reaction; but I saw none. *Mother,* Jim went on, and then with the same pause he'd used before—and you could have heard a pin drop in the room—he answered, in that same loud voice, *Elizabeth Milnor.* And that was that, except for Judge Miller suggesting that they were through for the day, and everybody who had no official business there took it as a hint to clear out. As I started to follow them the Judge called me back. After he had carefully closed the door, he took a key off his chain and opened the drawer of his desk and took out a bottle and a glass.

"John," he announced, "I think this day deserves a drink. Now you're a voter and a part of the town. Your father was a fine man and the town's lucky to have one more Tracy in it."

The only other time the issue ever got important was in the army, when a stiff-necked chicken-ass colonel raised a point of service propriety as to whether a bastard could, by act of Congress or designation by the President of the United States, be created into an officer and a gentleman. He didn't put it in exactly those words, but he almost did. After his genealogical grilling I was ordered to wait in the anteroom of his office. I was still waiting when the colonel crossed the office and went in to see the "Old Man"—

34

in most outfits the "Old Man" is the colonel. But we didn't think in terms of a regiment. We thought in terms of a division and later in terms of an army, and our "Old Man" wore stars. He also wore a couple of forty-fives, and an exceedingly thin temper. What I heard through that door probably wasn't very good for discipline, but the General had his own ideas about discipline. He sounded like Old Matt. He damned everything in sight. He damned colonels who bothered him with picayune details. He said he didn't give a damn where the hell a man came from if he could command a tank, and to hell with how many fathers he had or didn't have, what he wanted in his tanks was "bastards" whether they were legitimate or illegitimate ones; tough sons of bitches and bastards, that's what he wanted; that he'd personally supply the missing paternity of any bastard that was worthy to serve in his command.

The sergeant on duty was a good guy, and he was trying to keep a straight face; he was having a hard time of it until the General's door slammed open, and the General charged into the room. The sergeant's face was straight enough then. The General stood glowering for a moment, his hands caressing those forty-fives on his hips. "I know you," he finally said. "Milnor."

I said, "Yes, sir."

The next time I saw the General close to, was in the little village of Saint-Valery. A group of us had been ordered to meet at what was left of an inn that had called itself the *Colonne de Bronze*. It was one square back from the *quai* and of more than casual interest to the Jerries. Every once in so often, with no very definite time schedule, they would throw one in there, just on the off chance of catching something. It was a damnfool point to collect eight tanks for briefing, but the Old Man seemed to lead a charmed life so we weren't worried too much. He had his back to me when I came up to him; he was talking to one or two of his staff.

"It was a tough son of a bitch of a nut to crack," he was saying. "No time to get artillery on it and the road coming between those two towers where they'd once imprisoned Jeanne d'Arc. A hell of a high wall and a cliff on one side and the same high wall and a thirteenth-century tank defensive moat on the other and the Jerries down at the foot of the hill with a strong point covering their withdrawal. So what does this crazy bastard do? He grabs a two-wheel farm cart stashed away behind the wall, and he puts a couple of cans of high-octane juice in it and ties a bag of grain to it for a sea anchor to keep it on its course. Then he plugs the cans with a couple of shots, heaves a match onto the wagon and sets it off down the hill. From a strong point he turned it into a hot point. He fried the knockers off those Jerries and then he was rolling in on top of them and the town was ours. Give me a few more sublime bastards like that and we'll have this son-of-a-bitch war over so fast GHQ won't have time to get off the pot."

There was a crump and everybody ducked. The General turned around slapping at his boot with his riding crop. "Captain," he nodded, "I was just telling how you came through the Jeanne d'Arc towers."

Again I said, "Yes, sir." Then I added, "Thank you, sir."

He beetled his eyebrows and glared. "For what?" he bellowed.

"For the 'sublime,' sir."

The Old Man roared at that, and explained to the puzzled officers about him, "A private joke, gentlemen. A very private joke." And then we forgot about Saint-Valery and talked about how we would hit Abbeville. They gave medals for less, but I didn't get one at Saint-Valery—the General, however, had talked one hell of a citation. The ribbon I did get later was for just having been present while another show was going on.

Those seven words, incidentally, were the only words I ever spoke to the General. Beside whatever other opinion he may have had of me, he must have put me down for a laconic bastard as well. . . .

I flicked the cigarette out of the car window and let my foot down on the accelerator. It's strange how memories come flooding back on you, and in the passing of a moment whole chapters of your life can pass before your mind's eye.

I had to slow up at the village. The Allen boys at the garage raised their hands and I waved back and Eddie Connors waved from the doorway of his diner and then I was through the village and my foot was on the floor board.

There are no towns between Haviland and Poughkeepsie, just names of where villages had once been thought of, but had never grown to more than a few houses. But the names sounded important. Whaley, Stormville, Ludingtonville, and then the growing traffic of the county seat. I had intended to stop for a drink at the

Nelson House, but I glanced at my watch. As it turned out, I could have had the drink anyway, because the train was marked up fifteen minutes late.

All that evening and during the drive over, I had been shying away from the actual moment of meeting Frankie. What do you do when you meet an eighteen-year-old girl in the dark on a railroad platform with the news that her stepfather has killed her mother, and blown his own brains out? It doesn't make much difference that great love prompted a merciful act; it was still her mother and the only living person in all the world that she could call family. Of course, the news itself she already knew—that is, that her mother was dead; but you couldn't put the rest of what had happened into a telegram. At least I hadn't been able to. I must have written twenty drafts of that wire before I sent it, because I knew what it was going to be like when she got it. I had been working in a lumber camp in Montana the year after I left college, when Matthew died. Mrs. Haines had sent me one of those meaningless telegrams that told me nothing except that my father was ill, but with the color of urgency for me to hurry home. It had taken me hours to get to a town where there was a telephone, and then hours more to get through to Haviland. Those were some of the worst hours I ever spent in my life; in each one of them I prayed that I might be able to get back before he died, and then in the end I learned that he had been dead for two days before the telegram reached me.

Maybe it was the war that taught me that the truth, no matter how hard, is kinder than hope when there is no hope. Frankie was close to Matt, so I had had to give her both barrels, or she would have wondered why she was hearing from me and not from him. I had implied that it was an accident. I'd seen no harm in that.

As it happened, Frankie hadn't gotten the message until the next day. In these damned modern colleges for women, girls seem to be away from them more than they are in them, and Frankie had been off on some half-baked field trip with two other girls, leaving only a vague itinerary of the towns they'd be stopping at.

I was in the village attending to things when she'd finally telephoned. Elizabeth had spoken to her, and had left the story still with the color of accident to it. She asked Frankie to promise not to read the papers. The *Times* and the *Tribune* had been dignified and straight with their stories, but the tabloids were having a Roman holiday. The Tracys were a colorful tribe to uncover, and their women were pretty colorful, too. The libel laws protected Elizabeth and me, but Emmeline's shindig and spectacular divorce came in for a rehashing, and they did Susan's laundry over for her again. All in all, the story was hardly one that I liked to think of Frankie's reading on a train all alone as she came home.

The Albany express finally came roaring in, and the great driving wheels of the engine ground past me. There are two kinds of people; people who can guess which end of a train the sleepers will be on and people who can't. I never can, and some stiff-necked obstinacy or pride always prevents me from asking. I was way up at the forward end of the train, and perversely the New York Central had that night decided to put the Pullmans on the rear, so I had to hotfoot it all the way back to where Frankie was standing beside the last car with her luggage about her on the platform. I waved to her, but she couldn't have seen me. I slowed up to catch my breath, and also to catch my thoughts. It is strange how at certain moments inconsequentials are very vivid and stand out so clear to you. I was conscious of the cinder grits crushing and grinding under my shoes, and of the burned-out and used sulphur smell of a trainyard that makes the phlegm in your throat acrid and thick, and you know if you spit it will be yellow. And then she saw me, and half started toward me. I kissed her, because I had always kissed her when she went away or came home, but I was aware as I did it that it might take only a slight trigger in her present state of emotions to crack her up. It would have been better for her had I remained detached and undemonstrative.

Suddenly, the human mind having curious streaks of cowardice in it and subtle devices of evasion, my thoughts took escape to the previous summer when Matt and Alyse were giving their end-of-the-season party. Matt had done the honors of host, and then caught my eye and grabbed two highballs, and we had escaped to the garden and were sitting on the edge of the wall in the dark when Roger, Adelaide's husband, and Frankie had come up from the pool. Frankie was walking quickly, straightening her dress and putting her hair back in shape with short angry motions. Roger caught up with her just before they came into the light of the doorway, and took her by the shoulders and turned her to him and kissed her and said: "Don't be so upset, Frankie. After all, we are what we call in the South 'kissing kin.' "

Frankie had stared at him for a moment and finally said with a biting composure: "And what do they call incest in the South?"

Only when she had gone into the house did Matt speak. "Come over here," he'd said.

Roger started, and turned toward us.

"You cheap son of a bitch." Matt's voice was low and level.

Roger commenced to splutter, and Matt stopped him. "If it ever occurred to me as a good thing to do, I'd kill you the way I'd crack a louse between my thumbnails. Don't ever let the idea occur to me."

Roger opened his mouth to say something and then turned with his mouth still open and walked into the house, looking every inch a gentleman.

Yes, your mind can do tricky things like that when you want to evade the reality of the present. Then a porter was beside us, picking up Frankie's luggage, and we were walking toward the car and there were people about, and it was good for both of us, probably, not to be able to talk.

As I turned out into the traffic, Frankie asked: "Did she suffer?"

The driving was an insulation. "No. She didn't suffer at all."

"And Matt?"

"It happened very quickly."

"I bought a paper at Rouses Point, the *Tribune*. I didn't read it. I kept in on the seat beside me, but I didn't read it. And then when the train stopped at Hudson I couldn't stand it any longer. But there wasn't anything except the notice that the funeral would be held tomorrow morning. The story must have been in the day before."

"Yes, it was in the day before. —Did you have anything to eat?"

"I didn't want any supper."

"I'll bet you didn't have lunch either?"

"I tried. But I couldn't swallow. I just couldn't swallow."

On the Post Road, traffic stopped for a red light. When it changed, I turned right instead of heading straight across town.

"Where are you going?" she asked.

"We're going to stop at the Nelson House for a bite."

"I couldn't eat anything."

39

"I didn't have any supper," I told her. "Sit with me for a moment. I'll just have a sandwich and a drink."

"Oh. Of course."

There was an empty parking slot in front of the sheriff's office across the alley from the hotel. It was always safe from parking tickets. The cops assumed that any car left there was official, or the driver knew somebody; and they were usually right.

I glanced at the dining room but it was empty. There were people in the grill so we turned in there. I wanted people and sound. They could be antiseptic and impersonal and act as a stiffener on the emotions. A jukebox was playing, the bar was lined, and a number of the tables were occupied. I picked one a little out of the stream of things.

"Two bowls of soup," I told the waiter. "Any kind of soup."

"Bean soup," he said.

"All right, bean soup. And two steak sandwiches, rare, and two Scotch and plain water."

"I couldn't eat anything, I'd be sick if I ate anything," Frankie said.

"That'll be all right, too, but at least you'll have had some food inside you."

The waiter looked like he was going to say something and then just shrugged. A lot of dames had been sick in the Nelson House, and anyway it probably wasn't his job to clean up.

"Better make those double Scotches," I called after him.

"Tell me what happened," Frankie said.

"Let's wait for the drinks."

"I don't need that kind of courage."

"It isn't for courage. It's for being good for you."

She got part of a drink down, and put the glass on the table.

"All right," I told her. "Hang on to something, Frankie. —Did you know Alyse was sick?"

"Sick? No. She went into the hospital for a few days last summer for a check, but she told me everything was fine—just to watch her diet and rest a little."

"They didn't tell her, then. They told Matt. But Alyse was no fool, Frankie, I think she knew. . . . Matt couldn't be sure, but he thought so, too. Anyway she decided to make the last months of the summer the most wonderful ones that she could. For Matt, for

40

you, for all of us. She tasted and retasted every beautiful thing that lay within the compass of her life. I don't think she and Matt had ever experienced such happiness as this last summer. But still he couldn't be quite certain whether she knew or not. —Come on, drink that soup, Frankie."

I drank some of mine, and, obediently, she picked up her spoon. The most that could be said for it was that it was hot, and had what a camp cook would call "hair on it"; which was to say that it had that indefinable mucilaginous base of all hotel soups.

She put her spoon down again. "I think I know what happened, John. You don't have to tell me, it's all suddenly very clear. It's just the details—"

"A little while ago, Matt took her out to the Mayos."

"She didn't let me know that."

"There wasn't any use. When all the tests were made, they dealt her the ace of spades. They still didn't tell her, they told Matt. But she told Matt she knew, and after that there wasn't any more make-believe between them."

"Did she have much pain?"

"Very little, I think; that phase was just starting."

"But aren't there things they can do? Things they can give you so there is no pain?"

"More or less. But you lie on a bed and waste away, and torture those who love you, and in the end—you die anyway."

"You mean she didn't have the courage to go through with it?"

"There are different kinds of courage, Frankie. They gave her some stuff to take. A couple of weeks ago she tried to take too much."

"Oh."

"She didn't take enough. Then she begged Matt to help her. And he promised her that he would, when things got too bad. And even after that, they had some wonderful days, and the medicine saw her through the bad hours. Matt left a letter that told the whole story."

She had to wet her lips. "How—?"

There was really no way not to tell her, for eventually she would know. "They went for a walk together, as they often did. They walked up onto the crest of the hill at the edge of the woods, where the valley and the land they both loved was spread out before

41

them, and the bright light of the sun was on them, and love was in their hearts. Alyse didn't know that was to be the moment; Matt was always gentle with her. The shot that killed her went through her body and into his arm, so he must have been holding her. She died instantly. And then he blew his brains out."

"She couldn't have known that!" Frankie protested on a cry. "She would never have agreed to it!"

"No, she didn't know it. Matt's letter made that clear. But he didn't want any more of life after Alyse."

I thought that she would break at last; that the tense and brittle barriers she had erected would shatter and she would break; but quietly, and very simply, she said: "I wonder how often such love happens to people?"

The waiter was standing beside us. "Anything wrong with the steaks?"

"Nothing. I guess we weren't hungry."

Frankie didn't say much of anything on the ride back to Haviland. Just one or two inconsequential things. I remember that I asked her if there was any family in France that should be notified about Alyse.

"Nobody close," she told me. "They're all very old now—more connections than relatives. I'll write them in a day or two."

"You mean there isn't anybody on your side of the family?"

"No one, really."

"Well, you inherited quite a lot of Tracys," I said in an effort to cheer her.

She shook her head.

"Oh, come off. Elizabeth couldn't love you more if you were her own, and you've got me to fall back on *in loco familias*."

"You're naming all the Tracys that aren't Tracys. Elizabeth really isn't. You are, I suppose, but I've never thought of you that way, and I'd rather not, I'd rather have you as friends and not inherit you as family. Susan, Adelaide, Emmeline, even Constance —I don't think Mother or I were ever very welcome in their eyes."

"To hell with them. Anyway, they're never about much except in the summer—and as for Constance, she's so remote that she hasn't really been here for the past forty or fifty years."

"The Tracys weren't very good with women, were they?"

"What do you mean?"

42

"Except for Elizabeth and Alyse, they married bad. And except for Matt and you, they didn't beget much that was worth anything. They're a sort of patriarchal strain."

I controlled a smile. What a strange mixture of youth and age she was. "In this last generation, they were pretty patriarchal," I conceded.

"In the earlier ones, too, from what I've heard. They seemed to have concentrated all their strength and vitality in the male line."

"They bred great cows," I offered in jocular defense.

"They were more famous for their bulls." Then after a pause she said, "This is a stupid conversation. I suppose people talk about stupid things to avoid talking about things that hurt too much to talk about—"

Suddenly I could feel the convulsive spasms of her sobs, and heard the dry throat-aching rasp of grief welling up in her. We were just coming over the crest of West Mountain, and I pulled the car into a wide space on the side of the road. "Go ahead and cry," I said. "That kind of strength is really weakness."

The dry rack continued until my own throat hurt in sympathy. I put my arm about her and pulled her over to my shoulder. She resisted and fought against me, and I held her in both my arms. Gradually I could feel her fingers bite into me in utter capitulation to grief; she beat her head against my chest in a frenzy of violence, as if you could beat away the tricks that life can play on you. Then, finally, the choking bitterness went out of her, and the violence passed, and she was only hurt and young, and I was glad that for a space the numbness of fatigue was granting her a merciful respite.

Presently she straightened up, and reached over and took the handkerchief out of my jacket pocket and wiped at her face. "Silk isn't very good for this," she said.

I handed her a linen handkerchief and she went to work with that. Then in a casual voice she said, "There were civilizations that had taboos and superstitions about their hair clippings and nail parings. They felt that their souls were involved and that if anyone else ever possessed them they also possessed some part of their spirits and could hold them forevermore in their power."

I had to come out with it: "Your generation of young girl is educated in the damnedest things."

43

She ignored the comment. "I was wondering if they ever had a taboo about tears," she went on. "I mean, tears are really so much more important than nail parings or hair clippings, and when someone else possesses them—" She broke off. "Thank you, John. Thank you for a lot of things, a lot of things that I'm sure I must have forgotten to thank you for. And thank you especially for tonight."

I started the car down the mountain toward Haviland. "The Greeks had tear bottles," I reminded her. "I've seen them in museums, beautiful little iridescent glass bottles. They used to save their tears."

"Small bottles and big bottles for small griefs and big griefs, I suppose. And fancy bottles for show."

"And if their grief wasn't large enough," I said, "I imagine they used to put water in them. I don't suppose human nature's changed much in two thousand years."

She fell silent again, and then she said, "You haven't told me where they are. Are they at the Big House?"

"No," I told her. "They're in the village. There's official business and red tape to go through."

"The police, and things like that?"

I nodded.

"That must have been very hard for you. For you and Elizabeth."

"Not very. The police have been pretty decent, and Matt was well thought of by a lot of people who could smooth things over."

"I want to see Alyse," Frankie said.

"Tomorrow," I put her off. "They'll be at the house, then, and the family will meet there before going to the church."

"Let it be tonight, John. I don't think I could see her for the last time in front of the family."

"It's rather late tonight, isn't it?" She didn't answer me. She had already said all she had to say. "Maybe it isn't too late," I gave in.

When we came to the War Memorial, I turned left and pulled to the curb. Mooney's window was dark, but there were lights at the rear of the store. "I'll see if anyone's there," I told her, and I got out of the car and hurried across the sidewalk. The knob turned and the door swung open. There were voices from the back

44

room. "If he's got a poker game going I'll brain him," I muttered under my breath.

But it wasn't a poker game. Mooney and Doc Farnley and Jim Fletcher and Doc Harris and Lieutenant Costello from the Police Barracks were sitting around Mooney's desk talking. There was a bottle of whisky and some glasses in front of them, but they were just talking quietly, and in the back of the room on two trestles were the caskets. They all looked up as I came in.

"Some of us dropped in to sort of pay our respects, and pass a little time with Tim," Fletcher explained. "Tomorrow it will be a kind of Tracy show up on the Hill, and a lot of us wouldn't want to be intruding. Quite a few came by this evening, John. Some who did, would surprise you."

"Thank you, Jim—I've got Frankie out in the car. She wanted to see her mother. I just met her at Poughkeepsie, she hasn't been home yet."

They all got up. Mooney gestured to the bottle, but I shook my head. He slipped open a desk drawer and piled the bottle and the glasses into it, and then everybody went out to the street door. Farnley nodded to the car and said: "Shall I go out and get her?"

"That'd be a good idea," I told him. "This is going to crack her up pretty much."

He crossed over to the curb, and Costello and Fletcher and the others stepped a little aside, and lit cigarettes. Costello flicked his match in a glowing arc toward the Memorial. "Did you hear?" he asked. "They're going to put our names on the other side. 1917 on one side, and 1941 on the other."

"No, I hadn't heard."

"That'll leave two empty sides for two more wars," he said.

"Maybe they could think of some appropriate sentiments to inscribe," I suggested, "and call off the wars."

"That makes too much sense. They wouldn't ever do it that way. My name'll be up on that. I was in Matt's regiment, you know."

"Yes, I knew. But I didn't know you were from Haviland?"

"It's honorary. I left the force and went into the service from here. I come from Brooklyn, but who the hell would ever be able to find my name on a monument in Brooklyn? If you want to be a big frog, pick a small puddle."

45

"It's a small puddle, all right. Most of the names they'll put on the other side of that memorial will be the same as on this side. Matthew Tracy and Matthew Tracy."

"But only one Costello," he grinned.

"Maybe one way or another you'll get your name on the other two sides," I told him.

Doc Farnley touched my arm. "I think she'd like you to go in there to her," he said.

Frankie was standing beside her mother's casket, quietly looking down. As I came up to her, she reached out and touched a lock of Alyse's hair, and smoothed it over the left side of her forehead. "Mr. Mooney couldn't have known that was the way she liked it." She looked over to the other casket. It was closed.

I took her hand. "No, Frankie. Let's go home."

When we walked out to the car, the group of men were standing quietly by the door. Several of them simply said "Good night." The rest said nothing. Small towns can achieve a nice dignity about death. They live so intimately with each other that at the end, they don't slop over with a lot of loose sentiment and hackneyed phrases. They just accept it, and let life go on with its living.

When we got up to the farm, I passed the Big House, and Frankie looked at me inquiringly. "I forgot to tell you, Elizabeth had some of your things moved down to our place. She thought you'd be happier there." She nodded, and said nothing.

There were no lights on except in the lower hall. I opened the front door, and Mrs. Haines came out of the kitchen passageway with her finger to her lips. She put her arms about Frankie and then whispered to me, "Your mother got to sleep about an hour ago. I gave her some hot milk and she took one of her pills. She left one for Miss Frankie, too."

Joy, hearing us, came downstairs. She paused for a moment at my side, and then, seeing the door opened, dashed for it and was out into the night.

"Damn," I said. "She's off to the Big House, or up to the barn. Oh well, I have to go up to the barn anyway. Will Talcott will be expecting me."

"At this hour?" Frankie asked.

"Radiant dropped a fine bull calf, and in Will's mind it wouldn't

46

be right if a Tracy didn't give it the once-over. I'm elected. Life goes on."

"I'll go with you," Frankie said.

"You'll go right to bed with some hot milk," Mrs. Haines interjected firmly.

"I'm not tired. Maybe a breath of air will make me sleep better."

"Leave a thermos in the library, and you go off to bed. You need some sleep, too,' I told Mrs. Haines.

The air was crisp, and there was a crunch of frost on the grass as we walked across it. For quite a stretch we didn't talk, and then Frankie asked, "What will happen to all this?"

"Matt left a will. The land comes to me. I don't know whether that answers your question. It will just go on, for a while, anyway. It has a momentum, you know."

"It'll go on," she said.

"There was a trust set up in the will for you."

"I don't want anything from the place. It should all stay here."

"It isn't from the place," I explained. "It was set up a long time ago by Matt, for Alyse and for you, and now for you alone. You'll have enough—more than enough—to give you independence. It's all right for certain kinds of people to be independent; it doesn't destroy them or rob them of the impulse to do things for themselves. You're that kind of a person, Frankie."

"Do you feel that you're not?" she asked.

I thought about it. "I don't know. Maybe if I'd had to do things my life would have been different."

"You've done things."

"Aimless things. Different things. I haven't been a sticker, or one of the world's doers."

"You were in the war."

"So were five million others. Twenty-five million others, if you count those who were on all sides. It was part of our generation."

"This was enough of a job for Matt, and he could have done anything he wanted."

"But this was what he wanted," I reminded her.

The Big House was dark as we passed it again, but there was a shadow of darker darkness before the door. I whistled softly, and Joy came reluctantly toward us. Halfway down the drive, she

47

stopped and looked back. I whistled again, and then she came to me.

There was a glimmer of light from the barn. We stepped through the door, and the sharp bite of the night was drowned in a warm, moist earthiness. The long corridor between the cows was restless with quiet living, and the fragrance of grain and the ammoniac odor of the gutters had a seminal and fertile urgency about it.

Suddenly I was oppressed by the sense of the three hundred ton weight of hay that lay above the low ceiling, the fermenting hundreds of tons of silage that flanked the doors, and the fourscore of cattle that this single barn contained. All of it had come from the Tracy land, had come in an unending and repeating cycle through the generations, and if the cycle were ever broken there would only be futility and waste.

The light that was burning was at the far end, where you could hear a rustling sound of straw, youthful and out of place in the placid midst of all these quiet matrons of the herd. The Radiant cow gave a deep, almost inaudible low as we approached, and then, sensing no harm, fell to licking at the calf that stumbled against her on gawky and ungainly legs.

The door from the milk room opened, and Will Talcott came into the barn. "Evening, Miss Frankie. Evening, John." And then without a word of Matt, or of death, he turned to the pen. "There she is!" he announced proudly. "She's a great old lady, isn't she? And there he is, probably one of the greatest bull calves to ever be born in the breed. It's a great herd now, but if he proves out, it'll be the greatest herd in the country."

"How long will it take before you know?" Frankie asked.

"All depends. We'll get a clue in his daughters. That'll be in five years, maybe six. Their first lactations won't tell the story. But we'll really know in his granddaughters, say ten years."

"Then you're just guessing now?" Frankie said.

"Oh, it goes further than guessing," Will told her. "It's a sense you get to have. Besides, everything that could make him great is inside him right now. If he really has it—barring fate and accident—well, then it's happened. Only it takes a long time to prove out anything on a farm, a long time. And sometimes we don't live to see it happen. —You'll have to name him in a day or two, John.

48

He ought to have a good name, something like *Tracy's Radiant Victor*."

"Why assume that I'll be the one to do it?"

"There aren't any other male Tracys to carry on, are there? No one counts Miss Emmeline's or Miss Adelaide's husbands as Tracys, and the land has always followed the male line."

"So even a bastard is better than no Tracy at all." I didn't say it out loud.

Three

I gave Frankie the sleeping tablet when we got home, and she took it docilely enough. But as I was about to turn out my light, I heard a sound in the hall. I opened my door. There was no one there, and the house was silent. I looked toward Elizabeth's room to see if there was a spill of light across her threshold. It was dark; Frankie's door was dark, too. Then I heard a sound from the library below. I slipped on my dressing gown and went down.

I could see her figure, a dim shadow by the fireplace. She turned as I came in. "I was frightened," she merely said.

"Did you take the pill?"

"It didn't do any good."

"Give it time. I'll put a log on, and we'll sit here for a while until you feel sleepy."

"Thanks, John."

"But you mustn't talk, you must even try not to think. Just sit and watch the fire and let sleep happen to you."

"I'll try."

She came over to the couch and sat beside me. I handed her Elizabeth's afghan that was folded uncomfortably behind me, and she wrapped it about herself, like girls do at football games, and then curled her feet up under her. Neither of us said anything and the fire burned fitfully. Presently I was aware that she was crying silently. Her shoulders were still, but I could see the glint of tears running down her face. I reached out my hand and touched hers, and she slumped against me and I could feel the slight tremor that ran through her as I stroked her head. Then in a little while she was quiet, and I didn't realize that she was asleep until she turned in my arms, reaching gropingly in that foetal crouch of slumber of the very young. In turning, her robe and nightdress were pulled awry, and her breast was round and pink and small-nippled and formed like a woman's. Frankie was no longer the adolescent girl I'd always thought of her as being, and the knowing aroused in me a strange humility, and a desire to be tender; and at the same time I felt that glow of consciousness that wells up in you in the presence of beauty, wherever you come on it, whether it's in a painting, or a statue, or a sunset, or in the body of a woman. With a strange ambivalence I was suddenly angry with her. After all, I wasn't old enough for her to relegate me so cavalierly to the avuncular. Stretching a point, I was old enough to be her father, but I didn't feel it, and I didn't want to feel it. Then I realized that my anger was toward myself; maybe I'd turn into a nasty middle-aged lech like Roger, if I wasn't careful. Gently, so as not to waken her, I pulled her nightdress closed. My touch must have half-wakened her, though, for her hand reached up and clasped mine and held it there. Finally when her grasp relaxed I slipped my hand away, but still her arms encircled me. It may be a romantic image to hold the sleeping body of a lovely girl, but it's damned uncomfortable. I got a cramp in my back, and it felt like needles were being jabbed through my arm, and my neck ached with tension. But it was important for Frankie to keep on sleeping, so I didn't dare move. Before I knew it, I must have gone to sleep myself.

When I opened my eyes, there was the faint light of dawn in the room. It took me an instant to register that I was not in my own bed, but lying on the living room couch, with a blanket over me. And then I saw Frankie. She was sitting on the floor beside me, staring at me. When she saw that I was looking at her, she smiled.

"When I woke up you were asleep," she explained. "You sleep awfully soundly. I tried shaking you a little but that didn't work, so I got you a blanket."

I started to get up but her hand pressed me back. "No, go back to sleep. You've been through a lot, too. I'll wake you with a cup of coffee when it's time for you to get dressed." Her hand was still on my shoulder, and her face was very close. "Thank you again, John," she whispered. And then her lips touched mine and it wasn't

51

the kiss of a child, but the firm warm lips of a woman. An instant later she was gone. "God damn it," I muttered, and got stiffly off the couch and went upstairs to my room.

I thought of trying to go to sleep again, but I heard the whine of the vacuum cleaner from below, and an instant later it moaned to a stop. "Not today, Annie," I could hear Mrs. Haines say.

There's an odor of mortality that infects a house and the people who live in it when there's the business of death to be done. The overtones of life belowstairs ceased, and it was as if the house again slept. It was just shy of seven o'clock. "Oh, to hell with it!" I exclaimed, and hurled the blanket I had been carrying around with me like a toga, onto the bed. It was as if I were hurling Françoise away from me. A silly damnfool name to give a girl—Françoise. It probably hadn't seemed silly, though, when Alyse had given it to her, in the little gray and pink house under the hill at Saint-Cloud, where the Seine, wandering a lazy course beneath it, looks divorced and separate from the twentieth century. I can never remember whether at Saint-Cloud the Seine runs to or from Paris; it twists and turns so, you seemed to be crossing it whichever way you went.

Odd how you collect towns and villages and cities and make them part of your consciousness. You can know them ever so fleetingly, and yet they become a part of the tapestry of your being until you find yourself hemmed in and full of places that really have had nothing to do with your life. Sometimes I feel myself a walking atlas of sensations related to places, an emotional Baedaeker filled with the damnedest trivia; but it's the trivia that makes man unique, not the important things. The important things all happen to everybody and in the same way; but the trivia, they happen to only one man, and they happen alone. Pasted in the album of my memory there were a couple of trivia about Saint-Cloud.

It would have been 1937 or 1938; no, 1937—the next year I was a long way from France, and that was the year that Matt met Alyse, and met her in Saint-Cloud. But my business there, while part of the stuff of broad coincidence, had no real focus or relationship. I was in Saint-Cloud by accident, by the merest accident of having met a girl in Paris and falling in love with the idea of falling in love, and Saint-Cloud seemed to be an admirable place in which to do it. We didn't have too much time, and it wasn't to be a very great love affair anyway. Saint-Cloud was near, and it was early spring and a week end. When you cross the bridge, if you turn left, the road will take you to Versailles; if you turn right, it will take you to a little hotel just back from the river. It won't take you much further, because from that point on it ceases to be a main road, and piddles away into a village street—the village street that Alyse had lived on, and Frankie was born on. But that's another story; and it's Matt's story, not mine. It's funny, I can't even remember the name of the hotel. I guess it wasn't trivial enough. And gone from my memory, too, was the name or the shape or the color or anything about the gay young girl who had shared the room with me. I assume that she was gay and young, because the year was 1937, and I was twenty-three and the whole world was young and gay. On the first evening, with the lights out—if I had been older the lights would have been on and it never would have happened —I stubbed my toe, and an excruciating pain ran through me. Actually I'd broken it, and a little later, when I should have been feeling something decidedly different, I was feeling only an outrageously throbbing big toe.

Standing on that balcony in the spring of 1937, I could have looked down on the street below and seen a nursemaid. She would have been dressed in pale blue, and would have worn a bonnet with a flowing veil, and a cape, because the morning would have been brisk. She would have been sitting on one of the benches by the embankment, and toddling in front of her would have been a two-year-old child trying to command her awkard little legs into carrying her over to where a yellow butterfly would be hovering against the bole of a cropped plane tree.... Now that I have gone back in my memory, I can smell the sweet, vivid aroma of hot chocolate somewhere in the background. But the name of the girl, the shape and the color of her has shredded away. Probably she called "Johnnie," to let me know that breakfast was waiting and she was waiting, too. And about the bed, I can, oddly enough, remember the warm, human and very nice smell that fragrant bodies give to a bed they have slept in and made love in. And I think I remember a child's cry, gurgling into laughter as the butterfly floated off in the breeze, and the world became magical and beautiful to the child—and the child's name could have been Françoise.

The last time I saw Saint-Cloud a war had passed that way and a lot of things had happened. Alyse had written me a letter that had finally caught up with me the day Paris fell and we were entering the city. She asked me, if I were passing that way, to go to the little house she had once lived in, and snip a sprig of lilac that would be hanging over the garden wall, and send it to her. She had meant it as a bit of whimsy, but there had been a real touch of nostalgia in it, too. Her letter reached me in one of those low moments a man can get into. We were winning a war, but we were losing so much in winning it that there was a bad taste in our mouths. We found ourselves standing knee-deep in the rubble of a cockeyed, beat-up world, and suddenly it had seemed important to me to recapture some contact with another world that had once seemed to be going someplace good. On an impulse, I commandeered a jeep and a driver, and we went up the Champs-Élysées and out the broad avenue into the Bois. We were stopped at the bridge to Saint-Cloud, but our papers were all right—or rather, I had so many of them that their sheer weight carried us through; but we could see what the Germans had done to the little village. Their orders had been not to touch Paris; but this was not Paris, just a little village, and so they had turned their guns on it. It didn't even make important rubble; it was merely a wanton gesture of civic butchery.

The little hotel was not *marching,* as the GIs used to put it—a convenient phrase for anything that didn't function, that was *kaput,* finished, washed up and done with. From the top of the street it looked pretty much the same, but once I got close to it I could see that it definitely wasn't marching. Its roof gaped to the skies, and within its flame-smudged stone windows there was only gutted emptiness. Fire had seared the side of the building so that the word *Auberge* remained untouched, but the words that followed it were utterly obliterated—*Faison d'Or* or *Roi Soleil,* or some such. I could have found out by asking anyone in the street, but I wasn't in the mood. That was another of the trivia, that its name was lost, but the little balcony that hung like a quizzically raised eyebrow from a room on the second floor was still there.

With Alyse's letter and the description and the number of the house, I found it. Only it was fresh out of lilac that year; in fact it was fresh out of roof and windows and one wall. I had a camera with me to take a picture, and I set the diaphragm and focused and did all the things you do with one of those complicated small

54

cameras, and was just about to press the button when I stopped. There was enough misery and heartache in the world without adding to it. The Germans had gratuitously knocked Alyse's little home into a shambles, but there was no reason for me to gratuitously batter and break her memories of it. I used the film to take a picture of my driver for his girl, against a pile of rubble in the village square; he even borrowed my forty-five so he could look like he was taking the town single-handed. . . .

All of this I remembered, and yet I couldn't remember the girl's name. I called myself an appropriate epithet. When a man gets so he can't remember the women he's slept with, he's getting too old to think of—well, he's just getting too old.

There was a knock at the door. "I've brought your coffee," Mrs. Haines called in to me.

I poured myself a cup, then peeled out of my pajama jacket and went back into the bathroom to shave. I was halfway through when there was another knock, but the bedroom door opened before I could call out. Elizabeth came in with a coffee cup in her hand.

"I heard Mrs. Haines bring you your coffee," she said. "How did you sleep?"

"About as well as I expected to," I told her.

"I waited for you last night," she said, "but I must have dozed off before you got in."

With anyone else, it would have been a question. "We stopped for a bite to eat," I explained, "and then Frankie wanted to look at Alyse."

"I thought she would. —How did she take it?"

"Very well. Afterwards, she went with me to see the new calf, so it was later still when I came upstairs. I stood outside your door but you must have been asleep by then."

"Why do you shave with that kind of a razor instead of one of those safety things? Is it because they're the kind your father always used?"

"More than that. These are Old Matt's razors."

She smiled, but it was a smile of memory. "It's such little things that hurt so much. The way a man clears his throat in the morning, or whistles to his dog, or the way he holds the skin of his cheek while he shaves. When you were six years old, you sometimes invaded our bathroom to watch your father shave in the mornings, and I resented it deeply. It seemed a violation of a very wonderful intimacy." She cleared her throat, and took a swallow of coffee.

"Why didn't you slap my bottom and heave me out?"

"You had your rights too," she smiled. "Part of the adolescent initiation, I suppose the anthropologists would call it."

The door was open, so Frankie didn't bother to knock. She had got this wandering-around-in-the-morning-with-a-coffee-cup-in-your-hand habit of the Tracys, too. "I looked in your room," she said to Elizabeth, "and then I heard your voices in here. Do you mind?"

"Not a bit. —Only put some clothes on and be decent." Elizabeth turned to me.

"Oh, I've seen him in a bathing suit. Much more naked," Frankie said.

"Than what?"

"Than he is now."

"It's not the same thing," Elizabeth insisted.

"I don't see why it shouldn't be," said Frankie.

"I don't either," Elizabeth admitted, "but it isn't. Nakedness is very desirable in its place, but otherwise it's just slovenliness or bad manners."

"This is a very interesting discussion," I broke in. "But please remember that I was standing here quietly shaving when suddenly my privacy was invaded from all sides, and I became a focal point of female interest."

The words were hardly out of my mouth when Mrs. Haines hustled back into the room with a large pot of coffee. "Come right in," I said. "Join the crowd."

"I heard everybody talking in here and I thought you might want some more coffee," Mrs. Haines stuck up for herself.

"We do," said Elizabeth.

This time I closed the bathroom door and finished shaving and put on a dressing gown. Then I knocked. "May I come in?" I called.

The room was warm but Mrs. Haines had lit the fire for cheer, and Elizabeth and Frankie were seated in front of it. There was a quality of tension in the air that gave me a sense that something was starting that had to be stopped, even though it might hurt

56

intolerably for the moment. "Do you want to hear something funny?" I asked.

"I would very much like to hear something funny," Frankie said, and I noticed how sometimes there was a faint bilingual precision to her speech. Her eagerness almost halted me, as if she were hungering for something to make her laugh and break the band around her heart. It was going to be like hurting a child, but the hurt would be beneficent, and I made myself go on.

"Do you remember the first time we met?" I asked her.

"At the Haviland station," she answered promptly. "Matt and Alyse and Elizabeth and I, we all met you. You had been away for a long time, and you were wearing a gray suit and a gray tie, and as soon as we got back to the Big House I went out in the garden and picked a flower for your buttonhole to take away the grayness. I remember you kissed me for it. And I can tell you about the second time I met you," she went on breathlessly, "and the third time, and the nine thousandth time."

"You should get *A* in all your school work," I stopped her.

"It's college, not school."

"A slight problem in semantics, which we won't go into at the moment. But do you know when you first *could* have met me?"

"When I told you," she insisted. "I hadn't been in Haviland very long, and you were coming back after being away."

I shook my head. "No, we'd met a long time before that. I just happened to think of it this morning."

"It couldn't be. I wouldn't have forgotten."

"Do you remember the house you lived in at Saint-Cloud?"

"Yes—I can just remember it. What's that got to do with it?"

"Quite a lot. How much further back can you remember?"

"How much further do you want me to remember?"

"To when you were about two."

"That's not fair. Nobody can, really."

"Then I'll remember for you. —Did you have a nurse, and did she wear a light blue uniform, with a veil and starched collar?"

"Yes! How did you know?"

"Not very remarkable; they all did. —And did you ever play on the little gravel esplanade in front of the hotel, while your nurse sat on one of the benches under the plane trees?"

She gave a little gasp of memory and closed her eyes. "The

Auberge du Roi Soleil! The gravel walk, the benches, the plane trees with their tops cut off. —And you were there, and I was only two!" She opened her eyes and stared at me. "What a shame I was too young to remember. I would like to have known you when I was two."

I felt acutely uncomfortable for having wakened in her more than I'd bargained for. "Skip it," I called it off. "I was just making it up."

"The *auberge,* the river walk, the nurse in her uniform—you made them up?" Her stare widened. "But you couldn't have. It's real. They were there. And I was there, so you could not have made me up too."

"But I did. It was all a figment of my imagination."

Her mouth set, and the little laughter that had been in her eyes went away. Her hand shook as she put down her coffee cup. "There was something you wanted me to know," she said. "Something you started, and aren't finishing for some reason. It is important for it to be finished, if only because you have made it important."

There was the smart of anger in her, and suddenly anger bit into me, too, for she had made me feel foolish and cheap. There was only one way to break this crazy thing that was growing between us. I chose my words carefully. "If the little two-year-old girl I have just imagined," I said, "had looked up, she would have seen me standing at a window of the hotel."

"What were you doing there?"

"Just standing."

"I mean what were you doing in the hotel? What were you doing in Saint-Cloud?"

"I'm not sure that this is a seemly conversation to be holding with a two-year-old figment of my imagination."

Her hand gripped mine. Her eyes were like glints of blue flame, and then they quieted and she laughed lightly, but her nails still cut into my palm.

"You were there with a girl?"

"Why do you say 'girl,' not woman?"

" 'Woman,' that's more serious. Or was this serious?"

"Talking of seemly conversations, I don't think this is the sort of thing to discuss in front of my mother," I evaded.

58

"Elizabeth is far too intelligent to have foolish illusions, even about you, John."

"I'm not quite sure that I wouldn't prefer to speak for myself," Elizabeth interjected. "I'm afraid this whole conversation is pointless, foolish, and getting out of hand."

"He began it," Frankie maintained obdurately. "And it must be finished. Were you in love with her, John, whoever she was?"

"I don't think either of us was very deeply concerned on that score."

"Was she beautiful?"

"Yes, I suppose so. What I mean is, she must have been. I really don't remember."

"Beauty is always desirable in such matters, particularly if there is nothing else but beauty. Still, I suppose one can't have everything." Frankie walked over to the table and started to light a cigarette. She flubbed the first match, but got going on the second. "Was she good?"

"What do you mean, 'was she good'?"

"Just exactly what you think I shouldn't mean."

At this point Elizabeth put down her coffee cup. "I suggest that we drop this whole business," she said firmly. "It's got undercurrents that I neither understand nor like."

Frankie turned to her in swift appeal. "Please, Elizabeth, this could be important. I don't know how or why, but it could be. John has something in the back of his mind he wants to say, and maybe he needs help. —Was she good, John? Or don't you remember that? It all seems a little vague, so she probably wasn't very good, or you would have remembered it. You probably don't even remember her name! It's a pity. Oh, I'm not being moral. It's just a pity. And so wasteful of emotion. The poor girl, not beautiful enough to be remembered; not good enough to be remembered. Now if I were going off to a little hotel, I'd make very certain that the man would remember me. There would either be love, or I would be pretty enough to stay in his memory and—and I would make it my business to be good at what I was doing, so superlatively good that there would never be the remotest chance of the man not remembering."

"Frankie!" Elizabeth protested, not from shock or moral censure, but to break the child's hysteria.

59

"It is nothing to be shocked about," Frankie defended. "It's a woman's business and it's her right and obligation to be good at it. But all this is beside the point. The reason John started to tell this little story of his was not to make me laugh. And it wasn't to boast of his youthful amours. But it was to tell me that almost before I was born, he was going to bed with girls whose names he doesn't even remember now! He was afraid I might fall in love with him and he wanted me to see how foolish and ridiculous that would be."

She was standing in front of me now, and her voice had grown quieter until it was almost a whisper when she finished. And then, without so much as the flicker of an eyelid to give me warning, the flat of her hand came across my face with all the power and sting of a young animal, and she marched to the door. She stopped when she reached it, and her hand dropped to the knob. Then she turned and ran toward me and what she did next was as unexpected as her slap. Her arms went about me, and she was kissing me. But more than that, through the thin silk wrap she wore, her body pressed against mine with all the knowing of a woman. The knowledge was instinctive, but the instinct was there. Across her shoulder I could see Elizabeth stare at us, and then rise and walk toward the window and look out.

Then Frankie was gone and there was a dry choked sob in the hall, and the door of her bedroom slammed shut. Elizabeth turned from the window and came toward the fire. After a long moment she said: "If she hadn't slapped you I think I would have. In some ways, John, you are a fool."

"She's upset. Alyse, and all this rotten business."

"It would be abnormal if she wasn't upset. But all that had nothing to do with what just happened."

"But it's ridiculous!" I expostulated.

"Of course it's ridiculous. And not the least ridiculous thing about it is the way you've been acting." She started to fold up the blanket I had tossed on the bed. With the blanket off it, the bed looked arrogantly unslept in.

"I didn't sleep with Frankie last night! At least not the way that phrase means."

"I didn't ask you," Elizabeth said quietly.

"All right, but the idea crossed your mind."

"Naturally."

60

"Why, naturally?"

"People do, when they're in love. Sometimes when they're not in love."

"Look, I'm not in love with Frankie; and if she thinks she's in love with me, it's nothing more than a schoolgirl crush."

"Frankie is not 'just a schoolgirl,'" Elizabeth said.

"Nonsense. She goes to school. That makes her a schoolgirl."

"Your constant reiteration of that point of view doesn't make it so."

"We sat downstairs last night, talking. She was crying and finally she went to sleep. Later I went to sleep and she got that blanket and covered me. When I woke up she was sitting on the floor looking at the fire. That's all there was to it."

"That's all there was? There are some marriages that never experience even that much intimacy. And you call her just a schoolgirl."

"My God, are you crazy, too? A child, really nothing more than a child, whose mother's just died—a little too spectacularly—and I put out a friendly helping hand, an avuncular hand, and she goes off her emotional rocker. And so do you, philosophizing about marriage and higher intimacies. —I'm old enough to be her father!"

"So we all gathered from your little story. However, the matter of age becomes a diminishing obstacle, up to a certain point—but if I go on you will say that I am philosophizing again. From all this, though, I gather that you are both aware of the problem, and that it will have to be worked out some way."

"It's nothing that time won't take care of properly."

Elizabeth smiled in that remote way of hers. "Not forgetting that *time* is one of the involving factors."

"Look, let's be reasonable."

"I'm very reasonable," Elizabeth said.

"And let's stop being superior and remote. You talk as if it were possible for there ever to be anything between me and Frankie. As if it wouldn't be a cockeyed, crazy idea."

Elizabeth shrugged. "People find the completion of their lives in strange ways. And when something is right, it can be very right, even though the rest of the world might call it wrong. That's a piece of wisdom I had to learn a long time ago."

61

"I know what you mean, but it's still crazy. Sometimes I think this whole Tracy tribe is crazy. They've sat up here on their semi-royal backsides for so many generations making their own rules and doing fantastic things and getting away with them."

"Not forgetting that you are a Tracy," Elizabeth reminded me.

There was a knock on the door, and Mrs. Haines stuck her head in. "Mr. Mooney's downstairs, so is Miss Susan and so is Miss Emmeline, and your breakfast won't be any the better for being kept waiting. Will Talcott's fixing the stove in the church, it don't work—it never does, except for Will—and he wants to talk to you about breeding a cow, I don't remember which cow, but he says he'll talk to you about it this afternoon."

"Don't you ever take a breath?" I asked her.

Her answer was a snort as she took the spread off the back of the settee and smoothed it tidily over my bed. I waited until she'd finished and left the room. "Oh my God," I said, "Susan and Emmeline. And the damned furnace in the church. I suppose that's to be one of my concerns from now on—that and every cow that's bred!"

Mooney was standing beside the sideboard in the dining room when I got there, with Old Matt's Waterford decanters reflecting patterns of amber and golden lights upon the silver. There is a natural affinity of a drunk for liquor; even when he isn't drinking he likes to be near it.

"Have a bit of whisky," I invited him. "Or would you prefer coffee?"

"Well—" He put his derby hat down on a chair, and I gestured to one of the water glasses on a tray, and he took it, and poured himself what in any man's language would be called a drink. "Trouble in the sitting room," he said, and raised his glass.

"What kind of trouble?"

"Woman trouble. Emmeline's took over. As Matt's sister, she's appointed herself the head of the family. She's decided to run the funeral. Susan's been out to the cemetery, says she's to be buried beside Matt, and we'll have to dig another grave for Alyse. I was to the church and Adelaide was there. She ordered me to change the chairs where the 'family' are to sit. Four chairs, she wants. For her and her husband, and Emmeline and her husband."

"Well, why not let them run it? It'll save a lot of trouble."

"Now that's a damnfool thing to say, **John**. A funeral's got to be run with a strong hand, or you have a hell of a mess on your lap. What's more, it's got to be run by one person. And you're it. —I'll have another small drink, if you don't mind, just to take the taste of the last one out of my mouth."

He drew a chair over beside me and put his drink down in front of him and then produced an envelope from his pocket. There was a mare's nest of doodles and notes on the back of it. "All right, let's get started. Number one, the graves. They stay dug as they are. Susan's a pain in the neck anyway, and what's more she's divorced, she's lost her chance to be Tracy-queer. Right?"

"Right."

"Now the chairs for the family to sit in. There'll be three, not four. Right?"

"What three have you elected?"

"I haven't elected anything," Mooney said. Matt elected, so there'll be three chairs—for you and Elizabeth and Frankie."

"Why not let all of them sit there?" I asked.

"Because the whole damn church'd be sitting there. There's too many Tracys! Look, John, they got to learn sooner or later who's the top dog in this show, and there'll be less headache and fireworks if it's sooner." He took another sip from his glass. "Oh, yes, I almost forgot. After you'd left for Poughkeepsie last night, Miss Constance got around to deciding that it was Old Matt and not young Matt who was being buried. So she had me up to the Big House, and nominated herself for the head of the family pew. Elizabeth seems to be her favorite at the moment—claims Elizabeth is her daughter and she doesn't want any part of Emmeline or Adelaide. —How mixed up can you get?"

"That's quite a lot of mix-up, I grant you. All right, how do we start to straighten it out?"

"I'm just getting around to that, John. I suppose you'd call it psychology; though with this bunch of zany women you might wonder how anything mental would work. You're going to be at the church when they arrive, and you're going to be sitting where you belong. They'll recognize a fact when they bump into one."

"Tim," I told him, "just get this straight. I don't care what happens as long as there aren't any scenes or ructions. Matt and

63

Alyse deserve a decent funeral, and it'll be tough enough for Frankie without having the family raise hell."

"All of which brings me around to the end point," Mooney said. "This kind of a setup you never can tell what new problem will pop up right under your elbow without you know it's there. I'll do whatever I think best, and any question, I'll just say I was following your orders."

I smiled at him. "Comes there's a third world war and they can use old codgers like us, I couldn't want for a better adjutant."

Mooney rose. "I'll get rid of that hen party in the other room and send them off to the Big House. I'll drive them there myself." He stopped at the door. "Oh, by the way, about the bill."

"Do we have to talk about that now?"

"We don't have to, but I'd like to, just so we don't misunderstand each other, John."

"Go ahead, then."

"There won't be any. Oh, you'll get the bills for the caskets and the actual out-of-pocket expenses, but that'll be all you get."

I frowned. "I don't follow you. You're in business, you've got to eat, and God knows we can afford to pay."

"Oh, I know you can afford it," he said. "But with friends, it's different. You go fishing with a man through your lifetime and bird shooting each fall, you don't send him a bill when you bury him. There's enough sons of bitches in Haviland that I don't like, to keep me in business when they die. That's the way I did it for your father, that's the way I'm going to do it for Matt; and if I live long enough, which isn't likely, that's the way I'm going to do it for you, you old bastard."

I was still smiling when Elizabeth came into the room.

"What's so funny?" she asked. "I just got a cold snub in my own house from Susan and Emmeline."

"Just something Mooney said," I told her. "By the way, he insists that he doesn't charge for Tracy funerals; at least certain Tracy funerals. He says he buries their bastards free of charge, too."

"I'd be surprised if he had sent a bill," Elizabeth said.

"I don't get it," I told her. "Undertaking isn't exactly an eleemosynary following of man. Or have I lived too many years out of Haviland to know how it functions?"

64

"You've gone fishing with Mooney, Matt did, your father did. I've cooked breakfast for him at four o'clock on a fall morning. It's hard to mix business with things like that. For that matter, when did you get your last bill from Farnley?"

"I haven't," I told her. "Now that you mention it, I never have. I always sort of assumed that the 'Tracys' got a yearly bill and somebody else paid it."

"And you never got one from Doc Harris for your teeth. And you won't get one from Pop Sanford for the estate."

"Well, what do you know," I said. "It's sort of like the Chinese taking in each other's laundry. A gregarious man could starve to death in Haviland."

Elizabeth laughed. "If they didn't like you, you'd get a bill quick enough. A long time ago I was a problem in Haviland. Then I discovered that when you have enemies in this kind of a small town, that's when you discover who your friends are. They're strange people with strange prides. They don't like to make money out of the people they like."

At that point the door opened and Frankie came in. She closed the door, and stood with her back against it. "I'm ashamed of myself," she said. "I didn't know there was that much nastiness in me. John, I promise you that I will never strike you again, to my dying day."

Elizabeth rose and kissed her, but I downed the impulse to and patted her shoulder instead. "Uncle John forgives you," I said. "You know that by a long and circuitous chain of legal circumstance I am technically your uncle; perhaps not legitimately, but technically."

Her eyes wrinkled into a smile. "A slightly bawdy uncle, and quite naughty. I'm in luck, they make the best kind."

We were all laughing when the hearse stopped in front of the door, and a moment later Mrs. Haines brought in the eggs. She took in the hearse in the roadway, and then glanced from one to another of us. "The Tracys are different, Mrs. Haines," I smoothed her down. "They do things their own way. They laugh in the midst of tragedy; and when others laugh, they sometimes weep that laughter should be so rare."

Mooney stuck his head in the door. "Take your time, but it wouldn't hurt to hurry," he said. "There isn't anything going to start without me. And you, young lady"—he nodded toward Frankie—"get some food inside that string-bean carcass of yours." To me he just circled his thumb and forefinger. "After you leave, the car will pick up the ladies at the Big House."

I circled my thumb and forefinger back at him.

Four

There isn't the usual conventional solemnity about death at country funerals; it is, rather, a brief neighborly interruption in the day's work. For the most part, it's a woman's business, and when the funeral is for a woman, men seldom attend. But where the passing of a man is involved, his friends drop by as a matter of course to say good-by for the last time.

When Elizabeth and Frankie and I got to the church it was full to overflowing, with men from the Hill and from Haviland standing in small groups on the porch. I gathered that the stores in the village had been closed for this hour, and the bank too, unless Jim Fletcher had given some junior teller a drawerful of money to do whatever business might turn up while he was gone.

I was about to go in with Elizabeth and Frankie, but Mooney touched my arm, and they went on alone. Then Mooney went back and did things at the hearse, and the men got talking to me. We might have been standing outside the polls on election day, for all the mention or sense of death there was. Jim Fletcher commented on the state of the nation, and Alf Adams and Will Talcott were talking about a new way to treat manure to freeze the nitrogen content. After a short time, Mooney came back and touched one after the other of them, which meant he was selecting the pall-bearers. Up to now I'd managed to escape all the Haviland funerals, having always been away from the Hill at the Tracy deaths, and I suddenly realized that they did things differently in Haviland—maybe in all small towns like Haviland. For one thing, they didn't have paid attendants to carry the caskets, and honorary pallbearers to walk solemnly behind. A man's friends performed this service,

67

and they didn't perform it symbolically. I asked Mooney what he did if a man didn't have enough friends, and he chuckled. "There's always enough who didn't like the son of a bitch, to want to be sure he's well planted and to hell and gone underground."

I was conscious of his reasoning as he made his selections. Will Talcott first—because the Talcotts had always worked the Tracy land, and this was just another and occasional chore expected of them. Alf Adams and Charlie Turner and Hank Leigh, next, because they were land neighbors, and neighbors could always be expected to pitch in and help in time of need. And Doc Farnley, and Pop Sanford, and Doc Harris, and Eddie Connors, and Will Renney, and old George Jennings, who was a handy man around the village and had probably dug Matt's grave, and Marty Danis from the Fire Company, and Grady the cop. I had the sense that Mooney was drawing on instinct to pick those who, for one reason or another, Matt would have thought of as his friends. There were one or two who looked like they had expected to be chosen, but I guess it was more that they would like to have been chosen. Mooney didn't skip any that I knew had been very close to Matt, though one or two that he chose I hadn't known had been that close. Then he was tugging at my sleeve, and I realized that I was to be one of the casket bearers, too, and that the rest of them were waiting for me to lead the way down to the hearses. It seemed a sort of ghoulish performance at first, and then it seemed somehow right, a little old-fashioned in its concept, but right. It put death back into proportion, it made it just an ordinary part of the business of living; gave it a homely dignity, somehow, instead of the high-flown theatrical palaver that has come to be associated with the process. Death was something that happened to a family; it was just another problem to be solved, and you went about it in an orderly, decent way. It was something you couldn't handle alone, you needed friends and you needed help, but you didn't run away from it and let others carry on for you. I suppose that when Old Matt had died, Matt whom we were now burying had stood on this same church porch among Old Matt's friends, and then led them down to the roadside to perform this last service for him.

When we got to where the hearses stood, I could see the Reverend Penny sitting in his car where it was parked across the road. Mooney gestured for us to wait a moment, and crossed the road. He had to rap on the window before Penny rolled it down, then he stuck his head in and talked for a minute or two. After that he came back halfway toward us, and nodded to me to come to him.

"We got real trouble now," he told me. "Penny's got himself all screwed up in dogma and discipline."

Jim Fletcher joined us. "What's going on?"

"We got a hung-up funeral," Mooney announced. "I'll be a son of a bitch if I ever run one that's the least bit irregular with Penny again. He called up his bishop this morning."

"What's irregular about it?" Fletcher boomed. "It'd be goddamned irregular if there wasn't a service."

"I thought I had him under control," Mooney said. "But now he's insisting that it was—"

"Go ahead, say it," I told him. "What happened, happened, and dodging the word won't help any."

"He says it was murder and suicide, and the bishop forbids a service in the church."

Jim Fletcher shifted his unlighted cigar from one side of his mouth to the other. "I think I'll be having a few words with the Reverend," he said.

Penny had his window up, but he rolled it down again when he saw Fletcher coming toward him. What followed was a sort of one-sided eavesdropping. We couldn't hear Penny—he was one of the lambs of God that never bleated very loud—but we could hear Fletcher. It's a wonder they didn't hear him in the church. Penny must have had his day in court first, because to start off with, Jim just stood chewing on his cigar, until suddenly the heavens opened and the thunder roared: "You're a servant of God, not his prosecuting attorney. . . . If that's so, then there must be two Gods, the One you believe in and the One I believe in. . . . Well, the hell with the bishop, but I don't believe you told him the story straight; he's a human being, but I've got my doubts about you. . . . Authority? I'll be your authority! You tell the bishop that I told you to do it, and what I say usually happens in Haviland—God willing, and He usually is."

Then Fletcher opened the car door and bellowed, "Get out!" and Penny got out. Fletcher slammed the door after him so hard that the window glass shattered with a loud explosion. Penny said something, and Fletcher answered him with, "We'll settle with God's wrath later on. You'll settle with mine right now!"

Mooney spit in the road between his feet. "What I like about Fletcher," he said to me, "is he's so reasonable. He'd make one hell of a Secretary of State."

A minute or two later, we were bearing the caskets into the church. I was surprised that Matt's casket didn't weigh more, even with five other shoulders sharing its burden. It was hard to realize that just beyond the clean sharp edge of that mahogany was all that was mortal of Matthew Tracy, of the man who was my brother, of the man whom I had loved more than any other man but my father.

Penny was waiting for us before the altar as we rested the caskets on the stands. As I turned to take my seat beside Elizabeth one of those curious projections of time happened, where in a brief instant a whole synthesis of experience occurred. It is like the running backward of a film of a man diving into water, or of the breaking of a great window glass. All the fragments fly backwards and come into place, and there is a oneness and an entity. All these people of Haviland and the Hill suddenly assumed relationship, and became an integral and understandable part of the whole scene. And for an instant, the course and the tradition of the Tracys fell into ordered position, and there was meaning and purpose, and the uncountable Sundays that I had sat in this very church seemed all to have been a preparation and focusing toward this glimpse of understanding. It had happened and passed, in the moment of time that it took me to cross to Elizabeth's side, but I had a sense that, once seen, this shape of things could be recaptured again.

I glanced across her and saw that she was holding Frankie's hand on the arm of her chair, and I was conscious of the incongruity of our sitting in three chairs from the Big House in the space where a pew had once been, while everyone else in the church was sitting in the little penlike boxes, looking for all the world like sheep in a fold. Mooney caught my eye, and his lips worked in the suggestion of a smile. I half turned my head and came into the line of Adelaide's and her husband's stony stares. Emmeline and her husband were sitting beside them, and they were whispering together. In the pew behind, Constance was sitting alone with Mrs. Talcott and fidgeting with her hearing device. She gave a sudden start and I knew she had turned it up so far that it squealed. Behind her Susan sat completely alone in a pew. It wasn't that she was ostracized; it was rather a matter of protocol. As the divorced wife of the deceased—at the funeral of the one-time partner of her loins and the wife who had succeeded her—there was no proper place for her to be except alone; if indeed it was proper for her to be there at all.

Our church has a very beautiful and profound funeral ceremony. The old sixteenth and early seventeenth-century boys who had fashioned it had real dignity and courage. They stood up and they talked with God in good strong Saxon-drenched, short-syllabled words, and God must have been pleased with having fashioned such children. They weren't quaking and namby-pamby and queasy. They were realists, and death was a reality; they were standing up before their Maker, and offering themselves for an accounting. They felt that the soul of man must be good in the sight of God, and that He must respect courage as much as they did. They achieved a straightforward father and son relationship; they lived in their Father's house and worked His land; there was filial devotion and filial obedience, and if you love your Father you don't fear him, because you know that He loves you, even though you may have been a wayward son. Perhaps, in the way of fathers, He had a special affection and understanding for the wayward sons. That's part of what the language says to me, and I can never hear it without somehow hearing the echoes of Dr. Donne under the great vaulted dome of St. Paul's. Even when the bombs were there, the echoes were still to be heard. And in Penny's thin reedy voice the echoes were still there, though they weren't his, and never could have been; he was too frail an instrument for the sounding of such sounds. He reminded me of a small cur running with a pack of big dogs, who stops occasionally to bay in their tones, and is frightened at the sound of his own bell. He was now commending the immortal souls of Matt and Alyse to God the Father, and I started to stir, for the resonant periods were coming to a close.

But not Penny. Penny would write an epilogue to the Sermon on the Mount. He started on a sermon of his own fashioning: "We are solemnly met on this sad occasion of the passing of two misguided and miscreant children . . ."

I was startled by a sound across the aisle from me. Jim Fletcher

71

had cleared his throat; it was a prodigious piece of throat-clearing —you had a sense that the rafters shivered; they didn't but you had the sense that they did. It was the kind of a sound you never expect to hear in church. It was at once a rebuke and an order, and Penny stopped in his tracks. Fletcher began to heave his huge body ponderously from his pew and I thought it was to be a signal that the service had been abruptly terminated. But when he rose, he started toward the altar rail and Penny, now as white as the surplice he wore and with some instinct for self-preservation and maintaining his position in the eyes of the congregation, quickly covered himself. "A few words," he announced, "will be spoken over the deceased by Mr. Fletcher, a vestryman of our church." Then he gave way so that Jim stood in the center of the aisle facing the church, and I realized that as vestryman Jim was about as far up in our church as a man could go without wearing his collar back end to.

"A very few words," Jim said, and now there was a voice in the church. "Because for those among us, there is little that can be said of this man and this woman, which is not already in our hearts and minds."

I have attended services for dead soldiers on the edge of the field of battle, read by friends who were not priests or ministers of any faith, and they had this same curious dignity. Jim didn't say much, but he re-created the image of the man we had known and his relationship to us, and our relationship to some larger over-all purpose in life; and he acknowledged, in passing, a few of the usually unremarked virtues. Then he asked that we speak after him the Twenty-third Psalm, and there was the organ music of great thought and feeling in our midst. Then he said the Lord's Prayer, and Penny, standing beside him and a little behind him, clasped his hands and looked piously down, his lips moving; but Fletcher didn't look down, he looked straight before him, as if the Lord God Almighty might be standing at the door and he might be talking with Him. I felt that for the first time in my life I had heard that prayer spoken.

For a moment it looked as if things would bog down. There is a formula for ending such matters, and Jim was at a loss. Penny started to rustle forward as if to take up the reins, but he was too late. Jim cleared his throat again, and there was no doubt in anyone's mind that the service was finished. *Ita est.*

72

As we raised Matt's coffin to our shoulders, Mooney was standing behind me with his head close to mine. He said under his breath, "That son of a bitch could bury me any day in the week. We got things screwed up in Haviland. Fletcher should be the minister, and Penny should be the banker."

I nodded. Jim Fletcher could bury me any day in the week, too.

We drove slowly down the Hill Road, following the hearses. At the foot of the hill there was a hemlock grove. At least from the road it looked like a hemlock grove, with its formless bank of towering trees. Just a little beyond, at the bend of the road, there was the mill pond and the two old mills—the grist mill, which wasn't used any longer, and the lumber mill, which was used only when timbers for a new barn were to be cut or fence posts turned out. Twenty-two hundred heavily worked acres take a lot of fence posts. And then about once a generation the price of lumber would go skyrocketing and with the Tracy luck, the prices always seemed to boom about the right time of the growth cycle of the replanted timber trees. I remember being told that during the first World War lumber was in short supply, and old Matthew had cut and then thoughtfully replanted. Then in the fall of '42 Matt had written Will Talcott a letter.

The letter had been written from New Guinea. They were over the Owen Stanley Range by then, slamming down the Kokoda Trail and harassing and battering the retreating Japs, but part of Matt's mind was back in Haviland. He had written Will that he felt the price of lumber had peaked, and that there should be a cutting—or rather a half-cutting—leaving seed trees and taking out only the most difficult timber to get. Matt said that it might take more than one war to finish up the job he was on, and the next time labor and costs would be high, so Will was to be sure that the half he left was the easiest and cheapest half to get out.

The other part of the letter had had to do with a breeding plan. They were achieving high production, but there was a hint of udder weakness showing in the line. Matt had been thinking about this down under the equator and half a world away, and he had been remembering the deep and well-attached udders of two cows in the Victress strain. It was his feeling, he wrote Will, that male breeding from that particular strain should be reintroduced into the herd immediately and repeated again in the second generation; nor was Will to be afraid of the inbreeding, the important thing

73

was to get your results and then nail them down. Matt had closed by saying that he had no more time to write, they were going forward within the hour.

Odd to be remembering that letter on this slow ride to the cemetery, with the hearses ahead of us. If Matt had been killed that day the enemy would have picked up his papers and taken them back to Intelligence. I could picture the urgent, intense little Japs trying to penetrate the mind and the intention of their adversary. That letter would really have thrown them back on their heels. What kind of men were they fighting, who, an hour before dying, could think of trees that wouldn't bear timber for thirty years, and a cow's tits eighteen thousand miles away? But Jap Intelligence didn't get the letter, and Matt didn't die that day, though strapped to his leg was the forty-five that was to be the instrument of his and Alyse's death eleven years later.

When we passed the mill, I noted for the first time how it was still in order and repair, and how even the old grist mill was roofed and sided and painted, though it was now used only for storage. There wasn't another such mill in our county, probably not in our part of the state. The Tracys and their long view! Then we came to the hemlock grove, and that was another anachronism, a double anachronism. You don't expect to see a stand of timber like that, with trees, some of them a couple of hundred years old, growing beside a lumber mill.

The hearses slowed, and turned into the grove. We followed them up the road, until soon the mill and the Hill Road and Haviland were lost, and we were in the deep secret green of big trees; and then we were out in an opening of cropped grass, more than an acre of it, still green because the trees braked the wind and the sun was hot there even on cold days. Spread across the green were little clumps of marble stones, all of them marking Tracys, or the kin of Tracys, or those who had lived on the Tracy land and become a part of it, so that when they died it was fitting that they should still be a part of it. They weren't strung out in orderly rows, like stones are in most cemeteries. Even in death the Tracys were individualists. They had set themselves off in little clumps by generations, or by the offshoots of generations that had founded themselves families and then died off as the branch of a tree may die, with the parent stem living strongly on. Off in the far corner

74

the green was broken by two gashes of brown raw earth, which showed the striations of the depths they had uncovered, the dark rich loam of the surface soil, and then the gravel and detritus underlay.

The hearses drove on to the grave side—that was the practical thing to do—but the cars with the family stopped at the edge of the hemlocks. Adelaide and her husband and Emmeline and Roger passed us without speaking, and went on ahead. Then Susan came and finally Constance, flanked by both Mrs. Talcott and Mrs. Haines. The people from Haviland and from the Hill waited their turn, quietly walking to one side so they would not impinge upon the family, and Penny, whose nose was always red and running, was blowing it gustily on a large handkerchief, and bowing to people.

Constance was only a step or two ahead of Elizabeth, but she stopped and turned back, and put her hands on Elizabeth's shoulders and thoughtfully kissed her; and for a long moment she looked into Elizabeth's face and then she said quietly, "My dear." And her voice was strong and resonant and not the quavering timbreless voice that comes from those whose minds wander and are not in focus. For an instant, time froze. Everyone stopped, even Penny. They didn't stare, for country people have manners of their own; but all of them were conscious of this story of human passion. Old Matthew had died eighteen years before, and here standing before his grave were Constance, his wife, and Elizabeth, his mistress. It occurred to me that men die more easily than their passions. And then the moment was over; Constance turned and started forward again with Mrs. Talcott and Mrs. Haines, and we were all of us moving toward the open graves.

Will Talcott was walking just behind me. "How many sheep are we running now?" I asked him.

"Thirty-seven," he replied. "Just enough for what we consume, and a few too many for this." He gestured about him at the hemlock-enclosed burying field. There are some people who feel a distaste at the idea of animals grazing over the dead, but their names are not Tracy; nor did the lamb or mutton that appeared on the Tracy tables ever have a taste of mortality about it.

"We'll have to be getting another ram," Will said thoughtfully. "The one we've got will be covering too many of his daughters."

75

Every once in so often, Old Matt used to import an English ram; young Matt had himself bought one at an auction in London a year after the war. It had come to a pretty price before it cropped its first mouthful of grass on Tracy land, but as Matt used to say, "The good ones always pay for themselves." It wasn't real money, but it was found money, as slow-talking thoughtful old men came to the farm each year and picked out yearling rams and a ewe or two, haggling a bit for form's sake over the price before they reached down into their pockets and came up with hard cash and a lot of it, for an animal that had pleased their eye and promised to please their profits. They'd come from Vermont and New Hampshire and way west in New York State, because their grandfathers had come to Tracy land for stock. They could see a lot more Shropshires elsewhere, but Will Talcott always insisted that they couldn't see any better ones.

As Elizabeth and Frankie and I came up to the graves, Adelaide and Melvin and Emmeline and Roger and even Susan, who for the moment seemed to be joining forces with them, stood in a little block together, like a strong point of resistance, as if the idea was in their minds that they were the Tracys and Elizabeth and I were outlanders, and that they outnumbered us and would stand together. But as we came very close, they stepped aside—Emmeline and Roger going to one side, and Adelaide and her husband going to the other, and Susan went quite a little way off and stood by herself.

When you've seen bulldozers scoop out a trench of earth and a few minutes later push back the earth over the rows of soft unboxed bodies, the act of burial loses any further impact for you. It becomes just a final bit of business necessary to put something beyond sight, so that the process of putrefaction will become concealed and sanitary. Man's final act is when his soul, at the end, extrudes his whole body and says in effect, "There, that's something that must be disposed of and quickly." But Frankie had never touched death before. It was all an unbelievable dream to her until the handful of earth clattered down on the wood of the casket. Her intake of breath wasn't a cry, but it was audible, and her hand dropped and clenched mine in a spasm of agony as the realization of loss and grief shattered through her like breaking glass.

Then it was pretty much over. Matt lay finally at rest in Tracy ground, and Alyse lay in alien ground, far from the little town beside the Seine. On the other side of Matt lay Martha, his first wife; and beside their graves, alone and bitter, stood Susan his second wife. These Tracys and their women!

Those who had come from the Hill and from Haviland started to walk slowly back toward their cars. Elizabeth wandered over a few feet and stood quietly before Old Matt's grave, and Constance started to move away and then turned back and stood beside Elizabeth. She opened her handbag and put on her spectacles and peered at the stone for a long moment. As if she found the words difficult to read, she started to cross the grave, caught herself and walked to one side, skirting that four-by-eight-foot area that is all that man at the end ever holds in fee simple of this earth's surface. She stared at the words and then reached over and touched them with her finger tips, almost as if to prove to herself that what she read was not some figment of her treacherous mind. And as she traced them I, too, read the words for the first time in many years.

Here Lies All That Could Die Of
MATTHEW TRACY
1874–1935

It was a strange thing to have on a tombstone. Elizabeth had put it up just after he had died. The grave stood separate; there was room beside it, in their appointed time, for Constance on one side and Elizabeth on the other, and the arrangement of this had also been Elizabeth's doing.

Something had happened to Constance, or rather it was happening at that instant. She straightened, and the helpless, withered, invalid look seemed to pass from her, and the slackness of her face changed and became taut, and her eyes, that were the rheumy, clouded eyes of the clouded mind, became clear and rational. Mrs. Talcott had gone to her and was holding her arm, as someone always held her arm when she walked, but now Constance moved away from her and drew her arm free. Mrs. Talcott sensed some purpose, made no gesture to support her.

"That was thoughtful of you," Constance said to Elizabeth in a low, quiet voice.

77

The words sounded strange on her lips; they must have sounded strange to her own ears, too; and then as if with an urgency to speak before this new power left her, she hurried on.

"We've both lost so much. But I lost even more. I lost the opportunity and all those years."

Mrs. Talcott and Mrs. Haines looked frightened and Will Talcott looked puzzled. This was a new Constance, or perhaps the old Constance. Only they had never known the old Constance.

She turned to Mrs. Talcott. "I shan't need you to go back to the house with me," she said. "I shall be going back with Mrs. Milnor and with—" She looked at me for an instant. "And with John," she finished. Mrs. Talcott started to come forward anyway, because for years she had been doing what was right, and not what Constance told her to do. But Elizabeth caught her eye, and she and Constance and Frankie started off toward the car together.

Mooney and Will Talcott walked with me a little behind them, across the field. Mooney shook his head. "You're the damnedest people I've ever had anything to do with," he muttered. "People in my church would call it a miracle. Probably just took a little nudge to slip a cog back in gear."

As we were driving up the Hill, Constance said very quietly, "Of course this may not continue; or it may come and go."

"It may," Elizabeth said, "but I'm glad that we could meet this way, at long last."

Pop Sanford's car was ahead of me and he was driving slowly, so I slowed up too, and followed him. We were at the Corners when I heard Constance say: "You should have married Matthew, Elizabeth," and I felt that her excursion into the lucid had passed, and that she was off again into her world of confusion.

Pop stopped at the Corners to let a truck pass and I stopped, too. I looked back at Constance and she was gazing out from one side of the road to the other as if she were seeing the countryside for the first time. "There's been so much living on this land," she finally said. "So much living. Matthew was the kind of a man who needed a mate. There was just too much vitality inside him not to be shared with a woman. He should have divorced me and married you, Elizabeth—or can't you divorce a woman who has lost her mind?"

78

Frankie was sitting in the front seat with me and her hand went out and covered mine on the wheel. I glanced at her, and there were tears in her eyes; she wasn't crying, but her eyes were swimming, and she shook her head as if to clear them and her hand tightened over mine for an instant and then she asked me for a cigarette, and I had the sense that she asked for it not because she wanted to smoke, but so that Elizabeth or Constance or even I would not be sure that her gesture had meant anything more than catching my attention.

In the mirror I could see Constance and Elizabeth. Elizabeth was looking at Constance and Constance was staring straight ahead, seeing not what was before her, but looking down the long stretch of time. And then Elizabeth said: "It was all right. There isn't a single regret; I couldn't have had any more."

Constance nodded, but she repeated, "It would have been better, much better, if Matthew and you had married. Better for everyone and better all the way around."

And Elizabeth said, "Maybe there were times when I thought so, but looking back through the years, it all seems as if it had happened in another time and to other people. Nothing can hurt me now, and nothing really hurt me then."

"I was thinking of . . ." Constance started to say.

"I know," Elizabeth interrupted her. "We are both thinking of so many things. Someday very soon we must talk about them."

Pop Sanford had drawn up in front of our house and there were three or four other cars there. I could see Emmeline's and Roger's, and one of Mooney's cars that I thought I remembered Adelaide and her husband riding in. Pop signaled as I started to drive on with Constance up to the Big House.

I rolled the window down and he stepped to my side of the car. "There are certain members of the family who would like to get to the business of Matt's will." His face was gray and his eyes looked like they had been chiseled from steel.

"Now?" I asked.

"Now," he said, and his lips worked and he spat something on the ground. "I can show them Matt's will, but that would only be the beginning. In my experience I think it might be best for you to be there, and Elizabeth and Frankie too."

Pop must have had his reasons, and I guessed there was no

way out. There had never been much love lost between Emmeline and Adelaide and me, and I had a sense that after this day there would be even less. "I'll take Constance up to the house and be back," I told him.

"If this is to involve the family, I think I should be there," Constance said. "Matthew was my son, and Emmeline and Adelaide are my daughters. Yes, I think I should like to be there."

Pop studied her for a long moment, one white hair strayed down from his moustache across his lip, and his lower lip worked against it as he made the decision. "Yes, Mrs. Tracy, I think it would be eminently proper." He opened the door of the car and helped Elizabeth and Constance out. I beckoned to him and he dropped back to join Frankie and me.

"She seems lucid at the moment; but she can raise hell when she gets confused," I told him.

"There's going to be a lot of hell raised anyway, John," he said. "A lot of hell raised. Maybe it's a good thing to get it all out in the open."

Frankie took my arm and as we were going up the steps to the porch she said, "I don't know, John, but I think Mr. Sanford is right. Get it all out in the open."

They were all waiting in the library when we got there. Roger and Emmeline both seemed surprised to see Constance, and then Emmeline quickly went to her mother and put her arms about her and greeted her, and Adelaide, taking the cue, quickly joined her. Somehow, they managed to re-create the image of Mrs. Haines and Mrs. Talcott, and Constance seemed to retreat back into her usual tottering insecure self, as they led her over to a chair beside where they had been sitting. Pop Sanford nodded to me and crossed to the chair behind the desk, which left the other side of the room to Elizabeth and Frankie and me.

Pop made a great business of arranging a sheaf of papers and straightening them on the desk before him. Then he took a spectacle case out of his pocket and removed his glasses. He half turned in his chair and sighted the glasses out the window before he took a handkerchief from his pocket and meticulously polished the lenses, after which he breathed on them and polished them again. Roger crossed and recrossed his legs and Adelaide's husband, Melvin, took out his watch chain with the key of some

80

engineering society on the end of it, and whirled it about his finger, winding it up and then unwinding it in ever-increasing tempo. Finally Roger cleared his throat and said, "Surely this delay is not necessary."

Pop glanced at him and then, replacing the spectacles on his nose, carefully adjusted the earpieces and peered at Roger again, almost as if he were seeing someone strange and new for the first time. Then he picked up the papers before him and slowly commenced to read.

The opening paragraphs were the conventional and usual ones; maybe not so usual, because they were written in the terminology of the old-fashioned lawyer who spelled things out. The preamble had to do with Matt's sound mind and conscience, at the reading of which Roger cleared his throat and looked at Emmeline as if to say, "Point one for rebuttal."

After that, it passed on to the usual formulas for the payment of just debts and funeral expenses, and again this was spelled out with a repetition of synonyms that would have done justice to a legal lexicographer.

At this point Pop turned a page, laid the will down and carefully polished his glasses again, and I could feel from across the room the projection of a restless and growing tension. Then Pop went on: "Not unmindful of my sister Emmeline, now Emmeline Mumford (Mrs. Roger Mumford), I leave her nothing." Pop nodded his head toward Emmeline. There was a buzz from Adelaide and her husband, and Roger leaned over and whispered something to Emmeline.

Pop returned to the will: "And not unmindful of my sister Adelaide, now Adelaide Carter (Mrs. Melvin Carter), I leave her nothing." Pop nodded his head toward Adelaide.

Roger glanced over at Melvin and Adelaide, and taking from them some authority to speak said, "Of course we shall protest this will."

Pop smiled at him, but the smile came only from his lips. "You may protest it," he agreed.

And now Pop hurried through the rest of the will. Only fragments remain in my memory. There was mention of the trust made out at the time of Matt's marriage to Alyse, and reference that this trust flowed to his stepdaughter Françoise, to whom **in**

81

addition he left outright the sum of $100,000 and the life use of the house and the property known as the Jennings Place, where Elizabeth had first lived, and which Old Matthew had subsequently bought. To Elizabeth and Constance he left nothing, they having been amply provided for in the estate of his father.

Pop turned another page, and I had the sense that he was pulling the ring and tossing the grenade into the room. "To my half brother John Milnor," he read, "the natural son of my father Matthew Tracy and Elizabeth Milnor, born out of wedlock, I devise, bequeath and will my entire remaining estate, consisting of all property both real and personal of which I die possessed."

There was more legal business and then mention of the executors, who were to be me and Pop Sanford and Jim Fletcher.

Roger was on his feet. "What was the date of that will?" he demanded.

"You have interrupted my reading of that information," Pop said. "The will is dated two years, eight months and four days prior to the death of Matthew Tracy."

Roger turned red. "You don't think for a minute that it's going to stand up!"

"I have not one single iota of doubt that it will stand up," Pop said quietly.

"It was written by a man obviously not in his sound mind!" Roger's voice got out of hand. "A man whose reason stands self-indicted by his act of suicide!"

"The law happens to be very clear on that point." Pop's voice remained even. "There have been many rulings. Even insurance companies do not claim that suicide can be contemplated or premeditated over a period of two years."

"In any event"—Roger's face looked apoplectic at this point— "the property was not his to throw around like this! His inheritance of the estate ignored the dower interests of Constance. Emmeline and Adelaide are the daughters of Constance and the elder Matthew Tracy, and those dower interests cannot be devised against the interest of the other heirs of Constance Tracy."

Pop smacked his lips as he might after a drink of whisky. "I was forgetful, Mr. Mumford, that you were once a practicing lawyer. Are you speaking as the husband of Emmeline Tracy Mumford or as her attorney?"

82

"I'm speaking as both!" Roger answered with as much dignity as he could summon.

"May I say something?" Constance rose from her chair.

"What can an incompetent old woman contribute to this conversation?" Roger jumped in before Pop could grant her the permission.

I was half out of my chair, but Pop's eyes stopped me. "That she is a lady of advanced years, I will not deny," he said to Roger. "Though I must bring to your attention that wisdom has been known to increase with age. That she is incompetent is a matter not of personal opinion, but to be determined only by a judicial process. And I must also remind you, sir"—Pop's voice assumed the cut of a lash—"that you are a guest in this house, and it would behoove you to behave as a gentleman. Furthermore, and finally, please realize that you have no interest or business at this meeting of the relatives and heirs of Matthew Tracy." And then as if the incident had never occurred, he turned to Constance. "Of course, Mrs. Tracy, you may speak."

"I don't know whether I understand all this completely," Constance said.

"If you don't, we shall try to explain it to you," Pop said.

"What I understand"—Constance groped for her words—"is that Emmeline and Adelaide or their husbands feel that at the time of the death of my husband I was entitled to some interest, some considerable interest in the property, which I did not receive, and which it was not within the power of my son Matthew to will as he chose?"

"That I think is a clear and proper statement." Pop nodded to her to go on.

Constance seemed to gain confidence and decision. "Well, if that is the case, and certain of the property in Matt's will is really mine and not his to leave, then I can dispose of it any way that I want, and I would want it to be disposed of as Matt wished it to be—to Elizabeth Milnor's son, John."

"This is sheer nonsense," Roger exploded. "A woman who for years has been mentally incompetent cannot dispose of her property!"

Pop raised his hand and Roger subsided. "Thank you very much, Mrs. Tracy," Pop said. "Even though what you said has

83

no legal effect, it was gratifying to me to hear you say it, and gratifying to certain others in this room."

"Thank you," Constance murmured. She seemed for a moment to retreat back into the shell of her former being. She wavered toward Emmeline and Adelaide, and Emmeline patted the empty seat between them where she had been sitting. Constance stood, irresolute and confused, and then crossed to the sofa and seated herself between Elizabeth and Frankie.

Pop waited for her to settle herself. "And now I have another document which I should like to read," he said, and drew a paper out of the sagging pocket of his black coat. "This"—he tapped the paper—"is an agreement of record. It was drawn and executed between Constance Harper and Matthew Tracy, Senior, prior to their marriage. It is the instrument of a gift, in lieu of dower rights by Matthew Tracy, and a relinquishment of dower rights on the part of Constance Harper. It was recorded fifty-four years ago, and its terms are sufficiently generous to place it beyond the pale of question. I might also add that it would be extremely difficult, at this late date, to question the competency of the contracting parties."

Constance passed her hand in a dazed fashion across her temple. "My mind must be slipping," she said pathetically. "I had forgotten all about that."

No one seemed to have heard her. Matthew's sisters and their husbands were on their feet. "Then this is all?" Emmeline's voice shook.

"This is all," Pop told her.

"It's not all by a damn sight, I want to discuss this further!" Roger blustered. "I'll see you at your office."

"Anything can be discussed," Pop said drily, "and your attorney may see me at my office, but you would not be welcome there."

"I'm an attorney!" Roger was pretty sure he had Pop there, but Pop's reply carried a smile.

"Not, however, admitted to practice before the Bar of the State of New York," he said. "So I would advise you to secure legal counsel."

"I don't want your advice!" Roger shot back at him on the way out.

"In that case," Pop said, "it is retracted. I seldom give gratuitous advice."

Emmeline and Adelaide passed Elizabeth without speaking. At the door Adelaide turned back to Constance. "Are you going to come with us, or have you chosen to stay here?"

Constance withered in the coldness of her daughter's question. Then she stiffened and turned to Elizabeth. "I think I would like a cup of tea," she said.

When the front door closed, we all gave a sigh of relief, and Elizabeth rose to attend to tea. "I think I could be persuaded to take a drink of whisky," Pop said to me. I gave it to him, and he walked over to the fireplace and stood there warming the glass in his hands.

"What do we do next?" I asked him.

"We don't do anything," he said. "It's all done. There isn't a lawyer in New York that wouldn't laugh Roger out of his office."

"It seems then that Matt wanted things to be this way, and this is the way they are," I commented.

"Not only are, but will be," Pop agreed. "I guess Matt knew that there are bitches and sons of bitches—pardon the expression —in every family, and the Tracys, being abnormally endowed with the things of this earth, seem to have them in goodly supply."

Elizabeth smiled faintly. "I pardon the language."

Constance snorted, and we turned to look toward her. "I don't pardon it," she said, "I applaud it. I only wish Matthew were alive. Old as they are, he'd have spanked Emmeline and Adelaide's backsides so hard they wouldn't be able to sit down in church on Sunday, and he'd have thrown Roger off the place. —I'll have another cup of tea, Elizabeth."

I was thinking how, in these rare flashes of her former self, one could see a suggestion of the woman Old Matt had married, when Frankie suddenly spoke up from where she was standing at the window staring out across the valley. "I don't ever want to touch or be touched by the ugliness I have seen here today," she said, as if she had been mulling over the whole miserable business. "I have enough in what comes to me from Alyse. And if I had nothing, it would be enough. Anything that Matt wanted me to have should stay here on the Hill and stay a part of the Tracy land. It really belongs to you, John. You're a Tracy."

85

"As far as the land goes," Pop explained to her, "you only have a life interest in the Jennings Place." He chuckled. "The Tracys never, never give up any land—that is, really give it up. As for the other, that was Matt's wish."

"Pop's right," I said.

"He is," Constance unexpectedly contributed. "Come here, my dear."

Frankie went to her side. Constance looked up at her, frowning a little. "Are you sure that you are not Matt's daughter? No, I guess you're not—the Tracys breed wretched women. It's too bad. Kiss me, child, we must get acquainted."

She turned to the rest of us with a little sigh. "My mind isn't very clear," she apologized. "I find I have to keep my wits about me to keep things straight. —Mr. Sanford, is Doctor Farnley a good doctor?"

It seemed surely that she was slipping back into the mists again, and that Pop was humoring her with his grave reply. "Yes, Mrs. Tracy, Dr. Farnley is a very great physician," he said.

"Would he be respected in the outside world? That is to say, would a court perhaps regard him as a very fine doctor and respect his opinion?"

"Doctor Farnley would be respected and his opinions would carry great weigh anywhere," Pop told her.

"And are you a very good lawyer?" she asked him.

"In Haviland, Mrs. Tracy, there is only one other lawyer." He smiled down at her. "I am not only the oldest, I happen to be the best. And so, because I think that I understand your question, I can assure you that when I transfer property it stays transferred. Likewise, when I draw a will, it stays stuck, and when I sue a man, he knows that he's been sued."

Constance nodded slowly. "I'm glad to hear it. I should like to have you and Doctor Farnley call on me tomorrow; or maybe it would be better if you made an appointment for Doctor Farnley to meet me in your office at, shall we say, two o'clock in the afternoon?"

Pop gave the effect of bowing as he took her hand. "It would be my privilege to have you come to my office," he said.

"And will you have some people there?" Constance pursued. "A secretary or somebody?"

86

It was only then that I began to have a glimmering of what she had in mind.

"There will be people there," Pop promised her. "Certain people who knew you many years ago, and who were your husband's friends, and your friends."

"I'm glad of that. And one more thing, please be good enough to arrange for a car for me. A taxi from the village would be best, I think."

"That won't be necessary," Elizabeth broke in. "John could drive you down, or Will Talcott."

I touched Elizabeth's arm, and shook my head, and she fell silent and let Pop carry on. "I will see that a taxi calls for you, Mrs. Tracy," he said.

"And now"—Constance rose with difficulty—"I think I will be going home; I am tired. This has been a hard day." She turned to Frankie. "Ask Mrs. Talcott to take me home, my dear."

When Mrs. Talcott came in, Mrs. Haines was with her. She hurried over to me, and said in a whisper, "Mr. Semple is waiting, he says he has to see you."

"Tell him I'm busy now."

"He says it's important."

"All right. Later. In a few minutes."

When Constance had left, Pop turned to us. "I don't exactly know what she wants to do tomorrow, but whatever it is, she was thinking like a lawyer and taking care of every point. I never saw a more lucid or competent mind. There won't anybody ever be able to say she acted under influence or constraint."

I wanted to talk it over with Pop, but first I had to get rid of Walter Semple. "Don't go yet," I said. "I'll be right back. Walter Semple's outside, wants to see me about something."

Pop took off his eyeglasses, and began polishing them. "Walter Semple, eh? He's not losing any time climbing aboard, is he? Well, run along, might as well make it a day."

"But will you wait?"

Pop fitted the spectacles back on his nose. "Sure I'll wait," he said. "I wouldn't miss it."

Five

Walter Semple was sitting in the little office at the end of the hall that Old Matt had set up years ago. The business of the land is never conducted on regular hours. On a farm, things happen when they happen. Good men are hired when you come on them and, if need be, men are fired on the spot; and buyers of cattle and men making contracts for the farm's output often came from great distances and arrived at odd times. So that is why farms of any size, even in the old days, always had a farm office. It wasn't snobbism or that Old Matt thought himself better than the people he did business with, though he was better than a lot of them; but in the hours that a man spends with his family, he doesn't like the physical intrusion of strangers; and the men who came to the office often had manure on their feet, and barnyard stains have a way of not coming off fine rugs. For that matter, Old Matt and young Matt often had barnyard on their feet, and the office served them as a tiring room as well as a place of business, and was a place where guns and fishing tackle could be stored without getting in the hair of a wife or a housekeeper. It had one other virtue; it made a good drying-off place for wet dogs, far better than the kitchen. And that was where Joy was, when I got there. She had managed to break away from the kennels during the day, and as the office must have smelled of Matt, it wakened some sense in her intelligence that here was a place that he would come back to eventually, if she only waited long enough.

Walter Semple rose as I entered the room. He was a big man about my own age, a towering man, with a face full of features like an actor; I always felt that he was selling something, and that

that something was probably Walter Semple. In a cast of characters you would have described him as a florid man. "Sorry to disturb you on a day like this," he greeted me. "I was at the funeral, you know. I was one of Matt's closest and best friends."

"I didn't know," I told him. "I mean, I knew you were at the funeral; but I didn't know you were so close to Matt."

Semple had a trick of wrinkling his forehead, which made his heavy eyebrows bush out, and he would lower his head and look through the fringe of them. It was an effective gesture, particularly with large groups of people. It suggested a dynamic quality, a forceful character. Close at hand, however, a slackness of jowl and a self-indulgent dewlap beneath his chin denied his strength. "Yes," he boomed, "Matt and I were like that." He put his cigar in his mouth and held his two forefingers out toward me. "Like that!" he reiterated. "Like brothers. Yes, I don't suppose there were two men in the town who had the interests of Haviland so close to their hearts."

I was afraid if I interrupted the mellifluous flow of wordage, it would only make him the more long-winded. I tapped restlessly at the arm of my chair, which must have seemed like a signal to Joy, for she uncurled herself from the corner and came over and sat beside me, and presently I felt the heavy urgency of her head on my knee. I knew what she was trying to say, but it is difficult to reach the heart of a dog, and the only thing I could do for her was to stroke the high domed rise between her ears. It was second best, and we both knew it.

I was aware that Semple's voice was droning on. "Yes, when I first got into this political game, Matt was my staunchest supporter. He said to me, 'Walter, if I had the time, you wouldn't stand a chance in politics in this town, I'd be running for office myself; but with the farm and everything, I can't fit it in. But you *have* got the time, Walter, and it's your duty. Men like us have to serve the community. And you will always have my support.' "

"I can just hear Matt saying that," I observed. "He must have had a very great regard and respect for you."

"We were like that!" Walter repeated, only this time his cigar was between the two fingers he held forth to me.

"And why have you come to me?"

He smiled broadly. "I wouldn't be where I am today if I wasn't

89

smart, and didn't know things. All this is yours"—he made an embracing gesture—"and it means a lot in Haviland, Mr. Milnor. I don't have to tell you that."

"You still haven't told me why you've come to see me," I reminded him shortly.

"Well," he said, "I'm always a man for putting my cards on the table. I hadn't got around to talking to Matt about it, but things have cooked pretty quickly in the past few days."

"I haven't smelled anything cooking. But then I suppose the lid is on pretty tight. When it comes off we'll all smell it."

"Look here, Mr. Milnor, you seem to be antagonistic to what I'm trying to say."

"How can I be antagonistic, when I don't know what you have in your mind?"

His cigar had gone out, and he made quite a business of relighting it, and studying me while he did so. "You know the North Hill Road, Mr. Milnor?"

"You dignify it by calling it a road," I commented.

He laughed. "You're a quick one to catch on," he said. "Well, a little group of us have bought up a lot of the land along that road, and we have options on a lot more; and we've got an option on the Little Whaley Lake land—it's in the hands of bank trustees in New York now, you know. And the Tracys have a lot of land up there, which is to say that today you, Mr. Milnor, have that land."

"Yes?"

"Well, there's only one hitch in it all. With the kind of a road that goes up the North Hill, that land's as useless as it always was. So we're going to put a road up there."

"Who's *we?*"

"The State. That's where I come in. I'm a pretty powerful man in the legislature, and I have a lot of influence."

"Enough influence to build a road where it isn't needed?"

"Yes, Mr. Milnor, I've got that much influence."

"That may be," I granted. "But you haven't told me yet where I come in."

"It stands to reason. You own land up that way, and that land will become more valuable with a road through it. The Tracys are

90

a respected and important family; they stand for progress and forward-moving things."

"And—?"

"Well, because I was such an old friend of Matt's, I just wanted to cut you in on it."

"I still don't get it," I told him. "All I see is that the Tracy land up there will automatically profit. You aren't giving me anything that you can't help yourself from giving me."

"Well, now, here's the next step," he went on. "We want you to be one of the officers of the development company."

"The *we* is still you, I gather?"

"The *we* is *me*. Editorial pronoun, so to speak. I'm Mr. Big in this."

"You're very modest," I suggested. "And there would of course be some profits in this company, of which I would be an officer?"

"We'd have a pretty big melon to cut, a very tasty melon."

"And my piece of the melon would not be inconsiderable, I presume?"

"Very considerable," he assured me. "Only a little less than mine, but then it's really my baby. I've got an investment in it, and I'm the only one who can put it over up at Albany."

I took out a cigarette to match his cigar. "You're being very generous, Mr. Semple, but somewhere in all this there's something that you want me to do, only you haven't mentioned it yet."

He flicked a long ash into the fireplace before he spoke. "I was getting to that. But first I wanted an understanding between us. There's an insurgent movement in the Town Committee; in the County Committee, too, for that matter. We're right on the eve of election and there's a group who would like to pull a switch. One of the first things a man learns in politics is to build his fences. You might say that in coming to you, I'm building my fences."

"You are refreshingly frank. Are your fences badly down?"

"No, I'm just being foresighted like the squirrels."

"Nuts."

"What!"

"You mentioned squirrels, and I said *nuts*. It was an obvious *sequitur*. So in the town and county committees, you would like my support? But aren't you forgetting that I'm not a member of either of those committees? Nor was Matt."

91

His smile was slow. "I think you're smarter than that. What the Tracys want carries a lot of weight in this town. All you have to do is call up Jim Fletcher and let him know where you stand. That's all you've got to do."

"All I've got to do is just make one telephone call. Just how much is there in all this for you, Mr. Semple?"

"Look, I made a generous offer so we wouldn't have to bargain. I might sweeten it a bit more. But only a bit, mind you."

"It's very sweet as it is now," I told him. "And I wasn't trying to bargain, I just wanted to look at the whole picture. The telephone call insures your going back to the Assembly, and makes you a considerable profit in your land development company."

"Makes both of us a pretty profit," he amended.

"Of course, there would be other ideas like this from time to time?"

"Well, naturally one thing leads to another."

"Naturally. State Senator and then Congressman, perhaps?"

"You and I, Mr. Milnor, could run this county, if we played our cards right."

"I think there's more at stake than the county, Mr. Semple. There might even be the governorship or the United States Senate."

He shrugged deprecatingly. "All things are possible in a democracy."

"And it could all start from so small a thing as my picking up this telephone and calling Jim Fletcher at the bank?"

The ash on his cigar dropped to the floor in his eagerness. "Not forgetting that what could happen up by Little Whaley Lake wouldn't be a small thing by any means."

"No, I guess it wouldn't." I moved toward the desk. "Never put off till tomorrow what can be done today," I said.

He followed me. "You don't have to call Fletcher right off. Any time before they meet Monday would do, though of course the sooner the better."

"No, I'd like to do it while you're here, so that there'd never be any question in your mind what I'd done for you."

"Look," Semple protested, "a fellow trusts his friends, you know."

"A fellow in your business should never trust anyone."

A flat "Number please" came over the phone. "Helen, will you get me the bank?"

"You know, maybe it might be better for you to see Jim personally," Semple suggested.

"No, the phone will do very well. —Hello, Jim, this is John Milnor. I've just been talking to Walter Semple. He wants my support in the Town Committee. He wants to go back to Albany at the next election, he has some unfinished business in the legislature. He says there's a group that would like to snatch the nomination right out from under him. —Well, I want you to know that he hasn't got my support. —And you might tell Uncle Dan at your next meeting that we don't need a new road up the North Hill. Some of the boys might think they were doing the Tracys a favor. —No, I hadn't thought about it, I hadn't realized it was anything I was supposed to think about. But I would suggest your thinking about Mun Allen. He knows what the town needs, he's intelligent and he's honest; we could do with those qualities in our next assemblyman. —Semple? He's right here, sitting at my elbow."

There was a loud rumble of laughter that must have rattled the plate-glass window of the bank, and then under his breath, "Why you son of a bitch," Jim said, and he hung up.

Fletcher's voice came over a phone like a loud-speaker. Semple was on his feet like a shot, crowding up against me. "I'll say it too!" he roared. "And I won't say it laughing! You stinking goddamned arrogant bastards—all of you—sitting on your fat complacent asses up here on the Hill, the power behind the throne, calling the shots the way you want them! You decadent land-proud whoring sons of bitches, I'll get you if it's the last thing I ever do! And you, you aren't even a Tracy, just a bastard dropping out of that whore mother of yours that your father wouldn't even marry. And you probably doing the same thing with that little French tart you've got up here!"

Whatever else he had to say came only in broken obscenities from a mashed and bleeding mouth. Only part of me hit him; the other part of me seemed to be standing across the room watching, and wondering a little. This was the first man I had ever hit in anger in my life—in the war you could kill men, but without that kind of anger. I wanted him to fight back, but he wouldn't. He

93

dropped to the floor, his only defense being that he thought the kind of a man he supposed I was wouldn't hit a man on the ground. And I didn't, because of a silly code of breeding. I picked him up and knocked him down, again and again. Only when I was straining for breath did I stop, and only then I saw Pop Sanford and Will Talcott standing in the open doorway. I don't know how long they'd stood there, but long enough.

"I wouldn't kill him, John. He's not worth the trouble it would involve." Pop looked down at Semple groveling on the floor as he might have looked at what you find when you turn over a flat wet rock. "Nice fellow, isn't he? Couldn't help but hear him, he was yelling so."

I felt suddenly sick and empty. "Throw him out, Will. Don't show him to the door—throw him out so he knows he's been thrown out."

Setters are strangely sensitive animals. Joy was trembling. She walked over and sniffed at Semple on the floor. "I think I'm going to be sick," I told Pop. "The place'll be cleaner when we get rid of that thing."

I got to the hall washroom, with Joy standing beside me, still quivering. I didn't hear what Will did with Semple, but I heard the front door close. And then when the retching stopped and I'd washed up, I went back into the living room. Pop handed me a glass of whisky he had already poured. I glanced at Elizabeth and Frankie and I could see from their faces that they too had heard the things Semple had said.

"Even in a small town there can be the viciousness of the jungle," I offered inadequately.

They didn't say anything, but Pop said, "Even in Paradise there are obscenities. You find them in the dark places and the crevices; though it's drawing a long bow to compare Haviland with Paradise. —What did he want?"

"A deal on a new road up the North Hill, and Tracy support for him on the Town Committee."

"Stinks, don't it?" Pop said.

"I suppose I made a mistake. Matt probably would have handled it a different way."

"Matt would have killed him," Pop said. "But then he wouldn't

94

have come to Matt. He came to you because you were an unknown quantity. He thought maybe he could do business with you."

"I'm sorry you had to be in on it," I told Elizabeth and Frankie.

"I've had as much said about me before," Elizabeth said wearily. "You can't protect yourself from that sort of a person. Not even if you're what people call a *good* woman. Fortunately Semple's kind is in the minority; there are a lot more fine people in the world—" She smiled faintly. "I suppose I'm a little vulnerable, and you were born a little vulnerable."

"That's a new name for it," I retorted, and we laughed a little too hard, for what I'd said wasn't that funny.

"I'm sorry, though, that Frankie had to be smeared with that kind of thinking," Elizabeth went on. "The first time it happens to you, you feel like you'd been touched with some sticky vileness that you'll never be able to wash off."

"Yes, it's like that." Frankie spoke for the first time. "I'm afraid I'll be wondering what people are thinking when I pass them on the street in Haviland."

"No, you won't," Elizabeth said. "With a certain kind of man, a woman always knows what he's thinking. It's part of the business of being a woman." She touched Frankie's shoulder. "I think I'll lie down before supper. Don't you want to come up to my room with me?"

Frankie nodded mutely.

Pop stayed a little while after they'd gone, talking about the Tracy estate, and the Tracy lands and the Tracy obligations. He wouldn't stay to dinner, and presently he left. I stood and watched his car drive down the road toward the Corners, and for the first time since Matt's death the impact of deep loss came over me. There is a curious affinity that happens between brothers, even half brothers, such as we were. It springs from the growing up and the sharing of experiences, I suppose. Matt being the older, I watched everything that happened to boys happen to him first, and later, when they happened to me, he sort of guided and tutored me through them. Even in recent years, the elder-brother quality of our relationship continued. And yet for all his positiveness and strength, the family always used me as the instrument to soften things for him when the hurts of life began to hurt too much.

I was the one who had sat with Matt through the long night at the hospital in Poughkeepsie, and greeted with him a dawn that brought the news that his son was dead. And it was I who met him at the station in Haviland when Martha died. I remember, for we stopped at the Haviland House on the way home and drank a bottle of whisky between us; afterwards, we forgot about the car, and walked all the way to the Hill, taking the long way around by the North Road. And they had come to me, and not to Matt, the night Susan had really messed things up in Cold Spring. Costello had phoned me from the barracks, and we drove over to Cold Spring together. He told me what little he knew of the story as we went. It wasn't his police area, the boys from the Beacon Barracks had called him in on it. Whatever had happened didn't make too much difference anyway, because by that time Matt and Susan had broken. Nothing made too much difference to Matt in that in-between period, until Alyse. Alyse was the purpose and the meaning of his life. That was why she came straight to me after her first visit to the doctor in New York. How could we protect Matt and delay his knowing until he would have to know?

For all of it, though, I served merely as a buffer against the fates. There never was anything I could really do for Matt, except to be on hand, and sometimes help pick up the pieces. It was a strange and unexplainable exchange of strength between the older and the younger, and it brought us very close. Now all of that was at an end. He was gone, and there would be a great emptiness.

It was more than just Matt's dying, however. Life had taken a great spin, and when it stopped spinning, nothing was the same, even I wasn't the same. Everything was changed. For one thing, I had never before had any sense of possession. It had become part of a fetish of freedom not to have possessions. My life on the Hill had always been that of a guest. The land, the fields, and the work and the responsibility had been Matt's. I was there only between my being other places. Even Elizabeth's house I had never thought of as mine, or ours. Like the other "family" properties of the Tracys, only a life interest flowed to Elizabeth and to me. When we died the house would return to whoever then owned the Tracy land. But now, suddenly, it was different. The house, the land, the barns, the cattle, the Big House where Constance lived, and the houses that Adelaide and Emmeline and Susan lived in, were part

96

of the overreaching inheritance. But even so, I could not bring myself to a sense of possession in them, it was rather a sense of guardianship that I felt. And I realized for the first time that that was probably what Matt, and my father, and all the other Tracys had felt. You can possess a watch or a suit of clothes, or a boat or a horse, but anything as big as land, and that much of it, you could not possess. You simply had a trust of management.

Looking out over the immensity of the farm as it flowed across the great saddle of the Hill, the consciousness of this deepened within me, but at the same time I felt a resentment that it had demanded too much, of too many people, too long, and that I too was about to be hemmed in and crushed by its insatiable wanting. But the anger faded away almost as it had come, and in its place I knew that quiet warm sense that a man knows when he realizes that he is home, or that where he is, is home, and that he will never wander again, or need to.

Mrs. Haines turned up the lights behind me. "If it's all right with you," she said, "I won't even ask your mother, I'll just serve supper for the three of you in her room before the fire. If I ask her, she'll want to come downstairs."

I dragged my thoughts back into the room with effort. "That's a good idea, Mrs. Haines."

"This has been a time for her. Hard for all of you, but hard on her, most of all."

"Yes," I said. "Death has a way of delving back into the years."

"I guess your mother's had a pretty happy life on the whole." Mrs. Haines paused on her way out, thoughtfully twisting her apron. "But then I always say it's the happy things that hurt the most. The unhappy ones we can always forget."

I wondered about that as I started upstairs. I noticed Joy lying at the front door, her nose to the threshold, waiting. I snapped my fingers toward her and she rose and followed me to my room.

I took my time in the tub, as if a long hot sloshing bath would wash this day away. There was a lot to wash away. The knuckles on my right hand were swollen and blue. Damn Semple.

I damned him again when I passed Frankie's door a little later on the way to Elizabeth's room. It was open, so I looked in. She was pulling her stocking up and attaching her garter to it.

I would have been disappointed in her if she had seemed

97

flustered. "A gentleman knocks before he enters a lady's room," she merely observed.

"And a lady usually keeps her door shut," I retorted in the same vein, "especially when she's dressing and flaunting a beautiful gam around."

Frankie lowered her skirt and smoothed it around her hips. "Quite true. But I have it on the authority of a congressman that I am not a lady. I am a *tart.*"

She bent so quickly to tie her sandal I knew there were tears in her eyes that she was too proud to let me see.

"Oh, for God's sake, don't let that eat into you!" I scoffed. "And anyway, he's only an assemblyman; it's not quite the same thing."

She kept her head bent, and sent up a flippant tone. "You mean a congressman would know more about such things? That his wasn't an expert opinion?"

"I mean you should wash the whole business out of your mind."

"You know, it's funny," she came back at me.

"What's funny?"

"All this business that French tarts are more interesting, or tartly, or tartish." She straightened up, and there was a small, taunting smile on her lips. "Are there American tarts, John?"

"Now that you mention it, I don't think so. Not in the accepted sense of the word. We have *tramps.*"

She sat on the edge of the bed to think it out. "Not the same thing," she decided. "'Tart' is a gay word, mercenary but gay. 'Tramp' is a sad word, full of disillusion. It makes you think of a girl in a felt hat and a not too clean camel's hair coat; and expensive, very well made shoes that have been resoled; and very clean and very simple and once very expensive underthings."

There came into my mind the memory of a girl I had once known, and the girl's name was Angelica Barnes. "Tell me when you publish your thesis, it should make interesting reading."

"Those who can, do. Those who can't, write about it. Maybe I have a latent and undeveloped instinct for it. It *is* a profession after all." Again, there lurked in her flippancy the sting of Semple's brutal attack.

"I suppose they teach courses about it in college," I countered teasingly.

98

She shook her head. "No, it comes under the head of an extra-curricular research project. You'd be surprised how popular it is."

"The more I come to know you, the less surprised I am about anything in the younger generation."

"Which neatly puts me back in my age group," she said, and quickly changed the subject. "I was talking to Elizabeth after we came upstairs. I think it would be a good thing if she were to get away from all this for a week or two. I could go with her, and sort of give the trip a reason. She doesn't really want to, but she said she would."

"Splendid. Best thing possible for both of you. Only don't dawdle around, just get up and do it."

She wrinkled her nose. "Now? This minute?"

"No, I think you'd better have some supper before you go. —And maybe a little cold water on your eyes," I suggested gently.

Her smile was tremulous. "Thanks, John. I'll be back in a minute."

While I waited I looked around the room. It had overtones, but they meant nothing to her, for it had been Matt's room after we had graduated to separate quarters. It was just a room, and like all Tracy rooms, it was a man's room. Even Elizabeth's room had never been truly feminine; it was still marked with a man's having lived in it, and I don't think she ever desired it otherwise. Tracy rooms changed very little through the years, or through the generations for that matter.

I walked over to the window to see if the hole was still above it. Yes, it was there. The plaster had been repaired but the patching wasn't perfect, and I could see where the twenty-two bullet had gone flying out of the room. Except that I had jerked the trigger instead of squeezing it, it had been a perfect aim between Matt's eyes, of an empty gun. We had been playing cowboys and Indians, and it had been one very scared cowboy who had yelled, "That was a crazy damnfool thing to do!" And his high-pitched profanity hadn't been a patch on what Old Matt had had to say.

"Was this ever your room?" Frankie asked from the threshold of the bathroom.

I moved away from the window, almost guiltily. "No, it was Matt's for a time, when we were growing up."

I glanced at the pictures on the dresser—the ones that Elizabeth had had brought down from the Big House. I'd only seen one of them before, the picture of Alyse that Genthe had made. It, or a copy of it, had been on Matt's desk. The other two were blown-up snapshots; one of Matt and Alyse, sitting on a bench in the garden of the little house in Saint-Cloud, and there were lilacs leaning over the wall. The other was of a tall lean man whose face was unfamiliar to me.

"That was my father," Frankie said.

"You never knew him, did you?"

"No, I was only two when he died, but later when I knew what happened to him, it seemed that I must surely be able to remember."

I could tell that she wanted to talk about it, so I took out a cigarette. "It was an accident, wasn't it?"

She nodded. "Yes. Alyse was sitting on the sun deck of the hotel at Chamouni. I've been back there since, so it's all very clear to me—the scene, I mean. There's still the telescope, so that people who don't climb can watch their friends." She shuddered. "It must be awful to look through and see someone fall. The man who had been watching the day my father went up must have known who was climbing that aiguille, because he came over to Alyse and said, "Madame, something terrible is happening." She paused. "May I have a cigarette?"

I lit one for her. She drew on it, and then she went on, "I don't know how Alyse lived through it. Years afterwards, she told me how she made herself go to the telescope. . . . The aiguille was far across the valley and high on the mountain, but looking through the scope—I've looked through it since—you almost feel that you can reach out and touch the rock walls. She saw a figure hanging and swinging on the rope. And then my father fell."

"A strange and futile way for a man to give up his life," I mused.

"I don't know. I suppose Alyse felt that way at the beginning, but later she didn't. She felt that his death was just one of the risks of his being the kind of a person he was. He'd been a flier in the first war, and the world he came back to had lost its shape and meaning. I can understand how he felt that there was some-

100

thing pure and clean about mountains." She broke off. "In a way, I suppose, his death was inevitable."

I nodded. "The world of Europe was preparing the fates of such men. If not on the aiguille in Chamouni, then in some cellar in Paris or against a stake in some prison camp."

Her hand touched mine. "Thank you for understanding."

Mrs. Haines stood in the door. "I've announced supper twice," she said. "But of course, if you prefer to eat cold food, that's all right too."

"We'll be right in," I told her. I took Frankie's arm. "Come along, this is enough serious talk for one day, from anyone your age."

She yanked her arm away from me. "Why do you always spoil it! We begin to talk like two human beings, and then suddenly you retreat behind your thirty-nine years and call me a child!"

"Forty," I corrected her.

"Thirty-nine!"

"I have a birthday within three weeks, so for all practical purposes it is forty."

"And for all impractical purposes it is anything you want! John. Be honest. Do I talk like a child? Act like a child? Look like a child?"

"Sometimes. And this is one of them. If you want to pretend to be so old, I wouldn't lose my temper if I were you. It makes you look about twelve."

She refused to smile. Her eyes held mine. "What is it you are afraid of?"

"Me?"

"Yes. You're afraid of something. It isn't me, you just take it out on me. You've always been escaping from something. I've searched this house, and there's nothing in it of you, more than a guest would leave that came only for a visit."

Mrs. Haines was back at the door. "The soup is now vichyssoise, although it started out to be good plain hot potato and leek."

"Yes, come along," I said. "I didn't bargain for all this when I looked in at your door." I tried to hide it, but I felt oddly shaken. One moment she was a child, and the next moment she was as old and wise as Time.

Six

Elizabeth looked up as we came into her room. "Have you two been fighting?" she asked. "Has John said something to hurt you?"

Frankie shook her head.

"Then I might ask if you've said something to hurt John?"

It was my turn to shake my head, and suddenly all the tension vanished from the room. It's a trick that families that live very intimately among themselves possess. Elizabeth began to talk about the trip that she and Frankie had discussed—they wouldn't be gone more than a few weeks, could I manage alone? I said I could, and presently, we found ourselves speaking of Matt, almost as if he were up at the Big House and might be dropping in on us later. And then Frankie began talking about Alyse without the clutch of grief in her throat, and between the three of us the ghosts of Matt and Alyse were laid, and the fact of death was returned to its proper proportion.

When Mrs. Haines brought the coffee, she had Joy with her. "Will brought her down from the barns, she was up there looking again."

"Poor old girl." I reached over to pat her, and there was the crackle of paper in my pocket; I was wearing the same jacket I had worn yesterday when Pop had brought me Matt's letter.

"What's the matter?" Elizabeth asked.

"What do you mean, 'what's the matter'?"

"There was an expression on your face."

"I hope so." I tried to pass it off with a laugh. "I'd hate to go around with no expression at all on my face."

"This wasn't a pleasant one."

102

"I just remembered something I might have to do," I told her.

"Joy will be all right," Frankie said out of the blue. Her hand touched mine as she stroked Joy's head. "Dogs love so completely. I suppose that's why God gave them short lives, so that their hurts shouldn't be too many, nor last too long."

Elizabeth nodded. "It's nice to think so," she said.

It was hard for Joy to settle down that evening. She was restless, waiting to get back to the barns, where she thought that Matt might be. I took her for a long walk before I turned in. In this late season of the year the barways were open, and we walked out into the far meadows. Occasionally her ears and tail would alert to some small thing that scurried off into the dark, and twice she dropped at the scent of pheasant or partridge, but it was reflex action and there was no spirit in her heart for the game. We came to a rise of land. Far to the south, there was a twinkle of light from Alf Adams' house—or the barn, maybe; it was hard to tell which at that distance. To the right, where the land spilled off into the valley, I could see the little checkerboard lines of light that were the streets of Haviland. Turning back on our steps, there were lights at our own barns, and a light in the Big House, and a light in our house in the entrance hall, and one in my room, where Mrs. Haines was probably turning down my bed for the night. While I watched, the light went off, and only the fanlight over the door cut through the darkness.

The world seemed to diminish in size, Somewhere out beyond that rim of darkness were cities and many peoples and ponderous endeavors and vast conflicts. Out there were many lives to be lived, and some of them I had lived; but my life was now here and I was standing in the middle of it. I realized that never before had I been so free, because I had no desire to escape. A thought phrased itself in my mind, and it was formed and clear like a quotation: "For man has many lives to lose, but only one soul." It takes more imagination to put a boundary to the universe than to conceive it boundless. All that remains tangible is the vantage point of the viewer. He alone, and what he can touch, is real, and the conclusion presses in that he had better do his best with what he has. To be within his sphere is his purpose of being.

I clucked, as you do to a dog in the field when they've been broken to that signal, and Joy came swirling out of the darkness

103

to my side. We walked on. As we came closer to the house, there was the smell of wood smoke in the air, pungent and aromatic. On cold nights, in our part of the world, pine wood has almost the smell of juniper and eucalyptus in the desert, and if there is hardly any wind you can smell it for great distances. Maybe Constance was having a fire, or Elizabeth had thrown some more logs on her grate after we had left.

When I'd closed up the house and come to the top of the stairs I could see from the flickering light through my door that the fire was burning in my room. Mrs. Haines had evidently lit it, as much for cheer as for warmth. The hall was dark and there was no light from Elizabeth's or Frankie's room. Joy slipped ahead of me, and a moment later I heard her low whimper and then the thrash of her tail wagging against the sofa.

"I lit your fire." It was Frankie's voice from the dimness. My hand was on the light pull, and she said, "Don't turn up the light. The fire's enough."

"You ought to get some sleep," I protested. "You didn't get much rest last night."

"When you get sleepy yourself, drive me out," she said. "And don't be so stern and elderly. You breathe censure and disapproval."

"Just my normal breathing."

"Look, I'm sorry about this afternoon. I said a lot of things I shouldn't have."

"Forget this afternoon," I told her. "We're both nerved up and on edge."

"I know."

I sat down beside her on the sofa. "Can you spare the time from college for a couple of weeks, while you go away with Elizabeth?"

"I'm not going back."

"Is that a wise decision?"

"It isn't a new one, if that's what you mean. I didn't even want to go back after last Christmas, but I realize now that Alyse insisted on it so that I'd be out of the way, and not see what was happening to her."

"That's possible. But what's to be gained by growing up an uncultured, illiterate little brat?"

104

"As if there weren't other ways of getting culture," she pricked my stodginess. "Besides, I started out pretty well supplied. I came equipped with two languages and a smattering of two more. Also I have a singing voice with absolutely no talent, and I play the piano almost well enough to be a professional."

"And you don't want to go on with it—the piano I mean?"

"I said I played *almost* as well as a professional. There's a big difference."

"Don't you want to *do* anything? I thought your generation was hipped on doing things and being useful?"

"You mean like one of the 'ologies' or social work? No, sir, I've got something far more important to do than that."

"What have you got to do that's so much more important?"

"Woman's work. I'd make a swell lover. And don't ask me how I know. I just know. I think I have an instinct for it. More than for the piano."

"For the record, I wasn't going to ask you. You introduced me to your theories on this subject earlier today, remember?"

"And then," she disregarded the interruption, "I have the making of a first-rate wife in me."

"I hope you take up these careers in the proper order," I mentioned.

"Whatever the order, it will be proper for me, if it happens that way," she said. "And I would be good at having kids. I'm built right for it."

"Frankie, don't girls of your age have any reticence? Is there nothing you don't drag out and examine in public and discuss with strangers?"

She shook her head. "You're hardly a stranger. You're—" She stopped and lit a cigarette.

"Go on," I said.

"With my catalogue of virtues? —Where were we? Oh, yes, my pelvic structure; but that embarrasses you. I don't know why, but it does. You wouldn't buy a cow without assessing her as a functional animal. Why would anybody want to marry a woman without really sizing her up?"

"There's a slight difference."

"Not so slight. Alyse couldn't have any children after she had me; that was an accident, but it was a reality and something that

105

she and Matt had to look at. I don't mean that he wouldn't have married her anyway; but they would have been even happier if they'd had a houseful, and Matt would still be alive today. He'd have had a reason for living."

I found myself listening to her with increasing attention. It was her approach that threw me off my stride.

"I'm practically down to the end of my list," she went on, "so hang on to your sensibilities a bit longer. Last but not least, I happen to come of stock that ages gracefully; our glands seem to work pretty well. Alyse was evidence of that. It can be a very real asset, if two people are lucky enough to come to the close of their lives together. —It runs in your stock, too. Look at Elizabeth."

"Delighted to have you say so. I've a feeling that I shall be needing that gift rather soon," I said.

"Yes, you're just on the verge of being decrepit."

There was no use trying to drive a point home that she refused to accept. "What would you do, travel? There's still something of Europe to be seen."

"Sometime, perhaps, but not now. I have a European's sense of Europe, you know. It's a sick world. Its youth is gone and the days of its age are insecure."

"I guess maybe you're right about not going back to college," I gave in. "But I still want to know what's in your mind. Will you live in New York for a while? You must have a lot of friends you've made at school?"

"Not many," she said. "I began things a little out of step with those of my age, and I never quite got into step."

"Oh, come, isn't that taking yourself a little seriously?"

"Oh, but I do take myself seriously," she assured me. "I'm very important to me. No, I think I'll just stay here."

"I was afraid of that."

"Afraid? Why?"

"Because it isn't a place for anyone who's young. Like Europe, perhaps it's a dying world up here. We're a backwater, we're the vestiges of an old order, people who stay put, and don't change with the world about us. For the last two generations we've been farmers who didn't farm for money, but for a way of life."

"Are you trying to tell me that you'd give it up?"

106

"No, I don't think I'll give it up," I told her. "But the Tracys on the whole seem to have come to the end of the road. I don't even carry the name of Tracy and there's no one to follow me."

"There's no magic in a name," she said. "And if you had some unfinished business, you'd probably see to it that there was someone to carry on."

"Look," I chided her. "We started out to talk about you, and we end up with your talking to me like an old aunt. You know you're welcome here, but I don't think this house is the place for you, or the Big House either. Living alone with Constance in the other wing has nothing to give you. It would be a pretty grim business."

"I agree with you," Frankie said quietly. "It's not the place for me. I don't agree with you that it has nothing to give me, but at the same time I recognize that what it has to give me, I won't get while I stay here."

"That's too involved for me to follow."

"There was a little Hungarian in a play who summed life up in: 'There are two possibilities!' It rang a bell in me, because I am a European, too. We are down to two possibilities."

"And they are?" I asked her. "These two possibilities?"

"That I stay in the house and become something between a sister and a daughter to you and Elizabeth. I think I'll fix up the Jennings Place and live in it. That's the other possibility."

"By yourself? That's utterly mad!"

"Why? It was Matt's idea for it to be a place for me to come back to if I ever wanted it. Well, I anticipate his wish by never leaving. It's part of the Tracy fetish. Security. Everyone in the family must have some house to live in, so I'll simply take my security, now, if you don't mind."

A log fell in the fire; it flared for an instant, throwing a curtain of light and warmth out on us, and I could see Frankie's chiseled face peering deep into the glow; and then ashes crusted the embers and there was almost darkness between us again, and Joy's head worked against my foot.

"I'm glad it's dark again," she finally said. "I'm not as liberated as you think. Every time I say things that aren't what you think conventional for a girl of my age to say, it's like closing my eyes and jumping off a high place."

"Go ahead and say what's on your mind," I invited her.

"All right. That horrible man this afternoon—do people really think what he said of me—of us?"

"Don't let it get under your skin. There's a word for it. Trauma. You don't want to have to muck around with psychologists and analyists digging it out later on in your life. Much better never to let it get there in the first place."

"I don't want it to get down deep," she admitted.

"Then forget it," I told her. "Walter Semple is like coming on something unclean and nasty when you don't expect it. Don't let what he said stay with you."

"But it does stay with me."

"Why don't you talk to Elizabeth about it tomorrow?" I suggested.

"Because it hasn't to do with Elizabeth. It has to do with you and me."

"The foul mouthings of a foul man can have nothing to do with you and me."

"I'm not so sure about that," she said. "Haven't you ever thought about me like that? Doing what he said?"

I had to hold myself in; I almost shouted at her. "Are you crazy? You're a kid, and I'm a grown man! What the hell would I be doing thinking things like that about you? Why, you don't even know the words to be thinking the thoughts you're trying to think!"

"Very well. Don't answer the question, John. But I do know the words. They're one of the first things you learn when you go away to school. And in English they're not very pretty; or maybe they're only ugly because people use them in an ugly way. In the language I was born with, they're not ugly at all. Just the phrase *to make love*. It's as simple as that—and as lovely."

"It isn't as simple as that, because there are many kinds of love."

"But between a man and a woman it always comes down to that, doesn't it? Or am I not normal?"

"In the past day or so, I've begun to have my doubts."

"Well, then, normal or not, I'm me. I've thought of you that way, and it wasn't ugly or nasty. It just *was,* and it seemed right and beautiful."

108

"You don't know what you're talking about. This is getting all mixed up, and it ought to stop."

"Our not talking about it won't stop it," she said. "Last night when I was half-asleep in your arms, we were as close, almost as close, as two human beings could be."

"You were reading into it more than was there." I was aware of being brutal. "You were just a frightened lost kid, and I was a comfortable safe shoulder to lean against."

"I wasn't just reading something into it." She shook her head. "There was more to it than that. And we both know it."

"There was no more to it!"

"There was more to it, or you wouldn't have told me the story about the girl in Saint-Cloud this morning. There was more to it because a woman senses things, and I'm a woman, even though you may want to insist that I'm a child. There was more to it, because I wasn't really asleep when you pulled my gown about my throat, and when your hand covered my breast. That's why I'm going to live at the Jenning's Place."

I don't know how much longer I sat there after she left. I only know that when I went down the hall and stopped outside her room, the edge of the threshold was dark, and there was no living sound in the house, only a sound like a woman sobbing; but it was the sound of the night wind having its way through the elms. Later, I went to bed, and much later I fell asleep; but it wasn't a good sleep because I dreamed, and my dreams were troubled and full of the past. There was a laughing girl in New York, and her name was Angelica, and at the last moment her face faded and it became Frankie's face, and the censorship of dreams came down like a curtain and the image faded into another girl in a room somewhere, and the room had a balcony, and I saw the Seine winding outside the balcony, and I knew the room was in Saint-Cloud, and when I returned to her, the girl lying on the bed was Frankie and she started to laugh and it was no longer Frankie, but a child sitting there with a hair ribbon in its hair and playing with a toy. And there was the sound of crying and a whimpering that was like a heart breaking, and I wakened and it was Joy at the foot of my bed having the kind of nightmares that dogs have, her legs jerking and her lips fluttering and anguish working through her being. And suspecting what her dream was, I wakened her out of kindness.

There was the sound of a heavy door closing somewhere in the night, and I looked at my watch. It was quarter to six. I was glad the night was over. The men would be starting work at the barns, and I got myself out of bed to join them.

Seven

Will Talcott was trundling a feed truck down in front of the cows when I showed up, and Al Harris, the herdsman, was just coming out of the milk room clattering the tubes and cups of a couple of milking machines. Neither of them seemed to take any particular notice of my presence. I had the feeling they would have been more surprised if I hadn't been there.

"Oh, before I forget, here's the time book." Talcott pulled a notebook out of his jumper pocket. "I picked it up from Matt's desk. I found the checks for this month tucked inside. Matt made them out the morning he—that morning," he finished. "You'll have to sign them. Matt didn't sign them."

"I'll speak to the bank," I told him.

"I already spoke to Fletcher," he called back over his shoulder. "He said it was all right for you to go ahead and sign them, but you'd have to stop down one day and change over the account."

I glanced at the checks. They were written out in Matt's strong concise hand, in figures that looked like figures. Men who make figures like that don't very often go broke. They were postdated to this day. Matt was tidy; all the loose ends tied up. I slipped them into my pocket. This was no time for the past, the barn was teeming with the present. Al's assistant had already started his machines on the cows in the other line, and the calf-barn man—his name was Ted something—took over the feed truck from Will and went through the passage into the other barn. Will disappeared up the silo chute, and an instant later there was the great swooshing rain of falling silage, and the dull thud of it landing heavy and wet, filling the air with the sweet-sour smell of ensiled corn.

111

Al came over and handed me the weighing chart and a pencil, and as each milking bucket was weighed, he would call out the name of the cow and how many pounds of milk she had given that morning. It was a job that he usually did and could well do without assistance, but it was his unspoken invitation that if I was to have to do with cows, I'd better get to know their names and their production. Then the calf man was trundling hand trucks with the milk cans from the lower barn. The milk had been weighed there, and put in forty-quart cans and rushed to the upper milk room, where it was put into the huge water-spray coolers, and last night's milking rolled out onto the loading platform. Between weighings, I counted eighteen cans on the platform, and with this morning's milking it would come to thirty-six cans, or fourteen hundred and forty quarts. I did some figuring on the back of the weighing chart; that was better than a half a million quarts a year, and at sixteen cents a quart—milk was high these years—it was better than eighty thousand dollars a year.

"The Delight cow, eighteen point two pounds!" Al called to me. And while I found the cow's column to enter the figure, the pickup backed to the loading platform, and one of the poultrymen—I didn't know his name—nodded to me and said, " 'Morning, Mr. Milnor." I watched him unloading egg cases. Nineteen of them I totted off on the back of the milk sheet, and twenty-four dozen to the case—that made roughly four hundred and fifty dozen.

"How much are we getting a dozen?" I asked.

"Sixty-three cents."

As I figured it, that made around two hundred and ninety dollars in eggs, and around two hundred and thirty in milk. In other words, a daily cash crop of about five hundred and twenty dollars and a year's gross intake of better than a hundred and eighty thousand, assuming that this was average production, and these were average prices—which they weren't; they were pretty high. Anyway you looked at it, though, it was big business. With mounting costs, you wouldn't make a fortune, but you'd be far from a poor man, although with bad management you could lose your shirt. Even with good management and bad times, you could lose the tail of your shirt.

Harry, the tractor man, drove the big truck up to the platform

112

and started to load, and in a moment or two another truck—I could see Alf Adams at the wheel—came into the yard, made a wide swing up to the side gate, and began to unload his eight cans of milk and four cases of eggs. I suddenly realized that any storekeeper in Haviland or Jim Fletcher, looking out his bank window in the morning, could tell the state of a farmer's economic health as his truck went to the milk station each morning. A quick adjustment of the figures I had jotted down on the back of the milk sheets would give a financial statement of Alf Adams and his farm.

When he had slipped the tie pins into the hasps of the truck gate, Alf stepped over on the loading platform and joined me. "Good morning, John." There seemed to be a slight diffidence in his use of my first name.

"Good morning, Alf," I said, and only then did his hand come out in greeting.

"Your brother and I have had a working agreement on hauling my milk. Two days a week I haul—that's on your men's days off. If that isn't all right with you, we can talk it over."

"It's all right with me. Let's just assume that things will go on as usual."

"No two men ever worked the land the same way," he said. "I owe you some money, too," he added.

"I didn't know."

"Will Talcott'll tell you about it. Four cows and a young bull I bought from Matt three months ago. Matt took my notes on them."

"Anything you worked out with Matt is all right with me. And if it isn't all right with you, we can talk it over."

"It's all right with me," he said. "They were fine heifers."

The sloshing of water and the banging of milking utensils told me that the morning chore was finished. "I don't know too much about dairy animals," I told him, "but Will thinks we have something pretty special in the barn. You want to look at it?"

We walked back to the pen where the Radiant cow was. She lowed and came forward to the steel posts to examine the strangers who approached her young, and, finding them friendly, she stood aside and the calf, in little stiff-legged hops, came around to us. He tried to focus his deep irisless brown eyes on us, and then

113

thinking of better things to do, he butted his mother's udder, and she spread her legs a little to give him access.

"This one's got Victris blood in him," Alf said. "That white slash runs through the family. The bull I got from Matt was out of this cow, but with Design breeding to it." He studied the Radiant cow for a moment. "It's a fine thing to have bred and to own a great old lady like that. She's the picture of what a cow ought to be."

"I understand Mrs. Milnor's going away for a bit," Will said when we were alone.

"Yes, she talked about it last night."

Will smiled. "News gets around this place fast. Mrs. Haines told Mrs. Talcott. If you should want to be going too, I guess things could run themselves for a while."

"I think I'll be staying here," I told him. "There's quite a lot to learn about the Tracy farm."

"Quite a lot," he agreed. "Is Miss Frankie going to be staying at the Jennings Place?"

I looked up at him.

"Mrs. Haines mentioned something about it. About her being willed the place and probably going to live there."

"Nothing's been decided yet."

"Well, if she's going to, there'll be some things to be done. Water turned on, some repairs and woman stuff of house cleaning, and all. The place's been empty for a long time."

"We'll go down and see what's needed some day this week." I turned over the milk pad I had been figuring on. "How much stock do we sell in a year?"

He glanced at my rough figuring. "We can go over the books any time you want," he told me.

"No, I was just interested in a rough figure."

He took a well-thumbed notebook out of his jumper pocket. "Well, roughly from September to September—we keep our books that way, no good reason for it, but your grandfather started it— roughly twenty-two thousand, eight hundred and seventy-five."

"And that's roughly?"

He smiled. "Farming is the most accurate, inaccurate business there is. Awful lot of unknowns in it." He glanced at my figuring. "And then we had eighty-five hundred in beef. We don't do much

114

with beef; they just balance out a program that Matt started, improve the land and use slack labor. And seven hundred and eighty-four dollars in sheep, including the wool; and there's a few extras from lumber now and again. Last year"—he examined the next page of his notebook—"we took in two hundred and nineteen thousand, eight hundred and forty-two dollars and fifty-six cents."

"That's pretty big business!"

"I've known it when we took in half that, and it was bigger business, taking into account what was left at the end of the year for profits. Costs have been going up higher'n prices."

I fished the pay checks out of my pocket. There were eleven and they totaled close to three thousand dollars. "We always pay the men by the month, not by the week?" I asked.

"Tracy farm always pays by the month," he said. "Always has. We got steady men and once a month is often enough to get their hands on money; it helps keep them steady. Of course when we're cropping, we use day help, and they get paid by the week."

"Give me your pen."

After I'd signed them he said, "You want to stop at the Big House for a bite to eat? I haven't eaten what you'd rightly call a breakfast yet."

"I'll stop for a cup of coffee," I told him.

I ended up with a couple of fried eggs and bacon as well. When I finally left Will's kitchen and passed the front door of the Big House, Joy was holding her vigil there, still waiting for Matt. The second time I called her she came. As I walked home, the tremendous scope of the farm hit me anew. This was not only big business, it was a whole-time job. There was no hobby about it, no part-time occupation you could push the responsibility of onto another man's shoulders. There wouldn't be too much time left for the writing of books, or travel, though Matt had covered quite a bit of the world in slack seasons.

Elizabeth called to me from the dining room. "Breakfast's on the table!"

I stuck my head in. "I had breakfast with Will Talcott. Glad I did, because I'm not shaved yet, and I have to wash."

"Wash in the lavatory down here, and shave later. It's an old Tracy custom. Then join us for another cup of coffee, at least."

When I came back into the room, Frankie was at the table. We

115

looked at each other, but in the constraint of all that was unsaid between us, we didn't speak. We were both conscious of Elizabeth, so Frankie began to make conversation in a startlingly high voice. "I wonder why nobody ever started a new perfume business on a farm," she said. "There are such exciting and wonderful smells to hay and grain and silage."

"I gather I must be pretty high to have brought on the idea," I said.

"You smell beautiful!" she cried, and suddenly the constraint between us was gone.

"I can think of one or two farm smells that might be difficult to market," I ventured. "Even to give away."

"I don't agree," Frankie insisted. "It's just a matter of selling the public. After all, musk and whipped civet aren't very pretty, either."

Elizabeth smiled. "I may be perverted, but personally I'm very partial to a faint odor of skunk in the fall air. I much prefer it to tuberoses, or those sickly southern flowers."

"Fine!" I exclaimed. "When you get back from your trip, you can both start a new business. And by that time I should be something of an expert in farm smells."

"How are things on the farm?" Elizabeth asked.

"Everything seems in good shape. It bulks bigger than I thought, though. Matt used to mention figures, but suddenly this morning, fourteen hundred quarts of milk three hundred and sixty-five days a year seemed like a hell of a lot of milk. It also seems a lot more important than writing books that no more than a handful of people read."

Elizabeth started to speak, but Frankie got ahead of her. "You'll write your books."

Elizabeth just smiled. "Frankie and I were discussing our trip. —South seems the best idea."

"South is an excellent idea. You can lie on the beach, and get a good sunburn. Both of you."

I glanced at Frankie, but she seemed intent on stirring her coffee. I rose from the table. "See you at lunch."

I didn't get back for lunch, however. Setting up new accounts with Jim Fletcher at the bank took too long, and then Pop Sanford wanted a lot of papers signed that had to do with the estate,

116

so it was late when he and I went over to Eddie Connor's Station Restaurant for a bite to eat. Not thinking it would take so long, I hadn't bothered to change and I was a little self-conscious walking down the street beside the old gentleman, who in his starched white shirt and black broadcloth suit always looked like a Supreme Court judge ought to look. But if I was self-conscious, no one else seemed to be. I slipped in beside him at a stool in front of the huge horseshoe counter. Tim Mooney was there, and Sam Beaton, and presently Doc Harris came in, and it was obvious that this was a sort of inner circle of the town, a luncheon hierarchy. I had never eaten there before at that time of day, but despite my being an outsider, no notice was made of my presence. Everybody said hello, and presently I was somehow included and made a part of the conversation.

Mooney finished first and stood behind me, reaching over my shoulder for a toothpick from the shot glass in front of me. "In case it hadn't occurred to you," he said, "four days from now, at dawn, is the opening of the woodcock season. I have an idea that that dog of Matt's would work even better than she did last year."

"Joy and I could be induced," I answered.

"I notice I didn't have to break your arm," he grinned. "It includes Farnley and Doc Harris, too," he said. "It's a date of long standing. Matt never missed it."

I nodded. "Breakfast at my place, then."

"You're not inviting us. We're coming. It wouldn't be legal any other way."

When he got to the door, Sam Beaton called to him, "You and Farnley better arrange not to have any sick people or dead people next Monday!"

Moody looked him over carefully. "You strike me as being a bit peaked, Sam, but I reckon you'll last past Monday. And if you don't you'll keep till Tuesday anyway."

As we were leaving Doc Farnley came in to get his paper. He came over and sat beside me. "Tell me, how's Elizabeth standing up under all of this?" he asked.

"A little tired, but that's only natural."

"When I saw her day before yesterday, I told her I thought she ought to get away for a couple of weeks. Lie down on the flat of her back somewhere in the sun and just rest."

117

"She didn't say anything about your advising it. But she and Frankie are going away tomorrow. —Is it anything serious?"

Farnley was glancing at the headlines, and seemed to be paying no attention. "Well," he finally said, "it won't hurt her to take things a little slowly for the next few months."

"Is this serious?" I asked.

"Nothing too serious. People of her age and mine ought to slow up a bit."

When I got back to the place I stopped at the barns first to go over some things with Will Talcott, and we were sitting in the record room going over the month's business when Frankie appeared, dressed in jodhpurs and a leather jacket. "I was taking a walk and Joy told me you were here," she explained. "She was sitting out in front of the barn. She told me to ask you if it wouldn't be a grand afternoon for a ride."

"Tell her she's a smart dog," I agreed. I glanced down at my slacks and low shoes. "It won't take long to go back to the house and change."

"There's some trousers and boots of Matt's in the tack room," Will suggested. "I'll get the horses ready."

As the three of us were walking over to the barn I asked Will, "Don't you resent keeping the horses on the place? They take work, and they don't produce anything."

"Oh I don't know, they produce some pretty high-toned manure," he defended. "Anyway, it'd be a hell of a farm that couldn't afford to have a horse on it. Of course they're not work horses. Tractors have run draft animals off the farm—our kind of farming, that is."

"Alf Adams still uses horses," I said.

"But he really works his farm with tractors. He's just sentimental about horses, keeps 'em because he likes 'em. Your granddaddy bred trotters. So did Old Matt. Raced 'em at Goshen, and around. Won big money they say. Then he gave it up. Said that when professionals got their hands on horseflesh it was time for gentlemen to get out of the game. —I'll saddle up while you change."

He slipped a pair of bridles over his arm and picked up two saddles from the racks. While I was rummaging about in the

118

closet, Frankie was studying the ribbons and trophies that lined the wall, and the mounted bits and shoes that each bore the name plates of the horses that had worn them. "If you keep turned around," I said, as I found a pair of breeks, "I'll slip these on." I knew they'd fit, because from the time I was twenty, Matt and I could wear each other's clothes, and did.

"Are these really silver shoes?" Frankie asked, pointing up to the wall.

"When they're silver you never call them *shoes,* they're *plates.* Yes, they're silver."

"But they didn't use them?"

"They raced with them. When you had a champion you indulged the champion—and yourself."

"Actually used them?"

"They were softer and lighter than iron, and I guess there was a legend that they were faster. There were some men in those days who hung diamonds on their women, and silver shoes on their race horses. They're all buried up by the glen."

"Who are?"

"The horses; not the men."

"You're pulling my leg," she accused me.

"We'll ride up there this afternoon, and I'll show you. All the great horses the Tracys owned, and some of the ones they loved that weren't so great, are buried up there. The great bulls of the herd, and the great cows are also there."

"I still think you're joking."

"You'll see that I'm not. There's a simple stone with a name and date above each animal—not every animal that died on the place, but the ones that brought fame to the breeding, and wealth to the Tracys. And some that were just loved. It's sort of a *noblesse oblige.* A lot of farmers bury their fine animals; they don't just haul them to a far field and let woods animals eat them, or call in the glue man. But I guess only the Tracys, hereabouts, were sentimental enough to set off a piece of land and put up stones."

"It makes me want to cry," Frankie said.

I knew what she meant. I fastened Matt's trousers and mumbled under my breath, "Hold in your gut."

When we dismounted in the low corner of the meadow by the

glen, Frankie wandered along the line of small monuments, reading them. "Miss Emmeline—1873."

"It was a family name back in my grandfather's day," I explained.

A little farther down the row, there was the stone of the first great Radiant cow, the dam of her far-flung line, with her then world's champion lactation record for the breed. And there was my first horse, a little Morgan mare named Flavia—she had been as lovely to me as the Princess of Zenda—and the oldest stone there bore the name Lola Montez. "That was my great-grandfather's doing," I told Frankie with a laugh. "There's a family legend that the name was not just an accident of popularity, he was involved in more than horseflesh with the name of Lola Montez."

"It still makes me want to cry," said Frankie.

We took the glen trail which had been the first road up the Hill, and rode down across the fields into the valley. Some of the barways were open and we raced toward the ones that were closed, and jumped them. Then, finally, we walked the horses to rest them. They picked their way through a wood lot, and we finally came out in the meadow behind the Jennings Place.

"There's your new property," I said.

"I didn't know it had a garden on this side," she said. "I've only seen the house from the road. It's a lovely place. El'zabeth lived here and you were born here, weren't you?"

"No," I told her. "I was born in the house on the Hill, about thirty minutes after Old Matt carried Elizabeth there in his arms."

Frankie said, "I never really got the story of what happened except from Adelaide and Emmeline, and it seemed awfully garbled."

"From those sources, it would be."

"There was really a fire, though?"

"There was a fire," I said.

"But the house couldn't have been badly damaged? It seems so old and perfect."

The same thought was in my mind. Time can be so kind and healing to the land, to houses, and sometimes even to people. After the fire, Old Matthew had bought the place and repaired the damage; today no sign of it remained. And the tragedy and

120

the human violence that had played its brief scene there had also been repaired. There seemed no rancor left in Constance's heart, and certainly there was none in Elizabeth's, and the focus of that violence—Old Matt—had been dead for these many years. Only the legend still lived, distorted and ugly and violent; but that, too, was dying. Someday Emmeline and Adelaide would forget, or they would have no one new to whom to tell it.

The little garden was pleasant and serene, and we walked through it. Even in the winter, gardens keep their shape; their beds suggest the promise of what they will be in summer. Frankie broke off a sprig of holly and started to put it in her buttonhole. Then she changed her mind and put it in the pocket of her jacket instead. "I'll keep it," she said, "to remember my house with, while I'm away. You have to have a male and a female, you know, or it isn't any good. Alyse told me."

"You have to have a *what,* or *what* isn't any good?"

"You've got to have a male holly plant, or the female isn't any good. She doesn't grow right, she grows lopsided and stunted. And without the male you don't get any berries, either. Nature's pretty smart, isn't she?"

"Very smart," I conceded. I was thinking of Elizabeth, sitting in this garden in the first years she came to Haviland—beautiful and lonely and too young to have been so hurt as to seek this out-of-the-way corner where she wasn't known. I could imagine the moment when she and Old Matthew met, and the afternoons when he would pass the time of day with her in this garden, until the time of day was not enough to pass. —Well, it had been a knowing hand with nature that had planted the male holly beside the female holly.

"It must be full of old-fashioned flowers in the summer," Frankie said. "Hollyhocks, and sweet william, and rosemary and rue."

"A lot of rue," I said.

She looked up at me. "There are so many overtones to living where the Tracys have lived. I don't suppose I shall ever know them all."

I had no answer to give her. She got back on her horse, and we took our way home through the meadow. The light was softer now, and pale gray mists began to rise out of the low places, and along the stream. In the valley, someone was burning leaves, and the smoke of their burning mingled with the mist, and the pungency of their burning was heavy in the air and re-created all of the fall days of one's life. Of one accord, we walked the horses to savor the world about us the more deeply, and because the mood we must both have felt would have been shattered by a quick motion.

Finally I said: "I'd like to talk to you about last night."

As if she hadn't heard me, Frankie raked her heels back across her horse's belly. "I'll race you to the glen!" she called back to me.

My horse broke in pursuit and we were both galloping neck and neck across the fields, stopping only at the foot of the glen where the old road went into the wood. Then we rode single file. The road was badly washed, and not too easy going, and so we didn't talk.

Eight

After an early luncheon the next day, I drove Frankie and Elizabeth to the station to catch the two o'clock to New York. I dropped them off, and then pulled the car into an open space a little beyond and carried their luggage over to the platform. When I got there Elizabeth was talking to Henry Sanford and Frankie had gone into the Station Restaurant to buy some papers.

"Do you realize," Elizabeth was asking Pop, "that I've never gone away from Haviland or come back without your being at the station? Sometimes I suspect you meet all trains."

"Not all of them," Pop smiled. "Just all the ones you're on."

"Then this wasn't an accident? You really were here to say good-by to us?"

"The first time was an accident," he said. "Afterwards, it was by intention. And as a token of my intention—" He handed a little twist of paper in which was the kind of a nosegay Fred Renney's greenhouse would put up—little rosebuds and lilies of the valley. As Frankie came up, he handed her one, too, and then he and Elizabeth walked down the platform talking.

Frankie and I stood together in that uncomfortable constraint of leave-taking when there are so many things to be said, with not enough time to say them in. I was almost glad when from far up the cut came the long blare of the engine as it blew for the crossing at the milk factory. "I'll take care of her," Frankie said.

"And take care of yourself," I said, and then the train was on us and the spit of cinders was on our faces, and I said: "Oh, damn, I've got a cinder in my eye." I kissed Elizabeth good-by, and started to kiss Frankie and turned awkward and put my hand

123

out to her, and she suddenly realized that I was trying to shake her hand and she fumbled with the papers under her arm, and the conductor was calling, "All aboard!" and the train was pulling away, and Pop and I watched it disappear and we were standing alone on the platform.

"I'll drive you back to your office," I offered.

"I've got some things to go over with you anyway." He walked to the car with me.

There wasn't much to go over. Just some details about inventories, and the estate appraisal. While I was signing the papers I asked him about Constance's visit the day before.

"It was a very curious afternoon," he told me. "Farnley was here, and Fletcher and Doc Harris came in. We talked, all of us, about one thing and another. Up to a certain point, Constance was clear as a bell—up to the time of her trouble, that is. But there was no clear memory of the years that followed, just a vague confusion. She had been somewhere, and she hadn't been happy. And then beginning the other day— It really began the morning Matt died. He'd gone across to her wing of the house to visit her, maybe to say good-by. At that point things began to clear for her. It was as if she had walked through a room, and when she came out the other side she was an old woman, with more than half of a lifetime gone by. Old Matt was dead, and a man who was older than the Matt who had been her husband was talking to her and seemed to be saying good-by to her. The curious thing is that she could be as clear about things as she was."

"What about Elizabeth?" I asked.

"Elizabeth she could remember from the early days of her trouble."

"And me?"

"She found it a little difficult to really grasp who you were. That you were Old Matt's son, and Elizabeth's son, was a difficult piece of the puzzle to put together; but Emmeline and Adelaide weren't too hard for her. They'd been older than young Matt before her mind went away, and during the years in between, they had come in and out of the shadows to her. I can't say that she loved them, and whatever doors might have been open in her heart were closed by the way Emmeline and Adelaide and the men they married acted the other afternoon. Doc Farnley spent a little

124

time with her alone, and later she sort of conveyed the impression that if she wasn't in her right mind, then neither were any of us. And the memoranda of the dispositions she wanted made removed any last doubt that I might have had."

"If she's antagonistic to Emmeline and Adelaide, there'll probably be more trouble from that quarter," I said.

"Not too much. She'd thought that out, too. She said that she had no desire to will you and Elizabeth any litigation. She left a tidy little sum to each of the grandchildren—she had me go over their names to be sure that she hadn't missed out on one of them—and she left an equal sum to Frankie, setting her forth as 'her step-granddaughter,' which is a new wrinkle in the law. She left the others all the Harper jewelry—that's from her side of the family. The Tracy family jewelry that had come to her she left to you and Elizabeth, and the jewelry that Matt had given her personally she left to Frankie. All except one ring." He pressed a button on his desk. "The engagement ring Old Matt gave her. She wants you to have that now, prior to her death. She slipped it off her finger while she was here."

His secretary came in from the other room. "Margaret, will you get out of the safe that envelope I gave you to keep for Mr. Milnor yesterday?"

The secretary brought it. Pop opened the envelope and gave me the ring. I'd often seen it on Constance's hand, but I'd never looked at it closely before. It was a large ruby, old-fashioned in cut and in its setting of small diamonds.

"There was a card, too." Pop slipped a card from the envelope and handed it to me.

It has been burned free of heartbreak, the card read. *May the next woman who wears this know only happiness.*

"The whole thing's so strange," I said.

"Constance is a strange woman." Pop tapped the empty envelope against the edge of his desk. "She's clearing her decks. Tidying up her unfinished business."

"It has been burned free of heartbreak," I reread. "She was going back in her mind to the fire."

"I imagine. It wasn't something that anyone who touched the story would ever be likely to forget."

It occurred to me that I knew almost as little as Frankie about

125

what had really happened. "Have you got a little time?" I asked him.

"Never ask an old man if he has time." Pop smiled.

"I never did know the real story."

"You couldn't know all of it," Pop said. "It goes too long a way back before the fire. Before even the day Elizabeth came to Haviland. It goes back further than Old Matt, too. It rightly began, I guess, when Constance was knee-high to a grasshopper."

"That's the accepted theory," I murmured. "Her name was Harper, wasn't it, before she married Matt?"

He nodded. "Kinderhook people, they were. English stock, but they'd come up into the Hudson Valley on the heels of the Dutch and got their hands on a lot of land and begun to live like the patroon families."

"I've seen a little of it in my day," I said.

"Nothing like it was a generation ago," Pop said. "Van Brunks, Van Eycks, Ten Eycks, Van Rensselaers, Roosevelts—and mixed in with them, the Harpers. They lived like lords of the manor, and acted like lords of the manor. They were proud and arrogant and wealthy and ambitious. But as time went by their ambition died. They stopped having anything to be ambitious about. They had more than enough wealth, and too much pride and arrogance. You've seen it in the Roosevelt tribe. They even got so there wasn't anybody good enough for them to marry, except people with their own names; and in time, even with sound stock to begin with, that makes for overly sensitive and unstable people. In-grown. It was what defeated most of them in the end; they just petered out and got weak and sat in their overmortgaged homes and watched their lands dwindle away from them—most of them, that is, except the Roosevelts, and at the time I'm speaking of, the Harpers at Kinderhook.

"Well, in the fall of the year, before Matt and Constance were married, Matt drove into town in a racing cutter the day of the first real snow. He stopped here in the office to go over some things, but he didn't stay long; he'd been cooped up on the Hill for too many months and he was driving over to Poughkeepsie to a party, and after that there would be another one in Newburgh and another in Krum Elbow.

"I didn't see Matt for a good month after that, but I heard

126

about him. He'd met a Constance Harper at one of the parties, and he made it his business to be a guest at every party she was at that month. With the big houses people ran in those days, fifteen or twenty guests wasn't anything and they usually stayed the week before moving on to the next party. Going over to Poughkeepsie to court, I'd heard of this Constance Harper, and I'd heard of the man she was said to be in love with. In fact, he'd been pointed out to me. His family owned a big store in Poughkeepsie and he'd inherited it; his name was Markham. And Constance, going into the store one day, had met him and, one thing leading to another, she'd fallen in love with him, or thought she had.

"Poughkeepsie knew all about that story, but I don't think Matt did at the time; and I'm certain that the Harpers didn't. The idea of a Harper marrying a storekeeper was unthinkable, not only to the Harpers, but to just about everybody else in the Hudson Valley, I guess.

"Well, when Matt came home just before Christmas, he was engaged to Constance Harper, and the engagement was due to be announced at the turn of the year at a big party the Harpers were going to give at Kinderhook. Nobody knew then, but Matt learned of it later and told me; the Harpers had finally come upon the story of Constance and Markham, and they'd raised hell about it. Constance tried to revolt, said she was going to marry Markham and no one could stop her. But children didn't revolt much in those days, and to make things worse, the whole business had been pretty much talked about, and her name had been compromised. I don't think it amounted to very much; probably no more than they had gone driving, and a horse had cast a shoe, and she'd been late getting back to some house she'd been staying at.

"It was just about that time that Matt showed up at Kinderhook and asked Mr. Harper for his daughter's hand. Constance had been pretty well brought to heel by her father by that time, and, in the way of her generation, once the decision was made she accepted it. Moreover, I gather that she avoided talking to Matt about Mr. Markham."

Pop got up and stood at the window, his gaze wandering down along Railroad Avenue. "That's the beginning of the story," he finally said. "What follows is such an ancient history that I guess it can be repeated. Old Matthew never told it to me all at once, but

127

he'd unburden himself now and again, and the story shaped up something like this. I don't know quite how to put it," he said, "but fifty years ago sex was a pretty confused business."

I must have smiled, because he shook his head. "I know. It's still confused. But in the time I'm talking about, it was unhealthy, too. Ideas of sin bulked bigger in people's minds, and the women of those days were pretty thwarted and inhibited. They were raised to think that their bodies were obscene; some of them even took their baths in bathing gowns so their modesty wouldn't be affronted by their own sight of themselves. I know of one marriage in which the husband never saw his wife's body in the light of day. He never saw it for fifteen years, and when at last he did, the bloom of youth had passed from it. Too bad, because they loved each other." For a long moment he was silent, and then he turned from the window and came back to his desk. "The Victorians were nasty people, John." He offered me a cigar and lit one himself, and then forgot to smoke it. He just sat there, staring out across the room.

"I probably sound pretty garrulous to you." It was more of a statement than an apology.

"No, go on." I urged him. "Go on. These are things that perhaps I ought to know."

He nodded. "Yes, I think you should. These events have been in my mind for a long while, and for a long while I've tried to understand them. So what I'm telling you is not idle gossip, or the babbling of an old man with too many memories."

"Pop, I know that, believe me. —What happened after they were married? Old Matt, I mean, and Constance."

He dropped into the chair behind his desk, and placed his cigar carefully across an ash tray and made a tent of his fingers. "Well," he went on, "by the time they came back from the honeymoon, or shortly afterwards, she was pregnant and she and Matt were living in separate rooms. Apparently that was her decision and not Matt's, though he never told me in so many words. I gathered, however, that for a couple of years after Emmeline was born, their relationship was pretty difficult. I suppose Constance was what would be called today a frigid woman; which is a catch-all phrase to describe a conclusion which can be arrived at in a number of ways. I don't think her trouble was Markham; that affair didn't seem to have gone very deep with her. And I don't think it was a lack of restraint, or a heavy-handedness on the part of Old Matt. He was a passionate man, but he was gentle and knowing. No, I'm inclined to think that Constance's trouble was common to a lot of women of her generation. Prudery, pruriency, mixed-up religion, an inhibiting sense of sin, and Victorianism; the mixture was enough to ruin the life of any woman. It certainly ruined Constance's. In any event she and Matt had a couple of bad years, as I said before, and then things seemed to be getting better and she was carrying Adelaide, and it looked like everything might be all right again until young Matt was on the way. Shortly after he was born, they had to put Constance in a sanatorium. She was there for more than a year, and when she came back you could see that they hadn't been able to do much for her. She was established in the wing of the old house, with a nurse, and some evenings she'd be well enough to dine at the table and act normally. But the slightest thing might set her off. I saw quite a lot of Matt during that time. Farnley did, too. One or the other of us, or someone close to Matt, who would understand and not notice when Constance became difficult, dined with them a couple of times a week. She was better if there were outsiders around.

"Of course you'll be wondering what Matt was doing those years. Some men would have taken to drinking a lot, and others would have found themselves an arrangement—either a house-keeper, or some complacent lady in the village."

He caught my smile. "I'm serious," he said. "You'd be surprised how many arrangements have existed in Haviland. But, those weren't solutions for the kind of a man your father was. He threw himself more and more into the farm; that's when the big barn was built, and the herd was extended; he even bought more land. If during those years women touched Old Matt's life, they didn't touch it more than casually."

The old gentleman was silent for a long moment. He twisted in his swivel chair so that he was half faced away from me, and once more his gaze went out along the village street. I wondered with what figures and events he was peopling it.

"Constance grew worse instead of better," he finally resumed. "Some of us urged Old Matt to have her committed; if not for her safety, for his own sanity and peace of mind. The life he was leading was no life for any man. But he wouldn't do it, even though they hardly ever saw each other at this time. In the far wing of that house, Constance had retreated to a world of her own."

He picked up his cigar and made a ritual of relighting it, holding it out before him with the match below the tobacco until it became incandescent and then blowing out the match and carefully drawing on the cigar so that it would burn evenly.

"About that time Elizabeth came to Haviland. It's true, what she said today. I was the first person she saw at the station. About two days later, she came up here to the office and sat in the chair you're sitting in right now, and asked me if I knew of any small property she might rent. She explained without really explaining anything, that she wanted to spend a year in the country, and she liked the anonymity of this kind of a town. I had never thought of living in Haviland as achieving anonymity.

"She was quite businesslike about the whole transaction, and insisted on giving me references, and very special references they were—the Fifth Avenue Bank and the Debevoise law firm. She asked me if I knew them. To this day, I'm not quite sure whether she was that naïve, or she thought that I was."

"Naïve isn't exactly a word to describe Elizabeth," I commented. "I've never known anyone more direct or with less duplicity in her being."

"The only way I can describe her"—he seemed to reach for the idea—"is to say she was like a finely bred race horse. Everything about her was thoroughbred."

He lapsed again into a kind of reverie. "How long did it take her to find a place to live?" I cued him gently.

He looked up at me; there was a glint of humor in his eyes. "Not long," he said. "Not long at all. That same afternoon, in fact. Yes, that afternoon I showed her the Jennings Place. She fell in love with it. It wasn't furnished very well, but she said that was no drawback, she'd move her own furniture up from New York.

"I remember that when she signed the lease, she wanted to give me a check for the whole year instead of the first quarter, but I wouldn't let her. As a matter of fact, I went backwards on the deal, and before I signed the lease myself for the estate, I sent it down to her lawyers in New York for them to approve. I got a

130

letter thanking me, and telling me that any consideration or service I could render her would be deeply appreciated by them. The same thing happened with the bank downstairs. They got a letter from the Fifth Avenue Bank, the kind of a letter you could borrow money on. It said they'd appreciate our extending every courtesy to their client. Seems I've made a little too much of a point about something that isn't very important," Pop stopped himself.

"It's important," I told him. "It gives a fuller picture of Elizabeth."

"Yes, I know what you mean," Pop said. "In the weeks that followed, she'd telephone to ask if she could move some planting in the garden, or who was a good carpenter, or a good plumber—things like that. I began to worry that she was putting too much money into a rented house, and I stopped by one day to talk to her about it. She was about moved in by then, but still having things done to the kitchen and to the upstairs. It wasn't the *Jennings* Place any longer, it was Elizabeth's. The furniture was the kind of stuff you don't buy, you inherit; there were a number of fine pieces, and a lot of books, and a sense of home and peace and dignity about it.

"The next part of this," he went on, "isn't so easy to put into words. There's more of implication in it, than anything that happened, or even might have happened. From time to time through the winter and through the following spring and summer, when business took me past the Jennings Place, I would drop in just to see how she was, how she was getting along. Sometimes, if it was afternoon, I'd stay for a cup of tea. It was along around that time that Mrs. Sanford thought I was in love with Elizabeth. She didn't think so for long, but then the way she thought I was in love with Elizabeth didn't last for long either. I was very happily married to Mrs. Sanford, but for a few brief weeks I dreamed some dreams, though Elizabeth didn't know anything about it. Then I came back to earth and the practice of law in Haviland, which is a mighty earthy profession."

He got up and paced the room once or twice, and then, glancing at his desk, he seemed to be reminded of something and he called out to his secretary. Margaret came in, and he dictated a few notes to her as he checked items off on his calendar, and gave her a property description for a transfer to copy. I wondered if he

131

intended to go on with his story, or if he had come to the end of what he thought that I should know. I didn't want to ask him, or to hurry him.

Pop finally finished and glanced up at me as I twisted Constance's ring about my little finger. Margaret gathered the papers from his desk. He picked up the small envelope with Constance's wavering writing on it and handed it to her. "Have this photostated," he instructed her. "And make a memorandum for both of us to sign, that in our presence yesterday this ring was deposited with me by Constance Harper Tracy to be conveyed to John Milnor, as a free gift without consideration, and notify the insurance companies to make the proper transfer on their policies."

"The law makes for very tidy housekeeping," I remarked, as the door closed behind Margaret.

"It's too bad some of the Tracys didn't follow the law."

"For the good of the Tracys, or for the good of the law?" I asked.

"For the good of both, I guess."

"The law doesn't keep a man from making a damn fool of himself," I said.

"No, but it helps him out a lot, once he has."

"And you've had a lot of helping to do with the Tracys?"

"Some," he conceded. "But Matt and Elizabeth would have met one way or another in the end; they weren't the kind of people that could live in the same town and not have something happen between them."

Pop was back at the Jennings Place, and without a break in his stride. I slipped the ring into my watch pocket and crossed my legs to hear him out.

"There weren't any automobiles around here then, it was a horse-and-buggy world, and a mighty different world, John. We went the same places, but we didn't get there so quickly. The Jennings Place isn't too far from the village, and Elizabeth used old Henry Allen's livery when she wanted a carriage to go somewhere. But come spring of that first year, she asked me about buying a horse and rig of her own." He chuckled at some memory. "You know in my generation every man thought of himself as a judge and expert of three things, liquor, women and horses. I wonder what your generation has substituted for the horse, John?—You

132

know, looking back on it, I don't suppose there was a man in Haviland who knew less about horses, or women. But I wasn't admitting it in those days. Elizabeth and I sort of did it ass-backwards. We bought the rig first; at least it was a rig we started to buy and a gig we ended up buying, and a three-wheeled one at that."

I listen well, but Pop must have detected something in my face, because he interrupted himself. "No, I mean it. It was a three-wheeled gig. I sometimes think it was the only three-wheeled gig that was ever made, at least I never saw one before or since. Henry Allen had done some trading, and there it was in his barn, all sparkling and polished and black and yellow—and only three wheels, mind you."

"Black and yellow?"

"Yes, black and yellow. Why?"

"I didn't think there could be two of them. It's stored in the old barn up on the farm, with a linen cover over it in the back of the sulky room, and it gets cleaned once a year, and its leather dressed. But I never knew the story of it."

"Old Matt had strange sentiments and he indulged them," Sanford said. "But it wasn't the gig that caused the trouble, though it might have helped. It was the horse. I should have let someone who knew more about horseflesh buy one for a woman to drive, but then I considered myself an expert. There was a man at Whaley who traded in horses, and good ones. Well, the one that Elizabeth fancied—I must say I fancied, too. He was sound and spirited, only he wasn't an animal for a woman to drive. I didn't know it then, but he'd been mistreated at some time, and if he was standing and something frightened him, he'd shy, and he'd shy backwards, and man or God couldn't stop him, he'd go back.

"Well, for a couple of weeks everything went well. Elizabeth would drive through the village looking as smart and as pretty as a Gibson girl, and everybody would stop and stand and watch her go by. Then one afternoon, by the turn in the road where the old mill stands, she stopped to rest the horse before going up the hill. She told me later, she'd been sitting there for a minute or more, relaxed and watching the little waterfall in the ravine, when suddenly a partridge flushed from the side of the road just beside her horse's head, flushed with a drum and roar of wings, and the horse

133

started to back. There wasn't anything she could have done, and even if there had been, there wasn't time to do it in. The horse backed and that fool front wheel crimped. I suppose that was what saved her because, as the gig tipped, she was thrown first and landed on the side of the bank. But the horse and the gig went right on over, and landed in a tangle beside the stream. It's a good twenty-five feet of drop.

"The next thing Elizabeth knew was a twinge of pain, and there was a man kneeling beside her, working his fingers along her bare ankle. I only mention that because it comes into the story later. Her ankle was bruised and badly sprained, but no bones were broken. Then Matt went down to look at the horse, and from the top of the bank Elizabeth could see the poor beast thrash, and the bone was sticking through the flesh of its leg, and its screams were horrible. Matt managed to get the horse's head on the ground, and he quieted it, and then he took his clasp knife out of his pocket. Elizabeth tried to stop him, but he explained to her that it would take a long time to find someone with a gun, and that the quickest way was the most merciful. Even then, she still couldn't believe that he would do it, the horse was looking up at him with such trust and confidence in its eyes—with some men animals seem to instinctively have that trust. And then the blood started to gush out of the poor beast's neck.

"Elizabeth told me later what a coward she was. She couldn't look, she had to close her eyes. When she opened them, the horse was quiet. The blood was just barely pulsing from the wound into the great murky puddle about its neck. Matt was still kneeling beside it, gently stroking its head. Then there was a little quiver and the pulsing stopped, and Matt patted the horse's head and rose and came back to her.

"When he started to pick her up he noticed his hands and stooped and wiped them on the grass. It was only a few hundred yards back to the Jennings Place and no one had passed, so he put Elizabeth's shoe and stocking in his pocket and picked her up and started to carry her in his arms. His own saddle horse followed along behind them. Elizabeth isn't one given to hysterics, but she admitted to me that she was pretty close to it then.

"They hadn't gone far when she looked down and saw her bare ankle and foot, and she realized that while she was unconscious

134

this man had unfastened her stocking and drawn it from her. That was the trigger for her getting mad, but the real cause was probably the accident and the killing of the horse, because she didn't have that kind of cheap modesty in her. Anyway, she suddenly slapped Matt across the face. He stopped, she told me, and looked at her, and then he glanced down at her bare leg and ankle and started to laugh—not as she had ever known other men to laugh with their lips or their minds, but with a laughter that came from way inside him, so that she could feel it ripple along his belly and ribs as he held her."

"He was quite a lot of man," I said.

"He was," Pop agreed. "And it was about then that Elizabeth knew it. It was also about then that the strange thing that happens between a man and a woman happened. She wouldn't admit it straight off, of course. No woman would. She said she just acted like any other female. 'You're a heartless, cruel, callous beast of a man!' she screamed at him. She said he didn't laugh any more, he just looked at her with a curious expression on his face, as if he was looking right through her. And she said she felt more invaded and undressed than she had with the thought of a strange man taking her stocking off, and that made her feel childish and unreasonable, and she accused him of being capable of doing the same thing to her as to the horse, if she'd been hurt like that.

"He didn't answer right away. He wasn't even looking at her, she said, he seemed to be looking somewhere far behind her, and when he spoke, it was like he was measuring each word. 'If there was no other way out, and it seemed the right thing to do, and I loved you enough.'

"It was a funny thing, she told me, that although he didn't hold her any tighter, she suddenly felt the shape of his hand on her back; and then she noticed that there was blood on his other hand, and that some of it had come off on her dress, and she was conscious of the cleanliness of his nails, and his fingers, which were sensitive and strong at the same time. She even noticed that the dust of the road made little spurts and eddies about his boots as he walked. It's strange, the things that one notices at the important moments in life. A lawyer is conscious of that when he examines witnesses; they remember the damnedest things.

"Matt called Doc Farnley as soon as he got her back to the

house. Old Doc. —Young Doc was only in medical school at that time. As I say, Matt called the doctor, but the woman who did for Elizabeth called me as being the only friend she knew Elizabeth had in Haviland. Farnley had already examined her when I arrived, and he told me it was a bad wrench, with a lot of torn muscles and ligaments; but more than that, she'd had a bad shock, what with the accident and the killing of the horse. 'Damn fool thing for Matt to have done in front of a sensitive woman,' he said.

"I guess I knew the moment Farnley mentioned Matt's name what had happened. Old Doc's generation of physicians weren't the psychologists that young Doc's are now, and I sometimes think that at that period lawyers knew more about human nature than doctors. Elizabeth had met Matt as few people in a civilized scheme of things ever meet. The impact of his gentleness and his competence and his maleness had hit her all at once; and emergency and blood and death and gentleness are powerful sexual factors in the make-up of the human animal. She'd been exposed to all of them in one instant, and at the same time to the most male man that ever walked the earth of this valley.

"Elizabeth never talked to me about it until a long time later, when she was carrying you. Quite obviously carrying you, I might add. She was seated in the garden under an apple tree in blossom, and she told me the whole story, not to defend or justify anything, but just sort of to explain, so that I would know; and I guess she hoped that I was mature enough and wise enough to understand that when things are that way, there isn't any other way they can be. But the night the accident happened, she didn't say anything except to thank me, and tell me that it was good to have friends like me and Farnley. The woman who took care of her was tidying up and putting things away, and on the chair was a stocking that was torn and stained and a little blood-streaked; and as she was about to throw it away in a wastebasket, Elizabeth interrupted what she was saying to me, and told her to put it in the drawer of the bedside table. It was such a transparent and sentimental thing to do, I knew that somehow and somewhere it was all tied up with Matt Tracy and that a far-reaching chain of circumstances had commenced that would lead into many lives and have much to do with Haviland; and like all inexorable and inevitable things nothing that man could do would change or stop it, and they being the people they were it was probably right—the inevitable usually is.

"When I left her, I didn't drive straight home. I drove up over the Hill and made the great circle back to the village. I passed Matt Tracy's house. There was a light in his library window, but I didn't go in.

"Behind a horse it's a long trip from the Jennings Place around the North Hill and back to the village. It was very late when I got home. Mrs. Sanford must have sensed that something had happened, something more than Elizabeth's accident. I'll never forget how gentle and understanding she was. She slept in the spare room because she said that I had had a trying day and would need my sleep. And from that night, the very good years of my life with Mrs. Sanford commenced, and until the day of her death she was always one of Elizabeth's closest friends."

I rose and walked over to the window. Farnley's car turned the corner and headed down toward the station, and Mooney closed the door of his shop and started off down the street toward the post office. "There's an awful lot of living done in a small town," Pop mused. "A lot of it comes to nothing, but some of it is important and shouldn't be too quickly forgotten. I'm probably boring the hell out of you."

"Go on and tell me the rest of it."

"That's a big order."

"Well, tell me the important things."

"The trouble is that even at this distance, it's hard to determine just what is important," he said. "And then again, what comes to your mind is probably what is important, just *because* it comes to your mind."

"That's as good a yardstick as I could ask for." I smiled.

"Well, if you really want to go on, Elizabeth's ankle was some weeks in mending. It was a nice summer though, and in a few days she was spending most of her time sitting in the garden, or in the little covered terrace at the back of the house, and I'd drop around from time to time. She talked of Matt quite a bit, and I gathered that he would stop in as he passed—which must have been almost every day—and visit with her. It wasn't that she asked about him directly, but it seemed that no matter where a

137

conversation started, it ended up with Matt Tracy. There wasn't anything about him that didn't interest her.

"And then late one afternoon I was sitting on the terrace with her, and we heard a carriage stop on the other side of the house. Her ankle was almost well by then, and she jumped up and hurried through the house to open the door. I knew it could only be Matt to make her run like that, and I got up to follow her into the house to say I was leaving. I'd got to the living room as she opened the front door. Matt was standing there, and he had a book in his hand. He didn't come in, and he didn't say a thing, and she didn't say anything either; they just stood there looking at each other. Not a word was spoken, but they were saying so much to each other that I felt I ought to look away, that I was eavesdropping. I remember that I did a courtroom job of clearing my throat, but it didn't do any good. It was as if I were in one world and they were in another. They moved toward each other, and the book that Matt was carrying fell to the floor, and they were in each other's arms. They didn't embrace like people meeting or leaving each other, they—well they just embraced completely, and for all time, and it wasn't anything that anyone had a right to witness. I went back out on the terrace and lit a cigar.

"Presently I heard Elizabeth say, 'Matthew,' and Matthew say, 'Elizabeth.' That was all they said, and then I could hear their steps coming through the living room, and they were standing at the doorway of the terrace, hand in hand. If sin is ugly, then theirs wasn't sin, because I have never seen two people so touched with radiance and with beauty.

"Well, I guess I needn't tell you that I took my way to the door by myself. It was pretty close to dark, and I stumbled over something on the threshold—the book Matt had dropped and hadn't bothered to pick up. Its back was split and it was in two pieces. I gathered it up and took it with me, and that night I glanced through it in my study. Its title was *Prefaces and Dedications* and it had been assembled from the library of a man named Huth, and privately printed. It was actually Huth's own copy, it was signed *Henry Huth 1874*. Of all the books in the Tracy library, it was the damnedest book for Matt to have picked up that day to take to Elizabeth. I sent it away and had it rebound, and later I returned it to her. Bookbinding is a slow trade, and a lot of living had been

lived by then. Elizabeth looked at the volume, and then she handed
it back to me with a smile. 'You keep it, Henry,' she said. 'He was
a wise editor; only *Prefaces and Dedications*. No Epilogues.'

" 'But every story has to have an epilogue,' I told her.

" 'I know,' she said. 'I wonder what ours will be.' "

Pop got out of his chair and stretched his bones, as the old do,
and went over to the bookcase on the far wall. He took down a
short red book that stood beside the four tall volumes of his be-
loved Blackstone, and handed it to me. "You might as well take
it with you," he said. "Like Constance, I am of a sound and dis-
posing mind, and I am aware that the time has come in my life
to clear my decks. Anyway, that book belongs back in the Tracy
library, and the Tracy library belongs to you."

"Prefaces and Dedications," I read aloud. "And the epilogue
isn't finished yet," I added. "Or do you write epilogues down into
the second and third generation?"

"I guess you do," said Pop. "I guess you do—"

"What did Haviland have to say about all this?" I asked him
curiously.

"Oddly enough, it took a long time for the story to get into the
currency of public gossip," Pop said. "In a town the size of Haviland, very little that goes on between a man and a woman remains
a secret for any length of time. Of course Matt's people up on the
Hill were devoted to him, and they said nothing. And the woman
who did for Elizabeth was devoted to her, and she didn't say
anything. It was Matt and Elizabeth themselves who really told
the town. There didn't seem to be a devious or furtive bone in
their bodies. They just began to be together, that was all. When
Matt went to the village, Elizabeth drove with him, and when
Matt had business in the bank, she'd wait in the carriage, cr if
the weather wasn't pleasant she'd sit inside in what's now Jim
Fletcher's office. The very openness of it kept anybody from
thinking there was anything to think about, until presently the
town was so used to the idea that it wasn't worth thinking about.
Anyway you can't crucify a man with disapproval or ostracism
when he doesn't know he's being disapproved of or ostracized,
and what's more, doesn't care. Matt Tracy needed Haviland like
he needed the acreage the town was built on, which is to say he
didn't need it at all. While on the other hand, Haviland needed the

139

Tracys. It still does, John. You have to have some yeast in the dough to make good baking. The Tracys, I guess, have been the yeast of this town. There was another factor involved. In the moral economics of a small town, Elizabeth as Matt Tracy's mistress was less of a menace and a threat than Elizabeth Milnor, living alone on the old Jennings Place. All the old hens of the town felt that she was out of circulation, and that their husbands were safe. There was even an element of pride that Haviland had an honest-to-god lover and mistress living in sin in the community. And if a scientist of the social *mores* had counted the traffic that passed the Jennings Place, he'd have noticed that it increased when romance flowered there." Pop toyed with the old-fashioned nibbed pen on his desk. I didn't want Pop to be sidetracked. "Tell me about Carrick Finley," I asked him.

"What do you know of Carrick Finley?"

"Very little except that Elizabeth was married to him, that he died before she came to Haviland."

"Elizabeth never talked to me about it, except indirectly," Pop said. "I knew she was a widow when she came to Haviland, and through some legal papers I discovered that Milnor was her maiden name, which had been legally returned to her. But that's all that I knew. Actually, it was old Mr. Debevoise who told me the facts of the case. Not as idle gossip, you understand, but as one lawyer to another. He wanted to implement me in the protection of his client, should the story ever arise to hound Elizabeth here in Haviland. It doesn't make much difference now, I suppose, whether it's known or not. Scandal, when it becomes sufficiently venerable, is endowed with the dignity of history. The contemporary social inconvenience of Alexander Hamilton's bastardy is the pride to-day, I understand, of the Hamilton family."

"Time the great legitimatizer," I laughed. "My progeny in the second degree will proudly follow their line across the bar sinister to the Tracy quarterings."

"Forty years has already accomplished quite a lot in that direction," Pop said levelly. "But the murk and the scandal was not on Elizabeth's side in the Carrick Finley story. A generation ago, we didn't talk about the problems of the Carrick Finleys of life. Today you can't sit at a dinner table without hearing the subject bandied about. I don't suppose when Elizabeth married Finley

140

she knew that such men existed; her mother certainly didn't. I imagine Elizabeth was in love with him, or thought she was—a girl of eighteen in those days was far more innocent than a girl of fourteen today, and I gather her mother had more than a little to do with urging the match. Finley was seven years older than she was, quite rich and very handsome, from all reports. They had the appropriate honeymoon in Europe, and then came back to live in the Finley house on Thirty-sixth Street. It was a good address, the crest of Murray Hill, and what the Morgans and the Satterlees didn't own between Madison Avenue and Park, the Finleys did.

"A year or so passed, and though they lived under the same roof, and entertained, and kept up all outward appearances of compatibility, their marriage had gone out of the window. Divorce in that era, and in New York, was socially unacceptable. There was only one ground for it. You made your bed and you lay in it, or rather you moved into a separate room and pretended that you lay in it. Elizabeth must have assumed that there was another woman in Finley's life. Within the limits of her experience, that was the only assumption possible for her to make, and those who knew the truth couldn't find the language to tell her.

"As the story came to Debevoise later, Elizabeth and Finley were invited to some party down on Long Island at Easthampton. Elizabeth was to go on ahead, and Finley was to meet her. But the morning Finley was supposed to arrive, he telephoned that he was detained in town and she was to stay on at the party without him. She decided not to stay, however, and took the evening train back to town. Either the servants were out, or it was late and she didn't want to waken them—at any rate, she let herself in with her latchkey. The house seemed empty. She wrote a note to Finley so that when he returned he would know that she had come home, and she went to his room to leave it on his dresser. She discovered him with his lover, and his lover was someone who had often been a guest at her home. —It makes a murky story, doesn't it?"

"That's pretty difficult to stick," I said.

"Yes. She left that night. She went to her mother's, and the next day she went to see Debevoise. He wanted a little time to think it over—the grounds aren't exactly conventional for divorce

141

in New York, even now. But two days later, Finley wrote the end of the marriage himself. The people who lived next to the Finley house saw a figure hanging from a lower branch of a tree in the Finley yard. They didn't recognize who it was. They called the police. When the police got there, it was Carrick Finley all right.

"Maybe it was more than coincidence that Elizabeth's mother died that week. And maybe it was for the best, because there wasn't anything left to hold Elizabeth to her old life. A month or so later, she came to Haviland and rented the Jennings Place. —And that's the story, John. All of it."

"One thing puzzles me. Didn't Elizabeth have any family left when all this started between her and Matt?"

"Nobody near enough to care, just some cousins and a couple of old aunts. She was her own mistress, before she became Old Matt's. I suppose her lawyer, Debevoise, was closer to her than anybody else. She wrote to him some long months after the affair with Matt started—in the spring of the following year it was— and he came up here to see her. He came charging into my office the next morning, wanting to know what kind of a man I was, and why I didn't take a horsewhip to Matt Tracy. I told him that aside from its being out of style, I probably wasn't enough of a man to take a horsewhip to Matt Tracy, even if I could think of a reason for doing it, which I couldn't."

"Had he met Matt?" I queried.

"No. Not yet. And I suggested that it would be wise to keep an open mind until he did meet him. It was a beautiful spring day, I remember, not too bright; the kind of day you'd enjoy being on a trout stream, even if you didn't catch any fish. I had an idea, though, that a trout could be interested in a properly placed fly. So I reached into my desk and took this out."

Pop opened his top desk drawer and drew out an aged and patched pigskin fly book. It was the color that the bowl of a favorite pipe gets from long smoking and polishing against your nose, and it was bulging with its burden of feather and hook.

"I put it on the desk and pretty soon, as we were talking, Debevoise reached over and began to look at it. We were discussing Elizabeth and her problems, but as he talked he would take out a fly here and there, and hold it up to examine it. There

142

was one he didn't recognize, one of my own tying, and he looked at it closely and then nodded his approval. 'It's a Sanford Special,' I told him. 'There are some that call it the "Kiss of Death." How about going fishing?' I suggested.

" 'I have to be back in New York this afternoon,' he said. But he didn't take his eyes off that fly.

" 'That's the difference,' I said, 'between practicing law in Haviland and in New York. On a day like this, I can always occupy myself with the Last Will and Testament of one of the Salvelinus Fontinalis family. They're quite numerous in the neighborhood, and very demanding on the practice of a country lawyer.'

" 'I haven't any tackle with me,' he said.

"I reminded him that to my impoverishment I had enough tackle for four men.

"Before we left the office I telephoned Elizabeth that her friend Debevoise would be staying over, and that she could plan on having trout for dinner. She asked me if I could join them, and I was about to say no and then I thought that maybe it would be better if I did. Besides, it would mean that we could fish right down the glen stream to behind the Jennings Place, and that would give us the evening fishing, and if it was good, well we wouldn't be so terribly late for dinner anyway."

I laughed, and opened up Pop's fly book. He must have had some flies in there fifty years old. I held one up.

"That's the Sanford Special," he acknowledged.

"I remember Old Matt used to fish this. But he called it 'Murder in the Afternoon.' "

"That's the general, if bloodthirsty, idea," Pop said. "It's a habit in plagiarism to change the title. Your father stole one of those flies from me, but he never could tie them as well. I used to get that blue-gray hackle from a strain of chickens he raised on his own farm, but I never told him. He used to buy his feathers from Mills in New York, but they were never the same."

"Don't leave me in the middle of old man Debevoise," I went back. "Did you catch anything that afternoon?"

"It was great fishing," Pop said. "One of those days you never forget. The water was right, the whisky was excellent, and the fish were hungry. Late in the afternoon, when the light was just right and a hatch of gray flies were beginning to rise, we left the rig by the old mill and started to fish up to the big glen pool. Well, I was the host, so I let Debevoise fish it first. He laid down a very respectable fly, and at his third cast the water churned and a very large trout slashed at it and that was that. Debevoise broke his heart. He fished that pool every way he knew how, and he was no novice. But Mr. Fish had disappeared; he was done for the day. Finally Debevoise came up on the bank and had a spot of the painkiller that quiets remorse, and then after about half an hour when I figured a fish's memory might have dulled a bit, I tried my hand. I stalked that fish as I had never stalked a fish before. I guess I wanted to show Debevoise that besides Blackstone on Contracts I also knew something about Walton on Angling. But did I catch it? I did not. Everything was just right, and I was just putting out the cast that should have raised Mr. Trout when I sort of got overeager and flubbed the whole business. My back cast was too short and my fingers slipped and I shot out too much line and a mare's nest of leader dropped into the pool like my Aunt Nellie's drawers. I was licked, and I knew it; Debevoise knew I was licked and the trout knew I was licked. He made a lazy swirl a couple of inches from my tangled line and helped himself to some insect on the water, and that was that.

"Suddenly I heard the deep-bellied rumbling laugh that could only be Matt's. I looked around, and sure enough he was standing there on the far bank, watching the whole performance. 'You'll never do it that way, Henry, you've got to plead a better case than that!'

"Debevoise looked around too, and I knew that there was somewhat of an awkward introduction in order, so I compromised and didn't make the introduction; anyway Matt was on the other side of the stream. 'Mind if I try?' Matt called.

"I felt pretty much of a fool. 'It's your pool, and it's your fish!' I called to him. Which was strictly the truth since the pool was on Tracy land. —I'm sort of making a long story out of this," Pop broke off. "When you get to my age you either have no memory at all or your memory is so damned precise that it gets long-winded."

"Go on and catch your fish," I told him.

"I didn't. I was finished. But Matt dropped down and let him-

144

self into the water. He eased up to the foot of the pool, and looked about him. It was where the pool should be fished, but with the brush behind it, was an impossible place to fish it from. On his third cast, the fly was a living thing. It twitched and seemed to flutter its wings without moving, and then slowly swung into the current making fitful little darts. Then it happened, so quickly that I didn't see the start of it, I just saw the finish. The biggest trout I ever saw in Haviland waters curved out of the pool and slammed into that fly from above. He didn't want to eat it; he wanted to kill it before a gallery of his peers, so that there would be no remotest question in their minds as to who owned that ledge of the bank and would brook no interference.

"The next ten or twelve minutes was the best fishing of my whole life, and I was only watching. That fish was out of the water as much as he was in it, and he was pink and golden and speckled and full of glory. It was light tackle and skill against brute strength and the spirit of hell, but after a bit things quieted down and Matt drew him in close until he brushed against his waders and then he gave Mr. Trout the first bit of slack line he'd seen, and there was the swirl of tail, and then the pool was quiet, and Matt was laying the line back on his reel. 'With a barbless hook! My God!' Debevoise intoned. 'And you let him go!'

" 'I'm leaving him for Henry to tackle someday,' Matt answered."

"And then what happened?" I asked Pop.

"Well, Debevoise walked over to Matt as he climbed from the pool, and he put his hand out. 'I want to shake the hand of the finest fisherman I've ever watched,' he said.

"Matt hesitated for an instant, and his eyes crinkled with a sort of private joke—I guessed that Elizabeth had been talking to him —and then he put his hand out. 'As one fisherman to another, I thank you,' he said.

"Well, the evil hour was on me." Pop shook his head. "Eventually Debevoise had to know who Matt was. 'Mr. Debevoise, Mr. Tracy—Mr. Matthew Tracy,' I said. Debevoise gave a start, and darted a quick glance at me. He got free of Matt's grasp mighty quick, and his eyes narrowed, and he looked at Matt carefully the way you'd size up something you weren't quite sure of. Finally he said 'Hrumpf.' He said it three times, and each time

145

with a different intonation. The last 'Hrumpf' was sort of puzzled. 'That was a damned fine performance, anyway!' he brought out at last. 'Damned fine! Damned fine!' Then he stuck a cigar into his mouth and I offered him a light, but he refused it and dry-smoked the cigar as we climbed up from the stream. None of us talked as we walked through the fields to the Jennings house. It isn't far, you know."

"I know. I rode by there yesterday."

"Of course you know," Pop said. "Well, we none of us talked, but there was a lot of thinking going on. And then we came up through the garden, and Elizabeth was at the door with a bottle of whisky and glasses and a pitcher of water on a tray, and she greeted Debevoise and me, and then she put the tray down and crossed to Matt. She offered him her lips, and he took her in his arms and they kissed, and there was so much giving and so much taking in their kiss that we looked away, and the old man said 'Hrumpf' again and then he said, 'I'll take that light now, if you don't mind.'

"After he lit the cigar, he spotted a white rose in the garden and he led me to it, and named it a Prince Charles, and told me how it was one of the oldest roses there were. In the midst of telling about the rose, he broke off to throw a question at me. 'Why the hell can't he divorce his wife?'

" 'You can't very well divorce a woman who's lost her mind,' I told him.

" 'Then why doesn't he give her grounds to divorce him?' he demanded.

" 'It would appear that there are quite adequate grounds,' I said. 'But again it's rather difficult for a woman who's lost her mind to bring such an issue before the courts in her own interest.'

"He chewed his cigar and the idea over a moment or two, and then delivered himself of another 'Hrumpf.' 'This new generation is so damned impetuous,' he finally said. 'They go at things hell-bent for perdition.'

" 'Being different from the generation and the generations which preceded them?'

" 'Probably not, probably not,' he conceded. 'But we were more clandestine about it, a little more cautious.'

146

" 'Caution is a negative virtue,' I reminded him, and he grunted."

"It must have been quite a dinner party," I commented.

"Surprisingly," Pop said, "any constraint during the evening was on my part or Debevoise's. Elizabeth was as composed as you please. When she seated us at the table, she placed Matt at the head. It was an act of declaration; it was a way of saying that in the life of her kind of a woman, when she meets Matt's kind of a man, the head of her table, her heart, and her bed are empty unless he is filling them. It was as simple and clear and direct as that. And because they were so much in love, they had that wonderful insulated sense that nobody was seeing them as they were. They always had that sense."

"I know what you mean," I said. "They had it even when I was growing up. —Did Debevoise react to it eventually?"

"I'm coming to that," Pop said. "When it was time to go—I was to drive Debevoise back to the Haviland House—he turned to Matt and said, 'Have you a rig, Mr. Tracy, or can we drop you?' And then before Matt could answer him, he answered the question himself. 'No, of course you haven't, I was forgetting.' Then he said good night to Elizabeth, and stood in front of Matt and their glances met for an instant, and then the old man's hand went out and he was shaking Matt's, and saying, 'I'm very glad to have met you, young man. It's very difficult to have clear ideas about people until you do meet them.'

"At the road one of the harness lines had got itself twisted, and as I was adjusting it in the dark, Debevoise stood beside me. I heard him grunt and I looked up, and in the window we could see Elizabeth and Matt standing in front of the lamp, just looking at each other. When he walked over and took her in his arms, the way she went to him was an avowal without reservation, it was a complete giving of herself. And then Matt lifted her in his arms and he leaned over the lamp and blew it out, and Elizabeth's house was dark, and old man Debevoise said, 'May God have mercy on them.' And then he cleared his throat and said, 'The damn young fools, they ought to pull the shades down, they'll have the whole town talking.' I didn't tell him that the whole town was already talking some.

"And as for you, John"—Pop regarded me quizzically—"I

147

have a feeling that that's about the time you came into the picture. As things turned out, I don't mind saying it's my guess that you were probably conceived that night. There are damned few people conceived in love."

"Most bastards are," I said, and immediately regretted saying it because of the way Pop looked at me.

"It still burns into you?" he said.

"Sometimes. Not often. Anyway, I'll say this for myself, there are damn few men who have what practically amounts to an eye-witness account of their conception."

"Damned few," Pop agreed with a twinkle. "And by rights, that ought to make a fitting end to the story. Only it doesn't. Just about nine months later, I woke up around two in the morning, with the fire siren going full blast. By counting the blasts, I knew it was someplace on the Hill Road. I called the operator—it was Nellie Simpson at the time—and she told me it was the Jennings Place. Mrs. Sanford got dressed along with me, she figured she might be of some help. She figured right, too. All hell had busted loose when we got there. Everybody was running around, like they do at fires, and nobody seemed to know anything about Elizabeth. And then suddenly Matt appeared out of the darkness in bare feet, with his nightshirt stuffed into his trousers.

" 'Thank God you're here, both of you!' He had to shout to be heard, but he didn't stop to say anything more, he just herded us over to the foot of a tree on the other side of the road where Elizabeth was lying rolled up in a blanket in her nightdress. I was afraid she'd been hurt, but he said she was all right, but that things had started, and could Mrs. Sanford stay with her. Then he grabbed my arm and told me to go along with him. 'I sent for Farnley,' he gasped out, as he pulled me through the underbrush and circled the burning house. 'I may need you, too. I thought I saw her once, just after it started, but I couldn't be sure.'

"Suddenly, there was a horrible scream of laughter just ahead of us and we came on her. It was Constance and it wasn't Constance; it was hardly anything human, just a mad unreasoning thing that stood there chanting and screaming at the fire. She'd got away from her nurse and started the fire. She was too far gone by the time we overtook her to recognize even Matt, and from what we could make out of her confused babbling, we realized

148

that it wasn't Matt she had tried to destroy, it was her father. Somehow her tormented mind had accomplished a complete transference, although it wasn't until later that Farnley and the other doctors were able to piece together some of the contributing elements to her illness. A large part of it seems to have begun in her childhood, the way most mental sickness does. Her mother had been more or less of an invalid, which had thrown Constance and her father pretty much together through the period of her growing up. She was what you might call 'father's girl' up to the time she was about twelve—he was always present when she was bathed and dressed, and she frequently had breakfast in his bed with him in the morning. Then as closely as the doctors could ever get to it—I don't know what you'd call it, his ingrown Victorian puritanism turned around and bit him. That kind of thing could happen to people in those days. He went into a wallow of guilt and self-condemnation, and implanted upon himself and Constance and the whole household an implacable rigid discipline of restraint and inhibition. Sex turned into an ingrown toenail, so that it hurt with every step. And it's easy to see how, when the whole business was uncovered, it wasn't Matt at all, but old man Harper who was at the root of Constance's trouble."

I was a little stunned at this revelation. "That's something I never even vaguely suspected," I said.

"Nobody else in Haviland knew about it either," Pop told me. "Nobody, that is, except Matt and Doc Farnley's father and me. I'm not even sure how much of it Matt ever told Elizabeth. But it was past history at the time of the fire, and at that moment you were making future history. Matt got Jim Haines, Perry's father, to take Constance back to the farm by the old Glen Road—it was more of a road then than it is now—and we went back to Elizabeth. Her time was on her, and word had come back that Farnley was over at Whaley on a case but a message had been sent to him. The village would have been closer, but there was going to be enough talk as it was, so your father decided to bring her to the Old House at the Tracy place. He'd been living there for a year or so while Constance was so difficult. He carried Elizabeth upstairs in his arms and Mrs. Sanford and I were with him when he laid her down on his bed. Elizabeth was heavily in labor by that time. He never left her, and when the pains gripped her, she

149

clenched his hand and his just being there seemed to give her strength. Finally the two women exchanged a look, and Elizabeth said, 'I'm afraid we won't be able to wait for Farnley.' Her lips were bruised with her biting at them, but she managed a smile. 'He'll be very completely your child, Matt; I'm afraid you'll have to bring him into the world, as well. And if anything goes wrong—'

" 'There won't anything go wrong,' he said.

" 'But if it should, remember, darling, you can cut my throat if you have to.'

" 'She's out of her head with pain,' Mrs. Sanford whispered.

"Elizabeth heard her. 'No I'm not,' she said. 'That was something very private between me and my—between me and Mr. Tracy.'

"Then they set me to getting plenty of boiling water on the stove and a bottle of disinfectant from the barn. About an hour later you were born; and about a half hour after that Farnley came puffing up the stairs."

Pop leaned across the desk to turn on the lamp. "I guess I've *tired the sun with talking and sent him down the sky.* —That's a line from a poem by William Johnson. I found it in an anthology. I never could find anything else he ever wrote."

I wondered what echoes of memory those lines evoked for him, and I guessed that they must have rung some chord that carried his thoughts back to Old Matt. "Would you like to come up to the place and have dinner with me?" I suggested.

"Thanks. But my housekeeper will be having my supper ready shortly."

"It would be less lonely if you dined with me."

"There's nothing so terrible in loneliness, John. I rather enjoy it. Most loneliness is just a herd instinct that hasn't grown up."

The old man took his black hat off the tree and put it on, and then adjusted his sober black coat about his spare frame. On another man they might have suggested the preacher or the undertaker; on him they spelled that intangible dignity of the law, the stuff that makes judges. He waved me ahead of him, and we went into the outer office. Margaret was at her desk and Walter Semple was sitting in a chair across the room. Beside him was a glass dish filled with half-smoked cigarettes. He rose as we came in.

150

"My God, you fellows have been a long time. You must have settled all the affairs of Haviland."

Pop just looked at him and Walter seemed to subside within his collar and you could almost hear the false ebullience go out of him. "I want to see you," he said.

"I'll be going along," I said to Pop.

"I want to see you, too," Semple stopped me.

"Look, Semple," I told him. "As far as I'm concerned you ceased to exist the other night. You don't have, nor will you ever have, a reason to see me."

"I want to apologize for the other night. I lost my temper and I said some very hasty things." He glanced at Margaret and lowered his voice. "A man's got a right to apologize, you know."

"That was something I didn't know," I said, and I started for the door again, with Pop behind me.

Semple put his hand on my arm and as quickly took it away. "Listen, for God's sake, you two. Fletcher said I had to see you, you've got to let me say my say."

Out of the corner of my eye I saw Margaret get up and go into Pop's office and close the door behind her. "Fletcher says that I have to have the endorsement of both of you to be returned to the Assembly, or they'll force the withdrawal of my nomination," he bleated.

"You don't have mine," I said shortly. "Now you've had your say and I've had mine and I'll be leaving."

"Look," he pleaded. "The North Hill Road business is off. It's forgotten about, it'll be as if it never happened. I'm left owning a lot of worthless land up there and it'll practically wipe me out, but the business of the road is finished with and forgotten."

"Not by me it won't be forgotten," I told him. "And there are a lot of other things that will never be forgotten."

"You don't have to endorse me." He was begging now. "If you just let me alone it'll be all right. I can swing the committee."

"If you can swing the committee, then why are you coming to us?" Pop asked mildly. "We are not members of the committee."

"Well, there's a little friction there, and Fletcher says he'll play ball if you two come along or even just stay out of it. A split like this will bust the town wide open. Fletcher knows that."

Pop's eyes were gray and cold. "Maybe it would be a good

151

thing for this town to be, as you say, busted wide open. But whether or not, the answer to everything you've asked is 'No' and it's definite."

"I don't get it!" Semple's voice began cracking. "A man can give his whole life to the business of politics and the two of you who have nothing to do with politics can upset the apple cart with just a nod of your heads!"

"It wasn't a very strong apple cart, Walter," Pop interjected quietly.

"And you're not even a Republican!" Semple's voice got shriller.

"Not even," Pop acknowledged. "That's one of my lesser crimes. I am what is variously and humorously referred to in Dutchess County as a Democrat, and from time to time I serve a useful function as the seed of discontent and the *agenbite of inwit*."

"The what?" Semple asked.

"Translated from early English into later English, it roughly means the 'back bite of conscience.' It's a robust idea and it stings like hell, doesn't it, Walter?"

We left him standing in a kind of daze, with a lifeless look in his eyes as we descended the covered outdoor stairway leading from the office. "You threw me a little with the *agenbite of inwit*."

"I shouldn't have. A small-town lawyer has a lot of time between clients to read the damnedest things, and I've read 'em. But seriously, John, you'll have to watch your step with Semple. He'll never forgive you and he'll never fight clean. He'll try to get you in your short hair someday, some spot where you're vulnerable and where he can hurt you a lot; or maybe hurt somebody you'll want to protect."

I watched him start down the hill toward his little house on the edge of the village. He walked not with the feebleness, but with the dignity of age, with precise steps that had learned the lesson that wherever we are going we arrive there more certainly by a steady and inevitable progression. I wondered if the mantle of the law would cloak as majestically the shoulders of Bill Corley, when he got to be Pop's age and was the elder member of the bar of Haviland. It was as if my wonder had evoked him, for Bill's convertible swung at that moment around the War Memorial, slowed and stopped for an instant, as he made up his mind whether

152

to cross the tracks to the other side of town or turn left on Railroad Avenue. He bore to the right, and came toward me and his arm waved in greeting. I was about to answer when I realized that he hadn't even seen me. I looked behind me. Jim Fletcher was standing on the steps of the bank; he waved his cigar in answer to Bill's greeting. The convertible passed me, and only then did Corley catch sight of me. "Good evening, Mr. Milnor," he called out.

Jim Fletcher negotiated the steps of the bank with the dignity of an elephant and ambled over to my side. "Good evening, Mr. Milnor." A slow rumble of amusement welled from inside him like the roar of the evening train coming up through the cut south of the town. "We're being awfully damned formal this evening." His laughter got involved with a cough and he spluttered for a moment, spitting out shreds of tobacco from his chewed-up cigar, and then he thrust it back in the corner of his mouth. "You'll rate 'Mister' from a lot of people from now on, John. Most of them will be wanting something; they'll figure it doesn't pay to be too familiar with the head of the House of Tracy."

"You make me sound like the head of the banking firm of 15 Wall Street."

"Same idea," Jim said. "There has to be a point of general focus in any town, and the Tracys have been it for Haviland since the day when." He made a business of lighting his cigar. "Bill Corley would like to go to the Assembly," he said irrelevantly. "He has a hankering to go places and do big things."

Walter Semple had come down from Pop's office and was standing irresolutely on the sidewalk. He saw me and Jim Fletcher talking, and for a moment it looked is if he were coming toward us; and then he turned and walked down the street in the opposite direction.

"You and Pop were with Semple a long time," Fletcher remarked.

"Semple was waiting a long time," I amended. "We only saw him as we were leaving. What did you sic him on me for, anyway?"

"Because I don't run this town; it isn't a good thing for one man to run a town, even a small one. There's going to be some shuffling and changes in the County Committee—they're going to force Semple's withdrawal from the nomination. Walter wants to

153

make a fight for it—I thought he ought to find out where he heads in."

"I haven't got anything to do with the County Committee," I told him.

"Maybe," he said. "Maybe not." And then as if he was on another tangent, "As I understand Matt's will, you're one of the principal stockholders in the bank."

"I hadn't realized that. I haven't really looked into what the estate holds." I reversed his tangent. "I don't even know who the members of the town committee are."

"You will. They'll be making themselves known to you from time to time, wanting to know where you stand on things."

"Is Pop on the town committee?"

"Hell no! Pop's a Democrat. He *is* the Democratic town committee."

"And Walter Semple has to ask his endorsement for a Republican nomination?"

"I can't think of a better endorsement to have," Fletcher said. "Nothing wrong with that, is there?"

"Nothing wrong with it at all," I told him. "Except that it seems a little cockeyed and fanciful. Maybe even a little idealistic."

"Could be," Fletcher granted. "Just the same it works real well. There isn't a finer man in this town than Henry Sanford. If he's for a thing it's pretty near bound to be right, and it pretty near always happens, sooner or later. —What do you think of Bill Corley for the Assembly?"

"I haven't thought about it. Should I?"

Fletcher worked his cigar around to the other side of his mouth. "Corley's thinking about it, and he's got some others thinking about it. Myself, I think he's a mite too eager. You wouldn't want to go up there yourself, would you?"

"You really want to take me in and make me a member of the club, don't you?"

He nodded.

"If Matt were still alive, would you be asking me that question?"

That took a bit of cigar chewing and then he smiled. "Nope. But the way things have turned out, it looks like maybe you'll stop gallivanting and stay put here in Haviland. You've got a big stake in this town."

154

"Jim, I haven't made up my mind about that yet."

"Maybe."

"Maybe, what?"

"Maybe you have, and you haven't realized it yet. The roots go deep. Deeper than you think—but I'll be talking to you." He glanced at his watch. "Getting late."

"Yes." Railroad Avenue was almost dark, and the lights were on in all the shop windows. Jim hadn't talked to me as long as Pop, but he'd given me a lot to think about, too.

Nine

The house was empty and yet it was strangely full. I guess you have to dismantle and unfurnish a house before you can exorcise the living that has gone on in it. As Mrs. Haines served dinner, I looked about the room and the thought came over me that from the day the place had been built—and that would have been about 1758 or 1762, according to the records—there had been a slow process of Tracy accretion. At no time had the threads been broken, or the slate wiped clean. There was a collection of furniture about me that had never been moved out; its farthest travels had been to the center of the room once or twice a generation, to permit repainting or to stand by disdainfully while oil lighting gave way to the cumbersome home manufacturing of gas, or while the lead piping of the gas was ripped out to make way for the installation of electric wiring. People came to the room quicker and from greater distances as automobiles supplanted the horse, but the room, and the house that contained it, remained unchanged.

Mrs. Haines served coffee in the parlor, and I studied with new interest the coffee service and the silver. Elizabeth had told me that the Worcester was my great-great-grandmother's on the Tracy side. The blue and yellow Rockingham set—that would have been from Great-grandmother Tracy—was more familiar to me.

"Why Worcester, tonight?" I queried Mrs. Haines. "A special occasion?"

"It's nicer just for the family," she explained. "There isn't enough of it left for when there are a lot of people at the table. I'm more partial to it than that garish new Rockingham stuff, anyway."

I couldn't help but smile. A hundred and thirty years old, and it was still garish and new. I suppose that was part of the secret of the place. The old never really gave way to the new, and then eventually the new became old enough to be acceptable.

I tried to read the worn crest on the silver. As far as I knew the Tracys had no crest; at least nothing that they owned was marked with a crest.

"That's Milnor silver," Mrs. Haines answered my unspoken question. "It's proper to use the silver from the bride's side of the family."

Even when the bride was without benefit of clergy, I thought. "Yes, that's very proper, Mrs. Haines. Incidentally, I'll let you and Will Talcott know in a day or so what to take down to the Jennings Place. By the way, have you seen Joy around?"

"She was to the back door this afternoon and then I saw her going off to the Big House."

I knew I'd have to go out and find her or I wouldn't be able to sleep with the thought of her lying on some cold doorstep, before a door that in her dog thinking might open to admit her to where Matt was. I lit a pipe and went out to the porch. There was a chill in the night, but it didn't seem cold and sounds coming clear from the valley spoke the dryness in the air, so I turned up the collar of my jacket and started up the road. There were lights burning in Constance's wing of the house and as I came nearer, a dark shape detached itself from the shadows. A rustling in the shrubs near at hand, and Joy was at my side. She looked up at me, full of groping. I patted her head. "Come along, old girl. He isn't here." She heeled beside me. "This isn't a very happy life for you," I told her. "You'll have to break through it and come to grips with things."

It's silly to talk to a dog. They can't understand you, except the tone of your voice, but they know they're being talked to, and she whimpered a little in response. "Life switched the game on you, didn't it? Usually it's the dog who dies first; a man will have a whole lifetime of dogs, and each time they go it's a wrench and a kind of heartbreak, but this time it was the man who went and the dog's heart that broke." Maybe she understood at that, because as I relit my pipe she stood up with her paws against me and licked my hand. Some association of loneliness made me look up at Constance's lighted window. That was real loneliness. There

157

was no way for anyone to be close to her—no one but Matt, who had always treated her with a touching consideration, never failing to drop over to her wing of the house in the evening to visit with her. If you inherit a man's land and his estate, and even his dog, you inherit his responsibilities, too. I turned my steps back to the door.

Will and Mrs. Talcott had their separate living quarters in the house. I found them in their cluttered, homey parlor. He was reading a farm journal and making some notes, and Mrs. Talcott was sewing. She got up as I came in: "I'm glad you stopped by. I'm sure she's been missing Mr. Matt's coming over; she's been so alone since he died."

"Yes, I know."

Mrs. Talcott sighed. "This evening she began to slip back again, and she'd been making such good progress, it seemed to me."

"I thought so, too," I said.

In the passageway, I started to turn in the wrong direction, having never been to Constance's quarters. Mrs. Talcott took my arm and directed me to a closed pair of double doors and I realized that Joy was waiting there ahead of us.

"Just don't take too much notice of things," Mrs. Talcott primed me. "Let her mind go where she has a notion to let it go. I mean, don't draw her up sharp, it confuses her even more." She knocked; Constance's clear, timbreless voice called, "Come in!"

Joy edged in ahead of me and went directly to a small rug by the fire as if her coming here were part of a pattern and a ritual. Constance was seated in a large Queen Ann wing chair before a fine accordion Chippendale card table. She was dressed in one of those flouncy and very feminine dresses that I vaguely remembered women affecting in my youth. I suppose you would have called it a hostess gown, the kind of thing that women wear when men don't dress for dinner.

"Matt, my dear, I've been so wanting to see you."

Her voice was so even, and her manner so normal and untroubled that I didn't see how it could be anything else but a slip of the tongue.

I took her hand. "I've been wanting to have a talk with you, too," I said.

"You haven't been in to visit with me for days."

158

"Well, I . . . there may have been a lot of things . . ." Still I couldn't believe that this was any more than a superficial confusion. When you sit alone in a room with your own thoughts it's often difficult to gather yourself back to reality.

"I know, you've been away somewhere," she went on, nodding wisely. "You and Alyse, both."

"Yes, I've been away somewhere." I heard my voice, and it sounded normal, though I was beginning to feel far from normal.

"And how is Alyse? I've been a little worried about her. She's been so tired and she hasn't seemed well recently."

"She's . . . I think she's better now. I think she's all right now."

"Give me just a few minutes, Matt. I've been sorting out old papers and family things, and if I don't get everything right they'll be so mixed up, I'll have to do it all over again." She went back to making piles out of the papers on the table before her.

I was grateful for the respite, both to get hold of myself and to try to figure out the best way to follow her through the mist that she had again lost herself in. I moved away from her, to the farther end of the room. I began to recall that I had been here as a child, but my eyes had not been schooled to capture the beauty of its detail. The house had been built in 1805 by the then Matthew Tracy. There was a legend that it had been designed by Bullfinch or Asher Benjamin. My father had had a different idea. There was a cupboard full of architectural drawings in the library, all scaled out by Old Matt's great-grandfather, though none of them was related to the house. It was known for a fact, however, that he had built the old barn, and it was undeniable that its cupola and trim were related to, and as sophisticated as the detail in the house. "If Bullfinch did the house, then he also did the barn," Old Matt used to snort, "and that makes it the only Bullfinch barn in creation."

"Pour yourself a drink, Matt." Constance's voice came to me from the other end of the room, and I was suddenly aware that I had wandered over to a table laid out with decanters and glasses. I must admit I was grateful to the unconscious impulse, for I needed a drink.

"Will you have one?" I asked.

"Don't make a tippler out of your mother," Constance laughed. "I had my one glass of sherry before dinner."

I made my own drink a little stiffer, and when I glanced up, Constance had gone back to her papers, so I went back to studying the room. It hadn't always been like this—that much I knew. Originally it had been a ball room, befitting the broad crystal chandelier and the intricate breasted Adam fireplace, and the bold carved corner pilasters. But when Constance and Matt had first lived in the house it had been converted into this vast sprawling living room, and during the years when Matt hadn't lived here and Constance had been away, it had remained unchanged.

Looking about it now, I thought how well the Tracys did themselves. There wasn't a museum in the country that wouldn't give its eye teeth to have this room as it stood. The Sargent portrait of Old Matt as a young man hung above the mantel. It was done in the manner of the Ribblesdale portrait. As a matter of fact you had to look at it twice to be sure that it wasn't the Ribblesdale; Matt had the same lean face and hawk nose and the spring to his body that men who have to do with horses get.

"Peas in a pod!"

I started. Constance was staring at me from the table as I stood before the painting. "There's such a strong resemblance, sometimes when you walk into the room I find it hard to realize that it isn't your father coming in."

"What are you doing?" I asked, to break the thread.

"Going over things." She gestured toward the jumble of papers in front of her. "A lot of things." She tore a photograph, mounted in the old-fashioned way on a heavy embossed card, into small shreds and dropped it into the wastebasket at her side. "So many Harpers," she explained. "Cousins and aunts and uncles. I don't even know their names; I don't think I ever did. It's the kind of clutter people carry about with them their whole lives. Emmeline's children and Adelaide's wouldn't know what to do with it when I go; and of course the Milnors aren't even related to the Harpers so it wouldn't mean anything to them, either." She held out a photograph for me to look at. It was a picture of a woman dressed in one of those out-behind dresses that marked the period of the late 'nineties, standing in front of a rambling house that I guessed was the Harper house at Kinderhook.

"Emmeline has the instinct of a squirrel and a Chinaman's reverence for family. If she ever came on this she'd probably frame

160

it and hang it on the wall, thinking it was some great-aunt on the Harper side." She laughed. "It's a picture of Addie. You remember Addie, the maid we had up at Kinderhook? The one who got herself into trouble and married the coachman so suddenly. And there was such a lot of secrecy and to-do about it; there always was, when a maid got herself into trouble and married the coachman in a hurry."

"Always the same coachman?" My own voice sounded normal to my ears, and I realized that somehow I had been tricked into Constance's world.

"Oh, gracious no, it was always a different coachman—and a nuisance, too, because the community never knew whether it was the coachman or the young son of the family, and sometimes even the coachman wasn't sure. But I didn't have any brothers, and Papa—in the eyes of the community—was above reproach. But I really don't think it was Papa that time, because at that time he had some sort of an arrangement in Troy." She tore up the photograph and its fragments fluttered into the basket beside her. "Of course nice girls weren't supposed to know about such arrangements," she added. "But Papa wasn't a very nice man. Oh, I don't mean about the *arrangement,* though women resent such arrangements. They feel that they're being robbed of something, and they are. That's why they're so against it, even when it isn't their own marriage that's involved. But it really wasn't the arrangement, it was just that Papa made things ugly. I'd been touched by that ugliness before I came to you."

Her poor clouded mind was adding confusion to confusion. Now I had become not her son, but her husband. I tried to interrupt her, but she swept ahead. "No, let me go on, it doesn't hurt any more," she begged. "I know now that I wasn't a fit mate for you. I came to understand that during the time I was away. It would have been better if you hadn't been so gentle and so kind. Nothing ever came to the surface between us. I wonder sometimes if this young generation that has no reticence and talks about everything can really talk their way through the real troubles between a man and a woman. The troubles that we had, Matt."

I went over to the window, evading her eyes. A medical man might have welcomed her confusion, so that he could peer behind the curtains of her personality and perhaps help her. But I couldn't

161

help her, even if I had had the wisdom and the skill; Constance had lived beyond a point where help would be of any use to her—she had built her world of shadows, and was happiest there.

"I'm not Matt," I could only tell her gently. "If you try, Constance, you'll come to see that a lot of time has passed, and a great many things have happened, and I'm not Matt. I'm not even young Matt; he isn't here either. So much has changed. Maybe you didn't want it as it was, maybe you don't want it as it is; and that's all right, too. Life has been so fashioned for you that you can have it the way you want it on your own terms, on your own reality—if that is the way you want it."

"Yes—I know you aren't Matt."

I turned, then, to face her. Her words were so calm and her voice was so rational that I thought she had come back out of the vague places she retreated to.

"And I am not really Constance," she went on quietly. "Don't you see, Matt, the people we once were are so long dead that we can talk about them as if they were other people? Sometimes I wonder if your gentleness with me wasn't a mistake. Maybe if you had been different, you could have made me into a real woman; I mean while you still loved me. Maybe it's a mistake to be too civilized. I know that I failed you, but I didn't know it then; I was too selfish, I was only thinking of myself, my puny, mixed-up emotions. Yes, Matt, you should have been a peasant instead of a gentleman. When I locked the door of my room, you should have broken it down. You'd have broken down the inhibitions, too. Then maybe my body would have come alive to you, and we might have recaptured the other things—the love and the gentleness—but at least we would have had that."

Again I turned away from the naked pleading in her eyes. Frost glittered in the starlight and banks of shadow rimmed the fields that spread across the saddle of the Hill. I heard her words, but only with the top of my mind. This baring of ancient intimacies and thwarted lusts and ingrown love was not meant for me, and yet I knew that she would have to get them said.

"You weren't paying any attention to what I was saying." I looked up and realized that Constance had stopped talking.

"I'm sorry," I apologized.

"I don't blame you." She half smiled. "You see, I know when

162

I'm confused. At first it used to frighten me, and I'd fight against it. I don't any more, though, because I've found out things eventually straighten themselves out in my mind. I know now that you're not Matt; not young Matt either. I suppose my mind wanted to think you were, because it's so much easier to live in the past."

I started to speak, but she stopped me. "You're John Milnor and you sat in Matt's chair at the service, and there aren't any Tracys left. No, that's not so; you're a Tracy—it's just the name that's dead, and it didn't seem that it would ever die. Well, there's so much that's dead. Come over here and sit down where I can see you better. No, there, just a little more in the light." Her eyes seemed very clear all at once, and her gaze was simple and direct. "What are you going to do with all this?" And then before I could reply, she said, "No, don't answer that; you haven't had time to think it out yet. You see, Mr. Sanford told me about Matt's will, and I think he was right. Emmeline and Adelaide and their husbands don't think so, I imagine. Particularly their husbands. But they have enough, and they aren't Tracys, and besides, it will take a man to hold the place together."

Unconsciously I had taken the ring Pop Sanford had given me that afternoon, and was toying with it in my hand. I saw Constance watching me. "Are you sure you don't want to wear it?" I asked.

Without speaking, she took the ring from my hand and gazed at it for a long moment, then she slipped it on her finger and studied it. Her hand was the hand of age, and the ring was loose upon it. "No, I want you to have it," she said, and held it out to me again. "And now you'll have to excuse me. I'm very tired. Please ask Mrs. Talcott to come in when you go."

Suddenly I saw her framed in the whole reference of her past, and there was an ineffable loneliness about her. An impulse gripped me, and I lowered my head and at the same moment, as if she expected me to kiss her good night, she raised her cheek.

At the door she stopped me. "You may be wanting to live here?" she asked.

"No," I told her.

"Still, you may be wanting to. Of course Matt and Alyse lived in the other wing, but that might not be convenient for you."

"I'll be living down at the other house," I explained.

163

"Well, if you should change your mind—" She left the thought unfinished. Joy crossed over to her. Her frail hand reached out and caressed the dome of the dog's head, and then, the ritual of leave-taking completed, Joy came to my side and we closed the door and went down the hall. This, too, was to be part of the life of the man who held the Tracy land.

Ten

As I was undressing and hanging my things away, Joy came to the closet door and sniffed, and gave a little whine. I knew at once what was wrong, and I could have kicked myself. The day before, while I had been over at the barn, a drizzle had come up and I had slipped on an old Duxbak shooting jacket of Matt's. "All right, old girl, this is the best I can do for you." I pulled it off the hanger and spread it on the floor beside my bed. Joy crossed to it, and lay down with her head stretched out between her paws, and only her eyes moved as they followed me about the room.

"The Tracy spoor and scent is pretty deeply spread over this Hill, isn't it, Joy?" I said. "Matt and the Tracys—and the Tracys' ways—and the Tracys' unfinished business—they'll keep cropping up as the days go by." Her tail started to move and then she thought better of it and just lay still.

I lit a cigarette and glanced over the books in the case beside my bed. For a moment or two I let my thumb run over the leaves of *Walden*. I put it back and noticed an empty space next to it. Someone had taken, or I had mislaid, one volume of a set of Montaigne. It was irritating. People whose lives are involved with books are both jealous and possessive of them. To lose one—or worse, to have it mistreated—is like having a friend in straits and not being able to do anything about it. I pulled down one of the remaining volumes, as if to capture it before it, too, took to wandering.

In his own peculiar way, but without the transcendental overlay, Montaigne was Thoreau's spiritual father. When you crack the shell and get the meat of the nut, there was damn little that

165

Thoreau said that old Michel didn't say first, and often with a little more blood in his veins.

I was several pages into his chapter on Experience when the phone rang. I glanced at my watch; it was quarter past twelve. "You had a long-distance call earlier this evening, Mr. Milnor," Helen said. "The operator just put it through again. They'll be on in a moment." And then Frankie's voice came over the phone. "Hello, John."

My thoughts went to Elizabeth. "Is anything wrong?"

"Nothing," Frankie answered me quickly. "The operator forgot to cancel the call. Elizabeth tried to reach you around nine just to say hello to you, but she's asleep in the other room now." I was conscious that over the phone Frankie's voice assumed that curious rhythm of the bilingual, a precision in phrasing and meter rather than an accent. "I'm sorry the phone rang so late. It must have wakened you."

"It didn't, I was reading. One of your countrymen—an excessively wise old gentleman. I recommend him to your attention."

"John, you astound me!" Laughter bubbled up in Frankie's voice. "With your views of what is proper for young women to do, you recommend him?"

"Who?"

"Our old friend Michel who lived on a mountain."

"So you're the one who stole the volume!"

"Borrowed it. I left a note in one of the other volumes."

I riffled the pages of the book in my lap. A thin envelope addressed to me in Frankie's angular script fell out. Propping the phone under my shoulder, I started to open it. "I just found it," I told her.

"John, don't read it now, please. Not while we're talking."

"Why not?"

"It would embarrass me. If I could have said these things in your presence, I would have." There was a moment's pause and then, "You're not reading it, are you?"

I was, or rather I was beginning to. *John, my darling,* it started. *I shall not be here when you read this. You said that I was a silly young girl. I am young, and perhaps silly; but not in the way that you meant.*

I folded the letter and slipped it back into the envelope. "I'm

166

not reading it," I told her. Silence and a constraint that was almost physical separated us. "Are you still there?" I finally asked.

"Yes, I am still here."

"Well, if I must not read your letter or talk about it, what shall we talk about—Montaigne?"

"No, I want to talk about the letter. John, will you do something for me?"

"Yes, what do you want me to do?"

"Don't read it. Tear it up. Seal it in an envelope and give it back to me. But don't read it, because it was a letter that never should have been written." There was a click at the other end of the line, followed by Helen's voice from the exchange in Haviland. "Were you finished with that call, Mr. Milnor?"

"Yes, we were finished, Helen." I hung up and balanced the thin blue envelope in my fingers. Finally I slipped it into the book and turned the light out. Joy, stretched out on the floor beside me, fluttered her jowls; at last the house was settling down for the night. Only from where I lay, it did not settle down. The mind's vagaries are uncharted. You toss and turn and approach the borders of sleep, and the mind relaxes its sentinels and is borne away on the stream of memory. I was back in Saint-Cloud and still, try as I would, the name of the girl who had driven there with me from Paris would not return, she remained just a vague and indistinct image. I could recapture the memory of the odors that swept in through the balcony window. Lilacs and warming soil, recently drenched with night rain, and the dry dusty smell of pebbled pathways in the sun, which is no odor at all, and the membrane tickling of bright sunlight that brings you almost to the sensation of sneezing.

And I remembered a night when for a moment the world was stilled and quiet in the midst of its torment, and then a man groaned in his sleep somewhere nearby. The silence once broken, another who had too long bitten back pain screamed in agony; and somewhere a flare was fired that erased the stars and artillery action commenced that was like the thunder of a summer storm heard in the distance and then began to roll as curtain after curtain of fire fell ever closer, until the ground itself shuddered; and in an instant's stab of light you saw the second hand of your watch cover the zero hour and you cried, "Come on, let's go! Let's get the hell out of here!" And the gunned motors, resonant inside their thirty

167

tons of steel, drowned out all other sound. And, by the sheerest accident of being just where you were, you lived; and, by the same sheer accident of being where they were, other men as good and no less tenderly nurtured died as steel screamed through the night, and armor that was invincible suddenly shattered and exploded into high-octane hell.

And there was a girl to whom I had brought my heart. And I told her the story of Elizabeth and Matt, and she was shocked. "What would people say?" she asked, as she loosened the fastenings of her dress. As the pale light of the city crept into her room there was only a gray indistinct form lying across her bed with a dark shadow punctuating her loins and a darker, no less enigmatic shadow falling across her face, and she was no different from any other woman that one might casually embrace, and for a brief pulsing instant of time I reached toward the stars, but I could not, or did not reach far enough. Everything was strangely aseptic and surgical, the excision of emotion complete and almost painless.

And there was a girl named Angelica Barnes—but there are censors of the mind and I rolled over in bed and turned up the light and reached for a cigarette. Joy roused and rose, stretched and coiled herself in the opposite direction on Matt's shooting jacket. The copy of Montaigne lay on the table beside me, and bisecting its fore edge I saw the thin blue line of the envelope. *It was a letter that should never have been written.* I slipped it out from between the leaves of the book. *Tear it up.* The impulse stopped at my fingers. *Seal it in an envelope and give it back to me.* I drew out the pages and straightened them with my thumbnail across the hard back of the volume.

> *John, my darling,*
> *I shall not be here when you read this. You said that I was a silly young girl. I am young, and perhaps silly; but not in the way that you meant. I am young and perhaps silly in baring my heart so utterly and completely to any living being as I bare it to you.*
> *This is one of the letters that should never be written. If I speak to you before this comes to your hand, I may weaken and beg you not to read it. But if I have spoken to you and you are reading this, you will not have listened*

168

to me. Knowing you, I know that I will never have your scorn or your ridicule; nor your pity—that I could not bear.

A little over a hundred years ago there was delivered to Elizabeth Barrett, in a room in Wimpole Street, a letter from Robert Browning. Two days before, they had met for the first time. Much came to pass between them and many, so many, are the letters they wrote that we may now read; but that first letter we may not read. Was it lost? No, I doubt that Elizabeth Barrett could have ever lost it. Was it destroyed? Perhaps, but not from prudery and not from embarrassment. I think she locked its message in her heart and the letter, itself, returned to him, because it is unseemly that the complete nakedness of the human soul be seen by other than those single eyes to whom it is confided. I am not Robert Browning, my love, not yet Elizabeth Barrett. I cannot give you sonnets, though my heart is filled with them; I can only give you the heart in which they sing, and the body that holds that heart, and my mind, my humble mind, that cannot control its emotions.

You may say that I will outgrow this, that somewhere, sometime I will love another. That could come to pass; but should it, my love would only be the richer for having loved you, and I the poorer for not having you to love. In your eyes, certainly in the world's view, it is not seemly that a woman should be so forward, but I have a forward heart and the full giving of myself has conveyed all the maidenhood or virginity I possess.

We shall be apart for some time. When we meet I shall have disciplined myself and I will never again be an embarrassment to you. Know only that I am yours, now and always, should you ever want or desire

Your Françoise

My first impulse was to reach for the phone and call her back. Instead I reached for another cigarette. This was not anything that might be resolved with words over a telephone in the middle of the night. Joy, with an animal's instinct for troubled human emotions, rose and laid her head on the edge of my bed, her tail tentatively working. I patted her head and she lay down again.

I read Frankie's letter a second time, and then got out of bed and threw another log or two on the fire. From my window, mists softened the sharp outlines of the world and the rounding crest of the Hill. Haviland—a town, a city, a community of people never really sleeps. Spattered across the village, this house and that showed life; here and there some pain of the body or the spirit refused sleep and the oblivion of rest.

I knew, and for the first time, that I loved this child, and that I was probably a fool for what I was about to do. When something precious and beyond value is given to a man, why shouldn't he take it? I crossed back to the desk and addressed an envelope to Frankie and into the envelope I slipped her letter, and then for a long time I stared at a sheet of notepaper before I wrote:

> *Frankie my dear:*
> *The lost letter you wrote about was not lost. I think rather it was returned, as I return yours; only in this instance that you may have back your heart again, and in some future giving suffer no sense that it is not wholly yours to offer.*
> *I have lived one whole lifetime beyond you, and there is in store for you more and better than I could ever give. Let's have a compact between us— These letters were never written, these thoughts were never thought between us; we start again as friends—very dear and I hope very understanding friends.*
> *J. M.*

I sealed the envelope and started to put a stamp on it and then thought better of it, or rather I had a better thought to act upon.

Joy studied me as I dressed and when I invited her into the car beside me, there was question in her eyes. The clothes were not right and there were no guns; but still it was a car, and an invitation and cars took you places and somewhere—perhaps to what she was looking for. She sat rigidly beside me staring out between the beams of the headlights. As we passed the wing of the house

170

I could see a form standing at the window of Mrs. Haines' room. There will be unspoken questions about all this in the morning, I reflected. And then the car was gathering speed down the Hill Road.

There is something heady and intoxicating about driving at night. The world recedes and all that remains is contained within a lozenge of moving light. You drive faster and faster until the illusion comes that you are standing still and the world is rushing toward you, with dim landmarks hurrying past in the penumbra. Only occasionally an approaching lozenge of light raced from a pin point in the distance, growing projectilewise to explode for an instant in roar of motor and brighter light, and then hurtling past, diminishing, red-tailed, an earth-bound planet, almost instantly lost in its rearward flight to darkness. All the rest was emptiness and mine, until the villages began to cluster and the valley spilled out to the flat land, and the parkway extensions of the city streets slowed my purpose or my flight—I wasn't sure which.

The further that I penetrated into the city the more was I glad that I shared no part of it. But I had lived enough in it to have peopled it with ghosts.

The car slipped down the crest of Morningside Drive and caught a succession of lights over to the Avenue, and then with the wall of the Park echoing back the hum of rubber on asphalt, I started south. A cat materialized out of the darkness and disappeared, a gray streak into nowhere. Joy stiffened and immediately relaxed, having the natural disdain of the true working dog for all cats. In the upper seventies the lights turned, but my mind was elsewhere at the moment; the tires screeched as I flung on the brakes, and a policeman a half a block away turned and looked at me. Only as I was lighting a cigarette did I realize that I had stopped across the street from the Frederic Barnes house.

Something curious happens to houses when people do not live in them, some extra dimension departs, and their windows become lifeless eyes staring out into the street. The Barnes, I remembered, had simplified their lives; they all, all of them that were left, now lived in apartments scattered along Park Avenue. Someday they would devise an advantageous tax avoidance, and the Barnes Mansion would become, like its kind on the Avenue, the head-quarters of an organization sufficiently dedicated to some vague public interest to be beyond the reach of the tax collectors; or it might perhaps become the mausoleum of the Barnes Collection.

It was no secret that Frederic Barnes had been a man with grime under his fingernails when he first emerged from a small town. Grime under the fingernails comes in degrees of sanctity, ranging from the presumed honest grime of the soil to the presumed questionable stain of commerce and industry. Barnes' variety had started with the grease and grit of a machine shop, and before he had time to really wash his hands they had throttled half the automobile industry, and he emerged a giant in a world not peopled with pygmies. He spawned new carburetors, and motor designs, and systems of translating power. His was a genius of compression—you applied pressure and at the critical point loosed the ignition element; in the succeeding parturition there were born faster automobiles, boats and shipping, air conditioning and hydraulics and tall buildings and skyrocketing stocks in the Exchange. In the span of a single year, Barnes stock rose from three to fifty-three, and Barnes' personal growing pains took him from a humble third-floor apartment in a Detroit suburb to a whole floor at the Ambassador in New York. The house on Fifth Avenue and the palace on Long Island and the playland at Palm Beach and the love nest at Capri followed quickly. Somewhere in the early years, he had put down his micrometers and slide rules long enough to clasp his wife's loins in periodical outbursts of primal creative urge; or maybe he didn't put down his micrometers and slide rules, he may even have measured his passion, for it wasn't just diet and the masseuse who had fashioned Caroline Barnes' hips in the angular and starved outlines that were fortunately to become so fashionable. In any event, before he found more interesting things to do with his passion, Frederic Barnes placated Caroline with three children, Frederic, Jr., Caroline the second, and Angelica. —With his vitality and genius they should have been remarkable children, but those were the days when he was jealous of what he squandered. Like the Bourbon kings, with an empire to pass to his issue, the least of his creations was his own family. The end result was one physically prepossessing moron with a fair polo rating, one strikingly beautiful but thwarted and sexless daughter, and Angelica. The rest of the brood I knew only casually, but Angelica I had studied with some deep concern.

172

They used to call her Angel Puss when I first knew her; then there was a brief period when she toyed in a necrophilic way with the dying world of Europe, and she changed her name to Angélique. The columnists reported this new facet of her personality to a scandal-loving public. Then she returned to America and one of the tabloids christened her just Pussy Barnes; it was on the near side of slander, but it was ringed with truth. Angelica, however, didn't seem to mind the label, and her family didn't understand it, or pretended not to. But it was in the earlier phase that I knew her. By and large it was fast company, or rather at the time I thought it was; later it was really to be supercharged, but that was after my era, I really knew her in her champagne and innocence period. At first there was a degree of innocence, and a little champagne; later there was a lot of champagne and very little innocence.

"The lights have changed twice while you've been standing here." A policeman's head was at the off window. He seemed to be sizing me up and trying to relate a Gordon setter to a man sitting in a car on Fifth Avenue at one in the morning. "You're not sick or anything? Can you get home all right?"

"No, thanks, officer. Not sick, not anything. I'm as sober as a judge. I guess I was just thinking."

"Umm." He weighed the situation. "There's probably a law against that somewhere on the books."

"I'll get off your beat, and do my thinking someplace else," I apologized.

"Yeah, do that. The damnedest things happen when people think."

I slipped the car into gear. "Good night, officer."

"Good night."

In the rear-vision mirror I could see him standing at the curb, watching my progress down the Avenue.

Provender trucks in front of the St. Regis were unloading milk and meat and the necessities of the day to come, and behind them scavenger trucks were hauling away the noisome slops and garbage that are incident to the feeding of many people. To find a place to park, I pulled across the street and drew up below the entrance to Soule's Bar and Grill. The doorman came over to the car.

"I'm just parking," I told him. He looked at me with the jaundiced disillusion of his trade. I tossed him a half dollar and his

173

attitude quickly changed, he would gladly rent me seventeen feet of the city's curbing—for five dollars he would have sold it to me. A cab pulled up and a girl stepped out. The doorman seemed to know her and saluted her. As she paid the cab her glance wandered in my direction. She was still looking at me as she slipped a tip to the driver and another to the doorman, and turned away. The doorman looked at me, then toward her, then back to me as much as to say, "You want? Can get." Then he slouched against the doorway, and his face glowed as he puffed on a cigarette he had been cupping in his hand all the while.

I took the letter I had written to Françoise out of my pocket, and glanced up at the hotel. The dark façade of the building was broken by only two or three lighted windows. Behind one of those windows Frankie was probably spending her own sleepless night. One's barriers and inhibitions become relaxed in the small beginning hours of the day; the threshold of common sense recedes, the pattern of one's life assumes shapes and directions controlled by the wish and not by the probable, or even the possible. All that I had to do was to cross the street and call Frankie's room. Why not? Other men my age had married girls as young as Frankie. A pattern and a shape of life would have been given to me: Haviland and the Hill by Elizabeth and Old Matt; the Tracy heritage by young Matt; and of and by herself Frankie, with all of her youth and loveliness, untouched and unspoiled. And the remaining fraction of my life—no longer half but whatever fraction would remain to me—would be in a deep, safe and secure frame both full and good. But what would I bring to her in return? A life more than half lived, the jaded knowledge that so much that seemed so bright and clear to her was neither bright nor clear. I opened the door of the car and slipped out. Joy started to follow me, but I ran up the window. "Stay where you are, old girl, and any quail you see are not yours to flush."

"Miss Françoise Dumont," I said to the clerk. "She is registered with Mrs. Elizabeth Milnor."

"Yes?" His question was born of the time of the night, but it was not too direct; even the best of hotels require only outward decorum.

"Would you be good enough to have this letter delivered to her?" I asked.

174

He seemed relieved. "Certainly." He glanced at the clock. "The first thing in the morning."

"No, I think you better have a bellboy slip it under her door. I think she's awake."

The question in his eyes was unasked. It must be frustrating to be a hotel clerk and touch only half of the drama of people's lives that crosses your desk and to be able to supply the answer to the other half only with surmise and the natural cynicism of your trade.

Soule's doorman opened the car door for me.

"Do you know a bar where a man can do some serious drinking at this hour?" I asked him.

"You mean serious drinking? No chicks?" he asked.

"Quite serious, and no chicks," I told him.

"Billy's over on First Avenue. They never close until day after tomorrow," he said.

"I didn't realize he was still in business." There had been a time when some important moments of my life had been lived at Billy's.

Eleven

My sense of humor nudged me in the side, as I drove across
town. "Grow up! Stop play-acting. You did what you did, now
don't dramatize it. Sure you've got an empty feeling in your belly
and you want a drink. Go ahead and have one, but what the hell
makes with the self-pity."

I parked the car down the street from Billy's. The years had
passed, but the place seemed unchanged. I snapped my finger and
Joy slithered to my feet. "I guess they won't object to your coming
in with me. A lot of two-legged bitches used to be welcome here."

Joy plastered herself against my leg as I sat at the bar, her tail
carefully arranged out of the way of careless footsteps. Matt had
trained her in bar manners, I concluded.

Billy's used to specialize in laconic bartenders; it still did. I
asked for Scotch and his hand drifted down a line of bottles with
his eyes holding mine. When he came to Cutty Sark, I nodded and
he put the bottle in front of me; he put ice in a glass and held up
a bottle of soda. I shook my head and he placed a small pitcher
and a shot glass before me and then went back to polishing a row
of tumblers. The mirror behind the bar was tilted forward so you
got a strange perspective on the room, and an unusual angle of
yourself as you stared into it; without seeing your face you could
watch yourself drinking. A very acute psychologist tilted that mirror, I decided; anyone who really wanted to get away from himself
didn't have to sit staring at his own image. Just over my head, and
reflected from the far corner of the room, I could see a party of six
sitting at a table. There was something about one of the women
whose back was toward me—the set of her shoulders and the car-

176

riage of her neck and something about the trick of tossing her head as she talked, to make a point. And then, as she half turned to speak to someone, the hair rose along the back of my neck. People talk about their hair rising; it actually does at times, it's not merely a figure of speech. In a city of more than seven million people you don't just walk into a bar and cross the trail of your own memories within an hour's time. The odds were too long for it to happen, but the woman sitting at the able in the corner was Angelica Barnes.

I quickly finished my drink and reached into my pocket to pay for it and then in the mirror I saw her turn further in her chair and stare in my direction. She spoke to the man sitting next to her, and got up and started across the room. In the mirror I saw her take the seat beside me. She motioned to the bartender, indicated the bottle, and he put a setup in front of her; her hand poured a drink and returned the bottle. I had the sense of living through a dream. The whole thing was a stunt done solely with mirrors, a conjure trick of the imagination. If I turned it would not be Angelica sitting beside me, it would be a stranger.

"It's been a long time," Angelica said.

"A long time," I agreed. "The best part of a lifetime."

"Well, anyway, part of a lifetime," she conceded. "I wouldn't say the best part. —I suppose we begin by saying all the trite conventional things, or shall we be different?"

"And . . . ?"

"Just pick up from where we left off—let's say it was day before yesterday."

"Can you say that about twelve years?"

"I think so. After all, we didn't hurt each other."

"We didn't do each other much good, either," I told her.

"Perhaps we didn't," she conceded. "We did our best, and it wasn't good enough. You wanted something I didn't have. You were looking for something that wasn't there. —You never married; are you still looking for it?"

"It isn't something to look for. It either happens, or it doesn't happen," I said.

"With us it almost happened—I saw you once during the war. I was in a cab, you were getting out of one, and going into the Gotham. I had a date, I was going somewhere, but I told the driver to go around the Park. In the end he brought me back to the Gotham. The room clerk told me you were registered, and gave me a suspicious look. I even called your room from the lobby and then hung up before you answered. I wrote you a note and then tore it up. It wouldn't have been any good, would it?"

"Was it ever?" I asked.

"Yes, and you know it. It was almost right for both of us. Only, by the time I realized that, it was too late."

"Too late for what?" I asked.

"Too late for too many things. Life is like a fragile glass ball. If you play with it like a toy, you break it, and you no longer have something that's whole and complete; the entity of things is gone and you only have a handful of pieces, some pretty, and some ugly, and all of them with sharp edges that can cut and hurt you." Suddenly she shivered and for the first time our eyes met in the mirror in front of us. "This is like drunk talk," she said. "Midnight profundities at Cross Town Society, only I'm not drunk."

"Someone else is, though," I told her. "You're about to be interrupted." I could see her companion from the corner table weave his way across the room. He lurched between our stools and there was a yelp from Joy.

"Somebody's goddamn dog bit me!" he bellowed.

I snapped my finger, and Joy took refuge on the other side of me. "That's what happens," I said to her, "when you bring a lady into a place like this. She can get her tail into trouble." I stroked Joy's head to quiet her, but she wasn't in any mood for tail wagging. She curled her offended member tighter about her and hugged against my leg.

"Is that your dog?" the drunk demanded.

"Yes. She didn't bite you."

"Don't tell me what she did. I say she bit me!"

"She happens to be very particular about the people she bites. Now why don't you just run along and quiet down." This whole business was getting nightmarish. A bar brawl started by a drunk over nothing—you read about it in the papers, but it never happens to you.

"Please shut up, Jerry, you're awfully tiresome when you're tight." Angelica took his arm and tried to steer him away, and with the mercurial shift of the drunk, his mood changed. "Come

178

on back, Angel," he wheedled. "Don't walk out and spoil the party, it's a nice party. It's hardly got started and we've got so much to do tonight, you and I've got so much to do tonight." He put his arm about her. "Come on back, we're just getting to know each other."

She stepped away from him. "We've just stopped getting to know each other," she said.

He reached for her and his hand caught her dress. I pulled him around facing me.

"You keep out of this, you son of a bitch." His voice wasn't thick enough to excuse the phrase. He lunged for me and I ducked, that was all the trigger I needed, but before I could hit him the bartender picked up the bottle and very casually let him have it over the back of the head; then with his damp towel he wiped the bottle and replaced it on the bar. "If you do it right, they never break," he said. A waiter picked the drunk up. "What do we do with this?" the waiter asked.

One of his friends from the corner table came over and helped the waiter lead him out to a taxi, and the rest of Angelica's group followed them out to the street; no one spoke to Angelica.

"It looks like I'm alone," she said. "Will you take me home?"

"I'm sorry about all this," I said to the bartender.

He shrugged. "It wasn't your fault. You were just waiting for a streetcar."

"Here's my name"—I scribbled it on a piece of paper—"in case there's any trouble."

His towel wiped the bar. "That kind's apt to start trouble, but they never finish it." He slipped the piece of paper with my name on it under the edge of the cash register.

"Your friends are nice people," I commented, as I handed Angelica into the car.

"Yes, aren't they," she said.

"Where's 'home'?"

"The same place, or have you forgotten it?" As I started the car, she asked, "Where are you living these days?"

"Haviland."

She glanced at Joy in the back seat. "And Billy's Saloon is just around the corner?"

"I had to drive in for something," I told her.

"I read about Matt's death," she said. "I started to write you and then I decided not to. It was sort of agreed that when we closed the book, it would stay closed. But I'm sorry about Matt. I always sensed that you two were very close."

"We were."

"It wasn't his way of doing things. They must have been very much in love."

"Yes."

She was silent for a block or two, and then she said, "You can't turn time back, can you?"

A taxi cut in front of me; he wanted the whole road. I slowed down and let him have it, and then glanced over at Angelica. Her body was motionless and her face without expression, but the tears were rolling down her cheeks, and it wasn't alcohol, or any surface emotion. I made the turn into Park Avenue, and brought her up in front of her apartment house.

"You're staying in town?" she asked.

"No, I'm driving back to Haviland tonight, or rather in what's left of tonight."

"Will you come up for a drink?"

"I don't think I'd better. It's pretty late."

"Yes, it is late," she said. "Very late in the day between us. And emotions don't turn back, either. —John, do something for me," she digressed abruptly. "Drive around—anywhere—around the Park—down to the foot of the island and back—" She was on the edge of hysteria and I could see the effort strain her face as she tried to retreat from the brink. "I'm lost. —Do you know what it is to be lost? You've seen lost dogs. They get bewildered and they start to run. They panic and they don't know friend from enemy. They just run . . . they just run, and keep on running. . . ."

I glanced at the clock on the instrument panel. It read two thirty. Silently, I slipped the car into gear, and then her hand touched my arm to stop me. "No, don't, I've been talking nonsense," she said. "I'll get out. It's been nice to see you again."

I let the clutch in and the car started forward.

"Look, you don't owe me anything," she protested.

"Human relations at six per cent compound interest," I chided her. "Get out of the banking business, it doesn't become you."

180

Blocks later, as the car nosed north on the Express Highway, she asked, "Where are we going?"

"To Haviland," I told her.

"Do you know why?" she queried.

"Not very clearly," I said. "Does it have to be clear?"

"Just a chance meeting—after all these years our paths cross for the first time. It isn't a good enough reason."

"Have you and I always had good reasons for the things we've done?"

"They were good enough at the time," she said. "Or at least we thought they were."

"Then let's think this has a good enough reason," I told her.

Her hand touched mine on the wheel and then she was quiet. She took a cigarette out of her handbag and I pushed the lighter into its socket for her. She exhaled a lungful of smoke and it whipped in a swirling gray streamer out of the window. A little later I thought she said something, and I turned to look at her, but her eyes were closed and I couldn't tell whether she slept or not. She had slumped down in the seat and there was the slight pressure of her shoulder against mine as I took the turns in the road. It was the touch of her shoulder, I imagine, the trigger of physical contact that sent my memory spinning back down the corridors of my life, back to the beginning with Angelica. I hadn't wanted to fall in love with her, I don't suppose anyone beyond the age of adolescence *wants* to fall in love, but I suppose the circumstances were a little too flamboyant and colorful to make for common sense. . . .

Tommy Prentice had a plantation down in the South Carolina rice country, near Sheldon, and some of the best bird shooting in the United States. The day I met Angelica, I was shooting alone. Tommy had wrenched his back the day before. You never know when you start out when you may want to come back, so I had a slab of a sandwich in my pocket and a flask of whisky. It was along about noon and I was walking some upland cover. My dogs had worked over to my left, and then I saw a liver-colored body freeze in the brush as it came to point, and I lifted my gun. As I moved a little to one side I realized that it was a strange dog, either a wanderer that had joined my dogs or I had crossed some-one else's shooting. I turned to glance about me and saw the move-ment of a hunting jacket and the glint of a gun barrel. It was either

181

my turning or the lowering of my own gun that flushed the bird and it rose in a great drumming flutter and veered toward me and to the right. Before I could call out or drop there was a slash of shot through the brush, inches from my face, and the smell of powder and the rush of air was in my nostrils. A feather or two dropped from the bird, an almost miss, but its flight was unstayed. My emotions were a little mixed; partly anger at a dangerous carelessness, partly irritation at myself for not having made my presence known, and no little contempt for an easy shot bungled and a wounded bird. I waited for the second shot but the bird was already at the limit of range. Then, to prevent the bird escaping in a wounded condition but mostly out of anger, my gun raised and I fired and the bird stopped in its flight and then plummeted to the ground.

"Nice kill," I heard from behind me, and then a tall, slim, rather beautiful girl was stepping through the brush.

Her gaze was as quick as a computing machine. I was almost conscious of her thought process as she quickly added Peel boots and a Purdy gun and subtracted stained and patched shooting clothes. To all that she added the button in my lapel. "You're from the Prentice place. Sorry, close shot. I almost got you." She spoke with the leger and remote disinterest that must have tinged the voices of the French nobility just before the Revolution. She'd missed a pheasant and almost shot a peasant.

"Better luck next time." I noticed she was wearing a Barnes Plantation button in her jacket. "You were shooting at the bird, I presume."

Her eyes narrowed. "That time, yes," she said.

There was a rustling beside us in the undergrowth and her dog emerged between us and presented the retrieved bird to her. "It's your bird, you killed it," she said.

"It was your shot. Let's say I was merely the handler."

I could watch anger form in her face and then as suddenly as it had appeared a smile took its place. "I'm not sure that I want to fight with you," she said.

"All right, let's not." There was something infectious in her gaiety. I put my hand out. "I'm John Milnor."

Her hand clasp was direct and firm. "Milnor?" She seemed to taste the name as if she were trying to locate it in some past experience or milieu. "Philadelphia?" It was more as if she were asking herself the question.

"A little town you probably never heard of," I told her. "Haviland."

"I know Matt Tracy. He's from Haviland. I've been to his place to lunch."

The hackles rose a little on the back of my neck. "He's my cousin," I told her. I was watching the expression about her eyes. There wasn't any—but for a moment I had the vision of two strange dogs meeting and smelling each other and deciding not to fight. Then she stooped and received the bird and patted the dog's head.

"I'm famished," she suddenly said, "and I haven't the foggiest notion where the rest of my crowd are." She cupped her hands and gave a *halloo*; there was no answer and she shrugged.

"The Barnes place is over that way." I pointed east across the swale.

She seemed puzzled for an instant, and then, touching the button in her jacket, she said, "Oh, of course. A long way. My horse lamed, I sent him back with one of the handlers. I was going to walk—I must have headed in the wrong direction."

I was conscious that she hadn't introduced herself, or had forgotten to. "I only have one sandwich," I offered.

"Fine! A half a sandwich can be a feast, when there's only half a sandwich." She settled down with her back against the bole of a live oak, opened the brown paper parcel and broke the sandwich in two. I handed her the small pocket flask. She sighted through it and drained an exact half and returned it to me, and for as long as it takes to eat half a sandwich we sat there eating, without talking. My dogs had joined us by now, made friends with hers, and were working in ever-widening circles about us. Suddenly she rose and whistled her dogs to her. "Unless you'd prefer to be alone I'll work back toward the Prentice place—it's nearer—and call a car to come over for me."

"Good idea," I said.

We raised two birds a little after we started. Both of them were her shots. The first she missed clean, the second she touched and as it broke in flight and turned toward me, she fired again and missed. I waited until it was well into my quadrant and dropped it.

She broke her gun as she came up to me and didn't reload. "This is getting to be a habit," she said. "I don't like to do things I don't do well."

Someone's done a fine job of spoiling this young lady, I thought. We didn't talk any more until we came to the stream where I'd tethered my horse. There was a ford and a stepping-stone bridge and she dropped to the water and wet her wrists. "It's fresh and cold. My tongue's hanging out for a swim."

"Do you want to ride?" I gestured to the horse.

"No, we're almost there. But I'm going to have that swim." She crossed the stepping stones and headed up toward the pool that widened out above. "Want to join me?" she called.

Thirty yards upstream where the grass came straight down to the water, I saw her stop and begin to slip out of her jacket. I turned and went up my side of the stream to the foot of the pool and peeled down to my shorts behind the cover of a thicket. Before I got to the stream I could hear the splash of her plunge. When I reached the bank there was only the widening circles of her dive, and then far out in the pool I saw the shimmer of a long silver shape, and her head broke the surface and her laughter cut the stillness of the afternoon. I dove. The sharp clean cold of the water enclosed me, and the faint ghostly fingers of grasses swept along my flanks, and then I was near her and side by side we swam far up the winding reach of the pool until it shallowed, and then we turned and headed downstream. As we came near the ford I slowed, but she continued her smooth crawl stroke toward the shore. She might not have been an outstanding shot, but her swimming form was a perfect, slow, effortless motion that drove her through the water. Twenty feet from a shelf of rock that sloped down to the stream, she lay, her face in the water, and with her arms outstretched churned her legs until her finger tips touched the shore. Then she slipped out of the water and stood in the full sunlight. As if she was completely unconscious of my presence she let the edge of her palms strip the water from her belly and breasts, and then she stretched out like a lean-limbed cat on the rock. Her gaze seemed unfocused out over the pool, but I was aware that she was watching me. Suddenly the heat was a weight pressing down upon the stilled afternoon. I let myself slip down beneath the surface of the water to a pale, green-blue aqueous world with

184

a clear sand bottom. What sort of a woman was this? Was this some hybrid unconsciousness of body, some supérior and unfettered plane beyond convention? Was it an invitation, and if so an invitation to what? We had met scarcely two hours before, we had spoken no words beyond the brittle amenities of strangers. My long-held breath bubbled with quicksilver about my eyes and then the underwater shelf of the rock she lay upon came into my vision. At the very last moment, I turned and headed back across the pool. In the brief instant that I lifted my head from the water to breathe, I could see her still lying motionless on the rock. When I reached the opposite shore, without looking back I walked toward the thicket and started to dress.

I was checking the saddle girth when I looked around and she was standing on the other bank observing me with a faint smile on her lips. As I led the horse to her side of the stream, she took a package of cigarettes out of her shirt pocket.

"Cigarette?"

I took one.

"Match?" Her cigarette was pursed in her lips. I struck a light, and as I offered it to her I was conscious of her steady gaze. There were no words between us as we walked the rest of the way to the Prentice plantation.

Tommy was seated stiffly on the porch, propped up in a chair with pillows around him. His wave greeted us before we could hear his voice.

"This is . . ." I started to say as we came up to him, and only then did I realize that I didn't know her name.

There was the briefest pause, as he let me sweat, then he said, "Hello, Angelica!"

"We were strangers who met in the field," she explained. "May I use your phone to call for a car?"

"I'll drive you over," I offered.

She looked at me as if she were weighing my invitation, before she shook her head. "No, it will be better this way, less bother to you. We had a swim in your river, Tommy, thanks!" She ran her hands through her still-wet hair. "Is your powder room still in the same place?"

I didn't realize that even after she had disappeared into the house I was still staring after her, until I heard Tommy say, "Maybe

185

she won't do you no hurt—maybe." It was the tag of one of his favorite stories, and we both laughed.

"Angelica who?" I asked.

He raised his eyebrows. "Barnes."

"Oh . . ." She was one of those people who, if you read the papers and the gossip columns, you feel you know before you've met them. "Tell me about her," I said.

"*You* tell me about her—someday," Tommy suggested.

"I don't think so. I imagine her acquaintance and mine will be limited to this afternoon."

"Then why did you ask about her?"

"Just curiosity. You meet somebody, and you want to know about them. What makes them tick."

"I'm in the railroad business; I've got less curiosity than you."

In the end Tommy and I never did discuss Angelica. Her car came up the drive before she emerged from the house. I handed her into it, and held out my hand.

"Oh, we'll be seeing each other again," she said.

"I doubt it. I'm leaving day after tomorrow."

Her answer was the slightest of shrugs and a half-smile that played about her lips, and then I was awkwardly conscious that I was still holding her hand in my clasp.

But two days later I had not yet left. I eased my horse across the ford and out along the trail that led to the upland corner of the plantation. The dogs ranged before me and came to repeated points only to have the horse pass and the birds run away into the brush. I crossed to the far side of the swale where we had first met. A horse whinnied nearby, and my mount stopped, raised her ears and then answered. I let her have her head and presently we came into a little clearing. Angelica was seated in the shade of a moss-hung tree which grew on a little rise above a spring source that trickled away in the brush; her horse was tethered somewhere out of sight.

"Hello," she greeted me. "I was wondering if you would come."

"I was supposed to be on my way back to New York this morning."

"That was what you said the last time I saw you."

"Tommy's back was kicking up and the doctor wanted him to go up to Baltimore to a specialist and get it treated. He left last

186

night." I got off my horse and held its bridle. "He was expecting some guests in this morning and asked me to stay over and play host to them."

"I see." Something about her, or between us, created a constraint that made me feel like a schoolboy making his excuses or an explanation. "There was a wire from his guests this morning saying that their plans had gone awry and they would be delayed a week," I finished.

"So you'll stay on?" There was only half a question in her voice.

"I hadn't thought that far ahead," I told her, slightly nettled by her self-possession.

"I hate to plan things beyond the moment, too," she said. She brushed leaf mold off her riding breeches as she rose, and looked up at me and smiled. "I owe you a luncheon."

"I have two sandwiches in my pocket today," I told her.

"Forearmed for any eventuality?"

"Let's just say *forearmed*," I said.

"Are we ever?" Her mood changed. "The fact remains I still owe you a luncheon." She crossed over to the edge of the clearing and mounted her horse. "There's a trail that follows this water course."

It was a narrow trail and we had to ride in single file so conversation was difficult. We came to a gate and she tripped the release and we rode through. We were now on Barnes land and the trail improved and a little more than a mile beyond led down into a clearing beside a stream, and under the tall live oaks was a small pale-pink bricked building looking as if it had been amputated from the fringe of outbuildings of one of the early plantations. The windows and dormers and the detail of the cornice and the door spoke with the flavor of two hundred years. "You're right," she said. "It was moved up here from the plantation, even the old bricks. It's almost the corner of the property and it's ten miles from the main house." She dismounted and handed me her reins. "There's a paddock and a small stable in back. Will you tend to the horses?"

I unsaddled them and found a grain bin and gave them a measure each. As I returned to the house, I heard a splash from the stream and then the steady churning of someone swimming. A moment later, she was pulling herself up on the opposite bank of the pool

187

and straightening the edges of her bathing suit down along her thighs. "There are some swimming togs in the house!" she called to me.

The door was open. All the doors were open. I could see at a glance that there was a miniature kitchen and a bedroom, but it was the living room that held my attention. It was of good size, with painted pine paneling, and a fine mantel, and sturdy forthright Chippendale furniture—the kind of a man's room that a decorator with taste and an ample checkbook, a very ample checkbook, might achieve. And yet it was somehow meretricious. It didn't belong here, it had been assembled. The table set for two in the corner didn't belong either; and the elaborate hamper and thermos jugs were a far cry from a sandwich wrapped in paper.

With a sense that I had gotten myself into something, I went on to the bedroom in search of swimming things. This room, too, was in perfect and frozen taste. The bathing trunks were laid across the back of a chair. It was a man's room, with an immense Virginia walnut four-poster bed and crewel-covered early chairs, but there was also a perverse feminine quality to it—the soft colors perhaps, and the expense and fittings of the dressing table. On a luggage stand stood a small traveling case with a fringe of white silk and pressed ribbons hanging from its closed edge. The doors of the closets were ajar, and in one, lined with silk and heavy with sachet, her riding clothes hung, and over a rack the functional underclothes of a woman who rides. The other closet was heavy with the odor of cedar. Completely male, and save for a white silk dressing gown, completely empty. The whole thing was a little perverse and imperious, out of time and place; hedonistic and yet curiously unashamed. As I slipped on the trunks, I glanced into the bath; the twentieth had invaded the eighteenth century. It was a huge polished marble box, even to the ceiling, of pale figured *brèche violet* and the accessories and necessaries of dark green marble; a vast tub was let into the floor, and everywhere the bronze fittings were shaped into gilded dolphins; even the spout in the bidet was a bronze gilded dolphin. The Romans would have envied the excretory conveniences. This was Frederic Barnes' stud stall, and in his momentary absence, his headstrong and spoiled filly had the taste in her mouth to be covered in service.

My dive carried me to the rock where she was sunning herself, and at once there was the flash of her body curving into the water beside me. Her legs brushed against me, and then her head bobbed to the surface. "Don't look so solemn," she said, and flicked a handful of water into my face. I lunged toward her. She evaded me and swam away, and just when I was about to catch up with her, she upended and went beneath the surface. I tried to follow her and when I came up for air she was climbing out on the bank and hurrying up to the house. When I followed her a few moments later she was emerging from the bedroom dressed in a bathrobe and toweling her hair. "I'm famished. Martini or whisky?"

"Are there martinis?"

"There will be. Hurry up." She gestured toward the bedroom. I saw that the white silk dressing gown was laid out, invitingly, across a chair. I glanced at it, tossed my wet trunks into the tub and put my clothes back on.

She had her back to me and was pouring a cocktail into a glass as I came into the living room. She handed me the glass with the merest flicker of amusement in her eyes. "Dry enough?"

I tasted it. "It's as dry as . . ." I reached for a simile.

"It's as dry as an angel's . . ." She paused and there was a taunting look in her eyes. "As an angel's kiss," she finally completed. "Some people call me Angel, some call me Angel Puss. And then there are people who call me other things and other names. Would you like me to tell you the names people call me?"

"Do you want me to say yes?"

She finished her drink and put it down. "No, I don't think I do. But I'm interested in what you're going to call me."

"I haven't decided yet. If I were to continue to see you I might have to invent a new name, something unused and without finger marks on it."

The flicker of amusement gave place to a flash of anger and then it passed. "Let's eat," she said.

She had already unpacked the hamper. Caviar and vichyssoise and a cold roast fowl, a salad and a thermos pail of ice with a bottle of champagne. "You really camp out," I commented.

"What's the matter? Your social conscience bother you?"

"No, the best things in life, when they're available, I can enjoy quite as much as the next man."

"But they have to be the best?" she queried.

189

"This is rather generous interest to receive for half a cheese sandwich," I countered.

"And don't forget the jug of wine."

As I filled her glass she said, "It's rather obvious, isn't it?"

"What?"

"This place," she answered. "You don't like it, do you?"

"Is it something I have to like or dislike?"

"I think so, you being you," she said. "But it is rather obvious. You don't know my father, do you?"

"Only to know of him."

"He has many sides. This"—the movement of her hand included the room—"is just one aspect of him. It reflects only a single appetite."

"It reflects it from a singularly luxurious frame," I observed.

"He enjoys the symbols of his own success; that's another aspect of him."

"Gold-plated dolphins?" I suggested.

She nodded. "Again, symbols. He likes things in multiplicity, in quantity. Long ago, he had enough money to buy anything he wanted; he's really no longer interested in it for itself, it's the getting of it that fires him."

I had the sense that she was talking to herself and not to me.

"When I was a baby he made an automobile from the ground up, from bare steel, and he made his own tools with his own hands." She got up nervously and went to a long, flat, brassbound mahogany box on a table. "Come over here and look at this." She raised the heavy lid. Couched in baize was a set of precision instruments —gauges and micrometers and large caliper micrometers—all finished in bright-honed steel. I picked one up and examined it. It was engraved *F.B.* with a flourish.

"Interesting, isn't it?"

I chose to ignore the bitterness in her voice. "Very," I agreed.

"Wreck him on a desert island and give him a drum of gasoline and a handful of metal and he'd build a plane to fly himself off. Only now there isn't enough time. He doesn't want to build just one thing; he designed and built production lines so that they could be built faster. He dreamed of making five hundred cars a day and then it led to a thousand and then two thousand and now four thousand. His appetites have no limit. He's bought places like this,

190

whole plantations—and forgot that he owned them. He built this hideaway for a woman. When it was finished he probably didn't even remember her name. It takes forty minutes to get here from the plantation and forty minutes back. Nothing that he wants from a woman is worth eighty minutes."

"You sound pretty disillusioned," I said.

"Do I? I came back from school once—I was seventeen—and stopped by his office. There was a woman waiting to see him. They announced me, but he had her come in first. There were two doors to his office; one led to a suite of living quarters. I didn't have to wait long, maybe twenty minutes, and then the other door opened and she came out. I thought she'd look different, but she didn't; she just looked like a girl who'd done a day's work. Then a light flickered beside the secretary and I was ushered in to see my father. He was standing at his desk studying a sheaf of blueprints. It was a moment or two before he realized that I was standing in the room, and then he turned; his pants were still unbuttoned."

"Do you know why you're telling me all this?" I asked.

"Yes." She reached for a cigarette and lit it. "I know all the jargon, I read it in the books and heard it on the couches. It's part of our generation."

I smiled faintly. "Then I don't have to tell you what you did. And for what reason."

Her eyes narrowed. "What do you think I did?"

"You went out and hurt your father in the most obvious and direct way that you could. Later your analyst suggested that what you did was a symbol of murder, and in the end all that you did was hurt yourself."

She shrugged. "Not too much. After all, I am Frederic Barnes' daughter. It's tough stock, it doesn't hurt too easily."

"You'd like to make yourself think that, but you know it isn't true: day before yesterday, when we swam together; today, here. You'd even like to use his bed, it would make the murder more complete."

She walked over to the door and stood there with her back toward me. "You start out right; you end up wrong," she said.

"Aren't you trying to fool yourself? Or perhaps you find it necessary sometimes to fool yourself."

She turned, and now her back was against the door. "I never

fool myself. That's the only important thing Frederic Barnes ever gave me. It's worth more than anything I'll ever inherit from him."

"And today is different from the day we met?"

"What are your scruples? Moral?" she demanded with a hint of scorn.

"In the final analysis, I daresay they are."

"And you don't like women who throw themselves at you. . . ."

"You weren't throwing yourself at me. I was incidental. Merely an instrument."

"Then why didn't you go back to New York?"

"I told you."

"No, you didn't tell me; you told me reasons that had nothing to do with your decision. Do you deny that when you rode out to the same place we had met, you didn't hope to find me there?"

"Let's say I didn't *expect* to find you there."

"But you brought a packet of sandwiches, and from all the points of the compass you chose that one trail?"

"Maybe I'm a romanticist."

Her gaze held mine with the frankness of a man. "Yes, I suppose you are; but isn't everyone who searches for something? That first day, for example, when we swam together you could have made love to me. . . ."

"Do we have to use the word *love*?"

"I used it loosely."

"Very."

"There's another word I can use, four-lettered, and short. It's quite graphic and ungarnished with emotion—would you prefer it?"

"At least, it's an honest word, and it's lost a lot of its shock appeal."

"But *I* shock you?"

"Are you trying to? You really don't. I just didn't know you were that uncomplicated. Complicated people conceal their motives, they compensate by indirection, they deceive even themselves. You're as simple as a child who wants something and when it doesn't get it, screams and has temper tantrums and breaks things."

"What did I want?—What do you think I wanted?"

"Not me," I told her. "I was just an instrument you wanted to use against your father. You love your father; you wanted him to be something it wasn't in his nature to be; you wanted something from him that wasn't in his possession to give."

"Don't be so damned smug and knowing!" she lashed out at me.

"I didn't mean to be."

"I'm angry, because you're half right. But only half, mind you. If you'd had me the other day, you wouldn't have had anything, just a shell. And I wouldn't have had anything for you but contempt."

"But you're not often refused, is that it?"

"Almost never."

"And so it became more important than if anything had happened between us?"

"Yes, that's true. But not in the way or for the reasons you're thinking. For the first time I wanted to give and not just take. Something happened to me. I told myself a fairy tale—that you wouldn't leave, that you'd come back to try to find me again, that you'd want something from me that no one else has wanted, and that I would have it to give to you. I thought that you would know nothing about me; Tommy Prentice isn't the kind of a man who talks about women. I thought that we might start fresh and clean and from the beginning. I don't know why you came to me today; but whatever you came to find, it either wasn't there, or when you found it you didn't want it. Something impelled me to tell you things I've told no one else. You saw part of the truth, I tried to make you see all of it. And in the end, I see that there's nothing I have that you want. The tawdry thing I offered you the other day, you certainly didn't want. And what I had to offer you today —you didn't want that either."

She crossed to the table and put a cigarette in her mouth. Her hand shook as she lit it and then as she turned I saw that her cheeks were wet with tears. "I think you'd better go now," she said. "It was a nice luncheon party, and we got to know each other a little better. I don't owe you anything and you don't owe me anything." She walked out into the hall toward the bedroom. "Good-by, John Milnor." The door closed behind her, and I was alone.

I remember the late afternoon sun was brilliant with an eye-aching glare, and the shadows in the room were like the dark blue shadows of a room I had once seen in Arles, or maybe it was in a picture that was painted in Arles that the shadows were so blue.

193

Even vivid was the skin's tactile memory of the weight of the hot whiteness beating against my clothes. And the sound I was hearing were dry sobs from the other room. I don't suppose the shape of our lives would have been much different if I had done other than I did. The door creaked as I opened it.

Twelve

A night bird darted into the funneled beam of the headlights. It wheeled and for an instant or two took forward flight down the shaft of brightness and then as if confused it seemed to hover as the car quickly overtook it. There was a thudding impact as its body hit the windshield. The glass was unbroken but the mirror of memory was shattered and my thoughts retreated into the present. Angelica straightened beside me.

"One shattering instant, and then there is nothing! Do you think that's the way it is?"

I realized that she hadn't been asleep. "I don't know. Maybe it's best that we don't know," I said.

The high whine of rubber on concrete gave way to the deeper-pitched hum of macadam as I turned off Route 22 onto the Hill Road. When I slowed down at the Corners she said, "It hasn't changed much, has it?"

"Time seems to slow down when it climbs this hill," I told her. "A great many things have happened, but not much has changed."

I stopped the car in front of the house. "You still live here?" she asked.

"I'm living here again."

"Alone?"

"No, my mother lives here."

"What will she think of this—of me?"

"I'm never quite certain what Elizabeth is thinking," I told her. "But if she were here it would still be all right. —She's on her way down south."

"Oh . . ."

"That was a very elliptical *Oh.*"

"You suggest," she said, "that there would seem nothing unusual in your bringing home lost dogs."

"I haven't made a habit of it. Come on." I took her arm and led her toward the house, with Joy bounding ahead of us. "Was she lost, too?" Angelica asked.

"Yes, Joy was lost, too. She was Matt's dog."

As I opened the door, the impact of what I was doing struck me. I had acted on an impulse, and I wasn't sure where this impulse was leading. "Would you like something to drink or a bite to eat?"

She was looking about the hall. "No, I don't think so." She ran her hand over the surface of one of the pair of Goddard tables. "It's nice to have roots, isn't it?"

"I suppose so. Mine are rather one-sided, though; as you know, they spring from only one side of the family tree."

"Yes, I remember. Do you always go out of your way to remind people of that?—What happens to all this, with Matt's death?"

"He willed it to me—to do with as I please."

"And now the roots go down on both sides of the tree. . . . And what happens to us?" she asked.

"What do you mean, what happens?"

"You pick up a lost dog, and it's yours, you become responsible for it. When you discover it has no owner, you feed it and look it over and eventually you keep it or take it to the Bide-A-Wee and ask them to find a home for it or dispose of it. —Don't look so serious, I was only pulling your leg. I'm a special kind of a lost dog. Any time you want, you can show me to the door and I'll find my way home; I've done it before. —I just wondered, what happens next?"

"Nothing," I told her.

She raised her brows. *"Nothing* never happens between a man and a woman who have once been lovers. There's a potential between them; it either repels or attracts."

"You can't be always right." I took her arm and guided her to the stairway. "I'm going to put you to bed and tomorrow morning —very late tomorrow morning I would suggest—I'll see you at breakfast and we'll talk about a lot of things."

I grabbed a dressing gown and a pair of pajamas out of my room and led her into the guest room. "If you want anything or get scared, yell. If you yell loud enough you may wake Mrs. Haines. She'll look like she'll bite your head off—the likelihood is she won't, she never does."

Her eyes held mine, then she put out her hand, and it was damp and cold. She closed the door and I went back to my room. I glanced at my watch; it seemed hardly worth the effort to go to bed. I undressed and showered and was standing smoking a cigarette and staring out the window for the second time that night. There were still lights burning in houses in the village. Joy gave a low bark, and I turned and saw Angelica standing in the doorway.

"One of the troubles with lost dogs," she said, "they hate to be alone. Your light was on, and anyway you hadn't gone to bed. I'm out of cigarettes. Have you got one?"

I lit a cigarette and gave it to her, and then handed her a fresh pack. She slipped them into her pocket and walked to the window where I had been standing. "The night has a beauty of its own," she finally said. "Darkness is selective and can find loveliness even in the drab and ugly." Then she slowly turned and came back across the room. She stopped by the bedside table and her hand went out and crushed her cigarette in the ash tray; even after it was out she continued to grind its stubbed end into the glass until finally it crumbled in her fingers. Then with a sudden decisiveness she switched off the light. Only the fitful glow of the burned-out fire lit the room, that and the light which is no light that filtered in from the night. Then in the almost-darkness her embrace found mine. After an instant she held herself away, an ember flared and her eyes were tear-brimmed, and she shook her head as if to clear them. When I kissed her, her lips were salt-stained and they trembled for an instant, with some emotion which gripped them, before they took fire and passion captured them.

The room was still, the last embers of the fire were gray, the curtains stirred as some vagrant breeze moved through them, and beyond, a pale light fringed the eastern sky. Only an unheard and now quiet breathing betrayed the figure beside me. "What are you running away from?" she finally asked.

"What makes you think I'm running away from anything?"

"I'm a specialist in the business of running away from things,"

197

she said. "I've been running for years. I know all the symptoms and all the clues. I could qualify as an expert witness in the courts."

"Remind me to have my counsel call you in the case of *John Milnor vs Life* when it comes up on the calendar. I assume you'd be a friendly witness."

"Yes, I'd be friendly," she said. "Benefits remembered. Who is it? Someone I know?"

"Who?"

"The woman."

"Wouldn't it be a simple world if everything in life could be resolved into such simple terms—into this?" I evaded.

"There are other terms," she said. "Many other terms; most of them gravitate back to what you call *this*."

I reached over to the night table and pulled two cigarettes from the pack and lit one of them for her. "And everything can be resolved into sex?"

"No, not when you put it that way." There was an instant's glow about her face and then an orange arc as her hand lowered. "But in another sense, perhaps," she went on. "Human beings trying to find themselves through their completion with others; trying to discover a reason and a purpose for life, and for living."

I hummed a line from a popular song of a few years back: "Man needs woman, and woman needs man."

"Or a reasonable facsimile thereof," she said. "You almost have the line right. They need the other half of themselves. It's the girl who's staying in the room next to mine, isn't it? My room shares the same bath, her door was open. I suppose I was curious."

"Aren't you making up a lot out of thin air?"

"I can tell you a great deal about her; maybe even some things you don't realize yourself." The bed moved as she left me and I could dimly see her as she slipped on the robe she had worn, and then she was silhouetted against the light as she crouched on the window seat. "She's young and lovely enough not to have to worry about beauty. She's younger, I'm afraid, than I ever was. And she doesn't live here, she hasn't moved into the room; and yet she's moved into it more than a guest who stays for just the night. And she's a virgin—well, she probably is. She is in her mind anyway; her underclothes are simple and sweet; they're the kind of things

198

a woman wears when she knows they will never be seen by a man."

"You're very extrasensory this evening."

"I'm always very extrasensory," she replied. "Don't you remember?—Some people can play instruments, some can paint; I'm sensitive to people and to things about me."

"Sensitive perhaps, but certainly not very reticent."

"If I have any virtues, reticence is not one of them. Anyway I was curious, and as I told you I was looking for cigarettes." The morning was really breaking and the room was beginning to flood with light, but her face was still in shadow. "And she's in love with you." She ended so low I could hardly hear her.

"And just how do you arrive at that conclusion? Did you find it traced in lipstick in strong angular letters across the mirror?"

"It might as well have been." Her voice remained muted; she wasn't being put off by my casual lightness. "There's a fragrance, an aroma, an effluvia about a woman in love. It's something that can't be put into words, but it leaves its mark on her possessions, even on an empty room. Don't laugh—I'm not being nasty, and I haven't been reading books with Latin titles by German professors. There's a resonance, an overtone; your senses can hear it."

"And of course," I defended, "propinquity being the essence of these matters and my room being down the hall, I am the guilty one."

"Is anyone guilty in *these matters*, as you call them?"

"But why pick me?" I asked. "If she's in love, why not assume that she's in love with some college boy her own age?"

She leaned forward and her fingers worked nervously with a ring she wore. "There was a handkerchief in her bedside table with initials *J.M.* on it. —Women are such sentimental animals, and they're unbelievably primitive; they're fetichists. Men created the gods, but women offered the first votaries, wore the first amulets, hoarded nail parings and hair clippings of the ones they loved and used them in their witchcraft. Somewhere in the possession of every woman in love is some gift or something personal of the man she loves; she may have to steal it, but she keeps it near her."

The light caught her hand and was dimly reflected from the dull black pearl she was twisting on her finger, and I remembered the day I had given it to her. She seemed conscious of my glance and

199

her fingers turned the pearl until it was on the inside of her palm. That was why I hadn't noticed it earlier.

She jumped in ahead of me. "You mustn't read too much into things. It was just an accident that I was wearing it tonight. It's simple and I like it, and occasionally I wear it. And anyway we were discussing other things. Are you in love with her?"

"Look here, it's quite possible for a man to be my age and be reasonably adjusted to life and quite happy in the way of his life, without being in love."

"It's possible," she said. She shivered and pulled the robe closer about her and then got up and crossed to the sofa in front of the fireplace. "Somehow I get the picture that you went in to see her tonight; but you didn't see her. I suppose you have a sense you're too old; that she's fresh and inexperienced, and you've touched too much of life and your emotions are used."

"Aren't they?"

"No, my darling. Your emotions are very clear and clean and honest. But to go on. —You probably also feel that it would be somehow wrong to be a parent with more than forty years between you and your child; that someday this girl will still be young and you will be an old man. It always amazes me how little men really know about women."

"It amazes me how much women *think* they know about men," I told her. "What you've said could be a reasonable catalogue of what I might feel, assuming I were in love with her."

"Except . . ."

"Except what?" I demanded.

"Except that nothing is reasonable between a man and a woman."

"Certainly this night hasn't been an excursion into reason," I wryly commented.

"It hasn't been too successful an excursion into emotion, either," she said.

"You mean that . . ."

"I mean that a woman always knows, when she holds a man in her arms."

"You sound," I said, "as if you were trying to throw me at her head."

200

"I could no more send you to her, than I could keep you from going to her."

"The heart is its own wayward master," I chided.

"Something like that," she said. "Do you know why you brought me here tonight?"

"You said you were lost," I told her.

"And I told you that you owed me nothing. Was it something of an emotional rebound?"

"No," I said.

"And when a little while ago we were together, was it her you were seeking and finding through me?"

I crossed to stand in front of her at the couch. The room was now light and as she lay stretched out under the silk robe it was as if I could still see her body. "I'm not that complicated," I told her.

Her eyes were closed and all of the strain and tension seemed drained from her face. I paced over to the window and back. She said something, but I didn't hear it. "What did you say?" I asked.

Again her voice was very low. "Could it be that we're both lost, we're waifs and strays; spiritually and emotionally homeless? I ran away once, before I hurt you; I think I'd be strong enough to do it again. . . ." Her words trailed off and, as I watched, her hand relaxed, opened and slipped to her side. I got the blanket from the foot of the bed and drew it over her. She didn't waken.

"Damn it!" I said under my breath. "There's something about this house that makes women want to sleep on couches!" I lowered the shades and, picking up my clothes, went out into the hall. Elizabeth's room had been partly dismantled; the painters were going to work in there in the next day or two. Angelica might waken and come back into the guest room, so I picked out Frankie's room.

It was already seven. I tossed my things across the bed; there'd only be time for a shower before getting downstairs ahead of Mrs. Haines' morning ritual of the coffee tray. As I was putting my clothes on a few moments later, I slipped open the drawer of Frankie's bedside table and found it—a square of folded linen with my initials embroidered on it. It was crushed and still unlaundered from the night I had brought her back from Poughkeepsie. It smelled a little of tobacco, as a handkerchief will that has been in a man's pocket, and faintly of lilac. Folded in it was a sprig of holly. I put them back and went downstairs, closing the door of my bedroom as I passed it.

I stuck my head in the kitchen. "I'm down, Mrs. Haines. I'll have my breakfast in the office," I called. The rattle of a dish and an enigmatic grunt told me I had been heard. A few moments later she put a tray down on the desk in front of me. Out of habit she took inventory. "I forgot the sugar," she announced, as she clumped out of the room. Whatever was upsetting her, there was considerably more in store to upset her before this morning was over. She was back on the heels of my thought, and slapped the sugar bowl down on the tray so hard that the cream jug jumped and spilled. It was as if she had said, "There!" Then she took a position opposite me and folded her hands under her apron. That was the way Mrs. Haines usually started things. For those who insist that "York State" people are not New Englanders, let's say that there are nevertheless certain regional tribulations attached to having them for help; they're not servants and they get more ingrown and ingrained than family.

"There's a woman in your bedroom," she threw the bombshell. "Do you expect me to get breakfast for her?"

"Assuming that was a question," I told her, "yes." I heard one of the men in the kitchen. "If that's Will Talcott ask him to wait for me; I'm going over to the barns as soon as I've finished breakfast."

She was back a few moments later to snatch up the tray before I had finished my coffee. "Will Talcott says there's a man waiting for him at the barn. He'll see you when you get there."

I noticed a big new Buick by the barn when I arrived, and I found Will and a stranger leaning over a pen partition looking at some young stock inside. The stranger nodded to me but continued his talking with Will. "Nine hundred dollars a head is the best price you can make?"

Will nodded. "If it's too much, why don't you think it over? Or maybe, if you look around some more, you might find somebody who has some stock you like at a lower price."

The man turned to me. "Are you Milnor?" he asked.

It was my turn to nod.

"People say you own this place now."

202

"So people say." I could see Will smiling at me over his shoulder. "If I take all four of these heifers, what kind of a price would you make—if I take all four?" the man asked.

I could see Will shaking his head. I discovered why farmers chew strands of hay when they trade; it isn't because they like the taste of it, but it gives them something to stall with and a ruminative appearance at one and the same time. "Thirty-six hundred," I told him.

"Damn it, you people are hard to do business with. I ask you to sweeten the bargain and you don't shade it a cent."

"Look, my friend, if you don't think these heifers are worth nine hundred dollars apiece, I'd advise you not to buy them. If you do think they're worth that, I'd suggest you buy one or as many as you can afford."

"Thirty-two hundred. That's my top price," the man said.

I chewed on the strand of hay.

"I'll split the difference," he offered.

I remembered standing beside Old Matt in this very barn and it was his words not mine that I spoke. "Mister, there's one difference between buying something at the Tracy farm and elsewhere —and it doesn't split. There's one price and you, the devil or God Almighty will pay it or you don't buy."

"I won't pay it!" the man said. He stuck his wallet in his pocket and stomped out of the barn.

"You'll do," Will Talcott remarked.

I could hear the motor of the big Buick start in the yard. "I don't think I've got quite the Tracy knack for cinching a deal," I said.

Will cocked an ear. "The car's still standing there. He's thinking it over." He ran his hand over the flank of one of the animals. "When you've got something better than the next man, that's what cinches the deal."

The motor was silent now and the man was stomping his way back into the barn. He took his wallet out and extracted a check and handed it to me. "I'll take 'em," he said. "I'll haul 'em this afternoon."

I glanced at the check. It bore the day before's date and was made out for the full amount of thirty-six hundred. When the man finally left, Will glanced at me. "Maybe you inherited the knack for cinching deals, too," he said, and then his expression sobered. "It's not exactly my business," he went on, "but in one way and another, Mrs. Haines talks a lot. It's sort of like she was born with her tongue hinged in the middle."

"I see what you mean," I told him.

"I don't mean anything," he said. "By the way, Alf Adams was in this morning. He lost two of his cows yesterday; wire in a carload of Canadian hay he bought. I told him he better throw it away; damned expensive hay, anyway you look at it." He worked the stem of grass from one side of his mouth to the other and his hand continued to stroke the heifer that was nuzzling against him.

"Have we any bailed hay to spare, to help him out?"

"We've got some to spare. But he's in more trouble than hay, I'm afraid. He's overextended himself, a lot of paper at the bank, and that new barn piled up some other debts, too. This wasn't a good crop year, bought hay makes expensive milk and his production's fallen off. It'll fall off more with two cows less in the line."

"You picture him to be a pretty poor risk."

"Less of a risk than most. He's one of the best farmers in the county and he's got enough drive and ambition for two like him. He's down to see the bank. I told him he ought to see you."

"Is he going to?"

"I don't know. He would have gone to Matt, but he doesn't know you."

"Do you?"

"I'm getting to," he said.

We checked in at the milk barn and then he walked with me out to the road. "How many cows do we have coming fresh in the next week or so?" I asked.

He glanced at me and then took a notebook out of his pocket. "Eight—no nine, in the next week or ten days."

"How do *we* stand on production?"

"We always aim to exceed our quotas." He smiled. "It's a Tracy policy. I'll get them together so you can look them over."

Mrs. Haines must have heard me come home for as I put a call in to Jim Fletcher at the bank, she bustled in with a breakfast tray.

I raised my brows. "I've already eaten, or did you forget?"

"There's not much I forget," she said. She put a cup of coffee in front of me. "She's up," she announced with thin-lipped recti-

204

tude. "She's taking a bath—in the guest bathroom. At least she's got that much manners."

I glanced at the tray; it bore what you'd call a full-blooded farm breakfast, including griddlecakes and sausage. Angelica, I seemed to remember, ran to orange juice, a single thin slice of dry toast and black coffee. "And your impulse stems from manners or curiosity?" I asked.

"No matter what she is, she's still a guest in this house."

She flounced out of the room as Jim Fletcher's voice came over the phone. "I was going to call you this morning," he said. "Has Walter Semple come to see you yet?"

"No, and I don't think he'd have the gall to come up here."

Jim laughed. "You don't know Walter. Gall is something he has plenty of. He has a new bug in his bonnet. He wants to trade. Sam Jennings died last week; that leaves the Sheriff's office looking for a candidate. Walter has an idea."

"And?"

"Oh, I just thought I'd let you know what he had in mind."

"Well, he hasn't come to see me, but what I called you about was Alf Adams. How much of his paper does the bank hold?"

"He's in the other room, I was talking to him when your call came in. Twenty-six thousand all told in mortgage and notes."

"Are you going to renew?"

"We shouldn't renew the notes," Jim said. "They're overdue and he's in heavy. It wouldn't take more than a nudge to put him under."

"What's wrong, do you think?"

"Well, I'd say he overreached himself to begin with. And then a bad crop year. No one was expecting God Almighty to turn off the rain supply."

"How much does he need?"

"He thinks three or four thousand will see him through. But I don't know. I'm afraid he'll need more help than that."

"I guess you better give it to him," I said. "I'll sign his notes. You needn't mention that, though. And suggest to him that he stop by and see me."

"Umm," Jim digested the thought. "I guess that's what Matt would have done. The worst that could happen is you'd end up owning Adams' farm."

"That's the worst that could happen," I concurred.

205

When I got upstairs I could hear Mrs. Haines talking to Angelica in the guest room. I couldn't hear what they were saying, it was just the drone of Mrs. Haines' voice. When I'd shaved and put on a fresh shirt the drone had ceased and I knocked on Angelica's door.

"Come in!" she called.

She was in her skirt and was brushing her hair in front of the mirror, almost as a man might brush his hair. She was lovely.

She saw me looking at her and, half turning away, pulled on her blouse and buttoned it. "That's strange," she finally said. "I'm a little embarrassed with you this morning."

"I see Mrs. Haines relented and decided to feed you after all." I indicated the breakfast tray; even the griddlecakes were gone.

"Now that you mention it," Angelica smiled, "her attitude was that of matron in a jail when she came in. Then she started to talk and we had quite a talk; or rather she had quite a talk. —As you may gather, she disapproves."

"Even if there were nothing to have disapproved of, Mrs. Haines would have kept her dissenting franchise."

"I learned a lot, about a lot of things," Angelica said.

"Such as?"

"Such as, that her primary concern was to determine how bad I would be for you." Angelica folded a scarf and tied it about her throat. "I don't think she could quite make up her mind in the end. I never could quite make up my own mind, either, darling. She told me a lot about Frankie, in an indirect sort of way."

"Yes?"

"Mrs. Haines hasn't made up her mind about Frankie. She distrusts *furriners,* but as between the two of us she has her *druthers,* I imagine."

Angelica went over to the window and stared out. "I'm beginning to sense a lot of things about you I never understood before. Elizabeth, and what this place means to you, and this way of life you lead up here, the permanence, and the security and the purpose of it. I had the sense this morning looking out over this hill that for one who came here and for whom it might be right, it could spell passionate living, and great peace and serenity and contentment as well."

"Look, Angelica, do you suppose we could . . ."

206

She turned from the window and faced me and her gesture cut me off. "Pick up where we once left off? I don't know. Last night and this morning, I've wondered. Let's talk about it sometime."

"What do you mean, sometime?"

"When next we meet," she said. "I called the station. There's a train to New York in an hour's time."

"I'll drive you in to New York," I said.

"I'd prefer you didn't." She came to me; it was almost an embrace, but at the last moment her hands on my arms stayed it, and we stood there, very close and very far apart. "I told you last night, I'm a special kind of a lost dog. I'll find my way home, I've done it before. And, as it ever was, you don't owe me anything; the debt was always mine."

"I remember last night what you said just after that. You said, 'What happens next?'"

She shrugged. "So much could happen, or so little. We mustn't tempt the fates by asking. I have an idea I'll be going away for a little while."

"Where?"

"Just away, nothing dramatic; I'm going to try to find myself and make friends with myself. It isn't good for a woman to be a tramp; though with you, my darling, it's exceedingly pleasant and almost painless. And then someday if you decide you want me, just whistle —I might come running back." She took my arm and started out of the room. As we passed the door of my bedroom she stopped and glanced in and then turned and kissed me, and I felt her lips tremble beneath mine; and then before I could speak she hurried down the stairs.

Mrs. Haines was standing at the door talking to a man who stood blocked in the sunlight, and it was only when we came up to them that I saw it was Walter Semple. He looked from me to Angelica and back to me. "If I could see you for just a few moments?" he asked.

I decided that after all I had underestimated his gall. My impulse was to throw him out of the house. "I'll wait in the library," Angelica said.

"I didn't realize you wanted to go to the Assembly yourself," Semple said when we were alone. "Good Lord, man, if you'd said so, I'd have gladly stepped aside. We old-timers are always glad to make way for the new blood coming along."

"You're misinformed," I told him. "I don't want to go to Albany." I was conscious that he was looking beyond me at Angelica, who was standing at the library window.

He looked back at me. A smile started to work about his lips and then he seemed to think better of it.

"There isn't anything to this gossip that Mun Allen is being considered?"

"The way I heard it," I told him, "it wasn't gossip."

He studied me for a long moment. "Look, what I'm going to ask you . . ."

I opened the front door. "I haven't anything to do with who will be sheriff of this county, but if I did you know what my answer would be, and someday you're going to realize that you're not welcome in this house or on this land."

For an instant I hoped that he would speak his mind and give me the justification to throw him out of the house. Instead, without so much as a word he strode back to his car and started away.

"I heard part of that," Angelica said when I rejoined her. "I don't like that man. Can he hurt you?"

"His kind?" I laughed.

"I imagine my coming downstairs with you gave him ideas; his eyes when they look at you are like hands touching you."

I glanced at my watch. "We have more than an hour before your train, if you still insist on going back by train."

"It will be by train," she said.

"Shall we take a drive then?"

I thought she hadn't heard me and then her gaze seemed to return from some reverie. "Yes, let's," she said. "We took another drive once, only you were taking the train that time, and we were saying good-by, though neither of us admitted it. I wonder if we're saying good-by again this time?"

There was a knock at the front door. "If that son of a bitch has come back—" I muttered. "I'll get it," I called to Mrs. Haines. Only it wasn't Semple, it was Alf Adams standing there, and I could see his wife sitting in the car.

"I could come by later," he said, including Angelica in his glance. "Jim Fletcher told me you wanted me to stop by."

208

My impulse was to ask him to stop back later, but when you see a man in trouble you don't like to stall him off. "No, come on in now. And ask your wife to come in; it can't be too pleasant for her sitting out in the car."

"Well, I'd rather..."

"She can sit in the other room while we talk," I suggested. His face lightened and I had the sense from what I knew of Adams that he wanted to talk to me alone; that he was the kind of a man who found it bitter to parade his defeat in front of his wife.

"Mrs. Adams, Miss Barnes," I introduced them, and then went back to the office.

"Fletcher said he would renew my paper, but that's all he could do and that you would go signer for me," he started. "I told him I'd rather that waited until after I talked with you."

"Do you want to talk first?" I asked him.

"I'd prefer to. About the notes—he says he doesn't think the bank should lend me any more money. I'm sort of in up to my neck, and you might say I'm fresh out of collateral."

"That might depend on the point of view," I told him. "From things that my brother Matt has said—" The acknowledgment had slipped out unnoticed and I saw that he remarked it. "From what my brother Matt has said to me," I repeated, "you have some other very important collateral. Your land's one of the best farms in the town."

"It's mortgaged," he said.

"Only within reason, considering its value. And he thought you were one of the best farmers in the county."

He spread his hands out and I was conscious for the moment that my own were soft in comparison. "You don't borrow money on these," he said.

"Maybe not," I told him, "but you might go into partnership with them. Matt thought you were right to go in debt to build up your farm; the day of the hand-to-mouth farmer has passed in this part of the world. Farming's got to be big business or it's no business; but he was afraid you might get caught in the middle before you got on your feet. I think he would have done something like I'm going to suggest. We have sixteen cows and heifers out of a new breeding line. Matt thought he had a winner. You take six of those animals and a bull that's the right breeding for them, and

209

we'll prove the line out together. We'll do it quicker, and two heads'll be better than one. Extend your loans and get a few thousand more at the bank, and I'll sign for it. We have some extra hay in the barn, so you can haul this afternoon."

"What do I use for money?" he asked. "That's a big deal you're offering."

"You don't use anything for money. You take a chance. If the breeding line proves out you buy the stock for what they're worth. If it doesn't prove out, you've bought yourself six grade cows, and you'll pay for them what they're worth. Either way I don't stand to lose."

"I might go broke," he reminded me.

"I suppose that's a possibility. But look at it this way. According to Fletcher, you're broke now, so what have you got to lose?"

He put his hand across the desk. "You've got yourself a partner, John Milnor; and when the day comes I don't stand in your obligation you got yourself a friend."

It was a fine distinction in spiritual bookkeeping, and I could see what had made Matt like him. "I'm even up on the day," I told him, and picked up the phone to call Will Talcott at the barns.

Alf looked at me. "I passed Walter Semple as he came down the road." His comment was oblique, and I thought he was going to say something more, but at that moment Will Talcott answered.

Sylvia Adams and Angelica joined us in the hall when we came out of the office. I could see Sylvia search Alf's face.

"I think everything's going to be all right," Alf said.

Sylvia grasped my hand and said, "Thank you."

Suddenly I realized I hadn't introduced Alf. "Miss Barnes, may I present my cousin Alfred Adams?"

Alf's glance caught mine. "It's a very distant relationship. I've never traded on it."

"No, you never have," I told him.

As we were driving down to Haviland, Angelica looked up at me. "So that's the way it's going to be?" she said.

"What?"

"Your life. You've finally decided to come to anchor and make peace with John Milnor. When did it happen?"

"I suppose it happened a little while ago, but I wasn't sure of it until this morning," I told her.

210

"It's a good life; it has blood in its veins and three dimensions. This could be enough." I looked at her and she laughed. "I wasn't thinking of last night, or including myself, when I said that." And then her thoughts seemed to veer. "She's a strange woman."

"Who?"

"Mrs. Adams, and she's married to a strange man."

"What's so strange about them?"

"They're so clear and so near the surface. When we met I had a sense that she was looking right through me, and for an instant I was embarrassed; it was as if she had seen us in bed together last night. Women can feel that about each other."

"Oh, come now."

"No, it's true."

"And I suppose looking at her you could tell whether she had been to bed with a man?"

"That's strange, because I could feel that. Her man had been in trouble and he'd come to her. At least there aren't any frustrations there. Is he really your cousin?"

"You heard what he said," I told her. "It's very distant. The blood mingled a long way back, I guess."

"You come of good stock, John. I'd like to have his kind on my side when I needed it. I had a sense that this morning was the first time you'd ever used the word *cousin* to him."

"It was," I admitted. "There was never any reason to before. I've only known him very casually, but he's in trouble and it sort of slipped out."

She glanced at her watch. "We have a few minutes. Could we stop and talk before we get to the station?"

I pulled the car off to the side of the road. "Did you prove anything to yourself last night?" she asked.

"I wasn't aware of trying to prove anything," I said.

"I was," she told me. "I had a sense that you were trying to prove to yourself that you didn't love Frankie; that you walked with too many ghosts of the past; that there were too many tangled skeins of emotion." She put her hand on my arm. "I'm afraid it's later than I thought; too late to talk out things like this. We'd better hurry."

The train for a change was on time, but we still had five or ten minutes to spare and we used it up pacing the platform. Pop

Sanford and Jim Fletcher passed down the street, looked at us and, seeing that I was with a stranger, they nodded. I waved to them, but they kept on their way.

"Should we have been devious?" Angelica asked. "Maybe I should have let you drive me back to town after all. Your handing a strange woman onto the New York train may set a lot of tongues wagging and heads bobbing in your town of Haviland."

"I doubt it," I told her. "But if they enjoy wagging and bobbing, let them."

The train coming into the station cut short this fruitless conversation. As it pulled out, I turned around and saw Walter Semple leaning against the corner of the station reading a newspaper. I had a sense that he was waiting for me to see him and then he folded the paper, stared at me for an instant, and walked off down the street.

Thirteen

Three days later I had a letter from Elizabeth. Before I opened it I glanced through the rest of the mail to see if there was a letter from Frankie. There wasn't.

Elizabeth was going through her usual rebellion at pampering herself. It was foolish to have come, and a waste of time, and her health was splendid. She went on to say that she would plan to stay on anyway for Frankie's sake; that the shock of Matt and Alyse was only now coming to the surface. She mentioned that she had suggested that I join them after a few days, but that Frankie was so listless that that hadn't even stirred her interest, so I could see how low and unstrung the girl really was.

Then a week later she wrote:

> An old friend of yours, Angelica Barnes, was here for two days on her way driving through to Florida. We dined together twice. I was rather pleased for Frankie's sake to have someone a little closer to her generation to break the tedium of her isolation with me. They spent the better part of the time together on the beach in the sun, which I gratefully avoided; and Frankie's spirits revived. There was the natural letdown afterwards when she returned to being "old ladies' companion" to me. The Barnes girl seemed nicer than when you used to see so much of her. I don't suppose nicer is the word, but more at home with herself and less brittle; less combative with life and more acquiescent. Your reports of the Hill are sketchy, but I fill in the gaps. In the matter of Alf Adams I think you did what Matt would have done. . . .

There was more, but it was just personal stuff about the household, and how much better she was feeling, and she'd be coming back any day now. There was just so much of resort life she could take without rebellion.

A day or two afterwards, I found a letter beside my place at dinner with a Florida postmark and Angelica's square bold script across the envelope. Mrs. Haines glanced at it pointedly as she served me. I could see her curiosity working double time as I put it aside to read later in the privacy of the library.

It must have been a hard letter for Angelica to write.

My dearest John,

This is in the nature of a bread and butter letter. Thank you for coming upon me in a bad moment. Thank you for the warm friendliness of your handclasp, and for the brief hours that evoked the memory of all that we once touched, of all that almost was between us. But thank you, most of all, for holding me in your arms; there has always been more than lust between us. Yet even the lust was touched and fused with the strange, incomplete love we have known.

I told you I was running away. I was, my darling, from myself as well as from you. And now, I have stopped running. I have come to a place where the appointment with myself is the peaceful but desolate last inhabitable sandspit on the Atlantic Coast. Before me is a limitless ocean, behind me is the life of Angelica Barnes, which I have never dared to contemplate in full awareness before.

I might have fled in any direction; it was the accident of your mentioning where Elizabeth and Frankie were that led me here, because I wanted to know what I was getting into, or had gotten into, or should stay out of. If this is incoherent or doesn't make sense, neither did my reasons or my impulse, for I intended to stop over only for the night, but I stayed two days before going on. Elizabeth is too wise a woman to have believed that my driving through was only a coincidence, so I told her that I had bumped into you, and that you had mentioned where she was, and it had seemed a pleasant idea to stop

214

and say hello on my way south. There was still a question in her eyes, so I told her the rest of it, or rather as much of the rest of it as she would think it proper for me to tell her—simply that you had driven me up to the Hill and put me up for the night. We were alone, naturally, when I told her that.

With Frankie, my relationship was simpler—on the surface, that is. I was someone who had been a friend of Matt's and had known Alyse, and, not being exactly an elderly woman, I was within reach of her generation as well. We spent two days pretty much together, swimming and lying on the sand. It was a baffling experience. She seemed so young, so heartbreakingly young, and then suddenly, on the afternoon of the second day, she interrupted something I was saying and asked, "Why are you running away from him?"

I was taken aback, but I managed to make the appropriate denials. Throughout the conversation that followed, however, there was very little I could say, so I'll just give you the gist of what she said.

She started off with the unvarnished assumption that I was in love with you, and, moreover, that you had been my lover; and then without being conscious of the subtlety of her thought, she phrased it another way, she said that I had been your mistress. The old-fashioned word threw me off, and yet in our mixed-up world it seems a little more proper and organized, even, than what we were; and in some ironic way, it made me feel a little more decent about us. Not for long, though. I felt cheap and callow in my evasions, when she went on to say that we had made love the other night. "We needn't lie to each other," she told me, with scarcely a trace of emotion. "You slept with him. What has happened has happened. The point is that we both love him, and if either of us knew that he returned that love, we wouldn't be here, we'd be with him. But we don't know, and we've both run away."

There was nothing I could say to that, John. I sat there, like a child, while she became, suddenly, the wise and penetrating woman. She said that you and I were in

215

love once before, but not enough in love, because I wasn't good for you. "The question is," she said, fixing me with her straight, disconcerting stare, "are you good for him now? I know I would be. But if I thought you were better for him than I, I would give up. I have to know it, though, and until I do, I'm your adversary and competitor. It won't be an even fight. I have a few advantages, but you have most of them. For one thing, you're beautiful; I'm too young to be beautiful. For another, you've slept with him—he could have had me, but he wouldn't take me. And finally, you're as polished and experienced as a race horse." She stood up at that point, and pulled her robe about her. "I'm only a gangling colt going into her maiden race—but I'll run a hell of a race, and you might as well know it." Then she put out her hand to me. "The strange thing is, I like you." Without another word, she turned and walked back to the hotel.

And here endeth my tale. Except to say that the strange thing is that I like her too, John. I would like to change places with her, and be able to start my life over, as she is starting hers. I might make fewer mistakes. But as I think about it, my darling, it wouldn't do much good, for I'd only fall in love with you again.

ANGELICA

The letter was still in my hand when Mrs. Haines came in.

"I came to give you this. Will Talcott just stopped by with it. He got it in this afternoon's mail." She held forth a letter in Frankie's handwriting, addressed to Talcott. "You'd better see what's in it," she said, and emptied an ash tray and dusted the table, while I glanced through it. It was a short note, merely requesting him to have the Jennings Place in order with the heat on and the beds made, and would he ask Mrs. Haines to be good enough to lay in a basic supply of canned goods? Her plans were uncertain, she added, and when she did arrive, it might be late at night.

"Well?" Mrs. Haines' lips were set. "What do you think of it?"

"What should I think of it?" I evaded. "After all, the Jennings Place belongs to Miss Frankie."

216

"That's not what I meant. I mean, what do you think of this business of her living down there alone when she's got here to stay, or the Big House?"

"For reasons which I imagine are utterly different from yours," I admitted, "I don't think much of the idea."

"If you ask me—" Mrs. Haines was always one to take a hand if you gave her a finger. "Isn't it just another case of Tracy bull-headedness, living in separate houses and not speaking to each other?"

I raised my brows. "Are you really expecting me to answer that question?"

"This foolishness of having the house ready so as she can move in!" Mrs. Haines snorted. "All I want is my instructions what I should do."

"From me?"

"From who else? If there's anyone to make decisions, you're it, as far as I can see."

"Then my decision is that Miss Frankie's instructions are quite clear," I ended the discussion.

Actually, I was as much in the dark as Mrs. Haines concerning this whim of Frankie's, and wrote a note to Elizabeth before I went to bed, asking her what it was all about. My letter missed her though. It crossed her trip north, and she was on the phone to me the following evening from New York, where she planned to stay a few days before coming back to Haviland. Frankie, she mentioned in passing, had stopped off in Pinehurst for a short visit with some friends, so I decided that there was no point in going into the subject over the telephone.

A couple of evenings later I came back from Poughkeepsie, where I had gone with Pop Sanford to the county court to clear up some matters relating to the probate of Matt's will, and walked into the house. Houses have vibrations, as if they become attuned to the people living in them; even before I called to her, I knew that Elizabeth had returned. Nothing had been moved, there was no clue of gloves or handbag on the console table; but the house was again full, where it had been empty during the past weeks.

She looked better, better than she had in months, but I was conscious of a strange constraint between us—not so much an obvious dis-ease, as an abnormal normality. We were neither of us in the custom of small talk, but it was small talk that passed between us at dinner, broken by Mrs. Haines' repeated and often unnecessary sorties from the kitchen. When Elizabeth very casually alluded to Angelica's visit, I was conscious of an immediate rearrangement of the dessert plates on the sideboard. Elizabeth seemed conscious of it too, because she veered off into some unimportant chitchat about her trip until Mrs. Haines finally went back to the kitchen.

As soon as we were alone, I said, "Angelica drove up here with me and spent the night, a little while before she went south."

"She told me that she had," Elizabeth said.

"She wrote me that she had told you."

Then Mrs. Haines bustled in with the salad, and Elizabeth said, "I think I got the idea of a place in the south out of my system—a warmer climate and a softer life, but on the whole I find it pretty dreary, and anyway I like bad weather."

Mrs Haines snorted in comment, and again retreated to the kitchen. "She's developing all of the reticent little ways of an F.B.I. agent," I commented. "I suppose I should have written you about Angelica."

"Only for the reason that it's uncomfortable to be with people, and not be implemented to cope with situations which might arise. But it really isn't necessary to explain. And anyway I doubt that you would be as explicit as Mrs. Haines was this afternoon. I tried to stop her, but it was no use, so I just closed my ears. Mrs. Haines is the perversion of the three monkeys. In the Tracy world she knows all, sees all, and tells all."

"You wanted something?" Mrs. Haines stuck her head in at the swinging door.

"Not a thing, thank you," Elizabeth told her.

"Oh? I thought I heard my name," she insisted.

"You did." Elizabeth smiled at her. "I was saying how beautifully you took care of everything while I was gone."

Mrs. Haines seemed a little undecided, as if she expected that there was more to this than met the eye. "I did my best," she threw back over her shoulder.

"You may have gathered that she's 'agin it,'" Elizabeth observed, when we had again earned a degree of privacy.

"And you?"

218

"Me? Neither for, nor against. I've come to believe that there are unique and particular circumstances which control each human heart and action."

I reached across the table and covered her hand with mine for an instant. The swinging door to the kitchen opened again, only this time it wasn't Mrs. Haines, it was Joy who pushed her way into the room. She went straight to Elizabeth's side with a tail-wagging welcome; and then, that amenity being served, crossed to the window and put her head on the sill for a moment, staring out into the darkness before she came back to me, and sat pressing against my leg. I patted her head. "The wounds heal and the empty spaces fill, and we make do with what we have to, don't we, old girl?"

"If she could answer you," Elizabeth said quietly, "I think she'd say that the heart, once given, can never be wholly given again."

I made no reply, but as we were walking into the library I said, elliptically, "You were referring to more than Joy."

"If the thought has verity . . ." She left her answer uncompleted.

"What about Frankie?" I asked.

"It would be easy to evade you, and ask you what you mean," she said after a moment's pause.

"Don't. I want to know what's going on with the girl."

"The girl is a very unhappy woman." Elizabeth spoke slowly as if she were trying to organize her thoughts. "I'm afraid you have to face the fact, John, that she was always more than normally grown up for her age. The terrible shock of Matt's and Alyse's going merely hastened the maturity of her feelings toward you."

I started to speak but Elizabeth brushed my protest aside. "Oh I agree that it started out in a very young and obvious way," she anticipated me. "You were an image of romance to her, the Prince Charming, the Knight in Shining Armour, the *Chevalier sans Reproche*."

"All of which was really none of my doing—" I managed to get in.

"I dare say not. But after all, we're not trying to establish culpability."

"Just a case of negligence," I commented wryly. "Just the same, you haven't answered my question yet."

"You've been doing a lot of interrupting," Elizabeth reminded me. "Explicitly, what would you like to know?"

219

"Firstly, what do you think of this business of her living at the Jennings Place?"

"Not very much," she admitted. "She's too young to be living there by herself."

"That's my thought."

"Wait a moment, I don't think we're talking about the same thing. I have no doubt at all that she's quite old enough to take care of herself. What I mean is that she's too young, too outpouring a person to immerse herself in loneliness and introversion."

"You did."

"I tried to," she amended. "The cases aren't similar, though. I was hurt in a different way. I had to crawl off by myself and lick my wounds. Even so, it didn't work."

"And it won't work for Frankie," I said with finality.

"No, I imagine not for long," Elizabeth murmured.

"Look here, don't you go getting any ideas—"

"I haven't any ideas at all."

I got out my pipe. "When will she be coming back?"

"I don't think she knows, really. A day or two before we left she talked with me, and said that she wanted to get off the late train in Haviland some evening without anyone knowing, and take a taxi to her own house and discover whether she was as self-sufficient as she thought she was."

"It's a damnfool thing to do!" I exploded.

"Possibly," Elizabeth commented.

"Like a girl scout camping in the woods to see whether she's afraid of the dark. She'll never stick it."

"Possibly," Elizabeth repeated herself.

"A very agreeable mood you're in tonight."

"Would you have me any other way?"

"You know damn well what I mean—and don't say *possibly!* The point is, what am I supposed to do about all this?"

Elizabeth lifted her brows. "It hadn't occurred to me that you were supposed to do anything about all this. When Matt left her the Jennings Place, wasn't it implicit that she live there?"

"Yes, but I never thought she'd really go through with it. Look, did what happened between me and Angelica—"

Elizabeth stopped me with a gesture. "I spent the best part of this afternoon *not* hearing from Mrs. Haines what happened between you and Angelica, and I don't intend to discuss it with you either, John."

"So you do disapprove."

"You're not and never will be old enough to put words into my mouth. Let's say our last about this, and let me be the one to say it. I don't approve or disapprove. Give me a cigarette."

"You don't smoke."

"Occasionally I do."

I held a match for her. "Only on state occasions, and at moments of crisis."

"Neither of which this is. But I've discovered that it makes it possible to choose your words more carefully."

Even an awkward gesture by a graceful woman is not unworthy of note. Her fingers held the cigarette rather as if it were a clinical thermometer, and she drew in the smoke much as one might taste a new condiment, then expelled it without inhaling, in a thin soundless whistle.

She was aware of my amusement. "By now I should have very carefully chosen my words," she said with a half-smile. "Yes, I was a little shocked, at first, just conventionally shocked, a carry-over of my generation. It seemed bad taste."

"For that aspect of it, I'm sorry."

"I don't mean you to be. It was my limitation. This is your house as much as it is mine. Under the circumstances, more than it is mine."

I stopped her with my hand on her shoulder. "Please—"

"Oh, I wasn't referring to the Tracy law of primogeniture," she laughed, "or if I was, it was only in passing and in humor—we seem to be so serious this evening. What I mean is, this is your home because you were raised in it, born in it—I told you it was my limitation," she finished lamely. "Don't make me preach."

"You're not. We both know that morality isn't a code of rules laid down by others."

"Thank you. That makes it easier for me to say that it must be the standard of each individual's conduct, and certainly its simplest, maybe its highest statement, is never to do anything that you would not do in your own home."

"It has been more crudely stated," I remarked dryly. "Something about a bird not fouling its own nest."

221

Elizabeth shrugged. "If you will. After all, there are few verities that haven't been reduced to earthy terms." She put the cigarette out in an ash tray. "And now I've had my say."

"You're talking like a remote Chinese sage."

"Am I? That's one of the prerogatives of age. When you've lived as long as I have, you realize every once in a while, that you've already spent more of your living than you have left to spend. And you like to leave everything orderly."

"Pretty involved. And slightly lugubrious."

"Not at all."

"Could it be that I'm one of the loose ends that bother you a little?" I asked after a moment.

"Not any more. I think you've pretty much found your bearings."

"You might better say my moorings, my *snug harbor.*"

"Why not? Every successful voyage has to have its home port, a place to start from and to return to."

"And through the twisted fates of a handful of people I have inherited mine—direction by devise!"

"It still rankles—"

I pretended not to have heard her.

"I don't see why it should," she went on. "You had achieved your direction before Matt's death. This place is only a part of it."

"I want to talk to you about Frankie," I said. "Somebody has to assume some sort of responsibility for her, and I think it's more your job than mine."

Elizabeth gathered up her glasses and handbag. Joy shifted to my side, sensing that her evening walk was in store.

"All right, we won't talk about Frankie," I said, and kissed her good night. "And don't revert to your generation and say that life has a way of working these things out."

"I wasn't aware that the verities changed with each generation." She smiled at me from the doorway.

The days that followed fell into an uneventful but satisfying pattern. I was getting to know my way about the problems of the farm, finding that so much of it had been part of the fabric of my growing up, and my life at Haviland. What was new was the burden of responsibility and daily accumulation of small decisions, all of them seeming, as is the way with the land, not to be of the day alone but extending forward into the cycle of the years; on a farm no day is of itself, it is involved with the larger flux of time. I suppose that is why those who work with the land will always be the political conservatives of the world; they are wary of dislocations of the pattern, of quick panaceas and facile remedies.

Without Will Talcott to frequently guide my decisions, it might have been much harder. He was an able second in command, with that peculiar genius of good seconds in command. When it came to breeding stock, for example, he would unobtrusively take more time in arriving at his conclusions, and I was aware that when he explained his reasoning, it was just his way of sharing the implements of his trade. He gave me, too, the curious unspoken sense of being accepted.

One afternoon as I was passing the old Jennings Place I saw the farm truck beside the road. I slowed to a stop. Will Talcott turned the corner of the house and called to me: "Just tidying up the place a bit, but there are a couple of things I'd like to go over with you."

He had one of the men spading manure into the flower beds and the place had assumed an ordered look.

"If it weren't for the rear end of a cow, the world would be a far less pretty place to live in," he observed laconically. "These foundation posts of the veranda are gone with dry rot." He drove his penknife almost to the hilt before he came to sound wood. "Depending on what you want and how long Miss Frankie will be living here, we could do a patch job and it would last for a while."

"Let's rip it out and do it right," I suggested.

"I figured that's what you'd want to do," he said. "And that answers my other questions, too. Those gutter and leader pipes were put in during the war when we couldn't get brass, and they're about shot."

"Get the place in first-rate shape," I told him.

"I figured it that way," he said.

That evening at dinner I reported to Elizabeth what was being done down at the Jennings Place. "I wish we had some idea of her plans," I said.

"I have. She's staying on in New York awhile. Someone she knows is ill and she's standing by for a bit."

"Little Miss Florence Nightingale might at least let me know where she is."

"I believe this is the first time you've asked," Elizabeth said. "She's at the St. Regis."

I could feel myself getting more and more nettled. "When did you last hear from her?"

"I had a letter yesterday and I spoke with her on the phone this afternoon."

"You're two of the most secretive damn females!"

"I'm not being secretive about anything," Elizabeth said. "I merely waited for you to ask."

Before I went to bed that night, I sat down at the typewriter and got off a letter to Frankie. It started off by being a works progress report on the Jennings Place, and then drifted into being a long letter about the farm and life in general—an effortless kind of writing, as if she were in the room and we were talking, and it was easy to talk with her. I glanced at what I'd written before I sealed the envelope, and had only a slight sense of being a fatuous uncle. I added a postscript to counteract the stuffiness, and put the letter in the mailbag to go out with the milk truck in the morning.

The following afternoon I had a letter from Frankie. Her first words made me realize that our letters had crossed.

DEAR JOHN:
I've started this letter to you a dozen times in the past few days, but it is something that can't be written; I have to see you and talk to you. It is important or I wouldn't ask you to spare the time and come without delay. I only pray that you will be understanding and not feel that I have intruded in what I have done.

FRANKIE

I read the letter over, and its second reading made no more sense than the first. I picked up the phone and put a call through to her in New York.

I only hope that you will be understanding and not feel that I have intruded. I was still in the dark—the OSS could have used such genius in indirection during the war.

After a moment or two, I could hear Helen at the Haviland

224

switchboard talking to the St. Regis operator, who finally came back with the information that the room didn't answer. I decided not to leave a message, and said that I'd put the call in later.

I went upstairs to Elizabeth's room. Constance and she were seated in front of the fire with the tea things laid out in front of them. I had forgotten that this was Wednesday. In the weeks since Elizabeth's return, Constance had formed the habit of inviting herself to tea every Wednesday.

"Have a cup?" Elizabeth invited.

"No, thanks," I said. "I just stopped in to ask you to read this letter, if you don't mind."

When she saw Frankie's handwriting, she lowered the sheet of blue notepaper to her lap. "I do mind," she said. "I've always had an aversion to reading other people's correspondence; the letter one writes to one person is never intended for another's eyes."

"You can read this one," I told her, "without any fear of invading privacy. I want to know if it makes any sense to you."

Constance's hand touched my arm. "When is Frankie coming back?" she asked.

I was surprised that she had recognized Frankie's angular script across the table. "I don't know," I told her.

"She ought to come back," she said. "She isn't ready to leave here and start her own life yet. It takes time to mend things. A lot of time."

"Yes," I said, "it does. Maybe Frankie's too young to realize it."

Constance gave a half-sigh, half-smile. "Poor John, you inherited quite a lot when you inherited the Tracy clan. A fine mixed-up kettle of fish. And you'll really have your hands full when Emmeline and Adelaide come back next summer." She turned my hand over and looked at it. "Perhaps not," she said.

Elizabeth put Frankie's letter on the table beside her. She had read it and seemed equally reluctant to discuss it, and when a few minutes later Mrs. Talcott came to take Constance home, she still evaded the subject. "A very remarkable woman, Constance," she said, after the door had closed behind them. "Very complicated, but very remarkable."

"She's both of those things," I agreed. "And now reaching down into this 'fine mixed-up kettle of fish,' what do you make of this

225

particular mess?" I picked up Frankie's letter and slipped it into my pocket.

"I make of it that Frankie has something to talk to you about, rather urgently."

"Thank you, Mrs. Watson, for clarifying everything. Now I know exactly as much as I did before. Do you suppose this damn-fool adolescent has got herself in some kind of a jam?"

I had the sense that Elizabeth was studying me before she spoke. "In the first place I don't think you feel Frankie is a *damn fool adolescent;* and in the second place a girl *getting herself in a jam* was, in my generation, a phrase of art, and I assume you use it with the same connotation. No, I don't think Frankie has got herself in a jam."

"Well, she's damn well into something, and what I want to know is, why the hell doesn't she bring her problems to you instead of me?"

"Your father," Elizabeth observed, "was always infuriated with the obscure, and when confronted with it, invariably reverted to profanity. He never discovered that the only thing it accomplished was to raise his blood pressure."

"All right. My blood pressure's down and I stand rebuked, but the question still remains—why doesn't she bring her problems to you instead of me?"

"It could possibly be, because they're your problems."

"How could they be mine?"

"Why don't you ask her?"

"Damn it!" The tea service rattled on the table as my hand slapped down. "Damn it," I repeated with exaggerated control, "I tried to telephone her, but she was out, of course."

"That *of course* is a completely male functioning of your mind, and I don't admire it. Is there any earthly reason that she should be in just because you called?" Elizabeth's voice carried an edge that made me realize that I hadn't inherited my temper solely from the Tracy side of my line; the Milnors had some salt in them, too. I lit a cigarette. "Do you have any idea what this is all about?" I finally asked her more reasonably.

"I have an idea, yes. But I'm afraid I can't talk to you about it."

"Why not?"

"Because I'd only be guessing. And it's something that Frankie apparently wants to discuss with you herself."

I'd lived with Elizabeth too long to try to budge her from a moral decision. I brushed my lips against her cheek. "You're probably right, old girl, you usually are."

"What are you going to do?"

"I'm going to change my clothes, throw some things in an overnight bag and drive to town."

"Good," she said. And then from a pattern of habit dating from my college days she added, "Don't drive too fast."

"I won't," I promised solemnly. "I'll look in on you before I go."

As I was closing my bag I thought back to a night some several months before when I had read another letter from Frankie and driven to New York. That first letter had been an appeal, too, but this one was different, there was an urgency about it. When I went back to Elizabeth to say good-by, I said, "Are you sure that there's nothing I should know before I meet Frankie? So that I can be a little forewarned?"

"I told you before, John, there's nothing I really know, I've just been putting things together."

"Everybody's being awfully mysterious—" I started to say, and stopped short. "By the way, who were the damned people you let her stop off with in White Sulphur?"

"A friend Frankie made at college. Her family have a house there. And I really don't think they were *damned*. They seemed quite nice and wholesome, if a little on the conservative side. She'd spent enough time with me, and I thought it would be a good thing for her to be with someone her own age for a change."

"Then you don't think there's some man or other at the bottom of all this?" I persisted.

"No, I don't think it's some man or other. But whatever it is, and if Frankie really is in trouble, be gentle with her. And bring her back here; this is her home."

"Then for all your putting-together, you're not so sure you do know what this is all about?"

"The older I get the less sure I am about anything. Now hurry along, but not too fast."

227

Fourteen

The clerk at the desk told me that Miss Dumont had left word for me to go right up. I knocked at the door, and Frankie's voice called, "Come in!" I don't know what I'd been expecting, but the complete normality of the scene threw me. Frankie was silhouetted against the window. "I got the message that you had phoned," she greeted me, "but when I called back Elizabeth told me you had already started into town."

Her voice was controlled and poised, and yet the room seemed filled with constraint, only a part of which I had brought in with me. She stood there, remote and unapproachable, her hands braced against the window sill. Only one table lamp was lit, and I had a sense that she had chosen the protection of semidarkness. I noticed with relief that though she looked a little pale and tense, her eyes were clear, and her shoulders straight and natural and not thrown back in a dramatic posture of courage.

"Will you have a drink, John?"

"Do you think I'll need one?" I heard the tone of my voice and it was none of the ones I had rehearsed on the way down.

"It just sounded like the conventional thing to say," she answered.

"I don't think we have to be conventional with each other." A senseless wave of anger swept over me. Why the hell couldn't I get control of myself and handle whatever this thing was, the way it ought to be handled? "What's all this about?" I pulled her letter out of my pocket and threw it down on the table in front of me. There was a question in her eyes as she stared at me; I couldn't read it, but I knew that whatever had happened hadn't broken or bruised anything within her. "I'm sorry," I apologized belatedly. "I guess I must have been worried about you, and I took it out by behaving like a boor."

She seemed to sense my impulse to go to her side, because she raised her hand and said, "No, let it be this way. It's not going to be a very easy story to tell." I could see her arms stiffen as she gripped the window sill behind her. "It all started, I mean my part of the story, when Angelica stopped by at Sea Island."

I started to say something, but she stopped me. "No, John, please don't—not until I've finished. We spent the whole afternoon on the beach together, Angelica and I—and now I'm ashamed for some of the things I said to her. I was just young, and stupid—"

I had the growing premonition that somewhere in all this there was a problem that concerned not so much Frankie as myself.

"She mentioned," Frankie went on, "a little fishing harbor below Key West that she and her father had put into years before. It was only when I was with some friends on my way north that it was suddenly clear to me that Angelica wasn't running away from you alone, John; that is, if she was running away from you at all. She was running away from something else that she didn't want to admit even to herself—I'm not making much sense, am I?" she broke off lamely.

"I'm having a little trouble following you," I admitted.

"It's so hard to know where to start to tell it," she began again. "Anyway, instead of coming back to New York, I got on a train and went down to the little village where she was."

"Angelica?"

"Yes. It was a crazy kind of impulse; and she seemed angry that I had intruded, and I didn't blame her. There wasn't a train north before evening, so I just sort of wandered off by myself, feeling that I'd pushed in where I wasn't wanted. Then about an hour before the train left, Angelica found me. John, she looked terrible, her eyes all swollen from crying, and her lips so white and trembling that she could hardly talk. She begged me not to go; she said she needed to be near someone desperately. There was an adjoining room to hers, and the door could be left open, and if I'd only stay, please— Oh, John, I couldn't leave her in that condition—"

229

"Of course you couldn't, but for God's sake, Frankie, get to the point!"

"I am, the only way I know how." Her voice choked up, and I could see that she was trying not to give way to tears. "We neither of us slept much that night," she went on with effort. "We didn't talk, but I could hear her tossing and turning in the other room—and then early in the morning, she thought I was asleep, and closed the door, but it didn't stay closed. It swung open a little, and although I didn't mean to spy, I could see her stepping out of her nightgown with the sun full on her, staring into the mirror—"

An image wavered and then shivered into the focus of memory, and it was Angelica dressing the morning she left Haviland, and turning as she saw me looking at her, and hurriedly pulling on her blouse. What Frankie was saying came to me, but so remotely that it was as if I were remembering the words rather than hearing them.

"It was wrong of me to watch, but I couldn't look away. Even when I closed my eyes I was seeing her. John, I have to tell you this, because it's part of it—the way her hands moved over her body, and then all at once a shudder ran through her and she clenched her breasts until I could see the marks of her nails in her flesh. It was as if she hated her body, and wanted to tear something out of it. I jumped out of bed and tried to stop her—"

Frankie's voice trailed off into the sobs she could no longer control. I was across the room and at her side, but an instinct told me not to touch her. "Get hold of yourself, Frankie. Try to get it all said, and you'll feel better." I gave her my handkerchief. She used it unashamedly, and after a moment or two, managed a semblance of composure.

"The doctor came a little later, and gave her a sedative, and after she was quieter, she told me everything. She'd had a lump on her breast and she'd put off doing anything about it, hoping it would go away. I don't think she was afraid of death, John; I think she was afraid of losing life."

"Is there a difference?" I asked.

"With a person like Angelica, yes."

Her perceptiveness startled me. Frankie was growing up fast, I decided. "I gather that the lump didn't go away," I said after a pause.

230

"No. It didn't. She came back to New York and"—Frankie's hand rose unconsciously over her own breast—"and they wanted to operate at once. 'Amputate.' It's such a horrible word. Especially when a woman is as beautiful as Angelica was. I can feel how she felt—as if no man would ever want to look at her again."

"Nonsense."

"It isn't nonsense, John. It goes deep; terribly deep."

Again I was aware of the new and growing maturity within her, but I knew I had to remain objective. "It is nonsense," I insisted. "There are lots of women no man wants to look at, but if a man's in love with a woman she's beautiful for him, even if she's ugly. You're wallowing in romantic twaddle."

Her eyes held mine. "You know that isn't true, John," she said levelly.

No, it wasn't true. I was hoping against hope that Frankie had been leading up to something like, "Angelica's taking it awfully hard." But Frankie was suddenly silent, she didn't say anything.

"I gather," I said at last, "that she's already undergone the operation."

Frankie nodded. "Five weeks ago."

"I see." There was a look on Frankie's face that made it unnecessary for her to go on.

"And that's that," I said.

"That's that," she repeated. "She'd waited too long. It was all through her."

I lit a cigarette.

"Where is she now?" I finally asked.

"At her apartment. She didn't want to stay in the hospital. She's enjoying one of the few benefits of wealth; she can die where she wants." Frankie's voice was suddenly harsh and bitter.

"Who's with her? I suppose that damned family of hers."

"No, she's alone. I've been with her, but she's really alone. She made her doctors promise not to tell her family. They're in Europe."

"Does she want to see me?"

Frankie hesitated a little before she answered. "I asked her, but she says she doesn't. She only says it with her lips, though, John. It isn't easy to have to die alone. Even with the little that I've tried to do, I'm still a stranger, while you—you and she—what I mean is . . ."

"I know what you mean," I told her gently. "You were right to call me."

Her shoulders seemed to sag, all at once, as if a great weight of relief had lifted from them. "I was so afraid you'd think I was butting in," she said unsteadily.

"Frankie, I'm very grateful. —When can I see her?"

"Now."

I glanced at my watch. "Isn't it too late? Especially if she doesn't expect me?"

"I don't think so. She doesn't sleep very much; the nights are so long for her."

I reached for my coat, and she walked with me to the door. She looked suddenly small and lonely standing there in the impersonal hotel room. I put my arm around her. "It'll be a long night for you, too. Why don't you drive up with me?"

Her face lit up. "Oh, John, I'd love to, if you don't mind!"

In the car, I said, "Alyse made a great mistake."

One of the nice things about Frankie was her honesty. She didn't pretend not to understand. "I've thought of her so much these past weeks," she said. "If only she'd let me know. So that I could at least have been with her."

We didn't talk again until I was pulling the car into the curb in front of Angelica's apartment house. Then Frankie murmured, "There's a great change in her, John—"

I knew what she wanted to say. "I'll try not to show that I notice it," I promised.

"Keep looking at her eyes," Frankie said. "That's what I do when I'm with her. Her eyes haven't changed. They're still beautiful. Even more beautiful."

The doctor was with her when we arrived, so Frankie didn't go back to the hotel, as she'd intended; she waited with me in the living room. Presently a door down the corridor opened, and we could hear his footsteps in the hall. He caught sight of Frankie as he passed, and came into the room. Maybe I'd expected the old type of family physician, like Doc Farnley. Frankie had prepared me for everything except that Angelica's doctor fitted into upper

Park Avenue like a very supple and knowing hand fits into a glove.

"Doctor Paul Holloway," Frankie introduced us.

"Frankie told me that she was writing you. I think it's a good idea. I approve of it."

"I'm glad you approve," I told him. I could hear a kind of stupid animosity in my voice. I didn't give a damn whether Doctor Holloway approved or not.

Frankie looked at us a little puzzled and Holloway gestured her toward Angelica's room. "You better go in first and prepare her," he said. "She'll want to primp up and be female."

When we were alone he offered me a cigarette.

"What the hell is all this?" I asked him. "Is Angelica dying or are we just stopping by for a drink?" I was conscious of a surly impulse to dislodge him from his bland urbanity.

"It might be a good idea to keep the whole thing on as light a plane as possible." He lit his cigarette. "It's the way she'd rather have it. Yes, she's dying." His voice assumed the metallic snap of his lighter as he closed it.

Something of the vague legend of Doctor Paul Holloway came back to me. He had been in the army, all the way through the show; there weren't many glamour boys in the medical corps, but the names of the good ones got around. Afterwards, New York—and he became a sort of pet of the columnists, with his name always in the list of the first-nighters and from time to time in the rumor lists associated with one or another of the top lingerie drawers of the town.

"You operated on a friend of mine from my outfit at Anzio," I offered by way of amend.

"I wouldn't remember," he said. "For a time until we got properly staffed at Anzio I averaged better than twenty majors a day."

I fumbled for a cigarette and again he offered me one from his case. This time I took it.

Frankie came in. "She's waiting for you," she told me.

As I started into Angelica's room Holloway picked up his coat. "I'll probably be seeing you," he said.

"How long should I stay?" I asked him.

"What difference does it make?" he said brusquely. "And you better get out of here and get some sleep," he said to Frankie. "I'll drop you back at your hotel."

There was a faint light through the doorway at the end of the hall and as I came to it there was the white figure of a nurse who nodded to me and then was gone, closing the door behind her.

The room was drifted with the clear poignant odor of spring flowers. God, with what memories a man can remember certain rooms in his life!

"Hello!" I said. "You're a fine one, not letting anyone know you'd come back to town." I was looking at her, but I really wasn't looking at her; it's a trick you play on yourself sometimes. It's like a camera, you focus on the background and everything in the foreground is blurred and unreal. You see it, but you don't really see it. Her great broad bed was just a fogged image. There was a figure straightened up against the embroidered silk of the headboard and that was Angelica; I knew it was, but I wasn't seeing her. She had a trick of lighting rooms, and I was grateful for it; everything was subordinated to one or two focal points. The Boucher pastel of a young woman over the mantel was in high key and on a table across the room a light source bathed the Clodion figure of a girl lying on her back playing with a dog; but the rest of the room was almost in shadow except for the flickering of the candle flames in the sconces on the wall—those eternal damned candle flames without which she could never go to sleep; she was afraid of the dark.

"Let's don't start out by pretending," she said. "We never did, and it's an agony of human relations we don't have to commence at this late date."

I crossed over to the bedside and took her hand in mine. For a moment we were shaking hands like strangers and then it was suddenly different: we were holding hands as friends will, or lovers—there's not much difference in the basic impulse—with the touch of flesh on flesh saying all that words can never say. I stopped playing the coward and forced my gaze into focus, and I could see her unspoken question and I wondered if I could school my expression from betraying me. The invasion had been complete, the battle was lost. The old cliché, "While there's life, there's hope," is only a cliché. And then I was conscious of her eyes and I remembered Frankie's words: "Keep looking at her eyes. That's what I do when I'm with her. Her eyes haven't changed. They're still beautiful. Even more beautiful." The ravage of disease and

234

the stigmata of death seemed to vanish, and I didn't have to pretend; it was easier that way. I lowered my head to kiss her and she turned from me slightly at the last moment and my lips brushed across her eyelids and as I straightened up I could feel the wetness of her tears, but the salt of tears is something you can't describe; it's something you taste in your throat or your belly or wherever it is that you feel things.

"Is Frankie out in the other room?" she asked.

"No, she went back to the hotel. Holloway dropped her off on his way."

"She shouldn't have sent for you, but I'm glad she did. I'm glad we can be alone again, too. We haven't had too many moments in our lives; but they've been good ones, most of them—this is one, though, that I never expected. So I may not bring it off too well," she laughed.

It was difficult to talk against her overtones.

"I'm glad you have Frankie," she said.

"Look, I haven't *got* Frankie," I told her. "You're off on the wrong tack."

"Perhaps from where I'm looking from, I can see more clearly than you. Don't be a fool this time—life doesn't give us too many chances." Her hands worked at the coverlet. "Light me a cigarette, will you, John?"

It was an unconscious and ingrained coquetry. Angelica was one of those women who could do anything as well as, and some things better than, most men. She could mix a better martini than I could, but she always gestured toward the table, and it was I who had mixed the martinis we drank. There were certain little tricks of dressing and undressing that were very much a part of her. She would raise an arm, or turn her back to you to suggest a zipper or a hook that she could have very well unzipped or unhooked herself. I once chided her and told her that she should have been born in the era of the Grand Monarch and she had laughed and said that modern women were foolish to wear so few clothes; and then we had both laughed, because she had had exceedingly few on at the time. I picked up two cigarettes from the box on the table and stuck them between my lips and lit them and then passed one of them to her.

She hunched herself back in the pillows. A long billow of smoke wreathed out into the cone of light between us, held for an instant like a gray thunderhead, and then collapsed and fogged.

"I was a coward, I didn't want you to come," she finally said. "But now that you have, I'm glad. Only don't stand there so stiff and frozen. Pace up and down the way you used to do, just be normal and relaxed, be a caged lion if you want to—only don't stand there and stare down at me. They all stand and stare down at me, the nurses, the doctors they've called in—don't be like the rest of them; be like our old selves together."

I escaped to the other side of the room—she was right, it did make things easier to pace—and gravitated to the little Clodion statue, the little terra-cotta nude lying on her back with her legs up in the air and balancing a little puppy on her toes, teasing him to jump down into her waiting hands. She was so excessively eighteen and joyous and nude, nude to the last stark female detail of her vibrant and lithe and alive body. It was not something that everyone looked at without pruriency or a consciousness of nakedness, and yet there was something about the little figure that could never be conventionally lascivious; there was no inhibition to make it so, and no self-consciousness to subtract from its naturalness.

"John, let's just treat this as a shipboard going-away, one of those gay *bon voyage* parties that never happen any more." There was a brittle edge in her voice and then she seemed to hear it herself and she cleared her throat and went on a little more quietly. "Do you remember, it was one of the last sailings of the *Mauretania,* just before the war? You came down to see me off?"

"I remember."

"You thought there would be a lot of other people. Maybe you wouldn't have come if you'd thought there weren't going to be a lot of people. It was the only time I ever really consciously tricked you."

"Now that you mention it," I told her, "I was surprised. I had thought that there'd be a lot of people there."

"And we had champagne, lots of it. There always seemed to be a lot of champagne those days." She reached over and pushed a bedside bell, and while she was still ringing the nurse came in and she asked, "Isn't that ready yet, Miss Hudson?"

And the nurse said, "It's all ready, Miss Barnes. I was just about to bring it in." In a moment or two she wheeled in a

236

bar table and on it were two glasses and a bottle of champagne in an ice pail. She seemed a little reluctant and disapproving. "Are you sure it's all right?" she asked.

"Yes, I'm sure," Angelica told her. "Doctor Holloway specifically prescribed it; you heard him. I have no doubt that if you ask him tomorrow he will write it down on your chart for you and that will make it very proper—and very medicinal."

"I brought the corkscrew. Do you want me to open it?" Miss Hudson asked.

"No, Mr. Milnor will perform the honors."

Miss Hudson handed me the corkscrew as if it were a strange kind of surgical instrument. She glanced for an instant at the little Clodion statue. It wasn't a blush she gave, but it amounted to the same thing, a little nervous sound that was halfway between a laugh and a giggle and clearing her throat—if anything can be halfway between three things.

"Somehow I wouldn't expect that from a nurse," I said when she left.

"Each to his own limitations," Angelica said. "After all, nurses have an attitude toward bedpans that most people would find difficult to assume. It puzzles her though."

"What puzzles her?" I asked.

"The Clodion. She looks at it quite often. She's grown up and there were pictures in her obstetrics and gynecology textbooks, but this puzzles her; she knows it's beautiful, but she doesn't know why."

We were back to our old basis and we weren't talking about each other, we were talking about things, and it was easier.

"You're a nice girl," I said.

"Why?"

"It would have been such an easy joke, but it would have hurt. The corkscrew and the champagne. The joke that hurts is never a joke, it's a cruelty."

"But people laugh."

"Other people, not the one that's hurt. That's why you were a nice girl."

The cork popped the way a cork is supposed to pop and foam raced up the neck of the bottle and spilled out into the waiting glass. We raised our drinks and I racked my mind for something to say, but most things said over glasses of champagne are sentimental or senseless. It wasn't the moment for either mood. Angelica touched her glass to her lips, almost like a kiss, and then waited until I returned the salute. It was a hangover from the old days; it could say all the things you couldn't put into words, it could say them even in a crowded room and across people's heads; it said them now.

"I never thought you liked this stuff," I told her as I lowered my glass.

"I don't, I never did. You have to be awfully well-bred or awfully wealthy not to like champagne; I happened to be wealthy enough."

I looked my question into my glass.

"We've only drunk it at very special times. This is the third time, to be exact."

"Should I remember the other two times?" I asked her.

"There's no reason to. The first was at the lodge in South Carolina. At the time and for the occasion it seemed the conventional thing to do. Champagne for a seduction. I'm a very conventional person. And then the afternoon I sailed on the *Mauretania*. That was the conventional thing to do, too; going-away parties and champagne, they go together don't they— And now."

I didn't answer her, I finished my glass and refilled it.

"I never realized you were quite that much of a sentimentalist."

"It's a failing of the gender," she said. "We're all sentimentalists; our feelings are all inward." She looked at me. "Yes, I mean it that way, too; maybe that's why. I never told you about the sailing of the *Mauretania,* did I?"

"What was there to tell? She sailed and you sailed on her and I stayed in New York."

She looked at me for a long moment. "There was so much more to tell," she finally said. "But at the last moment I didn't tell you. Do you remember the ship was delayed in sailing? Some V.I.P. was late, or it had missed the tide or something, I never knew, but it just didn't sail. Everything got out of time and context. When you're that close to going, you've already gone. We'd met, you remember, to say good-by. But we'd already said good-by to each other; your coming to the boat, my asking you to come to the boat, was just an extra bit of self-inflicted torture for both

238

of us. We were being oh, so very well-bred and conventional; and I was, as you just reminded me, being sentimental. You remember that I excused myself to make a telephone call?"

"Yes, I remember," I told her. "It was while you were gone that I finally decided that what we had, in the nature of the way we had it, must end sometime—and when you feel that, well, it's time to end it." I turned to face her and leaned against the window sill. "Yes, I remember it very clearly. I remember your going out of the cabin and my walking over to the porthole. There was a gray-necked gull that swept down quite close and then seemed to hang motionless in the air, the way gulls will. And it turned its head and seemed to stare back at me through the porthole. I remember thinking that its eyes were beady and malign, and then deciding that they were merely the eyes of a bird fitted by nature to see small things at great distances. And that was a damned fool thing to be thinking when your throat was dry and choking and your belly was sick with the pain of what was happening. And then the gull sideslipped and was lost with a hundred other gulls, and I finished my drink and poured myself another one and a few moments later you came back into the cabin, and a little while after stewards were beating gongs and I went off on the dock, and I didn't wait, I just kept walking and I was halfway across town when I heard the deep-throated blast of a big ship and the little shrill yelpings of small tugs and I knew the *Mauretania* had sailed."

Angelica slowly spun the glass in her hand and then swirled it until the wine frothed up to the brim and then she drank it empty. "Yes," she finally said. "I went out of the cabin. I called a man who knew that—what was her name? Mrs. Shipley?— at the passport division in Washington. My God, she's still at the passport division in Washington! Wars go on and lovers break their hearts and Mrs. Shipley is still at the passport division in Washington; it's good to know that there are some things you can still cling to in a changing world. Well, I held on while he got through on another line to Washington. Yes, if you already possessed a passport things could be arranged so that a replacement could be delivered to you at Cherbourg. I explained that it was not for myself, but for a friend who might decide at the last moment to sail. That would be quite all right, too. *When better friends were built Barnes would have them!* And then I waylaid one of the pursers. There was nothing he wouldn't do for Miss Barnes. Later on during the voyage he tried to prove it—and I almost let him. He got out the ship's plan and by a curious coincidence the cabin next to mine was empty. I hurried back to you. And then—nothing happened." She held out her glass and I refilled it. "Just to think, if I hadn't gone out to telephone, and you hadn't stood by a porthole and looked at a sea gull, the whole story might have been different." Again she swished the glass, studying it as if it might tell her something. "Thank you, John, for coming in to see me off on this voyage, too." The bubbles had subsided and she drank the glass.

"Look," I said. "You haven't got a maudlin bone in your body. Holloway's a good doctor and . . ."

She shook her head and stopped me. "Let's not try to fool ourselves; we never did. Holloway's a good doctor, and this is a voyage, and it's not one that Mrs. Shipley can help with; I won't need a passport. I don't know what the ship's waiting for. Perhaps it just missed the tide and it's waiting for the next one. Anyway, there's nothing to do, until the gong sounds, but have a drink together and talk off the top of our minds about pleasant things and pretend that it's not saying good-by."

I half turned away from her and let my finger play down along the flanks of the little Clodion figure.

"Do you remember the day I got that?" she said. "You pretended it looked like me. And I insisted that it didn't, that I would never be that young again; and I started to prove it to you and you laughed and said, *'Who the hell's interested in statues?'* and you kissed me and we proved something else instead."

I turned away from the statue. "You haven't any whisky, have you?"

"On the shelf under the table," she said. "I'm sorry, I didn't mean to be maudlin. But it's strange this business of dying. Somehow you feel that your thoughts should be concerned with intimations of immortality, with God, and with the problems of your soul. Instead the damnedest things go through my mind. I could offer a field day to a psychoanalyst; but it would be a waste of his time. Holloway says it's normal, it's what happens when people die slowly; he sugarcoated the pill, but that's what

240

he meant. The *Magic Mountain,* a sort of Venusberg. It's hell, in a way. A sweet sort of hell, but still hell. The reliving of all the things you ever did, and wanted to do, and didn't do. My God, I'm a mess, and I always was one. Somewhere along the line I had a chance and I muffed it. I had a chance with you and I muffed it. I was going to say we muffed it, but that wouldn't be true; Angelica screwed up her own life all by herself, screwed it higher than a kite. The little girl who wanted the moon and didn't realize that the world was right there for the taking; but she didn't want the world, she wanted the moon."

I sat down on the bed beside her and her fingers came down and slipped over mine and then our hands clasped and again it was like the old days.

"You're nice," she said. "You don't tell me that I'm not dying." She reached over to the table and pushed the switch buttons and the room was lit only by the slightly guttering candles. "I'm still afraid of the dark," she said. She half finished her glass and held it balanced on the covers between her fingers. Her eyelids slowly dropped. "I feel drowsy," she said. "You won't mind if I doze off for a while? You'll be around when they ring the gong, won't you—that is, if it isn't too much nuisance?"

I took the glass out of her fingers and put it on the table, and then slowly bent over to kiss her. A tremor of passion went through her lips and then, as the cool shadow of a cloud passes over the sun on a hot day, her lips were still and she slept. I crossed the room quietly and eased myself out of the door, leaving it ajar. In the hall I glanced at my watch; it was twenty minutes to three. Miss Hudson hurried out of the library and with only a nod to me tiptoed into the room and the door closed with a muffled click.

I was putting on my coat in the library before I realized that Holloway was sitting in the big chair by the fireplace, staring at me. "She's asleep," I told him. And then when he didn't answer I said, "What are you doing here at this hour of the night?"

"I came back," he said. "In case she wasn't asleep. After all I didn't know what kind of a bastard you might really be." My reactions were slow; rooms sheltering the sick and the dying are separate from reality, you don't translate back too quickly into the everyday world. Before the words which were forming

241

came to my lips he said, "Let's go out and get a drink, a lot of drinks."

There was something about him that made me not want to say it after all. "There's some Scotch over there in the bar," I told him.

"No, someplace else, any place, but not here." He got up and picked up his coat.

"Do you want to go in and see her first?" I asked.

He shrugged. "You said she's asleep. That's all I could do for her, but I wouldn't have been able to do it the same way."

When we got out on the street there was a light rain falling. He glanced at his watch. "Later than I thought. We could go up to my apartment. It's just around the corner." He seemed indecisive. "To hell with it. I not only want to drink liquor, I want to smell it. You've got your car?"

We got in and headed over toward Third Avenue. People who do their drinking on Third Avenue like to do it late. It wasn't much of a place, but then we weren't looking for much of a place. I gathered Holloway wasn't exactly unknown. The bartender was familiar enough to reach out a bottle of Scotch at his nod, and put it on the bar in front of us. Holloway drenched the ice and let the liquor come halfway up the glass and then slid the bottle down the bar to me; this wasn't a bar that bothered with jiggers. He took a long gulp and then found a dime in his change pocket and started toward the phone booth.

"It's out of order," the bartender said, and lifted out a phone on a long cord from underneath the bar.

"How long has she got?" I asked.

"It was over days ago. It's all finished with. She knows it, too; she's one of the few you don't have to fool. Only she doesn't want to die."

"Who does?" I asked.

"In my trade I've seen a lot who did; they're usually the ones who have a tough time doing it."

"Has she got much pain?"

"What the hell do you think?" he asked. "That's my business and I know my business. It's just that she doesn't want to give up."

"There isn't any chance, at all?"

"Goddamn it, I told you there wasn't." He glanced at his watch again and then tapped his glass on the bar as if he was trying

242

to make up his mind about something. I thought he was going to say something to me, but he picked up the phone and dialed it. "Holloway. Will you call Dr. Nelson at six fifteen in the morning and tell him that he will operate on Mrs. Phillips at eight. —Yes, he knows all about it, he was going to assist. —Tell him anything you want; tell him I fell down a manhole cover on Third Avenue. —No, it's not too serious—yet. —The telephone number on the manhole cover is"—he leaned back to read the number on the instrument—"Circle 7-3128." He pushed the phone down the bar out of the way.

"How long have you known Angelica?" I asked.

"Not long enough as a doctor. If she'd come to me a year ago, maybe even six months ago, I could have saved her; as for knowing her, I've known her since the middle of the war. And I've known about you since then, too."

"Go on," I told him.

He traced circles on the bar with the wet bottom of his glass that made me remember a caligraph machine in the window of Wendle's drug store in Haviland; it demonstrated fountain pens that would write a line five miles long. Only, whoever wanted to write a line five miles long?

"I'll answer the question you've got in your mind," he said.

"I haven't any question in my mind."

"I'll answer it anyway. No, I never went to bed with her."

"Look," I told him, "I don't give a damn whether you did or not. It's none of my business, it's nobody's business what people do in bed. It's about as important as whether you brush your teeth up and down, or sideways; it's a very personal and private matter and it's nobody's damn business."

"Correction noted." He swirled his glass through the neat patterns he had made, blurring them into nothing. "The difference between us is that I was born a roughneck and you weren't. I haven't got any instincts that tell me there are certain things you talk about and certain things you don't."

"Oh, nuts!" I poured myself another drink and then I started to laugh, it was as if the chip on my own shoulder had slipped down and cracked my funny bone. "All right, tell me why you didn't go to bed with her?"

"It's none of your damned business!"

He poured himself a drink, but he didn't drink it. He just swirled the liquor around in the glass and stared at it. "I don't know what people mean when they say they're in love. Me, I wouldn't know, maybe because I think I know too much about it. I know the area of the brain where it starts, and I can draw you a picture of all the fancy little nerve ganglia at the base of the spine—it can start there too, it doesn't even have to begin in the mind—and all the glands begin to secrete and the drive and the urge starts, and there's only one woman in all the world that you want to go to bed with, and going to bed with her is more important than anything in the whole cockeyed universe."

"You make it awfully simple," I observed.

"Every complicated thing in the world is simple. Think about it and you'll see it's true."

"And conversely?"

"The converse is true, also. Only the really simple things are complicated. What a man and a woman want from each other is simple, what they do about it is complicated."

The bartender slid his wet towel across the mahogany in front of us, and seemed to register the trend of our conversation. He didn't approve, or disapprove, it was just par for the course; and then he returned to his solitary post at the other end of the bar.

"That damned bedroom of hers," Holloway went on. "At first I tried to pretend that I wasn't in love with her. I didn't have any time for that sort of nonsense in my life." He broke off as if he had lost the thread of his thought, and then he commenced on another tack. "There was a girl, her name was Mary Krakow; in the town I grew up in it would be Krakow. I was in high school and I knew I was going to be a doctor and not a coal hunky for the rest of my life. She was in high school, and she wondered what the hell she was there for, because she knew she was going to live on the company street for the rest of her life. The night before I went away to college we were together. We lay on a hilltop; if you looked in just one direction, just toward the river, you couldn't see a single damned pit heading cutting the sky with its dirty unpainted wood. She was wearing those cotton pants that you could see in the J. C. Penny windows—Jesus Christ Penny's penny-pinching panties! *Pure brushed cotton guaranteed to feel like silk, in three popular styles, briefies, scanties and*

244

skimpies, .69¢ Special. And they did feel like silk at that—or maybe in that town and at my age I didn't know what silk felt like. That was another girl I didn't go to bed with."

"You weren't anywhere near a bed," I reminded him. "You were on a hilltop not looking at coal derricks, or whatever they call those things that stick up like toothpicks all over that countryside of yours."

"Holloway's an idealist," he announced gravely.

There are certain people who, when they get a little tight, begin to talk in the third person.

"Then what did Holloway do?" I asked.

"He tucked in his shirt and he tucked in Mary Krakow's shirt and he went home and finished packing his suitcase and he went to college, and then he went on to medical school, and he never went back to coal town."

"—Why?"

"*Why,* what?" he asked.

"*Why* everything. Why didn't you lay Mary Krakow on the hilltop? What did you want from Mary Krakow that she didn't have to give you? Why do you start to talk about Angelica Barnes and end up talking about Mary Krakow—which is in passing a hell of a silly name—why are you telling me all this? Boil it down to one word—*Why?*"

He seemed to be staring at some point about six feet behind me. "Speaking as a physician," he finally said, "if you have anything serious to do tomorrow, I would advise going slow on that bottle. You seem a little drunk to me."

"I haven't anything serious to do tomorrow," I told him. "Sometime during the day I am going to drop in on an old friend who's dying and do my best to be witty and gay and make her believe that dying's not very important, that people do it every day, that it's as easy as slipping off a log. We'll try to pack everything we have to say to each other into the little time that's left; but there'll be something important that we'll forget to say, you always do. There's always something afterwards that you wish you'd said. She won't want me to tell her any lies just to make it easier for her; but I'll tell her that I love her, which in some highly involved way isn't a lie."

"Yes, you tell her that." He patted my arm. "She'd probably

245

like to hear it; and anyway, what have you got to lose?" He stared at me for a long moment. "Maybe you're not drunk," he observed. "In which case I would prescribe another drink; I'm speaking professionally, you understand." He pushed the bottle down in front of me. "Now, you asked me a question."

"Let's skip the question," I said.

"No, let's not skip it. I've given a lot of thought to your question. Not since you asked it—there hasn't been very much time to think about it since you asked—but for a long time before, I've thought about it."

"Suppose we both pretend that you've said everything you want to say," I offered. "Then you won't have to answer the question I really didn't ask. It could be as simple as all that."

"I was still in the service when it began . . ."

"Look, there's no law that says I have to stand here and listen to you. I could go out to the can and smoke a cigarette."

"I hadn't been back to New York in over a year . . ."

"I could go out and walk around the block. Every time I pass the window I'll look in and see if you're still talking to yourself and when you finally shut your goddamn mouth I'll come back and finish my drink. Or, better than that, I could really get lost, I could go back to the hotel and get into bed and go to sleep and Holloway could talk until his tongue got fur on it. What you need is an analyst, or maybe you have one and he's asleep and that's why you've latched onto me?—Say, what the hell were you doing back in New York, in the middle of a war, anyway?"

There was a sign at the back of the room that said *Gents*. It had an arrow on it. As I turned on my heel and followed the arrow, I heard Holloway begin, "At the risk of your making a long story even longer, I'll tell you . . ."

I gave him enough time, I thought, to write his Book of Revelation, and then I got tired looking at girls' telephone numbers and the varied and assorted art work scribbled on the walls of this particular gentlemen's retiring room, so I headed back to the bar. Holloway was talking along, oblivious to my absence.

"Just where are we now?" I asked.

"I've just arrived in New York in the middle of the war," he soberly explained. "I hadn't been back in over a year."

"You actually mean, that in the middle of the war you just calmly cut yourself a hunk of life and munched on it!"

"I had done something for the liver of a patient once who had told me that a drop or two of absinthe in a very dry martini would do strange and wonderful things."

"And between the strange and wonderful things and your patient's liver you didn't draw any obvious conclusions? I suppose you went right out and started doing a little research? Don't tell me you went to Twenty-One?"

"Who's telling this story, you or me? I went to Twenty-One for certain obvious reasons."

"You mean there are reasons that are not obvious?" I asked him.

"I'm only discussing mine. I'd heard about the place for years. At the beginning I could never afford it, and later I couldn't afford the time. Also, I suppose that sort of thing is a fixation with guys who come from small towns. Anyway I went."

"I get the scene," I told him. "Go on with the story."

"There isn't much of a story. After the fourth or fifth martini it was difficult to decide whether a single drop of absinthe floated on the top or a generous splash in the shaker was the right formula."

"Yes, that could get to be a problem," I agreed.

"And just then I looked up and there was a woman standing in the doorway. It was obvious she had a date with someone, but the chap was late. She was one of the most beautiful women I'd ever seen."

"Don't forget you were splashing the stuff in the shaker by now," I reminded him.

"Somehow I got around to suggesting that she arbitrate the matter. After several tests it seemed that the float and precipitation method was best after all."

"This is a dull story," I told him. "I've been counting your martinis. Pretty soon you pass out. That's a hell of a way to end a story." I glanced at the drink in his hand. "Do you pass out very often?" I asked him.

"Very seldom, as a matter of fact, but when I do it is a very complete and noteworthy performance. Well, one thing led to another . . ."

"What do you mean, *one thing led to another?*" I asked.

"Just that. I remember looking at my watch and deciding that the man she was going to dine with would show up sooner or later, so I suggested we go somewhere else."

"Sort of absinthe yourself? *Je m'excuse* the pun. You and your gal and a bottle of *in absentia*."

He winced. "You're about done with that nonsense, I hope?"

"It wasn't very good, was it? Let's forget it. You were telling a story—then what happened?"

"Nothing unusual," he admitted. "Two people under such circumstances seldom do anything novel. We went places and had things to drink and somewhere along the line the place we were at ran out of absinthe."

"And from then on you floated a single drop of your very small store of mutual illusions on the top of your martinis?"

"You're a bitter son of a bitch, aren't you," he said gravely. "Remind me to talk to you about you some day. Yes, we floated our illusions on the tops of martinis. They were lovely and bright and iridescent. One way or another, I got tight."

"You don't say."

"Only a little tight. I don't think she got tight at all. Not even after she began talking about you."

"We're back again!" I said. "I forgot. This is the story I didn't want to hear. Let's skip it. Tell me more about your experiences in the war, about the time you were surrounded at Bastogne— or was that another guy? And you said *"Nuts"*—or was that another guy? Or maybe you better tell me about the girl in Paris —or was it Venice—she was a Countess or a Marchese or something. Europe was lousy with Countesses or Marcheses, or maybe Europe was just lousy. And she was only eighteen and you felt like an old man. And she was a hell of a lay, but you were always in a hurry, because you had to get down to Rickey's bar and slug some guy who looked cockeyed at the two of you because she was only eighteen and you were a beat-up old Colonel with gray hair in various places. And after you slugged the guy you drank martinis, very, very dry, about fifteen to one with absinthe floated on the top of them. And she wanted to go to bed again because by and large you talked a better lay than you delivered; but you remembered that you had to save the world for—what was it we saved the world for the last time? And so you slapped the silken smoothness of her sleek little backside—by now you knew the difference between brushed cotton guaranteed to feel like silk, and the real thing—and you told her to run along and be a good kid and cool off until the next time."

I finished my drink and poured another one with the sense that I would be smart if I didn't; I had that much sense anyway.

"So that's what's bothering you?" he said.

"Nothing's bothering me. Go on with your story, Colonel."

"I had an idea that's what was biting you, but I wasn't certain," he said. "Frankie said something that made me think so, but I didn't put the pieces together. When you sober up try to remember the way your mind worked tonight. You might learn a few things about yourself."

"Aren't you being awfully obscure?—And omnipotent, too?" I asked him.

"Perhaps." Then he turned and ordered a couple of cups of hot coffee. The bartender shrugged and went off to a hot plate back in the corner.

"You're a cold-blooded character," I observed. "You hang on a beauty and then before tomorrow morning's headache is adjusted for size you proceed to sober up."

"To finish the story—" he went on. "I like to finish the things I start."

"You like to—but I gather that in some departments you don't always do it," I told him.

"To finish the story—" he went on. "She told me quite a lot about you, that first evening. Somehow I never expected our trails would cross." He grabbed my coat and pulled me about facing him. "Look, you ambivalent bastard, you two were never in love with each other; not at the same time, you weren't. When it began, maybe you were in love with her, or the idea of her, but she was just dancing to the tune of a lost generation—"

"Don't make it so special," I interrupted him. "Every generation get's lost; it's the privilege of growing up and no one generation has a monopoly on it. That sort of hogwash went out with Scott Fitzgerald."

"And then later, when she fell in love with you," he continued, "well, you had gone on someplace else; and so it never happened. That much I learned that first night, part of it I learned in that damn bedroom of hers as I was trying to make love to her. She didn't care if she did or she didn't, so I took a shower instead. Maybe I didn't want to pick up the pieces; maybe she didn't particularly want the pieces picked up. Anyway, I had a hell of a wonderful ten days in New York and in the end we just got to be good friends."

"You poor devil," I murmured.

"It would have saved her life if either of us had had the sense to get married. I might even have saved her life, if we hadn't become friends—she'd have come to me earlier. I don't tell patients they have cancer and to go off and think about an operation. I throw them into a hospital the same day; I slug 'em, I drug them, I have them committed as psychopaths, if they try to stall."

"Only she came too late," I finished for him.

"And now I want to talk about Frankie," he said.

"Stop playing God Almighty, Colonel; you're more becoming with a scalpel in your hand." I turned and walked out of the bar. I knew my dignity was showing and I walked very circumspectly; there was a pattern in the linoleum you could sight on and it helped you to walk straight. The car was parked at the curb and as I reached for the keys I saw Holloway standing at the door. I was, anyway, sober enough to know better than to drive. "You know what you can do about it, grandma!" I called to him and aimed myself toward a taxi that cruised up to the curb.

Fifteen

It was a good thing I didn't drive. Trying to put the evening together again later, there was a hiatus between Third Avenue and one of the upstairs corridors of the hotel. There was a lot of marble and a floral figured carpet, and somewhere there was a potted palm that got in my way, and there were long rows of polished brass doorknobs and doors with numbers on them and I had a key in my hand and was trying to match a number with a door. The desk must have thought I was more sober than I was, when they didn't send someone upstairs with me. Then I found a door that matched my key and I worked at it, only the damn thing wouldn't work because the door was already open, and as it swung in I almost fell on my face. And Frankie was standing at the window staring at me and the room looked like hers; only, in the same hotel, hotel rooms have a way of looking like one another. And on a table was a quart of Scotch, with a room service look about it, and a bucket of ice; there was also a thermos of coffee and a plate of sandwiches covered with a damp napkin.

What comes next isn't very nice to tell; but it's part of the story, so it might as well be told.

Frankie said, "I waited because . . ."

But I didn't let her finish. "Oh for chrisake stop being a girl scout; and stop trying to find out the *because* of everything. Sometimes there isn't a *because;* and sometimes when you come on it you wish you hadn't looked."

"There's some coffee on the table and something to eat. There's a drink, too. Room service was closing and I thought . . ."

"And stop being a Cinderella," I told her. "Grow up and stop

251

being such a starry-eyed and intense little mother. I got home all by myself. No, I don't want any sandwiches; no, I don't want any coffee; no, I don't want a drink; I've had a drink. As a matter of sober fact, and to mix a metaphor, I'm drunk. Or did you recognize that, my little Jeanne d'Arc; did they teach you about drunks up in that college of yours? Or was that part of your extra-curricular research? Oh damn it, grow up and don't cry about it."

"I'm not crying," she threw out rebelliously, "I'm weeping. There's a difference. I can't help what my eyes do. If they want to run over, that's their business and I can't stop them." She brushed at her eyes angrily.

It was only then that I noticed the door open into the next room. It, too, was a sitting room; and then I realized that it was Frankie's room. "Now isn't this—just too ducky," I said. "I suppose you told the hotel that your illegitimate half uncle-in-law twice removed would like to have the room adjoining yours. You'd be surprised how quickly they get such ideas even in a sedate old ladies' seminary like this."

My overnight bag was in the corner and I went over and picked it up. When I turned around Frankie was gone. "Oh, to hell with it," I thought. "I'll try to talk some sense to her in the morning," and I started to loosen my tie and get ready to turn in. A fireplace screen makes a very perfect silent valet and I remember that I arranged my clothes and neatly folded them over it; I'm very tidy; a place for everything and everything in its place. I also vaguely remember that I thought a cup of coffee might be good for me, and then that a little Scotch in the coffee would improve things; sometimes you get ideas like that. Only it wasn't a very good idea. The coffee tasted horrible with the Scotch in it; it would probably have tasted horrible anyway, just with the Scotch in me. Then I turned out the lights and headed for bed; it had been a lousy night any way you looked at it. I remember stubbing my toe against a piece of furniture in the dark, and I said some pretty fancy things about guys who always stubbed their toes at critical moments. I found the bedroom door and things were better; the faint glow from the window was sufficient to steer a safe course away from chairs and other obstacles to navigation toward the oblong white panel of the bed, and the sea seemed to get steadier as I lay down on it. And then I heard Frankie's

252

choked voice out of the darknes beside me saying, "Is this the way you want me to grow up, John?"

"Will you for God's sake get out of my bed, and get out of my life!" I bellowed. "And remind me sometime, and in a more fitting place, to tell you what a damn fool you are! What the hell is going on in that oversophisticated little brain of yours?"

The bed moved and a wraithlike form fled across the room. "Come back here!" I yelled. She stopped, and for a moment I thought she was going to come back. "You pull these crazy romantic stunts of yours, and someday somebody's going to call your bluff and you'll wish you hadn't." The door closed and there was a crack of light at the threshold and I could hear sounds coming out of her throat like sobbing and then she seemed to move away and the thin line of light under the door went out and the room was dark, and I closed my eyes and the next thing I knew there was a bell ringing somewhere, a telephone bell. There are some people who can't stand to hear a telephone bell ring without answering it; I'm one of them. I stumbled groggily across the room; the sitting room doors were open and the bell was ringing in the other suite. I wondered why Frankie didn't answer it. The bell was ringing in her bedroom and the door was open so I looked in. The room was empty and the bed hadn't been slept in. I answered the phone, it was the clerk at the desk. "Mr. Milnor, the man from the garage got a message to call for your car at an address on Third Avenue and he's here for the keys. Can we send up for them?"

That was a stunner. Courtesy of Doctor Holloway, I presumed. He was quite an efficient character at that. I told them to send a boy up for the keys and then started out on a tour of reconnaissance. This bedroom was empty and looked untenanted. The sitting room was a different story; my clothes were neatly parked about the fireplace and there was a thermos jug of coffee on the table, a bottle of Scotch and a tray of sandwiches. I got the car keys out of my pocket and waited for the bellboy. The coffee was lukewarm and the sandwiches when I turned up the napkin were loathsome-looking, the way yesterday's sandwiches always look the next morning, with their edges dry and curled up a little indecently, showing their insides. There was a knock on the door and I handed out the car keys to the boy; and asked him to send

253

up a bowl of ice and about a quart of orange juice and another quart of coffee. Then there was nothing for it, but to go into the other room. I didn't have to go in there; but it was a nice masochistic thing to do, and I felt it would be good for my soul. Jumping out of a high window would have been good for my soul, too, at that moment.

There was the tousled bed I had done some troubled sleeping in and there was also undisputable evidence that it had been Frankie's and not my own room into which I had blundered the night before. The closet was empty—she had apparently come in for her things after I was asleep—but the dressing table held some of her personal things and tossed over a chair near the bed were the stockings and undergarments she had worn the day before. Suddenly my good sense nudged me and I gathered up the few things she had left and tumbled them into my suitcase and then I went in and rumpled up the bed I should have been sleeping in. There would be no evidence to start the wagging tongues of chambermaids. I even closed and locked the doors between the two suites, closing her side first and then going out in the hall and coming back into my room and locking the door from that side as well. Long before my breakfast arrived I ran out of things to call myself, and I had fashioned some pretty extravagant phrases at that. With half a cup of coffee in me I decided to dot the "i" and I picked up the phone and called Frankie's room. The clerk told me that she had checked out very early that morning. Forwarding address? "Just Haviland," he told me. I hung up the phone. I don't suppose I had really expected she had gone anywhere else.

I had finished showering and was just about dressed when the phone rang again. It was Miss Hudson. "Doctor Holloway asked me to call you," she said. "He asked me to tell you that it might be a good thing for you to come up to Miss Barnes' apartment as early as you can." Her voice sounded choked and unnatural.

"Is Doctor Holloway there?" I asked.

"No, but he'll be back presently," she told me.

I stifled all the questions that sprang to my tongue. I didn't want the answers.

Holloway was there when I arrived. He was in uniform, which is to say that he was in the same clothes he was wearing the night before, only I knew he had changed. He must have kept a whole closetful of blue suits and white shirts and blue neckties. And he looked like he felt all right, which was more than I did.

"Thanks about the car," I told him.

"You better go in." He nodded toward Angelica's room.

"How about briefing me?"

"Don't be obtuse," he snapped. "You've seen people die before." He turned toward the window and stood staring out into the street. "She was borrowing time anyway."

Miss Hudson nodded to me and left as I came in. I had a strange sense of emptiness in the room, as if something had changed, as if Angelica had already left it. Then I noticed that there was a change. The corner where the little Clodion figure had been was empty. The table on which it had rested was still there, but the little laughing girl was gone. I brought my gaze back to Angelica. She had changed, too. What can you say at times like that? I stood at the foot of the bed and looked down at her. Her lips smiled at me; I mean that the smile was only on her lips, it didn't come from inside. And then she said, "You look like death, John."

We both laughed, only her laughter came from her throat as if it hurt to really let the laugh come free. It was better then, the ice was broken, but I still couldn't think of anything to say. She held out her hand and I took it and she said, "You could at least return the compliment."

We didn't talk very much and what we did say was probably very trivial, nothing metaphysical, no profound leave-takings. I've tried to remember just what we did say, but it only comes back to me in formless snatches. I remember she talked about a day's shooting we had once shared; and then she talked about a dog she'd owned that had hung itself on a slip collar; and once or twice she spoke about her father; her voice was low, but it didn't seem weak. There was very little I could say, I just sat there holding her hand and listening. She talked as one might turn over a photographic album, as if she were recapturing scattered memories that were trivial and unimportant to anyone else, but somehow important to her. In between times she would close her eyes and just lie there until I felt that she had fallen asleep, and then her jaws would clench as if she were driving pain back into

255

the shadows. Once or twice she glanced at the bedside clock. And then she mumbled something, but I couldn't hear it and I thought that she was delirious. She seemed to read the question in my eyes. *"Curite, curite noctis equi,"* she repeated.

"Hasten slowly, oh dawn."

"That isn't the translation, but it's the idea," she said. "I didn't know you were that good a Latinist."

"I'm not," I told her, "but I remember the poem and it was once translated that way."

"Then you know the rest of it?"

I nodded.

"Catullus in the arms of his lover and praying time to slow its course. Only time won't stay its course. That's a funny thing to come into one's mind at a time like this. It's a bastard of a pain, John."

"Do you want me to call Holloway?" I asked.

"In a moment," she said. Her hand tightened on mine. "It's been nice knowing you." Her voice was very level and controlled. "And it's been nice your stopping by to see me off; with all the other things we've been, we've been friends, too—and that's quite a lot in this jumbled-up world of ours. Holloway's a friend, too. That's all he's ever been, just a friend."

"Yes, I know," I told her.

She looked up at me. "I don't know why I felt I wanted to make that clear, maybe just to keep the record clean between us. Yes, I guess you had better ask him to come in, he said he'd be here when I wanted him."

And then Holloway was standing beside me and he asked her, "Very bad?"

"Bad enough," she told him, and then as if she had heard herself she added something, something very funny and wry and neither Holloway nor I could ever after remember what it was, but suddenly the room was filled with laughter. It was so funny that Holloway and I were both laughing long after she had stopped and then we weren't laughing any more and I was looking at Holloway and not at Angelica and I noticed for the first time how blue and cold his eyes were, and there was a white line across his jaw that seemed to twitch in the light. Without speaking he nodded to me to go back into the other room. Angelica's eyes were closed

256

and she gave my hand a little grasp and then relaxed and I had the sense as I withdrew my hand that she didn't know I was going.

Miss Hudson was in the living room. "I think the doctor may want you," I told her.

"The doctor will call me when he wants me," she said and she went on tapping her closed fountain pen against the hard binder of Angelica's case chart. I remember thinking that he'd got her damn well trained.

There was a clock in the room ticking its way inexorably through time. The silence became oppressive and the clock's ticking seemed to become louder. I remember muttering, "Go on tick, you fiendish mechanical bastard, and someday somebody forgets to wind you, and then what happens to time." I couldn't have said it out loud because Miss Hudson didn't look up. It was a foolish thing to have thought anyway, because clocks don't make time, they only mention its passing.

Fifteen, maybe twenty minutes went by and Holloway came into the room and told Miss Hudson, "You better go in with Miss Barnes, now." She got up and arranged the fountain pen and the case chart carefully on the table and then left us. I was sitting on the arm of a sofa and he was pacing the room; we neither of us spoke. Finally he came to rest staring out the window with his hands clasped in back of him and began to crack his knuckles. I watched him fascinated. He went through the fingers of one hand and then of the other and then started all over again. "For God's sake, do you always do that," I asked him, "or only at special times?"

"Only at special times." He turned with his back to the window and faced me.

"What are we waiting for?" I asked him.

"What do you think we're waiting for?"

I was trying to light a cigarette with the table lighter, but it wouldn't work, it was out of essence. That's what happens in a house—first somebody forgets to fill the lighters, and then they forget to wind the clocks, and then everybody forgets everything and strangers come in and paw over things and what the family doesn't take is sold; the places where people live can die, too. Except in Haviland—the Tracys were still waging their fight against change. Someday the Tracys would lose, but in the mean-

257

time death and time and change would know they'd had a battle. I finally found some matches in my pocket and got the cigarette lit. "Isn't there anything you can do?" I asked.

"I've already done it," Holloway said. I watched his hands, fascinated, as the joints of his fingers turned white and then all the joints in his hands seemed to crack at the same instant. "Goddamn it," he said in a low, weary voice and then he slipped a hypodermic case out of his pocket and returned it to his bag.

He glanced at his watch. "You better have a drink." He opened the drawer of a breakfront that contained a nest of decanters. He must have read my expression. "I know you know where she keeps her liquor," he said. "Let's not get started on that tack."

"I'm not starting anything," I said.

"Excuse me, I guess I'm scratchy and overly sensitive. But I still think you ought to have a drink." Then he turned and went up the hall toward Angelica's room.

I suppose the people who make nightmares their business have a word for those ghastly dreams that go on and on and will never finish, where the horrors pile up behind you and your only wish is that it will be over and finished with. That day was such a nightmare, punctuated by the sharp hurting impacts of things that really happened.

It could have been minutes, it was probably an hour before Holloway came back into the room. He didn't have to say anything, he just nodded. I remember looking at the clock and not being able to read its face. My eyes wouldn't focus; sometimes it's worse when the tears won't come and all that you can feel is the dull griping clutch of grief working in your entrails.

Holloway did some telephoning. Angelica's lawyer and then the undertakers. He told them to proceed with the arrangements that had already been made by Miss Barnes. Miss Hudson came in and handed him a form and he sat at the desk and filled it in and signed it and handed it back to her.

When she left he continued to sit at the desk drumming his fingers. He closed the fountain pen and started to put it in his pocket. Then he stopped and looked at it for a moment and hurled it back into one of the cubbyholes of the desk. It's a wry thought to think that your own fountain pen can write out your own death certificate. Finally he turned around to me. "Do

258

you want to clear out, or do you want to see the rest of this through?"

"What's the rest of it?" I asked.

"Angelica asked me to be sure certain things were done."

"I'll stick around," I told him.

The undertakers arrived first; theirs is a prompt trade. They inquired if either of us was "family" and then dispensed with their conventional unction. I suppose they like it best when they can just do their work, like any other work that has to be done, and not be forced to supply a lot of conventional grief for someone they've never known. Miss Hudson took them down the hall and they followed her, like a couple of contractors going off to measure a room for new wallpaper.

A little later a lawyer from Angelica's firm arrived. He was young and very efficient in his three-button suit and his short crisp haircut and he had that smell of caste and Harvard law school that takes twenty years to lose, if you're the kind of a person that ever loses it. He had a copy of the will and a letter from Angelica. "Mr. Thurston is in Washington and Mr. Hubbard is in Chicago," he explained, "or I wouldn't be here."

I knew what he meant. Angelica had been inconsiderate enough to pick one of the firm's busy days to die on. "I spoke to them on the phone, however, and they gave me full instructions," he went on. I'll bet they did; Angelica's estate would be a nice lucrative one to administrate. "When will the service occur?" Young Mr. Blackstone was out of his depth and knew it and I could see him figuring how quickly Mr. Thurston and Mr. Hubbard could fly back to New York.

"If you've read Miss Barnes' instructions you should realize that there isn't going to be any service." Holloway wasn't helping him any.

"I know," he said. "I realize I used the wrong expression." He braced himself and made a fresh start. "When will the cremation occur?"

"The undertaker tells me that it can be arranged for six o'clock," Holloway said.

"Well, then both Mr. Thurston and Mr. Hubbard will be able to . . ." and then he got the idea. "You mean six o'clock this afternoon?"

259

"Look," said Holloway, "I'm not a lawyer, but I assume that when a person leaves reasonable instructions about such matters they are to be carried out."

"I was only thinking of Mr. Thurston and Mr. Hubbard," the lawyer said. He had a commuters' timetable out of his pocket and was checking the trains to Greenwich or Stamford. "I suppose I could attend in their place," he said doubtfully. I saw his finger stop at a train and the question form on his lips of how long a cremation took; he didn't ask the question.

"I don't think Miss Barnes would give a damn whether you attended or not," Holloway said.

"My wife and I did have an engagement," he offered apologetically.

"And Mr. Milnor and I have an engagement." Holloway piloted him toward the door. "Good night, Mr. Thurston."

"I'm not Mr. Thurston," the young man protested.

"That's all right," Holloway told him, "you will be someday."

The thought suddenly hit me that we do these things better in a small town. In the first place everybody knows everybody else. Mooney wouldn't have worn striped pants and he might have had a few drinks under his belt, but he would have been more friendly and not so damned cold-bloodedly efficient and smelling of cologne. Nor would Pop Sanford have caught a train, even if he had a train to catch; his was the sort of personal law that not only drew your will, but would walk to your grave with you.

Holloway came back into the room. "I just thought of Frankie," he said. "She's been standing by during the last weeks. I wonder if she would want to be there?"

"She's up in Haviland," I told him. "That is, I think she is, which reminds me that I better phone." I thought he was going to say something, but he didn't.

Mrs. Haines answered the phone and then Elizabeth was on and after a moment of sparring on both our sides we could hear Mrs. Haines hang up in the kitchen. "Is Frankie there?" I asked.

"She had luncheon with me, but she's back down at the Jennings Place now."

"She told you about Angelica?"

260

"Yes, John. I'm sorry," Elizabeth said.

"You don't have to be sorry any longer. She died an hour ago."

"My sorrow really goes out to you," Elizabeth said.

"Tell Frankie about it in your own way. I'll probably be back in Haviland in the morning. And before you offer it, there's nothing that anyone can do."

Crematoria, like garbage disposal plants, are always on the outskirts of cities. This one was over in some dismal reclaimed swampland behind Long Island City. As Holloway and I drove out together he suddenly tapped my arm. "Look, let's stop for some flowers. I know it's sentimental, but to hell with that, let's stop for some flowers anyway."

It was a little run-down florist in a poor neighborhood. They didn't have much, just some simple inexpensive little things, but there was a jar full of yellow roses. "Let's have those," I said.

"They're not as fresh as they look and they won't last long." The florist was an honest little guy.

"They don't have to last long," I told him.

When we finally got there it was just the sort of place you would expect it to be, cement and stucco gothic with a lot of interfaith paraphernalia and symbols strewn about. "Shadow Lawn without the palm trees," I said.

We were standing in the middle of the room, both with flowers in our arms, when they wheeled her past. One of the attendants said apologetically, "The flowers are always removed, so there isn't any need."

It was all that Trigger Holloway wanted, to be told he couldn't do something. "This time they won't be removed!" He wasn't used to back talk from people, so he didn't get any. And yet, I think we both felt it was a futile gesture as we laid the roses over her. Fortunately there were enough; we had bought all the little shop had; and as they spread out they almost covered her and then Holloway shifted them so that they covered her face. If her eyes beneath those closed lids could see within the next minutes it would be better to see the wonder of a yellow rose. Then the doors closed, and presently the undertaker came to us and asked us if we would be waiting. "It takes about an hour," he explained.

261

"We'll wait," Holloway told him.

I didn't know there were so many things you can think about in an hour. Somewhere there was a dynamo or the humming of an electric motor and I shut it out of my mind. We each sat with our own thoughts and presently the attendant came back with a pad in his hand and I looked at my watch. An hour had passed. He didn't seem to know whom to speak to and he wanted instructions about what to do with the ashes. Holloway hadn't thought that far, neither had I.

"She said she just wanted to be lost someplace where the sun shines and there was grass and green trees," Holloway said. "I don't know. What ideas have you got, Milnor?"

"They would be sent to you in a suitable container"—the attendant looked at his watch—"tomorrow."

"John Milnor, Haviland, New York," I told him.

"No other address, no street or anything?" he asked.

"It's a small town," I told him. "A very small town."

"Thanks," Holloway said. "You'll know what to do."

The funeral merchant's car was waiting for us when we came out and the driver was trained, or maybe it was because it was late and the fellow had a date, or wanted a drink, or his wife had pot roast for dinner, but he slithered through traffic like an angry eel. We had come out to the tempo of the *Marche Funèbre,* we went back like the *Hora Stacatto.*

"I could stand a drink," Holloway said.

Oh, God, I thought, not another business like last night! We were in the middle of the Queensborough Bridge. "Let's go down to my club, it's better than a bar."

Holloway nodded and I tapped the window and slid it back. "Sixteen Gramercy Park," I told the driver. He cut right against a car that was breasting up to pass us and the squeal of brakes sliced the night; there was the throb of a diesel as we seemed to pass under the left front wheel of a trailer truck.

"This jockey could be an asset to the mortician's trade," Holloway drily commented. "I'd tell him to slow down, but I know his type—then he'd really have his foot on the floor."

Charlie was standing at the end of the bar. We shook hands and I introduced Holloway. As usual Charlie didn't get the name,

262

but he got enough to say, "Good evening, Doctor." He lifted a gin bottle and I nodded. Holloway nodded, too. They were very dry. Holloway put his glass down. "Do you mind if I phone my service?" he asked.

I gestured toward the back of the room. "Give the boy at the desk my name," I told him. Charlie drained a dividend into my glass. Suddenly I remembered an engagement I had for the following week. There was a breeding farm in Georgia concentrating in our blood line and they wanted to talk about another bull. This was one of the jobs that I had inherited from Matt; it was a date of long standing; I was going to have to muddle through it alone.

Holloway came back and Charlie automatically commenced another round. "Everything under control?" I asked.

He nodded.

"How would you like to take yourself four or five days shooting in South Carolina?"

"Is that a hypothetical question or are you asking me?"

"I'm asking you."

"Why not? When do we leave?"

"We could leave tonight," I suggested.

"Why not!"

Joe was on the switchboard. "Get me Mr. Thomas Prentice, Prentice Plantation, Prentice, South Carolina."

"You mean they forgot to name the state after him too?" Joe smiled.

"And when you've got that started, call Eastern Air and get two reservations on the next plane to Charleston. If I'm talking, write the departure and arrival time on a card and hold it up to me in the booth."

The line was clear through to Charleston, and then there was a humming as the rural circuits came in.

"Hello, Tommy!"

"How are you, young fellow— Now hear this! The Captain speaking!" It was an old gag between us. Something warm happens when, after years have passed, an old friend picks your voice up out of the night and you're right back where you were when you were last together. "What's on your mind?"

263

"A friend of mine and I have about four days free. You wouldn't like to give us some bird shooting, would you?"

"I'd love it."

Joe was outside the booth holding up a sheet of paper. I read his message. "There's a plane that gets into Charleston at quarter to twelve tonight."

"I'll meet you. A male or a female gazelle?"

"A what?" And then I remembered the story. "A male!" I realized the thought that was going through his mind. "Look, Tommy, it's about that, too. Angelica died this morning. I've just come back from her funeral."

"Oh." There was a long pause, and the humming on the line whined up and down in cycles and then the Charleston operator was asking, "Is this line free?" I knew it was the Charleston operator from the "you all" way she said li-on. "No, we're still talking," Tommy said, but he wasn't talking, neither of us were. Finally I heard him clear his throat. "What the hell can you say? Come on down here."

When I hung up I could hear Holloway in the next booth speaking to his service. "Tell 'em anything," he finished. "Tell 'em I'm big game shooting in Africa and I'll be back in four days—tell 'em my grandmother died and I've gone to the ball game. You've got the address?"

The door opened and he was glancing at his watch. "What about gear?"

"We'll live on borrowed gear."

"Then what are we waiting for? Let's go!"

There was the smell of hot oil as we stepped out of the plane and then a gust of wind and the sea smell of salt and sweet grasses, and the primordial breath of tidal flats. Tommy was at the foot of the steps, and he led us across to the station wagon. In a few moments the city was behind us and we were off across a lonely countryside.

We didn't talk much, and we didn't talk about Angelica at all. It was only when we were finally standing in front of the fire, baking the chill out of ourselves, that Tommy repeated, "What the hell can you say, John." Then he put his glass down. "You

264

look beat up. Both of you look beat up. Why don't you turn in—unless you want to talk, that is?"

Tommy wandered into my bedroom as I started to strip. "You know where everything is. If it isn't there look for it. If you still don't find it, yell for it." The phrase rang an echo of memory. That night in Haviland I'd said almost these identical words to Angelica. His hand rested on my shoulder for a moment and I thought he was going to say something, but instead he went out and closed the door.

Holloway was in the library with Tommy when I came down the next morning; he was wearing his borrowed gear and they were drinking their before-breakfast coffee. I poured myself a cup and then spilled a half jigger of black rum into it from the bottle on the tray.

"Quite an authoritative way to take your vitamins early in the morning," Holloway observed.

Tommy had been showing him the areas of shooting on a map which hung on the wall. "And over here"—Tommy's finger ran up along the east boundary of the Prentice plantation—"that's the Barnes land." I was conscious of Holloway's glance and I started to say something, but I had a mouthful of coffee and the coffee was on the near side of scalding, and then the moment passed.

"I've got to telephone New York." I left them and went into the other room. As the operator took the call I glanced at my watch. It was only quarter to eight—but what the hell, an undertaking establishment is like the Nevada roulette tables, they're never closed for business. There was an unctuous voice on the line, but it got very matter of fact and businesslike when he found out what I wanted. Yes, he had the change of address right. Air mail, special delivery. *The package* would reach me the next morning. I got the sudden impact of a cylindrical package; I'd seen them before and I knew what they looked like—like four quarter-pound tins of tobacco mailed to you by Mr. Smythe at Dunhill's. A boy would deliver it at the post office, and a man with a rubber stamp would bang on the cancellations and heave it into an air-mail sack filled with all the other unrelated things that people felt they had to have in a hurry. Maybe this was why I had come down here and I didn't know it.

265

"Get your call?" Tommy inquired when I came back.

"Yes, I got it. Let's eat!" I led the way into the dining room.

It was on the last morning. Tommy was to join us later and Holloway and I had started off alone. We'd had two good days of shooting and in the evenings—the line came back to me—*we'd tired the sun with talking and sent him down the sky*. We'd talked about everything; everything, that is, except one thing. We hadn't talked about Angelica. The package from New York had been delivered the day before with just a street number for a return address, and no other suggestion of its contents. Neither Tommy nor Holloway had given it a second notice when I picked it up from the hall table as we came in from an afternoon of shooting. I was reminded of it now; it was a little heavier and a little bulkier than the packet of sandwiches I carried in the musette bag slung over my shoulder.

Holloway glanced at me. "When you lay a ghost you do a very thorough job of it."

"It was probably a damnfool thing to have come down here. I didn't think it through—it was an impulse."

Holloway shrugged. "Where a ghost is, is where you lay it." We started down the swale. "*Exorcise* would be a better word to use." He was still pursuing the thought.

I missed two birds that were fair shots and I could see Holloway looking at me; the dogs were looking at me, too. I reloaded and then carried my gun, breech open, and worked over to the left and away from Holloway.

"There's some first-rate cover on the higher land," I called. "Then follow down to the woods road. You'll come on a bridge below a big pool—I'll meet you there."

Presently the ground dropped away and beyond the trees was the blue of water. I came out on the shelving rock. And then I knew it wasn't any good. Memory and grief start out by being hard sharp cores of pain, unspeakable pockets of agony that lodge in your viscera and knot in your throat; that's the way they start out. Then shortly, the anodyne of going on living overlays the pain until it's no longer pain, but just an inward part of yourself that you carry around with you: a phrase, a memory, a color, the way someone walks ahead of you in a crowd, the sound of footsteps of someone walking behind you in the dark; only now you're not really feeling things, you're just watching another part of yourself feeling something. I could make myself remember Angelica, but I couldn't make myself remember the sick emptiness of that earlier time when we'd looked at each other and seen that it had stopped being good between us.

I opened the musette bag and slipped out the cylindrical container. The paper was brittle and I slit a line with my thumbnail just beneath the lid. There was a granular sound against the tin as I turned it. She had been so lithe and wonderfully animal and her flesh had been sun-touched, all over; and I had fallen in love with her and hated her at the same instant—wanted her and run away from her. She had wanted things on her terms and not on mine, and later, much later when the chips were down between us, there weren't any terms to meet on. These things are done with ingredients of illusion; and without illusion—well, that wasn't what we had wanted.

The top of the lid came off. I didn't look down. I could hear it like sand and pieces of shell falling on the rock.... *n'enquerez, de septmaine.... Ou elles sont, ne de cest an.... Car ce refrain le vous remaine:... Mais ou sont les neiges d'antan!*

The empty tin can described the parobolic ballistic of a falling object, hit the water, seemed to hesitate for an instant and then slipped beneath the surface. I could remember the pale aqueous blue and the cold shimmering play of light against the sand and the way the reef of rock looked when I had opened my eyes beneath the water—only the tears men weep are hot—and then I was aware that Holloway was standing on the opposite shore staring at me. I started to walk down toward the bridge and my boots crunched something on the rock. I stepped back and turned around and crossed to the higher land.

Holloway was silent as he joined me, and we walked down along the little valley. He kicked aside a branch that lay beside the trail. "Maybe that's why you came here. It was better this way. The dead must be buried." We were both silent for a few hundred yards and then he said, "I can catch an early afternoon plane back. And you?"

"I still have to go down to Georgia."

"That can't wait?"

267

"It's something to do. The first thing at hand to pick up and go on with the business of living life."

"I guess you're right," he said.

We stopped at a little rise of land. It's a run-to-seed countryside, the soil has run thin, but it's still heavy with so much living that has been lived on it. "You'll probably never be coming back here," Holloway said.

"Yes, I know."

Tommy said something of the same thing that evening as we waited for my train at the station. He said: "This is sort of out of your orbit, John. I'm glad you came down, but we probably won't be seeing each other here again."

"I'll be seeing you up north," I told him.

"Yes, that's right. We'll be seeing each other up north. I want to see what you do with that farm of yours. I want to see what you do with yourself." The rails were humming at our feet and then the beam of the engine's headlight cut the night into sharp edges for an instant, a signal light turned from red to green. "Look, feller, I've tried to say it, but I haven't found the words that make sense. When the cards fall that way, what the hell can you say?" His hand gripped mine. He said something else, but in the thunder of the train and gust of wind and cinders I didn't hear him; and then I was aboard and it was moving, and time and the scene were cut by that goddamned lonely wail that a locomotive makes in the night. It can be bad when you hear it at a distance; it can be worse when you're on the train.

Sixteen

When I got back to New York it was as if I had lived through a week out of time and context. It could have been another year, another lifetime. Nothing happened when I passed Angelica's apartment on my way out of town. I don't know what I expected to happen—but nothing happened. For a moment I had the impulse to stop in for a drink at Holloway's place, but there was something else that I wanted more. I wanted—and for the first time in my life in such terms—I wanted to get back to Haviland; I wanted to be home.

It was past eleven when I swung off the main road and took the turning for the Hill. As I came up to the Jennings Place there was a light in the upstairs window and I slipped the car out of gear and let it roll to a stop. Sooner or later I'd have to face Frankie and clean things up between us, but I didn't think I would make a very good job of it that night. The car was starting forward again when I saw Frankie's shadow move beside the curtain. I pretended to myself that she wouldn't know it had been I.

In order not to waken Elizabeth I pulled the car up to the main barn and left it there. In the morning Will Talcott would find it and drive it back to the house, and Mrs. Haines would know I had returned and she would bring coffee up at seven and life would slip back into its normal course. I crunched out my cigarette on the gravel and stepped into the barn. It was warm and steamy and heavy with the smells of living. One old lady turned around nervously and then quieted as I put my hand on her flank and she recognized my voice. When I stepped out into the night again my breath hung like white cotton on the still air. There was a scurry through the bushes and a low dark form was wiggling toward me, the way only a setter does when it's glad to see you, and Joy was by my side, her nose nuzzling at my hand. Someone had let her out and she'd had business of her own that night. She ran circles around me as I walked back to the house.

There was a light on in my room when I got there. I'd sent a wire from Washington saying that I might arrive late, and there was a thermos of coffee with a plate of sandwiches and a decanter of whisky on the table in front of the fire. There was also a small vase of yellow roses. Why the hell did they have to be yellow roses? As I picked them up to put them outside the door, the smell of them almost made my stomach churn. A card that had been propped against their side fell to the floor. On it was written *Frankie;* just that, and nothing more. How could the poor kid have known what yellow roses would do to me? I felt a little like a dog because I knew why she hadn't written anything else; I'd made her self-conscious and gun-shy about the sentiments and the thoughts that came tumbling out of her heart. I heard Elizabeth's steps in the hall and then she was at the door. "I was awake. I heard you come in. The coffee was made just an hour ago, it should be hot."

"Woman's first preoccupation seems to be with a man's belly." I kissed her.

"Aren't you oversimplifying things a little?" Elizabeth smiled. "Actually, the coffee and sandwiches were Mrs. Haines' contribution. The whisky was mine. The flowers were Frankie's." She took them out of my hand. "You were going to put them out in the hall?"

"No, let them stay. They gave me something of a jolt. I got some flowers for Angelica the day of her funeral. All the man had was yellow roses."

"Poor Frankie," Elizabeth murmured. "She meant so well. That was all they had at Renney's greenhouse, too."

"It doesn't matter, let them stay."

"Do you want to talk?" Elizabeth asked.

"I'd rather not."

"If you do, come into my room, I'll probably be reading for a while." She stopped at the door. "When you get to my age," she said, "you feel that you have gone through enough to have discovered a pattern and achieved a wisdom and a philosophy

270

about life. All that you really learn is acquiescence; life happens and you accept it on its own terms and keep on going." Her hand brushed across my arm. "You also discover something else," she added.

"What?"

"That you become a little sententious and preachy in your old age. Good night, John."

"How's Frankie?" My question stopped her at the door.

Elizabeth seldom pondered her words, this time she did. "A little shaken. This whole thing has bitten pretty deeply into her."

"You mean Angelica?"

"Angelica, yes; and you, too. Or am I reading too much into it?"

"I don't know," I confessed.

"Then, too, I think that a lot she held back when Alyse died is only coming to the surface now. Try to be gentle with her, John."

"I'll be gentle with her." I patted her on the arm and a moment later heard her door close.

I was under the covers and the lights were out before I realized that Joy was sitting in her corner and hadn't bedded down. I got up and went to the closet and looked for Matt's shooting jacket, but it was gone. Mrs. Haines must have sent it out to be cleaned. "Too bad, old girl." I patted her head. *"Things* pass, too." I reached down a stained old coat of my own and spread it on the floor for her. She sniffed at it and looked up at me. "If I can't explain it to myself, I can't explain it to you," I said.

Only sentimental idiots pretend that dogs can understand the words men speak to them; that's nonsense, they don't, but they do understand the sense of things you say. She nuzzled the coat and made three turns about it and then curled up on it with her nose buried under her tail, but her eyes were open and following me across the room. "The heart once given, can it be given again?" The words Elizabeth had once spoken came back to me. "Yes, in a way, and without unfaith. Given the power to love we can love many things in their appointed time."

That next morning I was up at the barns a few moments before Will Talcott came. He nodded to me and drew me down the milking line.

"The old girl's done it again." He was standing behind the

Radiant Victris cow and she turned her head to look at him and then went back to chewing her cud in a smug self-satisfied way.

"Done what?" I asked.

"*Done* caught herself with calf; or I better give up farming and go to storekeeping."

I looked down the line. It was a very special line and the Tracy farm was proud of it; the Radiant cow and her twelve living daughters.

"She's a whole milk factory, all by herself." Will stroked her flank.

The line stirred with before-milking restlessness and the Radiant cow gave an impressive moo; the line quieted, the Queen had spoken.

"Life goes on." Will and I walked back down the barn. That was all he said, but I knew he was talking to me and not about the Radiant cow. Mrs. Haines would have told him about Angelica; it would be too much to expect of Mrs. Haines that she hadn't.

"The McClery farm in Georgia bought the young Victris grandson."

He looked up at me waiting for me to finish. "Your price, not his, I hope. McClery likes to spend anything but money."

"I wasn't in the mood for bargaining. They paid our price."

"That's the best kind of a mood to be in for bargaining," Will chuckled.

I ate a bite with the Talcotts and since my car was still at the barn I started for the village without stopping at the house. You can drive to Haviland two ways from the farm. One way is by Tracy's Corners and down into the valley past the Jennings Place; that's the shortest way. I took the road down the South Hill that goes by the Adams' farm and through Tabor Glen, and I admitted to myself that in some departments I was yellow and just putting off the hour.

I finished with the bank first and then went up to Pop Sanford's office and used his phone to call Mrs. Haines. "I won't be back for lunch," I told her.

"This is Miss Constance's night," Mrs. Haines reminded me. "So don't be late."

I'd forgotten. Constance and Frankie and Elizabeth; the table was going to be heavy with overtones.

272

"You ordered something from New York?" Mrs. Haines asked. "A big crate with a lot of excelsior in it, no name on it? It's cluttering up the front hall."

I recognized her curiosity. "Have Will unpack it and unclutter the front hall; it's probably something for the farm."

I walked up to the diner for a bite to eat with Pop, and while we were eating, Semple came in and bought a New York paper; he glanced in my direction as if he wasn't seeing me. Then he folded the paper and left.

"Semple's got some bee in his bonnet these days." Sanford looked after him for a moment and then returned to his corn beef hash. "Place smells fresher with him out of it," he disposed of Semple.

Later I drifted back to his office with him and sat about, talking for a while. Sanford is an easy man to talk to; his mind will go along with you, about anywhere you want to go. Finally, however, he looked over at me and said, "John, you give me the impression of a man trying awfully hard not to do something."

"You might be right. Unfortunately I'm not sure exactly what it is I don't want to do."

"That makes it doubly difficult, doesn't it?" He broke the ash off his cigar. "I suppose if it's anything I could help in, you would say so."

"And if not, get out of your office and let you get to work." I picked up my hat. "I'll be seeing you, Counselor."

Will Talcott hailed me in front of the bank as he made the turn in the farm truck. He had a load of fence wire in it. "You haven't forgotten that you have a date this afternoon with Johnson from the Connecticut College," he called. "He wants to check over our breeding records for that article he's doing."

My half-formed intention to stop by the Jennings Place and see Frankie went by the board. When I got to the Hill, I left the car at the house and walked up to the barns, just in time to meet Johnson. Talcott joined us later and it was the end of the afternoon and the milking had already started before Johnson left. Will and I saw him off and then Will turned to me. "For a quiet fellow you certainly can raise a lot of hell on your time off. Wait'll you get back to the house. Mrs. Haines is ready to pop."

273

"She's been popping ever since I can remember. What's it about this time?"

"Not that I blame you," he laughed. "As pretty a little heifer as you'd be likely to come on in a whole lifetime."

"I don't get it."

"You will when you see Mrs. Haines." He picked up a milking machine and headed for the barn.

Mrs. Haines came out of the dining room as I opened the front door. "Where're you going to put it?" were her first words.

"Put what?"

"*Her!* I don't know what's getting into this family." She led me to the living room.

It's something of a shock when a hand reaches out of the grave and touches you. On a table by the window was the terra cotta of the gay laughing girl that had been in Angelica's room, only now it was bundled up in a clean dust cloth and looked like someone trying to fight her way out of a tent. I unswaddled the figure. Angelica must have arranged to send it the morning of her death. A gift of loveliness for the things we'd shared or a plea to be remembered in gentle laughing terms? I wondered which. I handed the cloth to Mrs. Haines. "You forgot something."

"More like she forgot something." Her lips were very thin.

"She's quite happy with her clothes off, she was born that way."

"So was I," Mrs. Haines delivered. "But I was never for lolligagging about in the living room without a stitch on."

"No, I imagine you never have," I agreed.

"What'll your mother have to say to it?"

"Hasn't she seen it yet?"

"She was up in her room writing letters when Will unpacked it, and she's resting now before dinner."

"What do you think she'll have to say about it, Mrs. Haines?"

"If I didn't know this family so well, it would be easier to answer that," she said primly. "Where're you going to keep it?"

"You don't approve of it here, I gather?"

"With maids coming in to dust, and ladies here as guests? It ought to be stored away in the attic; you couldn't keep it in your bedroom."

"Why not? She came out of a bedroom."

"Then she ought to have stayed in it," Mrs. Haines affirmed. "Who would want to go to bed in a room with that in it ?"

I glanced at the little figure. "You'd be surprised, Mrs. Haines. I hope God has been very good to you and you've had a very rich life to make up for all that you've missed."

She gave me a look to see whether I meant what she thought I meant and then headed back toward the kitchen. "While we're on the subject, there's some things I put in your bureau drawer that you ought to look to before they become the talk of everybody in the house." She closed the door righteously behind her.

I gathered, as I started upstairs to change for dinner, that she'd unpacked my suitcase and come on Frankie's stockings and underthings that had been left in the hotel room that unhappy night. God knows what manner of legend Mrs. Haines would be building out of this bit of evidence.

As I was getting out a fresh shirt I saw that they had been stowed where I would be certain to come upon them. There's something about a woman's intimate garments that is poignantly defenseless and vulnerable. There are those who would call the thought obscure or try to explore its pathology, but it didn't come to me in those terms; it was just that the sight of a sheer silk stocking, empty and formless, evoked a passing and strange sense of pity and tenderness. I wondered why some poet had never taken this theme and then I remembered that at least one poet had. Herrick had had certain things to say about his Julia's clothes. There was the faintest odor of lilac, or some clear but indeterminate spring flower, that hung upon the room; not a sachet, but something that Frankie must have used on her body. I couldn't find anything else, so I took a scarf and made her things into a small bundle.

Constance and Frankie were downstairs in the library when I finally got there. "I didn't hear your car," I greeted Frankie.

"I walked up the hill. It's a lovely evening."

There was an indefinable constraint between us. We were both acting like guests who had just met in a strange house. Then Elizabeth joined us and I suggested we go into the drawing room for drinks.

"I'll have just a half a glass of sherry," Constance tentatively suggested as if she were inaugurating an innovation; I had the sense that she enjoyed the ritual of her sherry more than the sherry itself.

"I'm in the mood for a very dry, and very large martini," I announced. "How about you two?"

"A half a one," Frankie said, and Elizabeth added, "And remember you ought to show more than the label of the vermouth bottle to the shaker. Your father never cared for these straight-gin mixtures, or maybe the vermouth was better in those days."

The overtones were beginning to fill the house again. Elizabeth could talk of the lover who had been Constance's husband, and nothing stirred in discord within the room. Presently someone would speak of Matt and Alyse in normal terms and those ghosts would find their way back into our midst. I helped Constance out of her chair.

"Did either of you ever try a martini with absinthe in it?" I don't know why Holloway bobbed into my mind at that instant.

"Wouldn't they taste sort of—" Frankie crinkled her nose reaching for the idea of what they would taste like.

"Let's settle for their just being dry," Elizabeth suggested.

"Anyway we haven't got any absinthe," I said. "We'll float a single drop of illusion; lovely, bright and iridescent illusion on the top of them."

Elizabeth glanced at me and then toward Frankie. I seemed to be doing my best to make an awkward evening even more awkward. *When you sober up, try to remember the way your mind worked tonight, you might learn a few things about yourself.* That was what Holloway had said. Well, I was sober, but what the hell had he been talking about?

The drawing-room door was closed—Mrs. Haines had passed that way. I opened it and switched on the lights and headed for the bar table in the corner. I was conscious of the impact of the little statue on the three women as they crossed the room to it. Elizabeth's glance toward me was a question, which for the moment I ignored, and in her sentiency she didn't ask it aloud. Constance went over and circled about the table looking at it. Frankie held back a little and was staring at me; when I glanced up and caught her gaze she looked back toward the statue. There were too many questions in her eyes to be answered at that moment and

276

in that room, or maybe they were questions that would never be answered. I took the drinks across the room to them.

Constance put her hand out to touch the figure and then stopped. She seemed to look at her hand, dry and wrinkled, and stiff and heavy with years, and then she withdrew her hand and fretted with her evening bag. There are times when beauty should not be touched. She glanced at Frankie and then back to the figure as if she was trying to recapture the shape of a young girl's body.

Frankie had finished her drink and put the empty glass on the table. "I'm glad she sent it to you, John. I would like to be remembered like this by someone who had once loved me."

It was one of those small bombshells—I don't think she meant it to explode the way it did.

"It belonged to Angelica," I explained, and I could tell from Constance's face that she knew of Angelica. "She must have arranged to have it sent to me the morning she died."

Constance passed me on her way to the sofa. "You fool," she muttered.

"I think I'll have another cocktail," Frankie said. "A dividend! —A full one this time with a whole dash of illusion; lovely, bright and iridescent illusion floating on the top of it. They teach you about drinking at college these days. Or don't you approve, John? Would you rather that I mixed it myself?"

I mixed it for her. I could see Elizabeth trying to understand the implications of the outburst and obviously floundering because she couldn't know the whole story. Frankie took the drink from me and, half turning toward the little statue, raised it and emptied the glass before she took it from her lips. It seemed a little melodramatic, but I knew what she meant.

Mrs. Haines providentially announced dinner. There are strictures of discipline about a dining table that dictate social conformity. We all came under the spell of the ritual and things began to go better. Presently Constance started to reminisce about her early days on the Hill and to talk about Old Matt; she even touched on the days when Old Matt and Elizabeth had first met. And something was said about young Matt and Alyse and I glanced at Frankie—she was white but she seemed under control. Both Elizabeth and Constance had things to say about Matt's wife Susan and then they were back to Alyse and the first days of the "Frenchwoman" on the Hill. The ghosts were really walking this night. I noticed Mrs. Haines refilling Frankie's wineglass, and the question crossed my mind of how many times she might have refilled it. Finally dinner was over and by an unspoken mutual consent we all gravitated toward the library and not the drawing room.

I stirred up the fire and asked if anyone wanted a drink. It was a rhetorical question, none of them besides myself ever took a drink after dinner, but Frankie was still possessed with perversity and said she'd have one: "Scotch on the rocks." My hands were tied. That's one drink you can't dilute and fake. I made it as decently small as I could, however.

Elizabeth and Constance talked in a desultory way and largely about nothing. Frankie sipped at her drink and wandered in and out of their conversation. It had to do with Mrs. Renney in the village who did sewing, and whether it was better to mulch roses and have mice girdle them in the winter or not mulch and have them winterkill. Constance said that camphor placed about in the garden would keep the mice down. I found I had very little to contribute to all this. Once or twice I tried to talk to Frankie, but she turned monosyllabic and the efforts died stillborn. She finished her drink and this time she didn't ask me, she got up and mixed herself another one. I was aware that Elizabeth was aware, and that Frankie saw the glance that passed between us. Her answer was to pour a little more whisky in the glass. I opened the window—the room seemed surcharged and freighted with the currents of too many lives. Constance asked me to get her wrap, and Elizabeth asked me to close the window, and the sense of edginess increased. Finally Mrs. Talcott came in to get Constance, and Frankie put down her glass and said that she had better be going, too.

"I'll get out the car and drive you down," I offered.

"I'd rather walk," Frankie said.

"Then I'll walk you down the hill."

"Look, let's not be complicated about this, or conventionally polite. It's just down the hill to my own house."

"You're the one who's being complicated." My irritation got the better of me. "If you want to walk down the hill by yourself in the middle of the night and be a forthright feminist, go ahead! Break your neck for all I care; but I'd advise wearing flat-heel shoes!"

278

I thought she was going to lose her temper, but the high points of color in her cheeks faded and instead she slipped on her coat. "Thank you for offering, anyway."

Elizabeth tried to press a flashlight into her hands at the door, but she said there was a moon and she would only forget to return it.

"And besides, she wouldn't get her girl scout merit badge for walking home in the dark," I threw in.

I could sense Elizabeth's irritation at the whole silly performance, and her effort to keep it in check. Then the door closed and Elizabeth turned to me. "What are you and Frankie fighting about?" she asked.

"We're not fighting about anything. She's just being a damned difficult brat."

"And she hasn't got anything to be difficult about?"

"I suppose she has," I agreed. "Who hasn't?"

"Thank you for a very pleasant evening!" Elizabeth said. "A charming evening! Now what are you waiting for? For your pride to simmer down?"

"This has nothing to do with pride."

"Then stop acting younger than she is, and go after her. I will not have that child walking the roads alone at night."

"As if anything could happen to her on these roads. And look, let's get this settled once and for all. She's either a child or she's not. If she's a child, she shouldn't be living down there alone."

"She's a child!" Elizabeth said.

I looked at her and then capitulated. "All right, I'll take little Miss Moppet home."

I went up to my room and stuffed into my pocket the scarf with Frankie's things in it. On my way down, I passed Elizabeth on the stairs. "I won't be long." I kissed her.

There was a moon, but not much of a moon. Low scudding clouds whipped across the brow of the Hill and galloped in patches of blackness across the fields. I reached the crossroads and was starting down the Hill Road before I saw her in the distance, just at the turn. She seemed to be walking quickly, almost running, and then she was around the curve and out of sight.

"If you have any idea that I'm going to make an idiot out

279

of myself racing after you—" I thought as I quickened my stride —and then I found myself running, too. There'd been enough damn foolishness about this night and it was time for one of the two of us to stop it. It seemed I was elected.

I thought when I'd made the turn that I would see her in the distance ahead of me, but for an instant the clouds opened and the whole stretch of the road was clearly lighted and there was no sight of her. "She's also working out her merit badge for the hundred yard dash," I decided.

I slowed my pace and rehearsed all the things that I was going to say to Miss Frankie when I got to the Jennings Place. What she needed was a good sound spanking to knock some sense into her head; I recognized that as a considerably involuted metaphor. A spanking probably wouldn't do her much good, but it would have been a great satisfaction to me. I discarded the whole idea as not being a very good one. But I did make up my mind to one thing. Frankie was going back to college. That much was going to be accomplished in my talk with her. It would be passing the buck; but sometimes the only thing you can do is pass the buck. It would at least get her out of my hair, and it might get some sense into her head; occasionally colleges succeeded in doing that much.

The Jennings Place was dark when I came up to it, and I was in no mood to play hide-and-seek in the middle of the night. I knocked on the door and called to her but there was no answer, and then I tried the knob and found that the door was open. I felt she was probably sulking upstairs in her bedroom. I finally found a light and turned it on and went to the foot of the stairs. "All the funny business is over," I bellowed. "Come down here and we're going to thrash this out—and you'll be lucky if that's all that gets thrashed."

I think I knew at that moment that the house was empty, but I couldn't believe it; it didn't make sense. I went up to her bedroom door. "Frankie, come out of there," I called, "or I'm going to come in and yank you out."

The room was empty. Part of my mind tried to tell me that she was probably standing out in the garden letting me make a prime jackass out of myself, but in another part of my mind the certainty was growing that something was wrong here. My hand went out to the phone to call Will Talcott and get one or two of the men and then some self-protective better judgment stopped me. What could they do but search the road I had already walked down, and I'd better find out what was at the bottom of all this before I raised the countryside. I raced for the old barn behind the house. There was just a chance that she'd got back to the place ahead of me and taken her car and driven somewhere; but I would have seen the lights on the Haviland road. Even that thought vanished; it was still there, with the keys dangling from the switch.

There weren't too many possibilities, and they all passed through my mind. She could have stumbled and fallen into the roadside and I might have passed her without seeing her; but she would have had to hit her head and be unconscious—not likely. I scanned the roadside as I drove her car up the hill. Or she could have stepped into the bushes and let me pass and then returned to the Big House feeling that a bit of a wild-goose chase would be good for me. There was only the night light in the hall and the light in Elizabeth's room. I turned the car and headed back down the hill. I told myself that she must be at the Jennings Place when I got there. As I made the turn in the road the lights were on in the house and my heart lifted before I remembered that it was I who had left them on. My call again echoed through the empty rooms. I glanced at my watch. It was quarter past twelve.

Then a thought hit me; it didn't make sense, but nothing was making sense. She might have taken the old short cut, beyond the turn in the Hill Road, the one that led down to the glen and came out in the meadows behind the Jennings Place. It was rocky and steep and it would have been a crazy thing to do on a dark night, without a light and in high-heeled slippers, but at that moment I wasn't entertaining too high an opinion of Frankie's sanity. There was a flashlight on the hall table and I grabbed it and started out across the fields behind the house. To save time, I headed cross country and of course missed all the gates. Navigating the second barbwire fence I hooked my sleeve, and gashed my arm, and cursed Frankie—in that order. Then I discovered a spot of low ground in the pasture lot beyond, discovered it hock-deep in muck and marsh; that was a job we'd have to get to in the spring. And to make the evening complete, in the dark I couldn't find the stone bridge over the brook, and had to wade the ankle-deep stream; it was cold and damned unpleasant. Finally I found the foot of the old trail that led into the woods and up along the glen. There was a soft spot where the trail was clear and I played the torch across it; but there were no footsteps, so she hadn't passed that way.

"John Milnor, Indian scout—you'll get your Trail Blazer badge for this night's work." By now I knew it had been a stupid thing to try the old road; a waste of time, when time was probably an essential. I'd have to walk all the way up to the farm before I could get to a phone and a car—and then a nice business with everybody in the town looking for a lost girl, and wondering what lay behind the story. Damn it, nothing could lie behind the story but a spoiled brat who had blown her top and was trying to make a bid for attention. You just didn't get lost on the Hill Road between the farm and the Jennings Place! You couldn't do it if you tried!

I had to take it slowly because the path was rough. I was trying to hold my balance on a loose stone when there was a shrill, ear-piercing scream from almost beside me. When you're ready for something, braced for it, you can take quite a lot. It's the un-expected that throws you. I did what any green kid would do. My footing slipped, the light went clattering down on the rocks and I could hear the glass tinkle as it went out.

"Where are you?" I called as soon as I had regained my balance. There was a thrashing in the woods to my right and then her scream commenced again, and it never stopped. Just one un-ending high-pitched scream exploding out of an agony of terror, but it gave me a bearing to locate her in the dark and I struggled the fifteen or twenty feet through the brush and rough ground to her side. She was still screaming. I could see her, a blur of light-colored clothing against the shadows, and as I reached down to her I thought that a wildcat had suddenly attacked me. She was on her feet and a knee was into my groin and her fingernails were tearing at my face and trying to get at my eyes. Nice thanks for the good samaritan, I thought, and then I realized that this wasn't a fit of schoolgirl hysterics, it was terror—uncontrollable, blinding terror. I managed to grab her hands and got an arm

282

about her, but she sprang from me. She lurched and fell headlong and then she was trying to crawl into the brush away from me.

"Frankie," I yelled. "Snap out of it, you crazy little fool."

She couldn't have heard me, she was screaming so loud. Then I knew there wasn't anything for it but to let her have it. I tackled her and got my arm about her. It was an army judo hold; but either the hold was no good or it shouldn't be used on girls—she had her teeth into my hand. There was nothing else to do—I slapped her as hard as I could across the face. Her teeth came out of my hand and she started to scream again.

"Stop it, Frankie! For God's sake, stop it!" My hand was slapping across her face trying to drive the words into her head. "It's me, John Milnor! I'm trying to help you! Stop doing this terrible thing to yourself and to me!" My hand was stinging. I knew there must be some better way to do this, but I didn't know what it was. "Stop it, you crazy little fool, I don't want to hurt you, I love you!" I was wondering how hard you had to hit a girl to knock her out, and how hard you could hit her without breaking her jaw.

She ran out of terror and she ran out of breath at the same time, but she didn't run out of hysterics. The nice strong stable ones, when they crack, crack higher than a kite. The sobs just ripped through her in a convulsion. I've had dogs with convulsions and I know the only thing you can do for them is to hold them tight until it passes. And then I realized that she was quieting. Not completely; she was being sick first, all over my jacket; and then the shame of that quieted her.

Now isn't this just ducky, I thought. I get ripped on barbed wire and slog through a marsh, almost break my neck on the rocks, get clawed up and have my hand bitten—and then, as if the evening were lacking something, I get sick on.

She was quiet now, except that a chill worked through her and her teeth chattered and her limbs were shaking—somehow she'd lost her topcoat. She was clutching me in a torment of despair. I tried to disengage myself enough to get out of my jacket and I finally managed it, one arm at a time, and after cleaning it off a little on the ground, put it about her shoulders.

"Come on, let's get out of here. You've got a chill, you're going to catch pneumonia or something."

"There's a man here in the woods." Her whisper was dry and cracked.

"Sure there's a man here in the woods, me."

"No, there's a man. He followed me on the road, that's why I ran down the path."

"Is that what this is all about?" I asked her. "I was the man who was behind you on the road."

"No, there was someone else, it's the man who's been writing the letters. Ssshush . . . listen now . . ."

The woods were quiet; that is, the woods are never quiet, nature has a life of her own, but there was no alien sound—and then close at hand I could hear a purposeful rustling through the thicket. For an instant the hair rose on the back of my neck. This show with Frankie had got my wind up, too. Then I relaxed.

"It's a porcupine," I told her. "A very unsophisticated or a very old and deaf porky, or he'd be in the next county with all the noise we've been making. Come on now, get up, I'm going to get you back to the house."

All this was going to make a pretty weird story to tell Elizabeth and Mrs. Haines in the middle of the night, and it pretty much spelled the end of Frankie's living alone down at the Jennings Place; that much would have been accomplished. I pulled her to her feet. As I started to lead her back to the path she crumpled with the first step. "I can't," she whimpered, "—my ankle, it won't hold me."

I found her leg in the dark and she shuddered and tried to pull away from me as I slipped my hand down to her ankle. It was swollen like a baseball. I couldn't tell whether it was broken or not, but I could guess how much it hurt. I cursed myself for the job of smashing the flashlight.

"I'll make you comfortable and go and get Will Talcott and one of the men." I could feel the tremor go through her body and the sharp intake of breath; she was right back on the edge of hysteria. "All right, I won't leave you, but what in the world are you afraid of? It isn't like you. You're only a few hundred yards from the farm." She was sobbing now and holding onto me. "I won't leave you, but I've got to get you out of here."

I picked her up in my arms and managed to get back to the path. It would have been nearer perhaps to go up the hill to the farm, but it would be a steep climb and the rocks in the dark would be difficult to navigate. I started down the path back toward the Jennings Place. Frankie was quieter now, but she was still gasping in her breath in broken half-sobs and she was clutching me like a frightened child. Once I almost stumbled and as I regained my footing I tightened my hold on her. She gave a little shuddering cry and pulled my hand up along her side. I was conscious of the softness of her breast. "I hurt my side when I fell. Something cracked. It hurts way inside."

This time I found the stone bridge and the farm road that led through the barways; and I was thankful that at this season of the year they were all open. The clouds were still racing across the sky neck and neck with their shadows that plummeted across the fields. Once we were out of the woods, the wind was cold; I didn't feel it with the exertion of carrying her, but Frankie shivered in my arms.

"It's better now." She told me in something more like her normal voice, "I couldn't have stayed in the woods alone. You can put me down here and I'll wait if you want to get someone."

"It isn't far from here, and you don't weigh anything. It's better this way." It was true, she seemed to weigh nothing at all. Just a gawky frightened kid who had tried to be grown up, and had got lost in the woods and become terrified. "Just a little bit further. How do things feel now?"

For a moment she didn't answer and then her head pressed tighter against my shoulder. "I'm trying to pretend that it never happened, trying to pretend that it doesn't hurt. I'm sorry I lost my head and went all to pieces."

"Stop thinking about it, in a few minutes everything will be all right."

"I didn't think I'd ever be so chicken and helpless."

I patted her, the way you might pat a child or a horse that was frightened—you don't need words, just the touch of a hand to let them know that they are not alone.

"John . . ."

"Yes?"

"I'm sorry that I . . . that I was sick. It's so messy and humiliating, and unlovely."

"You silly kid!" But it was a good sign. When you can get

285

angry with your body for the tricks it plays on you, well then, the terror is past. "I've had worse than that happen to me."

I had, too. The human animal can be pretty undignified when it's scared. I had a tank driver who was one of the bravest men I ever knew. He used to mess himself when things got very bad, and he'd sit cursing and the tears running down his face and he'd kick the controls in and drive on forward, when every instinct and every nerve in his body was screaming to get the hell out of there, and get out fast. Then one night it happened to me and I said: "You son of a bitch, it's contagious!" And he laughed and somehow the fear vanished and he shoved the throttle forward and yelled, "O.K., you kraut bastards, now it's our turn to scare living hell out of you."

"I've had worse than that happen to me," I repeated.

"But I can't forget it," she said.

"Yes, you can. You can forget a lot worse than that."

I kicked open the garden gate. "Is the back door open?"

"No, it's locked. I've been keeping it locked. The keys were in my coat and I lost my coat." She looked up and saw the lights in the house, and a tremor ran through her. "There's someone in the house." Her voice was harsh and dry with fear.

"No one's in the house," I told her. "The front door was open and I left the lights on."

"I couldn't have left the door unlocked."

I was circling the house. "You did, nevertheless." I kicked the door shut behind us and looked down at her, seeing her in the light for the first time. Her dress was torn and she'd lost one shoe and her face was muddy and tear-streaked and her hair was snarled with leaves and twigs. I didn't imagine I looked much better myself.

"We both look like a couple of refugees from a disaster area," I told her as I carried her upstairs and put her down on her bed. "Now let me look at this ankle of yours." I reached for her stocking and she stiffened. It wasn't pain, it was something else and it was pretty obvious what it was. Somehow it surprised me; it made me angry, too.

"Come on, grow up!" She shut her eyes and I could see her knuckles whiten as she clenched her hands. "How the hell stupid can you be!" I undid her stocking and slid it down over her foot.

286

The ankle was swollen and purple. I started to articulate it gently and there was no sense of broken bones, but a grunt of pain escaped through her gritting teeth. I went into the bathroom and let the cold water run and dumped a towel into it. When it was good and chilled I wrung it out and then dampened the end of another towel. Her eyes followed me across the room as I came back and put the cold compress on her ankle. Then I took the damp end of the towel and started to repair her face. Her eyes were swimming with tears and she shook her head to clear them, and her lips tried to smile. Finally I gave her the towel, to tend to herself, and went over to the telephone.

Helen was on duty. "Get me Doctor Farnley," I told her.

"He's in Poughkeepsie. Ruth Hawkins is having her baby tonight. If it's urgent I could get you Doctor Miller, he took a call about half an hour ago."

I glanced down at Frankie. For a cracked ankle Miller would be good enough, but there was something more to all this than met the eye. "I can reach Doctor Miller?"

Frankie shook her head. "Can't you get Farnley?"

I turned back to the phone. "Helen, do you think you could reach Farnley at the hospital, or if you can't, find out how soon he'll be back in Haviland?"

It took only two or three minutes and then Farnley was on the wire. "I'm down at the Jennings Place with Frankie," I told him. "She's had a fall, rather a bad one, and smashed her ankle. She's also hurt her side, up along her ribs."

"Does it hurt to take a full breath?" I relayed Farnley's question to her. The wince she gave was her answer.

"Just about half a breath and then it hurts. . . . Yes. . . . Yes, I know how to do that. . . . Exhale and then good and tight—and long strips. . . . I'll see if she has some. . . . Right!" I put down the phone.

"Farnley'll be here in about two hours," I told her. "He doesn't want you to be moved too much until he gets here, so that rules out getting you up to the Big House. Do you want me to ask Elizabeth to come down?"

"No, don't," she pleaded. "I've made enough of a nuisance out of myself tonight, and it would only upset her—and for what?"

"Mrs. Haines would be a damn nuisance . . ."

287

"I don't need anybody," Frankie insisted. "And she would be a 'damn nuisance.' "

"Have you got any adhesive?"

"There's some in the first-aid kit."

I started for the bathroom.

"It's in the hall closet downstairs," she said.

I started for the stairway.

"My ankle's all right. It doesn't have to be taped up, it's fine with the cold towel on it." She was talking off the top of her chest in an unnatural voice.

"Relax, Florence Nightingale. Just pretend that for once in your life you don't know all the answers."

"Don't leave me." Her voice broke and I turned around at the door and looked at her. Her chin was trembling. There was something, way under the surface, working here and I didn't like it—something more than a girl with a cracked rib and a twisted ankle. This was terror and fear. I went back and stroked her forehead and she quieted and the fear left her eyes. "Be a good soldier," I urged her. "I'm just going down to the closet in the hall. I'm not going to leave you alone. I'll whistle all the way down and back." She gave me a smile; not a very good one, but it was a smile.

When I got out in the hall my mouth was dry and my lips seemed to pucker up and I couldn't whistle to save my soul. When finally it came, it wasn't much of a whistle, but it was a noise —and then I couldn't remember a tune to whistle.

"I can't think of a damn thing to whistle," I called. "How about the Gettysburg address?—*Four score and seven years ago...*" There were three doors in the hall and the one I first opened was the closet. The thought crossed my mind that I had almost been born in this house. Why shouldn't I know which was the hall closet—an extrauterine perception. The whole business between Elizabeth and Matt had started with a sprained ankle. Who was the little girl among the Three Fates, the one with the scissors who snipped the threads—Lachesis? Well, come on sister, get to work with your shears; this is one pattern that doesn't get repeated. It's beneath you! Too corny! "*...one country, indivisible...*" I came back into the room. "Can you beat it? I can't even remember the end of the Gettysburg address, and I got a prize in school once for reciting it! Open up your dress. I want to look at your side."

"I can't . . ." Frankie was clutching at the top of her dress.

I looked down at her for an instant and started to unroll a length of adhesive tape. "What is making you act like a little damn fool?—Why can't you?"

"Because . . ."

I tore off the length of tape and pressed its end to the edge of the table and started to unroll another strip. *"Because*—why?"

"Because I haven't got anything on underneath. I haven't even got a bra on. . . ."

"Oh, that!" I hung the second piece of tape on the table. "Well, it'll teach you to wear one the next time before you go charging around in the woods. —Why the hell haven't you?"

"Because I don't need one!" Her eyes were blazing with fury. "And I don't intend to be touched or mauled by any man, least of all you. If you were the last man in the world . . ."

"Oh, shut up and grow up!"

"And stop telling me to grow up!"

"I'm sorry for that last," I told her. I had three strips of tape on the table by now. "But I want you to quiet down and listen to me. I'm not the least damn bit interested in your body, as a body. You've probably cracked a couple of ribs. It's one chance in fifty that the bone has splintered and can cause you some real trouble. There's no point in taking that one chance, so I'm going to put some tape around you—oh hell, do I have to spell it out?" Her eyes were clenched shut and her hands were stiff along her sides. "That's better." I started to unfasten her dress. "Look, you wouldn't have any feeling about this if I were a doctor, or some stranger helping you in an accident . . ."

"It's different."

"Well, just keep thinking of the similarities." Her slip raised a problem, so I broke the ribbons at her shoulders; it was torn anyway from when she'd fallen. Her eyes were still shut and she gave a shudder.

"Keep on talking," she said irrelevantly.

"All right, this may hurt a little, but it will feel better right afterwards." I drew her slip down to her waist.

There was an angry purple bruise running along her rib case

289

from her side to almost under her breast. It looked like a greenstick fracture, but I couldn't be sure that it hadn't splintered inward. Her eyes were open now and she was watching me, not looking down at herself.

"Roll over on your side," I told her. "You can grit your teeth, this is going to hurt. Now breathe out. All the air in you, breathe it out." I slapped the first piece of plaster about her. "Hold it!" I got the second and third pieces of tape in place. I smoothed the adhesive across her back and then eased her over. Her gaze caught mine and she stared up at me. Then I looked down and straightened the ends of the plaster across her chest. For a brief instant I was seeing her body, I couldn't help it, and then I drew her dress up about her.

I found a cigarette and lit it. "No, I guess you don't have to . . ."

"Have to what?"

I hadn't realized I'd spoken the thought.

"Oh . . ." The color rushed up to her face.

I patted her cheek. "You'll do," I told her. "You'll do fine." I reached into the closet and handed her her nightgown. "Slip out of your clothes and into this, but don't try standing on that foot." I went into the bathroom and did a survey of her medicine chest. "Have you got any sleeping pills?" I called in to her.

"I never use them," she said.

"No, I was afraid not—you're too damned healthy. Can I come in?"

She took a moment to answer before she called me. She looked a little white.

"Hurt much?"

"My chest feels better, but my ankle won't work."

"I told you not to stand on it."

"I just tried."

This is the point that storytellers and novelists always avoid. They get a man and a woman into a jam like this, or even better, alone in a lifeboat and then they ignore the physical functions.

"Do you want to go to the bathroom?" I asked Frankie.

"No . . ."

"You're lying. Your back teeth are floating. Put your arm about my shoulder and I'll help you in."

"No!"

290

"Sometimes you exasperate me!"

"And don't tell me to grow up and don't tell me that you're old enough to be my father!"

"Thanks for correcting me. I was just about to do just that."

"And stop being so smug and superior and self-satisfied!" she cried. "I can't take it any more! I've stopped being your problem child. Yes, I had a crush on you! I thought I was in love with you. What's wrong with that? Every immature, adolescent girl goes through that phase. Well, I'm through it, and well out on the other side! You've screwed up your own life—nobody's going to screw up mine. You've never really fallen in love because you didn't have it in you to fall in love. You've never *done* anything! Everything's always *happened* to you! Well, it doesn't go for Frankie! So you were born a bastard, and let it bite into you! That doesn't mean you have to be a son of a bitch as well! A smug son of a bitch to boot! So you're thirty-nine—and you want to call it forty! You can't wait to become a benevolent old uncle. Well, you can't be my benevolent old uncle . . . !"

The thought crossed my mind that if she didn't watch out she wouldn't have to go to the bathroom. But I was glad that whatever had snapped, had snapped. This was more like the real Frankie.

"Oh you make me sick! All you've got is a handful of memories that you pull out and look at. A girl in Saint-Cloud! And a girl who wouldn't marry you because your father and mother weren't married!—I've got a better reason! And Angelica! Maybe you were poison to each other, maybe it would have busted up! Well then, it would have busted up and you would at least have had that much together. But not Mr. John Almighty Milnor. Sit on your damn mountaintop! And breed your damned cows—that's all you'll breed! Damn you! You almost had me buffaloed. . . . And now I'd like to go to the bathroom."

The only trouble was that I started to laugh. I couldn't control it. As I leaned over to help her up, her hand came across my face. "That's in part payment for your slapping me up in the woods. —No it isn't, it's because I'm damned good and mad."

It was difficult helping her. I supported her, and she hopped on one foot—it hurt her side and she yelped with pain. So I picked her up in my arms and carried her in and deposited her on the john, and then I handed her a mirror and pushed her toothbrush and all the cosmetics that were lying about loose over to her side of the basin.

"You don't intend to stand here?"

"No, I don't. I scarcely imagine that comes under the heading of avuncular duties. Call me when you want to be helped back into bed."

I started to glance at my watch and discovered that I must have lost it in the scrimmage in the woods. It was one thirty by Frankie's bedside clock. I picked up her clothes—they were a mess, rumpled and torn—and tossed them into the closet. Farnley should be showing up within an hour or so. Only the bedside lamp was on and the room was otherwise dark. I lit a cigarette and walked over to the window and looked into the night. It was clearing and the moonlight was bright. Out of the corner of my eye I thought I saw something move by the side of the heavy planting near the road. It happened quickly—between two shadows there seemed to be an image and then there wasn't anything there. I strained to see, and something seemed to move into the deeper shadows. Your senses play tricks on you; when you start imagining, you can imagine a lot of things in the dark. Remembering the ruinous state of Frankie's face, I decided that her vanity would be occupied for some time, and I quietly walked out to the hall and down the stairs. There had been an extra flashlight hanging in the hall closet. I let myself out the garden door and circled the house. There was still a lot of wind; I couldn't hear anything, and nothing seemed to move against the background of planting and shrubs. You don't stalk well on a dark night with a white shirt on, but I had marked the place where I thought I had seen movement and I quickly crossed to it. I let the torch play across the ground. I didn't really expect to see anything, but there in the soft earth was a fresh footprint of a man's shoe. I clicked off the flash and stood waiting. There was no sound. Then I tried a trick they taught us in advanced training; as a last resort, make a noise in the brush and drop to one side. If the other fellow is jumpy or you catch him off guard he moves, and then you have him. That's the principle of the thing. Nothing happened. If he was still there, he wasn't being caught off guard; it was more likely that he had seen me at the window and had gone away.

I was at the head of the stairs when Frankie called me. Her voice sounded cracked and strained, and it was more a dry whisper than a call. "John . . . are you there?"

"Ready?"

"Yes."

She was standing on one foot in front of the washbasin and her face was chalk white and she was trembling. "I saw a light out on the lawn . . ."

I eyed her for an instant. "I lost my watch somewhere tonight and I was out there looking for it."

"Out there? You weren't out there earlier."

"I was when I first came looking for you. I thought I saw something . . ."

"What did you think you saw?"

"Something shining on the ground. It was just a piece of broken glass. I didn't find my watch."

"Is that all you thought you saw?"

"Oh come off it, Frankie, what else would there be to see?" I picked her up and took her back in to the bed. Her arms were about my neck when I put her down and for a moment they held me there. "I'm sorry I let you have it," she said. "I didn't know I had all those things in my mind. I sort of blew up and spattered the countryside, didn't I?"

"Forget it." I brushed a kiss across her brow. *"In hysteria veritas."*

"That wasn't truth, it was anger. And where did I get anointed to be so worldly-wise?"

"Half-truths are better than no truths," I told her. "Anyway, forget it! —I wonder if you remember something you said up in the woods tonight?" I pulled a chair over to the side of the bed.

"I remember something you said," she told me quietly.

"What? . . . Oh, that. Well, there'll probably be a better time than this to discuss it."

"You didn't mean it, did you?"

"I thought you just admitted you weren't anointed to be so worldly-wise? You said that there was a man there, *the man who's been writing the letters.*"

"Did I say that?"

"You know you did."

"Well, it was a foolish thing to say. I don't know why I said it." She looked up at me. "It hasn't got anything to do with . . ."

"With what?"

"There wasn't any man. You told me so yourself. My imagination started working overtime, and I lost my head and went into a blue funk."

"What letters? What man, Frankie?"

"If I wanted to talk about it, I would. But I don't want to. I've had my session of high strikes and it won't happen again."

"I don't intend that it shall ever happen again. That kind of fear is bad. It eats into you. I've seen people who emerged from fear—they'd lost something that they could never regain." An ugly thought crossed my mind and I seized on it, it was the only thought I had. "Are you being blackmailed about anything? If you are, tell me about it. Whatever it is, it doesn't make any difference. Whatever it is . . . I'll get you out of it."

"No! —Leave it alone, John, and stop poking into it."

The bedside lamp shone full on her face. I reached up and turned off the switch. The room was in half-light from the moon, but her face was in the shadows. "What letters? What man, Frankie?"

"Oh, God, don't go into it. Believe me, it's all right now. There's nothing I'm going to be afraid of."

"Are they letters that hurt me, or hurt people that you love?"

"No . . . ! No . . . ! They're letters to me—about me—they don't hurt anybody else but me—they don't even hurt me! Please believe me and let it alone!" Her hand clutched at mine across the covers.

"What kind of letters, Frankie?"

"Letters . . . just letters."

"When did you first start getting them?"

"While I was away, or rather when I came back and was staying in New York. —The first ones were forwarded to the hotel in New York."

"And they kept on coming?"

"Every other day or so . . ."

"And when did you get the last one?"

"Day before yesterday . . ."

"Did these letters threaten you?"

294

"Yes . . . no . . . they're crazy, insane letters . . ."

"Have you talked to anyone about them?"

"No, how could I? They're . . . they're . . ."

"What kind of letters are they, Frankie?"

Her head pressed against my hand and I could feel the sobs work through her.

"They're nasty letters . . . ugly letters . . . they're like having dirt and filth heaped on you . . . they're poisonous and slimy and put images in your mind that soil and besmirch everything you ever felt was clean and lovely . . . they're unspeakable things . . . they're things you can't talk about . . . they make the human body monstrous . . . you're afraid to go to sleep because they infect your dreams . . . they make you want to vomit . . ."

"And you couldn't talk to me about them?"

"Least of all, you!"

"Or Elizabeth or Sanford?"

"Oh, John, they're fiendish, they make it so you can't talk about them. They're about Elizabeth—and you and Angelica—and you and me—and they're about me and whoever writes them. Nothing in them is true, but to have anyone read them would be like standing in front of them naked and doing all the things they describe . . . that's why they're fiendish, because you can't go to anyone about them . . . you'd never be able to face anyone who ever saw them without wondering what thoughts were going through their minds, what images . . ."

"You have a surprising lack of faith in the better aspects of the human soul."

"It isn't their souls, it's their minds. The mind isn't like a slate. You can't draw pictures on it and then wipe it clean with faith or trust; something of the picture remains."

"Why did you go on reading them?"

"Because they're threats, not really threats but implications and shadows of threats . . ."

"Let me see them, Frankie."

I could feel her tense.

"I've destroyed them . . ."

"All of them?"

"All of them . . ."

"You're lying, Frankie. You haven't destroyed all of them."

295

"I destroyed the first of them . . . I've kept the rest. I don't know why I've kept them . . . maybe they were even less horrible on paper than my memory of them . . . it's like being hemmed in by evil . . . now I can't even bathe and feel myself clean . . . somewhere, someone is thinking those things, and writing them down and today or tomorrow I'm going to get another one of them, and never knowing who it is . . . it may be someone I know, or pass on the street, or brush against in the bank, or someone who fills my gas tank—until I can't look at anyone without thinking the thoughts . . ."

"Let me see the letters, Frankie."

Her cheek was against the back of my hand and several times I could feel her lips start to speak but the words were never uttered. Finally she straightened against the pillow and let go of my hand.

"You've got a strength that I haven't got, John. You don't always use it, but it's there and you're using it now. Let me say this, and then if you still want to read them they're in the top right-hand bureau drawer—the key is in the bowl on the mantel."

"Go ahead," I told her.

"I promised myself that I would never be saying these things to you again, but this time you force me to. . . . It all started out as a schoolgirl crush . . . and then I was really in love with you . . . I couldn't help that . . . you didn't want it, you don't want it—that's something that can't be helped . . . but these letters have invaded even the things that might have been . . . I never thought I would be so involved and perverted that if you touched my body I would cringe and freeze . . . that happened when you took my stocking off . . . it happened even worse when you put the tape around my ribs. There are things that happen when people love each other—I know them from books—I know them from my instincts—they could never happen now between me and any man I might come to love without the images being there, without what should be clean and lovely becoming soiled and ugly. . . . I'll never be washed clean . . . if you read those letters I'll never be able to raise my head and look into your eyes again."

I got up out of the chair and leaned over her. "This is sick and unhealthy."

"I know it's sick and unhealthy."

296

"Look, Frankie, sometimes things like this can get too big to handle yourself, and you have to have help from someone. They get out of hand and you can't go it alone." What I wanted to say was too unformed to put into words; even if I had found the words she was too confused to understand them. I reached into the shadows to grip her shoulders and try to press into her consciousness what I meant. She must have sensed my movement and as she squirmed away from me my hands touched her breasts through the thin silk of her nightgown. I felt her stiffen and freeze. I wanted to take my hands away from her, but I knew that I mustn't. This had happened, and now that it had happened it must be met head on. Maybe the learned analysts would call it a cockeyed therapy, but it was the only therapy I knew. I could feel the beginning shudder of hysteria go through her, and the sharp intake of breath that would explode in maniacal screaming.

This was the stuff of tragedy and it was all so clear. Frankie was at a crossroads. I hadn't intended to touch her this way, it was an accident, but I was at the crossroads with her. If I were to draw back my hands and let her go? The image of Constance crossed my mind, Constance, who had destroyed her own life and almost destroyed Old Matt's. Poor warped Constance, whose sex had got mixed up and who had wasted a lifetime until the passion was spent from her bones, before she emerged from the shadows. And Angelica, who had taken the other tangent and tried to lose her body in the arms of many lovers, until the day came when she wanted only one man and she could no longer trust her heart or her soul. The opposite sides of the same medal, frigidity or the using of your body as an instrument to punish and exorcise the perversity that had come to inhabit it.

"Frankie, I didn't mean it to happen this way." My voice was level, but it took all my discipline to control it. "It was an accident. I wanted to touch you because I wanted to say something to you, and in the dark my hands touched your breasts."

The scream broke from her lips and her body twisted and writhed to escape me. Blindly she reached out in the dark and her fists futilely pummeled against my face and then her hands were tearing at mine.

All the Constances in all the world, all the warped, twisted and frigid women, the women that break when they have their first

297

child, that crack and go to sanatoriums in their menopause, the women that lead men hellish lives and lead hellish lives themselves —and Frankie could be one of their legion.

"Frankie," I pleaded, "come back out of the dark places. Don't get mixed up and lose yourself. I didn't want it to happen this way, but we've got to go through with it. It isn't a callous experiment, or a brutal short cut to a quick cure. Yes, I want to touch your breasts; I want to hold your body in my arms—but I didn't choose or intend this moment. But if I let you wall this up inside you it will fester and grow like a cancer until your whole being will be warped and you'll never be able to be whole and healthy again. Frankie, Frankie my darling, listen to me, of all the people in the world I'm the last who would hurt you."

I could feel her will herself back from the threshold of hysteria. Her breath was a dry hoarse rattle in her throat and her body stilled, but lay trembling beneath my touch.

"They're lovely breasts, Frankie— No, listen to me. That's right, put your hands on my arms and hold on tight and don't push me away from you— They're lovely breasts, and they were given to you to be touched. They were given to you to be touched by the lips of your children; but before that by the hands and the lips of the man who loves you, and will find your body lovely, and will give you those children. And open your mind to this thought and believe it. There isn't a word or an image or an act that the human mind can conceive, that in its rightful moment—that in the arms of the man who loves you—will smirch or defile you. And if you can't bring yourself to believe this, then take it on faith, because I love you, you little damn fool."

She was still, utterly still, and I could sense no reaction from her. The moment stretched and with it the tension until I felt something must break.

Finally she spoke and her voice was almost a croak. "That's what you said in the woods. *I'm not going to hurt you, I love you* —only you didn't mean it. These are just words, and you're saying them to help me."

"I meant it," I told her, "only I didn't know how much I meant it. And I mean it now!"

She didn't say anything, but I could feel her slowly relax until there was no fear or restraint between us.

"And this is how much I mean it . . ." I lowered my face into the darkness toward her and kissed her. Against my lips I could feel the tremor of tension and withdrawal. She held her breath and I could feel her heart hammer and then slowly she exhaled her breath and her limbs were like a swimmer's who floats on the water, but her heart kept pounding. After a long moment her hands reached up and drew away the top of her nightgown and held my head against her; it was her only way of saying what she wanted to say.

"That's the first time you've ever kissed me as a lover, John."

"This Tracy clan was always a little premature." I heard my voice and it was husky.

Then I found my way across the room to the bureau and turned up the light.

"John!"

Her hand was up as if to stop me, and then it slowly dropped to the covers. Her nightgown was disarranged and she didn't seem to notice it and then her hand came up and very naturally and without shame or self-consciousness she drew it up over her.

There were six letters in all. Two with New York postmarks, three with Haviland cancellations—that told a story in itself—and one without any stamp at all. They were all typed. The thought of fingerprints passed through my mind—that was not likely, but I read them holding onto the edges of the paper only. It was the only way to hold them; there can be excreta of the mind, too.

"This son of a bitch is ripe for killing," I said in a low voice. I was talking more to myself than to Frankie. I glanced up at her and she was lying there with her eyes closed. When she had first talked I had thought she was exaggerating, that her youth and inexperience had led her into enlarging this. But she'd had the whole book thrown at her, all the books—Kraft-Ebing, de Sade, Crébillon père et fils, Restif de la Bretonne—and a good sluicing of a foul sewer as well. I played a not inconspicuous part, and Elizabeth walked through the shower of filth; but it was Frankie who got the full treatment, she was the imagined partner in a kaleidoscope of perverted insanity. She was right; they weren't the kind of letters you would be likely to show to anyone, they weren't the kind of images that you would ever want anyone to hold about you. There was threat in them, too; implied threat,

299

the things that were written could happen, might happen—they made Frankie's hysteria in the woods very understandable and excusable. A good clean rape would be a breath of fresh air beside this.

There was the sound of a car down the road, and I slipped the letters into my pocket and walked over to Frankie. Her eyes were still closed. I bent over and kissed her. She started and then relaxed; her lips were half-open, but she didn't realize it. "Eventually the Tracys, even the half-breeds, get around to 'first things.' That's Farnley coming up. I'll go down and let him in."

Farnley was at the door when I opened it. He handed me an envelope. "This was on the porch," he said. Frankie's name was typed across its front; it had been delivered by hand.

When he'd finished examining her, Farnley asked, "What did you fall out of? An airplane? You've got a fine sprained ankle. I'm not quite sure of the ribs; I'd like to get some pictures of them in the morning." He poked an exploratory finger about her face. "You're going to have something very close to a black eye in the morning, young lady."

"I thrashed about quite a bit after I hurt myself."

"I hit her," I explained to Farnley.

"That was *after* I hurt myself," Frankie said. "I sort of lost my head and didn't know what I was doing."

Farnley glanced at me. "Ummm . . ." was his only comment, but he delivered it as if great sense had been made. He didn't ask any questions. "Is anybody here? You've got a woman in the house?"

"No," Frankie told him. "Mrs. Harper won't be in until morning, she comes by the day."

"Ummm . . ." Farnley seemed full of *ummms*. He glanced at his watch. "Three o'clock! There isn't much more left of tonight. I'd rather she quieted down and didn't get joggled around any more than is necessary. Pretty late to get anyone in. Any good reason why you can't stay around until morning, John?"

I shook my head.

"Ummm . . . I could give her a pill." He took a syringe out of his bag. "This will be quicker. I'd stay myself, but it isn't that serious." He absent-mindedly jabbed the needle into Frankie's

300

arm. "If you've got to go to the bathroom, I'd advise your going before that shot gets to work."

"I've been," Frankie said.

"Ummm . . . They also taught you how to put adhesive on in the army, John. Quite a liberal education."

I took him to the door. "In my office about nine in the morning. We'll get those ribs X-rayed." As he slipped on his coat, he glanced about the living room of the Jennings Place. "I got the impression from my father once . . ." His voice drifted off and he left the thought unfinished.

"What impression did you get?"

He seemed to think better of what he had been going to say. "It was just an impression— How's Elizabeth?" he added irrelevantly. And then at the door, "Look, I don't think much of the idea of a girl like Frankie living down here alone. I don't know why I should be butting into your business—you're the head of the family now. However, I suppose you'll get around to doing something about it."

Frankie was groggy and her eyes were heavy from the shot when I got upstairs. I turned off the light. "What are you going to do?" she mumbled.

"I'm going to sit here in the chair beside you and watch you sleep," I told her. "I'll hold your hand if you like."

"I'd like, but I'm not going to let you do it." She edged over in the bed. "Lie down here. You've got to get some rest, too."

"Remember the last time, it didn't work out so well. I'm not sure that I like the idea of your growing up so quickly. By the way, I'm awfully sorry about what happened that night in the hotel. This isn't the way I wanted to say it, but I'm sorry. I was tight and it was a stupid, blundering thing to do."

"I was a fool the last time. I've grown up a lot since then." She smiled. "Each day I seem to grow older." Her hand reached out and pulled me toward her.

"The idea is to watch out for you, I'd probably go to sleep."

"That's the idea," she mumbled.

It was only a moment or two before I felt her hand relax and knew that she was asleep beside me. There was very small danger of my falling asleep. A little later she whimpered and began to toss about; it was either pain or a nightmare and I wondered whether to wake her, but in an instant or two she screamed and woke herself up. For a moment she seemed disoriented and as if she didn't know where she was, and then she saw me beside her and her hand clasped mine again. "It's all right," she whispered. "No fears . . . nothing mixed up . . . it will be all right between us . . ." Her voice trailed off and her head dropped to my shoulder and I thought she was asleep. "Any time . . ." she murmured, and then she was asleep.

I watched the dawn come up and then I watched the clock crawl slowly to seven. I disengaged my arm from beneath her head without waking her and tiptoed into the bathroom. This young generation of girls have the virtue of using man-sized razors. The shave felt good and the shower felt better. A damp towel and a brush took care of my coat, and for the rest of me I could pass without advertising the fact that I had slept in my clothes. I was just about finished when Frankie called in to me.

"When does this Mrs. Harper show up?" I asked her.

"About eleven. I get my own breakfast . . ."

"This morning, I'm getting it. Coffee coming up." I had the kitchen in a fine mess even before the tray was finished, and while the eggs were boiling I picked up the phone and called the State Police Barracks. My mind was very clear about what I was going to do, about what we had to do. "I want to speak to Lieutenant Costello. . . ." While I was waiting I reached over and slipped the eggs out of the water, only cracking one, and half cooking my fingers in the process.

"Hello, Costello. Milnor speaking. Could you meet me in Sanford's office a little after nine o'clock? It's something very important to me and I'd rather you handled it than anyone else."

While Frankie ate her eggs she said, "I'm glad to find something you don't do well." When she was finished she swung her leg out from under the covers and looked at it. No miracles had occurred, it was still as big as a baseball. "I'm afraid you'll have to do it again?" she asked. As I carried her into the bathroom she said, "I've never been so stiff in my life. I feel as if I'd really fallen out of an airplane."

I telephoned Elizabeth while Frankie was in the bathroom. Mrs. Haines answered at the same time, of course. There must be some way of getting Mrs. Haines off a phone, but I've never learned

302

how to do it. Elizabeth was the archdiplomat. "Oh, I'm glad you're on the phone, Mrs. Haines, I'll need a fresh pot of hot water for my tea." Mrs. Haines hung up with a projection of ill grace that I could feel even down at the Jennings Place. "I'm bringing Frankie up to the house this morning," I said. "Will you have Mrs. Haines get her room ready?"

"What do you mean?" Elizabeth asked. "What's happened? Where are you?"

"I'm at Frankie's. She had a fall and sprained her ankle. It isn't too serious, but she can't stay down here alone. Farnley looked in on her during the night and as soon as we leave his office I'll be bringing her up to the Hill—about ten or ten thirty. I'll tell you all about it later."

"Why didn't you let me know?"

"Well, it was pretty late before things got straightened out."

"John, there's more to all this . . . ?"

"Considerably."

"Is she all right?"

"She's all right," I assured her.

"And you're all right—you're both all right?"

"We're both all right."

"Let me talk to her?" Elizabeth asked.

"She's in the bathroom," I explained.

"I'll wait. I'll go with her to Farnley's office."

"I don't think that'll be necessary. I'll tell her to call you later. She's in the bathroom and I sort of have to carry her." I don't know what struck Elizabeth so funny, but she started to laugh and then it was as if she couldn't stop. "Things have the damnedest way of happening," she finally said when she got her breath. "Take care of her, John."

"John," Frankie called to me. "I didn't organize this very well. Could you get me some clothes out of the bureau?"

"What kind of clothes?"

"One of everything and two stockings."

Getting breakfast was simpler. "What do you use to hold your . . .?" and then I saw a garter belt tucked into the corner. I had a handful of about everything I could think of except one thing and I went back over the drawer. "Hey, don't you wear pants?"

"Of a kind," she answered me. "Bottom drawer, left side, back."

"Do you call these *pants?*" I handed the collection through the door to her.

"And the gray dress, the one you like."

"How do you know I like it?"

"The way you looked at me when I wore it in New York." Her hand came out of the door and took the dress.

"Look, you're not going to a ball, you know; you're just going to the doctor's office."

"Before I come back here I may be going to more than a ball."

I took the tray downstairs and came back. "Aren't you ready yet?"

"No, and I'm in trouble. I'm so stiff and my side hurts and I can't raise my arms."

"So don't raise your arms. Just get your clothes on and let's get started."

"That's the point, you dope. I can't get into my clothes," she bleated. "I'm stuck."

"Do you want me to come in and help you?"

"No, I don't want you to come in and help me—but somebody has to get me unstuck. Oh damn it, and I wanted there to be some romance left between us."

"Close your eyes!" I told her.

"Why should I close my eyes? You should be the one to close *your* eyes."

"Close 'em, you'll be happier. I'm not very good at dressing ladies with my eyes open; think what a mess I could make of it with my eyes shut." She *was* hung up, too. She was standing on one foot with her head down and her arms out in front of her as if she was about to take a high dive, and her slip was stuck and her dress was stuck. I couldn't help but laugh. "I repeat the question, do you call these pants?"

"Damn you!" Her voice was very close to tears.

When she finally straightened up, her face was flushed, and it was also something else. I turned her around so she could see herself in the mirror. "Milady has a very lovely little mouse under her right eye."

"I could spit," she said.

304

Seventeen

Costello was waiting for me in Pop Sanford's office. "You haven't murdered someone?" Pop asked.

"Not yet," I said.

He looked at me for a moment. "Well, it sometimes helps to have a legal opinion."

"Are you married?" I asked Costello.

He nodded.

"Have you got a sister, by any chance?"

"Yeah, I got a mother, too. I come fully equipped. What are you driving at?"

"Can I show you something that makes a decent girl look like something that even a Front Street whore wouldn't spit on, and then can you wipe it out of your mind and give me your slant on how we're going to handle it?"

He twirled his hat on its lanyard. "You really want me to answer that question?"

"No, I was just telling you what kind of a guy you are." I handed him the packet of letters.

He balanced the packet in his hand. "One of those things, huh? Pictures? Blackmail? Dirty letters?"

"No pictures—and blackmail doesn't seem the pitch."

He riffled through the envelopes, noted Frankie's name, and then the postmarks. "Local job." He looked up at me. "Did she get these, or did you intercept them?"

"She got them."

"Too bad! Lousy, isn't it? She probably feels like she's been pushed down into a public toilet."

"Read them."

"I'm going to, but I don't have to. I've seen things like this before; makes you wonder if God was off duty when he let that part of the human race happen." He began to go through them.

"Any chance of fingerprints?"

"Yeah, there's a real chance. Not on the letters themselves, but on the gummed flaps and under the stamps; that's where you sometimes get some beauts. There's one here that hasn't been opened."

"It arrived this morning."

He opened it and I watched his face get a little redder over the neck of his shirt. "This one's the lulu."

I reached for it.

"I wouldn't advise your reading it, unless you don't feel you're mad enough already." He tossed the letters over on the desk. "Sanford might have some ideas, if you feel he's old enough to read this sort of filth." He walked over and stood looking out on Railroad Avenue. When he heard Pop put the letters down he turned around and sat on the window sill.

"You want to kill the guy, of course. Next, you'd like him punished. And you want to stop this business dead in its tracks. Except for killing him, it isn't easy. The Counselor'll bear me out in this. Make a report to me, and it goes on the book and starts through channels. F.B.I. on the fingerprints. Post Office Department for using the mails. District Attorney's office and all his little legal squirts and every newspaperman in the county—copies of these things get kicked around and before you know it the bartender in the Nelson House is passing them out to traveling salesmen. If you're lucky, you catch this character, and he gets himself a smart lawyer and a jury trial, then they have the typewriter experts—by this time everybody including your Aunt Hannah's read these letters. Miss Frankie and everybody that got mentioned in them is dragged through the sewer. That's how these guys get away with it—there are too many good reasons for not turning them in."

Sanford nodded his agreement. "It adds up to about that, John. The only trouble is that until you know who it is and what you're dealing with, you don't sleep well; you don't know how much of a real threat it is."

Costello stared out the window. "Any idea who it might be?"

306

"Not really . . ."

"It could be anybody out there." He gestured across the village. "Almost anybody. Screwballs are where you find 'em and you find 'em in some of the damnedest places. There was a minister down at Cross River—he was real fancy. —What did you mean, *not really?*"

"It was just an idea, I'd hate to even tie a man's name to a thing like this until I was sure."

Sanford picked up his phone and called Fletcher in the bank downstairs. "Jim, could you send up to my office your folder of correspondence on that recent loan application by Semple? Yes, right away if you don't mind."

Costello whistled under his breath. "Very thin ice! And he's still got friends in Albany. This isn't some pimply-faced little degenerate you can take off on a side road and talk to."

Margaret brought the folder into Sanford's desk and the old gentleman put on his spectacles and slipped a letter out of the file. He put one of the letters that Frankie had received beside it.

Costello studied the two pages. "You're into marshy ground. It took two trials and, with all the typewriter experts in the country, they never really hung it on that guy from the State Department. —Me, I'd say the same machine wrote both of them."

"Marshy ground," I said. "I thought I saw someone last night outside Frankie's house. There was a footprint in the ground."

"That works real fine in television and the movies," Costello said. "Sometimes it helps to get a confession, but it's nothing you like to go into court with."

"You mean in a case like this your hands are really tied?" I asked him.

"That's about the only thing that isn't tied. If you're sure you're right, beat the—you know what out of him. Excuse the word, Mr. Sanford."

Pop polished his spectacles. "Under certain circumstances it is a very useful, forceful, one might almost say pungent, word. No objection in that particular context, Lieutenant."

"The trouble is, in a setup like this *my* hands are tied. Manual confessions don't stand up in court. Of course, if someday when I'm off duty if the character was stupid enough to find himself across the state line in Connecticut, it wouldn't hurt my conscience

307

a bit." He looked at me. "Only you've got to be awfully sure of yourself. Tell me all about last night and let me see if I get any ideas. I'll be checking with you this evening."

Frankie was sitting in Farnley's surgery when I got there, and Farnley seemed very pleased about something. "Her ribs are cracked all right, painful but not serious. Her ankle will get well in a day or two, no matter what I do to prevent it."

"What have you done for her black eye?"

Farnley laughed. "There are a lot of old wives' tales about beefsteak and leeches. In my experience they go away when it's time for them to go away. Women are luckier, they can use make-up. Don't hit her so hard the next time."

"You ready?" I asked Frankie.

"Just a minute, hold your horses," Farnley said. "And stick out your right arm."

Before I knew what was happening he had a needle into my arm, and a column of blood was rising in the glass tube. "What's this all about?"

"Obeisance to the sovereign State of New York and to guarantee that you breed nice healthy children."

I looked down at Frankie. She was as red as a beet and about as vocal as one. Her mouth opened, but only funny little strangling noises came out of it.

"All right now, pick her up and get her out of my office. I've got work to do." Farnley's hand was on my shoulder. "I couldn't be happier, John. And speaking medically, she's about a hundred and five per cent woman and in first-rate working order."

Frankie was stiff and seemed to hold herself away from me as I crossed to the car; it would have been easier to carry a rocking chair. I started the motor and she reached over and turned off the ignition. "Look, this is all a mistake," she said. "And let's get it straightened out before it's too late. Farnley'll be spreading this all over town—he's probably already called his wife."

"Spreading what?"

"You're not making this any easier," she pleaded. "It was all a mistake and he jumped to conclusions."

"And transfusions," I amended.

308

"When he finished with my ribs and ankle I just thought I'd . . . I'd get some free information."

"Very thrifty—your French blood coming out."

"It came out, all right. I just wanted to know, *if* I got married someday, *whether* I . . . you know what I mean—it's a woman's job in life . . ."

"And you scored a hundred and five per cent. Very nice."

"John, please . . . I want to talk to you about last night . . . only now that it isn't just words and ideas between us any longer, I'm finding it isn't so easy."

"We don't have to talk about last night."

"Yes, we do. Up at the house at dinner last night, you weren't in love with me, you didn't want to marry me . . . or anything. I don't know why you came after me, but I don't think it was because you wanted to. Elizabeth probably insisted."

"What I really wanted to do was kick your tail." I reached for the ignition key, but her hand stopped me.

"That's what I mean. You weren't in love with me."

"Furthest thought from my mind . . ."

"John, that's what I'm saying. And then you found me . . . and I was a mess. . . . Somehow you managed to straighten me out."

"Apparently I didn't straighten you out very straight—you're not making very much sense. Are you finished?"

"No, I really haven't begun. I wish it wasn't so light, I feel myself getting embarrassed."

"Let's go somewhere where it isn't so light, then," I suggested.

"No, that wouldn't be any good—it might be worse. I'll get it said now, or never. —John, you don't have to marry me."

"I know I don't *have* to, unless you feel yourself compromised after our having spent the night together."

"And don't try to be funny! I don't know why it should be so difficult to say. Let me start again. . . . I'm all right now. . . . What a girl reads and hears and thinks doesn't prepare her for what you did for me last night. You gave me something . . . gave it to me outright. You didn't make any promises, so there aren't any promises to keep."

She wasn't very pretty. The tears were running down her cheeks and her black eye seemed puffed and the powder was streaked over it. Mrs. Fletcher came down the street. She saw us sitting in

309

the car and started to speak to us, and then she saw Frankie's tear-stained face and thought better of it and passed as if she hadn't seen us.

"What I'm trying to say, John, is that I don't want to be just another thing that will have happened to you . . . just an accident in your life, practically willed to you—and as if that weren't enough, throwing myself at you. You said you loved me, but you were probably only sorry for me . . . don't wake up and be sorry for yourself. You didn't ask me to marry you, you don't have to—you must know that by now. If you want me to get out of your hair and go back to college, I will."

I reached over and pulled her toward me. "Come over here, you little idiot. Maybe I've been waiting for something. Maybe I had to find it before I knew I was waiting for it. If this doesn't tell you, I'm licked because I haven't any better words to use." I kissed her, and nothing happened. She was a girl letting herself be kissed. Her lips were unresponsive and her cheek was wet against mine. "Frankie, for God's sake come back, I want you—you, damn it. If you thought I kissed you without passion last night, you don't know what passion is."

Her lips opened, they had to, because she was saying, "I do now." I couldn't remember which side was hurt and I was afraid to hold her tightly. Her hand raised mine against her breast and pressed it there. Suddenly there was laughter on her lips. "And you still haven't asked me to marry you . . ."

"Haven't I? What do you think I was just saying?"

"Oh. I understood that, well enough . . . you made yourself very clear—but I didn't know you were including marriage. Sometimes you Tracys don't get around to that . . ."

"There've been enough bastards in this family," I said.

"The illegitimate son of the illegitimate son of Napoleon," she chanted. "You're really sure you want to break the tradition?"

"Quite sure!"

"Well, I guess you're right, there can be too much of a good thing. And there is quite a lot to be said for marriage—so they say. When?"

"Fairly soon, I would suggest."

"In view of one thing and another, I think that's a very good idea and exceedingly moral. How about three days?"

310

"Why the long delay?" I chided her.

"Well, for a number of reasons . . . trousseau . . ."

"That sounds pretty conventional for you."

"Time to invite the guests . . ."

"That sounds even more conventional."

"I'd like to be able at least to limp down the aisle, and I'd sort of feel embarrassed at your seeing me with a lot of adhesive tape holding me together—also I gathered from Doctor Farnley that it takes three days to do it legally."

Elizabeth was at the front door when we drove up. Mrs. Haines was her fluttering adjutant in the background. It would be too much to ask that there might be at least one crucial moment in our lives when it would be Mrs. Haines' ankle that would break.

As I carried Frankie over the threshold she announced, "I feel like a bride!"

"You don't look like one," Elizabeth observed. Mrs. Haines merely pursed her lips.

"Put me down in the library," Frankie demanded.

"I'll put you down in bed."

"What's a girl to do? He's been talking like that all morning." If she had any intention of shocking Elizabeth she failed. Mrs. Haines thinned her lips a little more.

"Is she badly hurt, John?"

"It's a mortal wound," Frankie interrupted me. "From which I'll never survive. As for the rest of it, I'll be as fit as a fiddle in three days and ready to dance at my own wedding."

Elizabeth plumped the pillows and got a coverlet. "Now tell me what this is all about."

"Shall we begin at the beginning, the middle or the end?" Frankie asked.

"At the beginning."

"The end is more fun."

"Just begin," Elizabeth said patiently.

"Well, to commence at the denouement, Mrs. Milnor, may I ask the hand of your son in marriage?"

"Make sense," Elizabeth said. "What happened to your ankle and why are you breathing so strangely?"

"Oh, that? I fell down and made a big noise. It's just a twisted

311

ankle and a couple of cracked ribs. It's nothing at all. The important thing is there's going to be a wedding in the family."

"When did all this happen?" Elizabeth demanded.

I put my arm about her shoulder. "I guess it's been happening for a long time, one way and another. We got around to talking about it this morning. I asked Frankie if she'd marry me, and she said yes. It won't change things very much."

"The hell it won't!" Frankie exploded.

"Did somebody say 'three days'?" Elizabeth asked. "Where did you get that black eye?"

"John hit me!"

"Did you hit him back?"

"Yes, later—but I don't think my aim was very good."

"Three days!" Elizabeth got the impact of it. "That isn't very much time and there'll be so much to do."

Women are strange creatures when it comes to marriages. Elizabeth's curiosity about what had happened to Frankie and how it had happened vanished for the moment. She examined Frankie's eye. "It will hardly show at all in three days. We'll have the wedding late in the afternoon and the lights will be dim."

"I'll bet it's the first wedding they ever had to dim the lights for," Frankie said proudly, "so the guests wouldn't notice how badly the groom had beaten up the bride."

"Take your clothes off and get into bed," Elizabeth commanded.

"I don't want to take my clothes off and go to bed. I'm fine! I feel fine! I never felt better in my life!"

"Do as I say," Elizabeth insisted. "You need the rest; this is going to be a very trying time. And I want to look at your side."

"It isn't going to be a trying time at all!" Frankie protested. "I'm a healthy young animal and . . . oh, all right."

"Now clear out!" Elizabeth shooed me toward the door.

"I don't want him to clear out," Frankie yelped.

"Oh, you two . . ." Elizabeth's thought broke in mid-stream. "You two aren't married already, are you?" And then without waiting for an answer, "Well, anyway turn around, John, or you shall embarrass *me*."

I turned around.

"Elizabeth . . ." Frankie's voice was very gentle and understanding. "We haven't . . . I mean we're not married; but it wouldn't

312

make very much difference, would it? We're very much in love, and that's all that's really important, isn't it?"

"Yes, that's all that matters," Elizabeth said slowly.

The memory of a breakfast tray crashing to the floor years ago crossed my mind. And Old Matt and Elizabeth laughing, and then only Elizabeth laughing and then her laughter dying away. I wanted to put my arm about her and kiss her. I would later, and she wouldn't know exactly why.

There was a rustling of clothes and then Elizabeth said, "Farnley put that tape on awfully tight."

And then from Frankie very clear and boastful and happy, "John put that on last night."

And then Elizabeth's "Oh." She said it very simply as if she understood everything. "You didn't hurt your . . . ? A blow there can be very dangerous later for a woman."

"No I didn't hurt my . . . my breast is fine! John, tell Elizabeth my breast is fine."

"Her breast is fine, Mother."

"Look, both of you!" I could tell by Elizabeth's voice that she was back in her stride again. "You don't shock me, either of you. I can't help it that I was born in the Victorian age, it's just that I find myself embarrassed in certain situations. Frankie, with Alyse not being here, I'm the nearest thing to a mother that you have and there are certain conversations that I intend to have with you before you're married, and I intend to have them with a degree of privacy that does not include John."

"Oh, that," Frankie said. "Doctor Farnley started to talk to me and I shut him up. I can't wait to get pregnant. I'm going to have a baby every year for the first five years, just like the Radiant cow, and I bet you I lactate like a dream. They'll be giving me blue ribbons and hanging my picture in the barn with the rest of the brood matrons."

"I give up." I heard the slap of Elizabeth's hand against what I assumed to be Frankie's backside. "Here, put on this nightgown and get the covers over you."

"Elizabeth . . ."

"Yes?"

"I'm not really as flippant as I sound, you know that," Frankie said. "Nor half as sure of myself. It's just a front that I put on. I'd like to have that talk with you. Loving someone, and marrying them, is a very important thing and there's a lot that I don't know about it. I'd like to know how to be as fine a woman as you are."

Mrs. Haines came to the door with the tray and surveyed the scene behind me. "I was going to knock," she said with innuendo, "but of course if people don't close doors . . . I brought a cup of tea and a coddled egg."

"I'll do without the egg," Frankie told her.

"And I'll do with a change of clothes," I said.

A little while later when I came out in the hall the door to Frankie's room was closed and I could hear her voice and Elizabeth's in low conversation. I went downstairs and up to the barn to check things with Will Talcott. I told him about the marsh ground in the pasture behind the Jennings Place, and to pick up Frankie's keys and lock the house when he passed, and to tell Mrs. Harper just to look in for cleaning—that Frankie would be staying at our house. He gave me the time slips and we made arrangements about shipping the young bull down to Georgia. As I was leaving to go back to lunch I said: "Oh by the way, Will, Miss Frankie and I are going to be married in a few days." —At least I'd get that in before Mrs. Haines.

"I know," he said.

"What do you mean, you know?"

He laughed. "Mrs. Haines telephoned Mrs. Talcott, and Mrs. Talcott came up to the barn to tell me just before you got here. I wouldn't ever want to get my leg over the traces with Mrs. Haines in the same county."

"Then I suppose Miss Constance already knows?"

"I suppose." He put his hand out and clasped mine. "I'm awfully glad it worked out this way. A farm is no good without it's going someplace."

I had almost passed the Big House when the image hit me of Constance sitting in there alone. In a sense she was the queen dowager of the tribe. The front door was open and I let myself in. Constance was sitting in the drawing room in a stiff pale-blue dress playing patience before the fire. She looked up and saw me and put the cards down in a neat pile.

314

"I wanted to tell you that Frankie and I are going to be married. I'd like to give her your ring to wear, if you don't mind."

I leaned over to kiss her, but she took my face in her hands and kissed me instead. She looked at me for a long moment and then finally she said, "Matt and Alyse should be very happy." There seemed to be no shadows left in her world; Matt and Alyse were at last decently dead.

As I was leaving, I turned at the door. "Why don't you come over and dine with us tonight?"

"I had dinner with you last night. Wouldn't you and Elizabeth and Frankie rather be alone?"

"No, there's enough aloneness in life that we can't escape."

"I would very much like to," she said.

Mrs. Haines was just about ready for luncheon and I noticed that there were only two places set. When Elizabeth came down she explained that she had given Frankie a sedative and she was asleep. "She wants to get up for dinner, though."

When we got up from the table Elizabeth asked me if I could spare her a few minutes before I went out again. We sat in the library and she asked me to close the door.

"Frankie and I had a long talk after you left," she began. "Mostly about you."

"I should have thought you'd have other things to discuss besides me."

"Frankie is mostly concerned about you. I haven't been unconcerned either."

"Look." I turned to her. "I'm sorry I didn't get a chance to talk to you about this first; but things started to happen, and they happened rather quickly."

"So I gathered. . . . She told me about a lot that I've only guessed at. She's very young, John, but she's older than you realize. She has all the the patter that comes out of books, but underneath there is a wisdom that comes from way inside. Maybe it's because she carries the heritage of a more ancient people than ours. In some way she's older and wiser than I was when I met your father."

I threw on a fresh log and stirred the fire into flame.

315

"I've been afraid for years that you were going to pay the penalty for the sins of your parents."

"Is that the word you want to use?" I asked.

"No, I spoke it in quotes, it's the word the world would use."

I put my arms around her and kissed her. "That's for a very special reason, and it goes back many years," I told her.

"There are, nevertheless, penalties. From the time you were a child you let things happen to you; you didn't happen to them."

"Frankie used that same expression," I said.

She nodded. "Frankie's an intuitive and very knowing person. What I mean is, you stood back and let life flow about you, you were a spectator."

I had seated myself at the desk. The sun had lowered until a shaft of light cut across Elizabeth's face, and it was kindly and gentle to her. The years had been very friendly; perhaps that's something that happens when a woman has been deeply loved. "Assuming that is true—and I think it is—what are you trying to say?"

"I'm not saying it well. I have had a sense up to now that there was something still unformed and unresolved within you. Young Matt was the seemingly strong one; all that he ever wanted he had and took from life. The only trouble was that in his taking he never knew what he wanted. What he did at the end wasn't strength, it was really evasion and weakness. Sometimes it's easier to die than it is to live; I've learned that lesson. You were really the strong one. Frankie told me about last night . . ."

I looked up at her.

"She had to talk to someone, her heart was so full. And the things she didn't know how to say, I could have said for her, because I have known them, too. What you did took the courage and strength that a woman wants in the man she loves."

"Aren't you reading a lot into all this?" I asked her.

"Yes. There's so much to be read into it. And now everything's all right. Nothing in the world could keep you from Frankie. You know what you want and life will never happen to you again, you will happen to life."

As I walked out into the hall with her, she looked up at me. "Your father never had any question in his mind that you were the

316

son of his heart. If he could be here this day he would be very happy, too."

Frankie had found a cane that afternoon and she was downstairs when I came back from the farm. "At least you won't have to carry me down the aisle." She got up and showed me how she could manage it.

"You look like a delegate to a D.A.R. convention, one of the charter members."

Constance arrived shortly and Elizabeth joined us. Constance in a strange burst of responsibility toward her branch of the family had taken it on herself to telephone Emmeline and Adelaide.

"Oh, God!" Frankie exclaimed. "Wouldn't it be simpler to just go away somewhere by ourselves and elope? We could take Elizabeth and Constance along, so it wouldn't be so much of an elopement."

"Adelaide and Emmeline won't come," I told her.

"Of course they will come, John." Constance was beginning to enjoy the position of dowager. "I ordered them to come. After all, they're your half sisters."

"In a manner of speaking, they are," I admitted. "But I've never thought of them that way. By the same token, neither have they."

"Then it's time you began," Constance said firmly. "Someone has to be the head of this family and keep them in line. They've been having things too much their own way too long, especially their husbands."

I glanced over at Elizabeth; she was smiling. Once the Tracys faced reality, they faced it with a bang.

"Who'll be the minister?" Constance asked. "I suppose Penny. I've never liked Penny."

"Not Penny," Frankie protested. "I'll never forgive the way he acted at the funeral. He's such a little man—I don't think God pays much attention to him. I'd rather be married by Mooney."

"Mooney buries people, he doesn't marry them," Constance explained as if she were making great sense.

"Even so, I'd feel more married. Look, I'd be very happy to jump over a broomstick if it would simplify things."

317

"Doesn't Henry Sanford hold some office," Elizabeth suggested, "that would permit him to perform the service?"

"That's my choice." Frankie grabbed at the idea. "It'll be Sanford or the town clerk, but not Penny."

"If Frankie wants Sanford," Constance said, "do something about it—only the marriage will have to be in the house and not in the church, but that's all right."

"What do you suggest doing?" I asked.

"I'm sure I don't know," Constance replied, "but your father would have known what to do."

I picked up the phone and called Jim Fletcher. "I want a favor," I told him. "What would Henry Sanford have to be, to perform a marriage?"

"Congratulations!" he boomed. "I gather, from something Mrs. Fletcher said, that they're in order. Well, in the first place a minister of the gospel, and then in descending order, President of the United States, governor, judge, town clerk ... you want him to perform the marriage?"

"That's the general idea," I told him. "How do you suppose it could be arranged?"

"It would be rather difficult to appoint him President of the United States and it would take time to make him a judge. However, on the day in question there's no reason why Burt Wheeler the town clerk shouldn't take a trip to New York and the mayor could appoint Henry acting clerk. Being as I'm the mayor, it would be legal as all hell. Glad to oblige."

"You see?" Constance said.

It was after Constance had left and Elizabeth had gone upstairs, leaving us alone in front of the fire in the library, that I took out of my pocket Old Matt's engagement ring to Constance. "Constance wanted the woman I love to wear it."

"I like it any way you say it," Frankie said.

I slipped the ring over her finger and the ruby seemed to come alive in the firelight, as if it were telling an ancient story. Frankie stared down at it. "I'm a little scared."

"Things moving too quickly? Want to slow them up?"

"No, it's just that this is so much for keeps. It's like taking your place in a long procession. Usually a woman marries a man and they make their own lives together. But when I marry you,

I not only marry you, but I marry the Tracys, all of them, even to Alf Adams and his wife Sylvia down the road, and the place, the farm, the land, even Haviland. There's not much of that sort of thing left in the world. . . ."

"Thus spake the young chatelaine of the Tracy land."

"You know what I mean." Frankie slipped her hand into mine.

"Yes, I know what you mean."

"And if I go whacky...? Promise me something. Be old-fashioned, do it the Tracy way. Don't divorce me—I don't believe in divorce. Just stash me away somewhere like Constance; maybe I'd get unwhacky and you'd find you could put up with me again sometime."

"Are you planning to get whacky, as you call it?"

"No, I'm serious. Beat me up, kick me around, mistreat me—do anything you want, only don't ever put me out."

"You're fairly safe," I told her. "The Tracys don't believe in divorce. The only one we ever had was Matt divorcing Susan."

"Yes, that's true," Frankie said. "I forgot. You know, in some strange way you are more Tracy than Matt was. —It's strange, mother and daughter marrying brothers . . ."

"Lafayette should have announced his beachhead." As I leaned down to kiss her there was the sound of a car pulling to a stop outside the house. "We're about to be interrupted. That's a man I have to see. Turn up the light and read yourself a book for a few minutes."

"There isn't a book on all the shelves that could match my dreams," she said.

Costello didn't speak until I had closed the office door. "I found these." He handed me my watch—the strap was broken—and Frankie's topcoat. "I went back along the path where you found her. Are you sure you didn't go up the path beyond that point, or enter it at the top from the roadside?"

"I'm sure," I told him. "Why?"

"Because there were prints of a man's shoes higher up on the path and you could see where he had broken down the bushes looking for her. I found her shoe, too." He took it out of his pocket and put it on the desk.

"You mean that part of it wasn't her imagination; there was someone actually there."

"It looks that way. It's been more of a threat than just filthy letters. This guy is nuts. He really wants to get you, but he's getting at you through Miss Frankie."

" 'This guy'? You haven't any doubt who it was?"

"Oh, it's Semple, hands down. The only question is, can we get a case, and then do you want to go through with it?"

"You're sure?"

"Motive—typewriter—he's a juicy character. While I was waiting for him I sort of went through his desk. He's got a collection of art work in his drawer that would make a whore blush."

"You went to see him?"

"Just routine. The character has a pistol license that expired last week. It's unusual, but it's still routine to stop by and pick up the gun pending a renewal."

"But you haven't got any real evidence on him?" I asked.

"Could get," Costello said. "Could easy get."

"And could easy get your ass in a sling, too."

He smiled. "It's been in a sling before. But this is your show. There's another element. He's got the wind up. Right out of the blue he brought you into it. Said that you were trying to get him on something. He's got a lawyer, Bill Corley."

"For what?"

"Just for instance. He probably figures we've got a cellar down at the barracks, or he might want a *habeas corpus* in a hurry. He's doing a lot of thinking. Like I said, he's got the wind up. Anyway I'm glad I got his gun. I don't like feather merchants packing artillery in my area."

"So what do we do?"

"The things I'm thinking, I shouldn't say. But we don't have to do anything tonight. He got in his car and went over to Poughkeepsie about six o'clock. We had him tailed as he got in the city and he's registered in at the Nelson House. He used to have a woman over there—I'll know more about him tomorrow." Costello slipped into his coat and started to go.

I offered him a drink and he took it. "I'm sort of off duty," he said. "I've been sort of off duty all afternoon."

"Do you really think he would have done anything to Frankie?"

"When it comes to nuts," he said, "I don't like to think and I do mighty little guessing. Did you ever hear that Semple has a

320

little place down in Florida, a place to retire to when he gets finished being a son of a bitch up here? I guess no one should ask too closely where he got the money to buy it ..."

"Go on," I asked him.

"It was just an idea ... sometimes I get ideas."

I opened the front door for him. "Oh, by the way, I'm being married Friday."

"Yes, someone told me. Police work gets to be pretty easy in a small town. Will you want any of my boys to handle traffic?"

"No, but I'd be pleased if you'd be there in an unofficial capacity."

"Thanks!" He put his hand out and grasped mine. "Thanks, I'd like to." The door closed behind him.

"Who was that?" Frankie asked when I came back into the library. She was taut and tense again.

"Just a man about a dog."

"It was about the letters, wasn't it?"

"No," I lied. "Just a fellow who's doing me a favor."

"You seem to get an awful lot of favors done for you."

"How would you like to do me a favor?" I asked her.

"Gladly!" She opened her arms. "I'm full of favors."

"The favor I was going to ask you, is to forget about those letters. Wash your mind of them, as if they had never existed."

"I'll do that, too," she said.

The fire had died down and there were only one or two small embers fitfully flaring. "I'm glad I didn't go around kissing and being handled by all the boys who ever took me out. It's much better this way. It was worth waiting for."

I could sense the thought lurking at the back of her mind. "Frankie ..." but her hand came up and covered my lips.

"I didn't mean that. Really I didn't. You would be a very strange man if you had never loved before, and I don't know whether I would like you so much. It's different with a man than with a woman; I don't know why it should be, but it is. I only meant that I was lucky, and that I'm glad ... You wouldn't want to do me a favor, would you? You wouldn't want to carry me upstairs?"

"What's the matter? Have you been on your foot too much tonight?"

"No, I just like it, and I won't have the excuse much longer."

She insisted that I put her down at the top of the stairs. Joy came to the door of my room, looked at us, said hello with a tail wag, and then went back to her bed.

"She's setting us a good example. It's time to turn in," I said, but Frankie wandered into my room.

"Where will we live when we're married? I mean what house will we live in?"

"Maybe the Jennings Place," I suggested. "I talked to Elizabeth about it, but she didn't like the idea. She wants to clear out and let us have this house."

Frankie was wandering about the room. "No, she should stay here. All of her life that means anything to her has been lived here. Anyway, in practically no time at all this house wouldn't be big enough for us." Her thought trailed off as she circled the room. "This has always been your room?"

"Since I was a boy."

"It's like a portrait of you in a way. And I'm an interloper. I'm not anywhere in the portrait, am I?"

I pointed to a leather folder on the desk of photographs of Old Matt and Elizabeth. There was a snapshot stuck under the edge of the frame and on top of the glass. I had been so used to it that I had almost forgotten it.

"Where did you get that picture of me?"

I slipped it out. It was a picture made a couple of years back of Frankie standing in the garden of the Big House. The long dress looked strange on her; she must have been about sixteen. I turned it over and glanced at the back of it. *Frankie sends her love, Alyse.* I handed it to her. "Alyse sent it to me a couple of years ago when I was abroad."

"I was sending you my love even then," she smiled. "You never stood a chance, did you? Why did you keep it here?"

"I'm wondering that myself. I told you before, sometimes we wait for things without knowing that we're waiting. On the other hand maybe it was an avuncular impulse."

"Have you any *avuncular* impulses now?" She slipped the picture back into place, and I looked at her. It came as something of a shock that I had been thinking of Frankie as a young girl all these years and she was now a woman. "Françoise . . ." I said.

"Why did you call me that?"

322

"I wanted to taste the name on my lips."

"And . . . ?"

"I like the taste of it."

"My father used to call me that, but no one else since I was a little girl."

"You're not a little girl any longer."

"I was always embarrassed with it over here, and at school."

"Why?"

"Oh, it was foreign-sounding, and people always seemed to stop and take a breath before they said it. It made me different, somehow, from other girls—and I wanted to be the same."

"It's a nice difference."

She smiled up at me and continued her tour of exploration. Suddenly, by the window, she stopped and turned. "There are ghosts in this room."

I knew what she meant. "Not many."

"Angelica was here?"

"Once."

She looked out into the night. "I thought that was going to hurt," she said. "Somehow, it doesn't." She went to the door.

I put my hands on her shoulders. "Françoise . . ."

"Yes?"

"I'll tell you day after tomorrow."

"You've already told me," she said. "Good night, John. Do you know, Elizabeth's a damn poor chaperone."

"Or perhaps Elizabeth's a very wise woman," I said.

"Yes, I guess that's it," Frankie smiled. "You wouldn't mind leaving your door open . . . ?"

"Those letters still under your skin? You're still afraid?"

"A little," she told me. "But mostly afraid of being afraid."

I nodded.

Eighteen

Thursday things really began to get hectic. Adelaide and Roger would arrive by the evening train and Emmeline and her husband would be in the following morning. Mrs. Haines brought the telegrams up with my coffee, and told me that she would bring my breakfast tray up to Elizabeth's room. Frankie was there, propped up on the couch, when I wandered in, and Elizabeth had her tray across her knees in bed. Frankie's kiss was all mixed up with grape jelly.

"The service will be downstairs at four thirty," Elizabeth said.

"We're discussing a marriage not a funeral," I reminded her.

"There's so much to be done . . . " Elizabeth seemed distracted.

"You sound as if you wished I would absent myself and arrive with the guests."

"It would help." Elizabeth had the phone in her hand and was talking to Miss Hawley at the Bon Ton beauty parlor. She and Frankie, I gathered, would need Miss Hawley's whole morning.

I tried to get a word in edgewise, but Elizabeth had the dressmaker on the line; that apparently would take care of the afternoon. Mrs. Talcott came bustling in with a large cardboard box and there was much rustling of tissue paper and the faint smell of sachet in the room as she held up a dress. "It's Alyse's dress," Elizabeth explained. "She was married to Frankie's father in it."

"Is this the way you want it?" I asked Frankie. "All the fuss and feathers?"

"Of course she does," Elizabeth interjected.

Frankie nodded. "Fuss and feathers and all the fur and trimmings, and the frosting on top of the cake."

324

"Which reminds me," Elizabeth said. "I've got to call the bakery."

Frankie took my hand. "I'm only going to do this once in my life, and I want to be done up brown. Of course, if you'd prefer a broomstick—"

"It's your wedding," I told her.

"It's yours too!"

"You must tell me about it sometime."

"Which is the Renney who's the photographer?" Elizabeth asked. "Haviland's so full of Renneys."

"Harry," I told her. "Photographs?"

"Of course," Frankie said. "Don't you want to be able to remember how your bride looked on the happiest day of her life?"

"I have an idea," I told her, "that I'll be able to remember. Where would you like to go?"

"Where would I like to go—where?"

"On your honeymoon! It's customary, you know. People get married and they go away together."

"Oh, that . . . !"

"Yes, that! And don't be so cavalier about it."

"It's all arranged," Frankie said.

"And when was it all arranged?"

"This morning, before you woke up. Every last detail is attended to."

"You wouldn't want to let me in on the secret?"

"I'd rather not," Frankie said. "It is sort of a secret."

"You don't want me to make any reservations or get tickets?"

"Everything's arranged for," Frankie explained.

"I'm expected to come along, I assume?"

"It wouldn't be much of a honeymoon without you."

"Does she know what she's doing?" I asked Elizabeth.

"Yes, I think she knows what she's doing," Elizabeth said. "After all, she's had as much experience in honeymoons as you have. And now finish your breakfast and clear out."

I found I had a lot of things to do myself that day. Sanford had phoned me that he wanted me to go over some papers in his office, but that he wouldn't be ready with them until about six o'clock. As I was signing them, I said, "These don't look very important to me. They could have been signed tomorrow."

325

"You'll be pretty busy tomorrow."

"Next week, then."

"Tidier this way." He took each page out of my hand and blotted my signature.

"Well, they're signed anyway. And now I've got to dash up to the place for dinner."

"We have time for a drink together." He started to put on his hat.

"We'll make time. What's the matter, the bottle in your desk drawer empty?"

"This is a very special drink, John," the old gentleman said. "The kind that ought to be drunk with your foot on a brass rail and your elbow on a mahogany bar."

"You're a sentimentalist."

"Did I ever deny it?" he admitted. "Let's get going!"

I had a sense that the Haviland House bar was crowded. About everyone I knew in town seemed to be there, but no one turned around when we came in, and then I spotted the figure of Holloway talking to Farnley and Mooney. I turned on Sanford. "Who rigged this up?"

"I plead guilty to the charge," he smiled. "I'm sort of a second offender. I did this once before in my life, for your father. Elizabeth had a little bit of a hand in it, too."

At that there were only about twenty and it wasn't as difficult as I expected. Jim Fletcher made room for Sanford and me at the bar and these men who were my friends circled around with their glasses in their hands and said, "Congratulations and good luck!" I noticed Holloway in the background, grinning at me and taking in the scene. The Allen brothers from the garage and Will Renney were there. Burt Wheeler said, "Glad I could make it. I've got a very important trip to make out of town tomorrow; but I suppose the acting Town Clerk will be able to handle things." He winked broadly.

Holloway finally came up beside me. "So I see the *rara avis* in its own habitat. Quaint tribal customs! I've been talking to the opposite ends of vital statistics in Haviland, the doctor and the undertaker—they're nice guys. You know, you're a smart bastard. What would any other place have for you that this town hasn't got?" He clicked his glass to mine. "You're smart in other ways too; and lucky."

"How did you horn in on this?" I asked him. "You're the only outsider here."

"I'm a small-town boy, myself, didn't you know? Frankie called me and invited me. Maybe she wanted some sober character to drive you home tonight."

Costello edged down the bar to me. "Can I talk to you?" he asked.

I introduced Holloway, and he turned away for a drink.

"We've got our case," Costello said. "Semple mailed a letter this afternoon in Poughkeepsie. The post office people over there were stuffy. They wouldn't let us pick it up. Maybe it's just as well. With a cancellation and delivered in Haviland it'll tie things up just the way we want them. Do you want me to intercept it?"

I looked about. Fred Clum, the postmaster, had been just down the bar a moment before. I caught his eye.

"I already spoke to Fred," Costello said.

Fred nodded.

Eddie Connor came up to me and explained the dinner. "When Sanford called me and asked me to cater this, I said *sure*. But what's the use of kidding, there isn't any restaurant in town that can cook a decent meal, including mine. So I got the steward over from the country club in Poughkeepsie and we've got the damnedest menu. Mrs. Milnor sent down the wine."

It was, too—"the damnedest menu"! Sanford and Holloway and I stayed pretty much sober. No one else bothered to. "This is an evening that will remain in the memory of living man," Sanford observed.

"And from the condition of most of those here, it will be mentioned now and again by their wives for a long time to come," Holloway added.

When we arrived at the house later I told Holloway, "Fix yourself a drink, I'll go upstairs and see Frankie."

"That's all you'll do," he said. "I left her some pills to take. She should be sound asleep."

She was. Holloway lingered in my room. "I had a talk with Frankie when I arrived this afternoon. Is something bothering her?"

"Why?"

"Look, I'm a doctor, not a grocery salesman. And it isn't a cracked rib." He eyed me. "Do you mind if I butt in?"

"No, did she talk to you about it?"

"There wasn't the time, and it wasn't the place. Is the business of Angelica upsetting her?"

"No, that's not it."

"You seem awfully sure. Sometimes . . ."

"I'm not so sure about anything," I interrupted him. "But there's something else." I told him about the business of the letters.

"I was forgetting," he said. "Small towns have everything. Speaking as a physician, you know these things can have a warping and disastrous impact on a sensitive woman, if she's not pretty solidly put together emotionally."

"I know."

He studied me for a moment. "I could leave you some sleeping pills, but I don't suppose you need them," he offered.

But I didn't go to sleep right off. I guess that the night before your marriage you don't sleep too well. At the important moments in a man's life he is likely to do a little spiritual bookkeeping.

Mrs. Haines stopped me as I was about to knock on Frankie's door the next morning. "It's bad luck for the groom to see the bride before the ceremony."

"It isn't bad luck at all." Frankie opened the door. "See, no cane, no crutch and hardly a limp. And feel . . . I took off the plaster. You wouldn't have any alcohol, would you? Some of the gummy stuff is left and I look like a busted statue that's been repaired."

I looked at her eye. "You look otherwise damaged, too. Like something picked up at a fire sale."

"Thanks for the compliment. I'll give you one. I decided last night why you're marrying me—just to get the Jennings Place back into the Tracy lands."

"I was wondering when you'd discover that."

Out of deference to Mrs. Haines and a busy day we ate breakfast downstairs.

About halfway through breakfast Mrs. Haines brought in the mail and put it down on the table beside me. "Will Talcott met Miss Emmeline on the early train and picked up the mail," she explained. The phone rang and she went into the office to answer it. "It's for you," she announced a moment later. "A man for you."

I shoved the mail into a stack and put it under the paper. "I'll be right back," I told Frankie.

It was Costello. He was urgent. "Something slipped up. Before Fred Clum could tell him, one of the clerks gave your mail to Talcott early this morning. —That letter from Semple was in it."

"It's all right," I told him. "Mrs. Haines just brought the mail in. I'll catch the letter before Frankie gets it."

Usually, normal living doesn't operate on such close schedule. Frankie's face was drained of color and she looked up at me with a startled, almost guilty look on her face. She was holding a letter in her hand and her hand was shaking, her whole body was shaking. She tore the letter in half and shoved the fragments into her pocket. She picked up her coffee cup but her hand was shaking so badly she spilled it across the table. She tried to hold it in both her hands, but she still couldn't control herself and a little of it spilled across her shirtwaist. In desperation she dropped the cup on the table in front of her and started to run out of the room. I caught her at the door. Mrs. Haines, hearing the clatter, came into the dining room. I nodded to her to leave us alone and for once in her life she got an idea quickly.

"What's this all about? I thought we'd settled the business of these lousy letters."

"It has nothing to do with the letters," she protested. "I just suddenly don't feel well."

I reached into her pocket and took out the torn letter. "I knew about this," I told her. "It was arranged that you wouldn't get it."

"I had a sense that there'd be one of them this morning. John, what have I ever done to get these horrible things sent to me?"

"You haven't done anything. It's somebody that's hitting at you to get at me."

"And now he'll try to get at you some other way." She clung to me and I could feel her fingers bite into my arms. "Promise me you won't get yourself mixed into all this. Turn it over to the police. I don't care who reads them only don't get yourself mixed up in this. Something terrible will happen to you. John, I'm pleading with you, promise me. Everything that's in those letters could actually happen to me, and it wouldn't be worth your being hurt."

329

"I've already turned it over to the police," I told her. "Stop worrying."

"Then that's what Costello was up here for two nights ago?"

"Yes. And stop worrying. You'll never get another one of these."

We could hear Holloway coming down the stairs. "And promise me something else," she pleaded. "You won't read this letter—not this particular day. It's bad enough that one of us has read it."

I patted her shoulder and gave her my handkerchief.

Holloway glanced at us. "We fight like cats and dogs," I told him. Then Elizabeth came down and things got back to normal. She glanced at Frankie and then at the mail and then back to Frankie and Frankie nodded to her. Families develop their own particular kind of telepathy; ours was working overtime this morning. After a moment I excused myself. "I've got some telephoning to do." I was aware of Frankie's glance following me out of the room.

I took the letter out of my pocket and put the torn pieces together on the desk. It was a sweet piece of sadism to send to a girl on the morning of her wedding. In a gibberish stew of filthy images it robbed marriage and sex of their last iota of normalcy and beauty. Even animals—especially animals—couldn't be like that; it was the regurgitation of all that was perverted in the human mind.

There was a sound at the door and Elizabeth came in. I folded the fragments of the letter and put them in my pocket.

"Do you know who it is?" Elizabeth asked.

"Semple."

"He's a beast. Well, it's better knowing. . . . John, Frankie is worried. I'm worried, too. Don't get into this yourself. Let Sanford handle it and take it up with the police."

"I already have," I told her.

"The man is insane, you know. He's crazed with hatred—if it didn't come out that way, it might come out another, an even more ghastly way."

"Stop worrying." I led her back into the dining room. "I'm going to show Holloway about the farm and then I've got to go down to the bank and cash a check. Does anybody want anything in town?"

330

"I want you to stay out of trouble," Frankie begged.

I took Holloway about the farm as I checked over things with Talcott, and then we headed into the village. We had turned into Railroad Avenue and were about a block away from the bank when I saw a State Police car parked at the curb with Costello at the wheel. I pulled in beside him and got out.

"Frankie got the letter this morning, after all. Here it is. You've got your case all wrapped up. Book a charge and give him the works."

Costello took the letter. "And if we get a conviction, he might get sixty days. They'll try this case in Poughkeepsie."

"Are you suggesting . . ."

"I'm not suggesting anything," he interrupted curtly.

There wasn't anything more to say so I started for the bank. I didn't get further than Mort Tanner's store, when Semple and Bill Corley came out of Corley's office down the street. Before they realized I was there they turned and started toward me. Something snapped inside of me. It can happen that way; it just snaps. You don't think it out, all the pieces just fall into place. There's such a thing as being too civilized; I didn't feel civilized at all. I suddenly knew I couldn't live in Haviland if this man lived in Haviland—it was as simple as all that. The town wasn't big enough for both of us. Frankie would never have to walk down the street under his gaze. It didn't seem to make very much difference whether I killed him or not.

Something else happens at such moments. Your memory does a freeze; it's like taking a photograph with everything in focus. I could see Costello sitting in his car at the curb. Jim Fletcher was standing on the steps of the bank talking to a fellow by the name of Griffin who lives on the other side of town. The watchman at the railroad crossing was swinging his sign at his side waiting for the 11:32 to blow before he stopped traffic. Grady, the cop, was palming a cigarette and surreptitiously smoking it in front of the firehouse across the tracks. Pop Sanford was sitting at his window with his heels up on the sill and his hands folded behind his head. Then Pop's heels dropped and he swung upright in his chair and was staring down the street. Mort Tanner was standing in the doorway of his store, almost beside me. The letter "M" on the plate-glass window of Mooney's furniture and funeral em-

331

porium was askew; I'd never noticed that before. The clock outside the jewelry store read 11:29. It was like a photograph of Haviland taken at exactly 11:29 of this particular morning. I would have made a hell of a witness in court on the accident that was about to happen. Only it wasn't going to be an accident. Then time started to move again. Holloway was a couple of steps ahead of me before he realized that I had stopped. Semple and Corley were talking and didn't look up until they were almost abreast of me, then Semple must have sensed something because he looked up and stopped.

"I want to see you, Semple, alone. I have some business with you."

"You haven't any business with me," Semple blustered.

"Watch your step, Milnor." Bill Corley's voice was raised. "We've been expecting something like this. You've physically assaulted my client once before." He seemed to want the whole town to hear what he was saying.

"I said I have some business with you, Semple, and we'll conduct it alone."

"I have a court order of restraint," Corley was yelling, "and I'm serving it on you." He whipped a paper about under my face. "There are witnesses to this service and if you ignore it you will be in contempt of court." He thrust the paper into my hand.

I tore it up and dropped it on the ground.

Semple turned and started to make a break for it. I put my foot out and he came down on the sidewalk with a crash that knocked the wind out of him. Corley yelled, "Police!" and started running toward Costello. I saw the State Police car back away and drive off as Corley reached the curb. He turned around and started back. "Stop him, somebody." He reached down and picked up a paving stone from the side of an excavation where they were putting in a new water main.

"Take him, Doc," I said, and turned my attention back to Semple. He was on his knees and then he was on his feet and I knocked him down again. Mort Tanner stepped back into the shadows of his doorway. Mooney came to the front of his store and was looking out through the window. Fletcher was still standing on the steps of the bank. Sanford was now leaning out of his window.

332

Somebody's going to try to stop this, I thought. I yanked Semple to his feet and shoved him into the doorway past Mort Tanner. "Let me use your store for a few moments, Mort." He stepped out on the sidewalk and I reached behind me and released the Yale lock on the door. I guess I didn't duck quickly enough; a heavy mixing bowl glanced across the side of my face and crashed to the floor. Semple was backing away. It took a moment to see in the dimness of the store. He had a revolver in his hand.

"Make one step toward me, and I'll shoot you," he said.

This was too damned crazy for words. To get shot in the belly by Semple! And on the morning of my wedding! And for a handful of filthy letters! Oh, for God's sake give up the heroics, I told myself. Let the law handle this. But it wasn't any good. One of us could live in this town, but not both of us. It was as simple as that.

"It wouldn't do you any good," I told him. "That's only a thirty-two. It wouldn't stop me. You'd have to be awfully lucky to kill a man with one bullet, and you aren't that lucky, Semple. You aren't lucky at all. If you were lucky you wouldn't be alive to have happen to you what I'm going to do to you." I was walking toward him and he was backing away until he came against the counter at the back of the store and couldn't back away any further.

"I'm going to shoot!" he yelled.

"No, you're not. You'd only get one bullet out before I reached you, and then I'd kill you. You haven't got the guts to pull that trigger." He didn't, either. The gun went off as I grabbed it out of his hand, but the bullet went into the floor at my feet. I threw the gun across the store behind me and slammed him in the face. He put his hands up over his mouth. "I'm going to make you wish you'd never been born, but at least try to defend yourself. You're as big as I am, you're young enough—are you yellow all the way through?"

His foot lashed out, driving between my legs. I only just managed to escape the full force of it, and I grabbed his foot and pulled. He came crashing down against the counter to the floor. He lay huddled there for a moment and then started crawling toward the door, calling for help.

"You're asking for it. I'll use my hands as long as you stand up. You're not fighting a gentleman. There aren't any rules."

He got to his knees and backed away from me.

"You know why I'm doing this. And you're going to tell me why before I stop."

"I haven't done anything to you!" he screamed. "You'll go to jail for this!"

"No, I won't go to jail. I might go to the electric chair for killing you—because I'm going to kill you if you don't talk."

"You're crazy! You're mad, insane!" he slobbered.

"No, I'm angry. There's a difference. You picked the wrong man and you're going to pay for it." I could hear pounding on the door and through the glass pane I could see a crowd of people, and one or two faces with hands cupped about their eyes peering against the light into the store. There was a curtain on the bottom of the door, a roller curtain. It pulled up with a cord that went through an eccentric roller and locked it in any position. It was an old-fashioned thing; you don't often see it nowadays, but then Mort Tanner's store is sort of old-fashioned. I went over and rolled up the curtain. I remember thinking how strange it is that a pane of glass can be as strong as a steel plate—people have a stoppage about breaking a pane of glass. When I turned around Semple was crawling across the floor behind me and his hand had almost reached the revolver. I ground his outstretched fingers under my heel and he yelped with pain and staggered to his feet. His ripped fingernails hung in shreds from his hand.

He picked up a broken shard of the heavy mixing bowl and I let him come for me and then drove my fist into his mouth. I could feel teeth go through his lips and into my knuckles. He slipped to the floor. The pounding was increasing at the door behind me.

"You haven't got much time left to talk, Semple. They're going to come in here and try to save you, but when that door breaks there won't be anything left to save. You better start talking. You wanted to play in the sewer, I'll play in the sewer with you." I kicked him and a bloody slobber slathered out of his mouth with his howl. "The next time I kick them off," I told him.

"I did it," he gasped.

I pulled him to his feet and let him have it in the mouth again.

"Talk quick and talk straight. You haven't got much time. You did what?"

"The letters—don't hit me again—I sent them."

Everything drained out of me at once. It was finished. He could have stopped it at any moment, right from the beginning, just by talking.

"What are you going to do?" he gasped.

"Nothing. It's all finished. You just retired, you retired from Haviland. You've got a place in Florida—you're leaving for it within three hours and you're never coming back here, because if I ever see you again I'll finish this day's work."

I turned from him and went to the door and snapped back the lock. The noise of the crowd dropped to a hush. Some of them were my friends, some of them weren't—there aren't too many that you can call friends. Fletcher and Sanford were standing nearby and Holloway was beside Corley. None of them spoke. Over their heads I could see Costello running up the street. He pushed his way through the crowd and then stopped as he saw me at the door.

"Someone reported there was shooting," he said.

"Nobody's been shot," I told him. "Will you come inside, Lieutenant, and you, too, Corley. I think Semple would like to see his lawyer. Pop, I'd like you to come in."

As they passed through the door, the crowd started to move forward and I beckoned Fletcher to my side. "Jim, would you ask these good people to stay where they are; we're conducting some private business inside." I closed the door behind me.

"I demand that you arrest this man." Corley pointed at me.

"Oh, pipe down, buster," Costello said. He walked over and picked up the revolver. "I'm a lousy cop," he said to me. "Never dreamed he had two guns. I could have got you killed."

Corley bristled up to him. "I'm going to prefer charges against you, Costello. I'll have your job. Dereliction of duty. I have a court order of restraint against Milnor."

"Sit down, Corley." Pop Sanford spoke gently. "You're going off half-cocked, it's a bad thing for a lawyer to do."

I pushed Semple into a chair. "You've got work to do. Get some paper and a pen, Corley."

335

Corley fumbled in his pocket and Sanford handed him a notebook and pen.

"Now start talking, Semple."

"This kind of a confession won't stand up in court," Corley spluttered excitedly. "You're all witnesses to the illegality of this. Sanford, as a lawyer, you're an officer of the courts . . ."

"We're all aware of the extralegality of this," Sanford said wearily.

"Start talking, Semple," I said.

"Don't say a word. You're acting under the advice of counsel," Corley said.

"I made you a promise, Semple. Start talking. Court orders won't save you. You're just stalling off a very evil day."

Semple stared at me through glazed eyes and his fingers reached up and pulled his lips away from a jagged tooth that was sticking through. He looked at Corley.

"This man needs a doctor," Corley said.

"He'll need a minister to make his peace with God, if he doesn't start talking. This is not a confession, it's a statement. Start talking."

"I'll talk," Semple said.

"This is it," I told Corley. "Write it down."

Corley looked with indecision first at Costello and then at Sanford.

"I'll help you get started, Semple. Why are you making this statement?"

He looked at me and then his eyes dropped. "Because I want to . . ."

"No, let's have the truth Semple. That's not why you're making this statement. You're making it because I beat you until you thought I was going to kill you. I told you I was going to kill you if you didn't talk."

Sanford was shaking his head at me. Costello said, "Don't write that down, Corley, that's not Semple's statement."

"No, write it down," I told him. "Is that the way it happened, Semple?"

"That's the way it happened."

"And I told you that I would give you three hours to leave Haviland and that if I ever saw you again I would kill you?"

336

"Yes, that's right," Semple said.

"My side of this is all on the record, Semple. Now, you begin to talk, and talk it straight and quick!"

His lips worked but his throat didn't and then the words began to come. "I wrote some letters . . ."

I saw Corley scribbling across the notebook. "What kind of letters . . . ?"

"Letters . . ." He stopped.

"I wouldn't want to live either, if I were you, Semple. But I wouldn't want to die the way I'll kill you if you don't talk. —What kind of letters?"

"Letters to your niece . . ."

"She's not my niece and I'm marrying her this afternoon. What kind of letters . . . ?"

"I made sort of implied threats in them . . ."

"What kind of letters?"

"Sexual letters . . ."

I came across the side of his face with my open hand. "Come on, talk! Talk plain English! —They were perverted letters?"

"Yes."

"They described acts which you knew she had never performed?"

"Yes."

"They were anonymous and she couldn't know who was writing them?"

"Yes."

"And you described things that you were going to do with her and to her?"

"Yes."

Corley was staring at him. "Do you want me to go on writing this stuff?" he asked quietly.

"Yes, go on," Costello said. He took the torn pieces of the letter Frankie had received that morning out of his pocket and straightened them out on the counter in front of Semple.

"Did you write this particular letter?" he demanded. "Read it carefully and be sure."

Semple nodded.

Costello took a pen out of his tunic. "Then sign your name to it! Write *Written by me and mailed in the United States mail.*

337

Write that on the letter and write it on the envelope. But only write it if it's the truth. At this moment you're under the protection of a police officer—Milnor, I mean this. Nobody's going to touch you, Semple." Semple took the pen and began laboriously to form the words and then he signed it. "And on the envelope, too." Costello pushed it in front of him. When Semple finished, Costello said, "I want to have something out of this cockeyed statement that will hold water in court."

I reached over and picked up the papers Semple had signed. Costello looked at me and for a moment I thought that he was going to blow his top. Finally he subsided. "You can do anything you want with them, but that's all the confession I'd want to take him to trial."

He glanced at the gun he had picked up off the floor. "Anyway, this, damn it, will stick! The Sullivan law has a punch in it that will even go upstairs and get an ex-assemblyman."

"That gun belongs to nobody," I said. "You found it on the floor, that's all. And I wouldn't delay Semple, he's leaving town in a couple of hours. He's starting right now."

I pulled Semple out of his chair and started him toward the door. He saw the shadows of the crowd against the curtains at the window and stopped.

"There's a back door," Sanford said quietly.

Semple turned and stumbled out into the alley behind Mort Tanner's store.

"I'm sorry," Corley said. "I didn't know anything about all this." He gestured with the notebook.

"You got any questions left in your mind?" Costello asked him.

"No, none," Corley said. "I had a louse for a client and some of it started to rub off on me." He handed the notebook to Sanford and I gave Pop the letter Semple had signed.

When we came out on the street the crowd, as crowds will, had grown. There were just the four of us and, somewhat puzzled, they peered over our shoulders into the empty store. "I think I owe you for a mixing bowl," I told Mort Tanner. "I tossed a salad and it got dropped."

He smiled. "If I remember it, I'll put it on your bill—if I remember it."

Holloway and I walked back toward the car. We were well out

of town before he spoke. "There's a lot to be said for small towns," he said. "By the way, that shot really went into the floor. There's a *corpus* and it isn't *delicti?*"

"It really went in the floor."

"You better get that hand of yours under cold water—it's beginning to swell up like a ham. And don't look now but you've got a peach of a black eye."

We were almost back to the house when he chuckled. "Come on, give! Where did you hide the body? What became of Semple?"

"There's a lot to be said for small towns," I reminded him. "We hide our bodies well."

The legend of a bride's privacy permitted me to get to my room without seeing anyone. I could hear Elizabeth and Frankie in her room. I closed my door. "Come on, Holloway, make this like a busman's holiday and get me into shape."

He studied me. "You look all right from the left side. It's a pity you haven't got two left sides."

The astringent stung. He poured a drink for both of us and then thoughtfully slipped the ice out of his and wrapped it in a handkerchief and applied it to my eye.

"Take a bath," he advised, "and change your clothes. I'll do the same and come back for you before the show starts."

When he came back into the room he was smiling. "I've seen everything. It's about time for you to go down. They're all there. I met Mrs. Tracy, your father's first wife . . ."

"My father's only wife," I corrected him.

"That's right, I forgot. You keep these things straight in your family."

"It's an effort, but we keep them straight."

"She's quite a character. And then there were two other characters and their husbands. They're exactly what to you, Milnor?"

"Half sisters," I told him. "How did you like Tex-as?"

"The bluff, hearty one? I suppose you have to have one stuffed shirt in the collection. About half the crowd that was standing on the sidewalk this morning are there, too—that banker fellow and the undertaker."

"Mooney."

"Mooney, yes that's his name. Quite a useful citizen, he found a drink for me."

"And one for himself, no doubt," I added.

"He looks like he could hold it." Holloway straightened my tie. "Look, John, it's none of my business to say this. I'm speaking as a medical man, but I wouldn't be speaking at all except that I'm your friend. Frankie may have a hard time to work her way out of this. It's the kind of a thing you can talk through and think you've licked and then it snaps up in your face. What I'm trying to say is, be very understanding if—well, just be understanding."

"Thanks, I know what you're trying to say."

We were at the head of the stairs before I remembered that I had forgotten to buy Frankie's wedding ring. "Just a minute," I told him, and went back and knocked on Frankie's door. Elizabeth answered and slipped out into the hall.

"We've got a problem," I told her. "I haven't got a ring."

"What have you done to your eye?" she demanded.

"Forget about my eye. It's all right. What do we do about the wedding ring?"

She looked down at her right hand and slipped off the little circle of diamonds that she wore. "It isn't really a wedding ring." She held it in her palm for a moment, looking at it, and then slipped it into mine. "But it isn't unknowing in the ways of love, either. I'd like Frankie to have it today. Your father gave it to me."

As I walked up to join Sanford, who was standing at the far end of the drawing room, I was conscious of the eyes that searched my face. Roger stared at me, and Adelaide and Emmeline looked at me quizzically. Of those from Haviland—most of them must have heard the story by now—it was just a general native curiosity and mostly on the distaff side. Then presently there were the sounds of Frankie's and Elizabeth's heels on the stairs and Elizabeth led her through the room and up to Sanford.

Frankie smiled and I forgot and turned toward her. She saw my eye and the side of my face and her smile died. "Oh, darling!" she cried. "You're hurt, something awful's happened!" Her own eye was not too well concealed; we were a fine-looking pair.

"Shut up, and let's get married," I whispered.

Sanford was watching us in amusement, and then remembered

that he had other things to do and he opened a book with the Episcopal service in it. Everything went fine until he came to "Who gives this woman in marriage?" I guess he hadn't realized that this service hadn't been rehearsed, and more than a ring had been forgotten. There was a silence in the room, the silence became a moment, and then it was shattered by Constance's reedy voice saying: "I give this woman in marriage." And, as if she expected someone might dispute her, she added, "I'm her grandmother. Who has a better right?"

Jim Fletcher cleared his throat with an amen quality. From that point on Sanford took off his spectacles and dispensed with "the book." He gave a little sermon at the end that had some very old-fashioned and very, very beautiful things to say about the estate and dignity of marriage. You can't read deeply among the fathers of English law without shaping your tongue to the full resonance and power of the language; Blackstone would have been proud of him. And then he was saying, "In accordance with the powers temporarily invested in me I pronounce you man and wife."

I waited for Fletcher's prodigious phlegm-stirring. It came, and there was no remaining question in the minds of Haviland that Frankie and I were married.

Marriages are unique I suppose in their similarity. Frankie kissed me—rather shyly—and then there was a general rustling. I noticed Mrs. Fletcher and Mrs. Farnley weeping; for that matter there were tears in Elizabeth's and Constance's eyes as well. People began to shake my hand and to kiss Frankie. Roger bristled forward, announcing, "Well, don't I get a kiss from the bride?" He saw me looking at him—there are some people who think I look like Matt. He shook Frankie's hand instead.

I came in for some kissing myself. Emmeline rushed up to me. She dabbed at her eyes with a handkerchief. "I'm your sister, you know." Adelaide just kissed me and said nothing. Across her shoulder I could see Constance nodding as if she'd just tied something up in a package, and approved it.

Champagne appeared, and everybody began talking at once and Elizabeth mentioned to Frankie that there were some presents in the library; in a town the size of Haviland you thank people in person, you don't write them letters.

341

Mooney had evaded the champagne and armed himself with a glass of whisky and was waiting for Frankie to notice a long slim aluminum case. "It's an ounce-and-a-quarter Leonard," he told her. "You'll cast a real dainty fly with it. If John hasn't got the patience to show you how, you come out on the stream with me this spring."

Mrs. Haines was unwrapping a package that had just been delivered, lifting out of the wrappings a large common earthenware mixing bowl, with a card stuck to it. "From Mort Tanner." Pop Sanford smiled, and Frankie looked at me. "There must be more to this than meets the eye," she said.

"Very aptly stated," Sanford murmured, and walked away.

Elizabeth was looking over at me and I nodded toward the stairs and she nodded back. "I think we can clear out of here without hurting anyone's feelings," I whispered to Frankie.

"Good. It'll only take me a minute or two to change. Will Talcott's already taken care of the suitcases. Yours, too."

Costello touched my arm as Frankie left the room. "It might interest you to know," he said in an undertone, "that Semple and his sister stopped in Brewster for gas at three o'clock this afternoon. His car was loaded with luggage and they were driving south."

I grinned. "It interests me very much," I said.

Out of the corner of my eye, I could see the usual expectant gauntlet forming, with rice and old shoes and even a cowbell smuggled here and there. Mrs. Haines came to my side and said, "Miss Frankie—I mean Mrs. Milnor wants to see you upstairs."

Frankie was talking to Elizabeth in the hall; they stopped talking when they saw me, and I tactfully didn't notice. Frankie said, "Wouldn't you rather go down the back stairs and escape all the rice business?"

It was sort of a dirty trick, but I wasn't looking a gift horse in the face. "I'd rather," I said.

We both kissed Elizabeth. "We'll see you when we get back," I told her.

"Yes, you really must do that," she said with great formality, and I was almost sure she winked at Frankie.

"What was that all about?" I said as we were stealthily navigating the kitchen.

342

"Just a private joke," Frankie said. "While you were raising hell in Haviland this morning Elizabeth and Constance and I were having a different kind of a time for ourselves up here; we were glad to get you out from under foot."

"How'd you know I was raising hell?"

"Oh, I managed to get part of the story out of Pop Sanford," she returned airily. "You'll be keeping no secrets from your wife."

"You seem to be keeping one from me," I commented.

"Not for long! —Let's take the back way to the Big House, shall we?"

"Why? Isn't that a little roundabout?"

"Maybe. But if we take the car at the front door, they'll all be waiting for us—"

"That makes sense," I said.

Joy scurried out of the shrubbery and came bounding to us. I patted her. "Go on home, girl!"

"Oh, let her come," said Frankie.

We had reached the garden of the Big House when Frankie stopped me. "Give me a present," she said.

I didn't feel like clowning over a funny lump I was getting in my throat, but I said, "Anything your little heart desires."

"Let this honeymoon be what you want, too." By the tone of her voice she didn't feel like clowning either.

"I'm not sure whether I understand," I said slowly. "But I think I do."

"I didn't want to go away, John—"

I swallowed hard. "Is Constance going to be with us?"

She choked back a giggle. "She'd prefer to be with Elizabeth, I think."

"And what about Elizabeth?"

"She wanted it that way, too. We talked it all over, the three of us—"

"While I was in Haviland—" I inserted dryly.

"No, yesterday. You see it was really Constance's idea to move down with Elizabeth. She said that this was your house, and you ought to live in it."

The lump in my throat got bigger. And I thought it was best not to try to talk over it. I found her hand in mine.

The rose trees were tied and bundled against the winter like sentinels, and we walked between them to the house. I picked her up and carried her over the threshold. "I'm so glad you did that," she whispered.

All the lights were on, and in the huge drawing room a fire was burning and a table was set with sandwiches and salad, and a cooler of champagne. "Elizabeth," said Frankie softly.

We made a pretense of eating, and then I moved the table away, and turned down the lights, and we sat on the sofa with our arms about each other, watching the fire dwindle away. I was conscious of Old Matt's portrait above the mantel, and I had a sense of the living that had flowed across this land, and through this house. There had been good times and bad; times of peacefulness and acquiescence, and times of strife and bitterness. The Tracys had had it all. But life flows in cycles, and I had the feeling that these were again to be the good years, rich and quietly satisfying. My arm tightened about Frankie. "Do you want to go up first?"

Frankie stood up, and looked down at me. "I'll bet you read that in a book," she said.

"I did," I admitted.

She stretched her hand out to me, and I could feel the strength in her.

As we were passing through the hall, there was a whine at the front door. I opened it, and Joy came in and passed us a little reproachfully as if to remind us that the night was cold and she had been waiting overlong. She went upstairs ahead of us. When we reached the upper landing she was bedding down on my shooting coat outside the big bedroom. I took Frankie in my arms. "That wasn't Elizabeth's idea," I said softly.

Joy thumped her tail and then curled it about her nose. Her eyes followed us to the door. Yes. These were going to be the good years.

(1)

344